An Unofficial Minecrafters Graphic Novel for Fans of the Aquatic Update

MARINE MADNESS

THE S.Q.U.I.D. SQUAD #6

MEGAN MILLER
NEW YORK TIMES BESTSELLING AUTHOR

SKY PONY PRESS
NEW YORK

Copyright © 2022 by Hollan Publishing, Inc.

Minecraft® is a registered trademark of Notch Development AB.
The Minecraft game is copyright © Mojang AB.

Sky Pony Press books may be purchased in bulk at special discounts for sales
promotion, corporate gifts, fund-raising, or educational purposes. Special editions
can also be created to specifications. For details, contact the Special Sales
Department, Sky Pony Press, 307 West 36th Street, 11th Floor, New York, NY
10018 or info@skyhorsepublishing.com.

Sky Pony® is a registered trademark of Skyhorse Publishing, Inc.®, a Delaware
corporation.

Minecraft® is a registered trademark of Notch Development AB.

The Minecraft game is copyright © Mojang AB.

Visit our website at www.skyponypress.com.

10 9 8 7 6 5 4 3 2 1

Library of Congress Cataloging-in-Publication Data is available on file.

Cover design by Kai Texel

Cover and interior art by Megan Miller

Print ISBN: 978-1-5107-6501-6
Ebook ISBN: 978-1-5107-6576-4

Printed in China

Introduction

It is a dire time in the world. The Evil Pillagers are conquering villages and destroying the villagers' culture and libraries.

But far out at sea live the Book Guardians, a secret group of miners and villagers helping to save the libraries' precious books. The Book Guardians bring chests of books, before they can be destroyed by Pillagers, secretly by boat to their hidden underwater ravine headquarters. Here a small group of three families collects the books and stores them for better times—for when the Pillagers are defeated.

While the grownups are checking deliveries, securing books, making plans, and double-checking those plans, the children—Inky, Luke, and Max—are meeting new friends and solving mysteries!

And that's not all. After helping the dolphins, they were gifted with the GOLDEN DUST MAGIC OF SPEAKING TO CREATURES. So, yes, they can talk to their underwater neighbors: the creatures, fish, and squid with whom they share their new home.

After escaping from a Pillager pursuit, the troop of Book Guardians are making their new home and headquarters at Ocean's End. But when some new faces show up to join their crew, things start to go awry. The adults are acting like children, leaving the S.Q.U.I.D. Squad to pick up the pieces. The worst part is, the new kids might be to blame!

Meet the S.Q.U.I.D. Squad

INKY

Clever. Enjoys organizing stuff. Pulled one too many squid tentacles. Knows what words like *acronym* mean. Mostly likes to play by the rules.

LUKE

Also clever, a little rebellious, and enjoys delivering a good speech. He sees himself as the leader, but Inky and Max have other ideas.

MAX

Brave. Leaves Inky and Luke in the dust when it comes to crafting stuff really, really fast. Their secret club name was his idea - the Super Qualified Underwater Investigation Detective . . . er . . . quad. Just say "Squid Squad," it's easier.

And also, meet ...

EMI

Lives in a cottage on the other side of the coral reef. Has a lot of informative books about the life aquatic that Inky, Luke, and Max need to read, like, STAT!

SOFI

Inky's mom. She's good at redstone and can spot a secret redstone door a mile off. So she has ALREADY figured out that Inky, Luke, and Max have made their OWN secret underwater cave headquarters INSIDE OF the Book Guardian's own secret underwater ravine headquarters. She hasn't even told anyone else about it!

ABS

Sofi's brother. He's really nice and can haul chests of books like you wouldn't believe.

ZANE

This is Max's dad. He goes on a lot of secret boat missions to find new villagers who want to save their books.

NEHA

This is Zane's sister. She's pretty nice, too!

PER AND JUN

Luke's mom and dad. Per is also fond of speeches and Jun tries to let him know when they go on too long. They go out with Zane on his missions sometimes.

MABEL

Friend to the Squad, unafraid to say what she thinks!

Chapter 1
Arrival

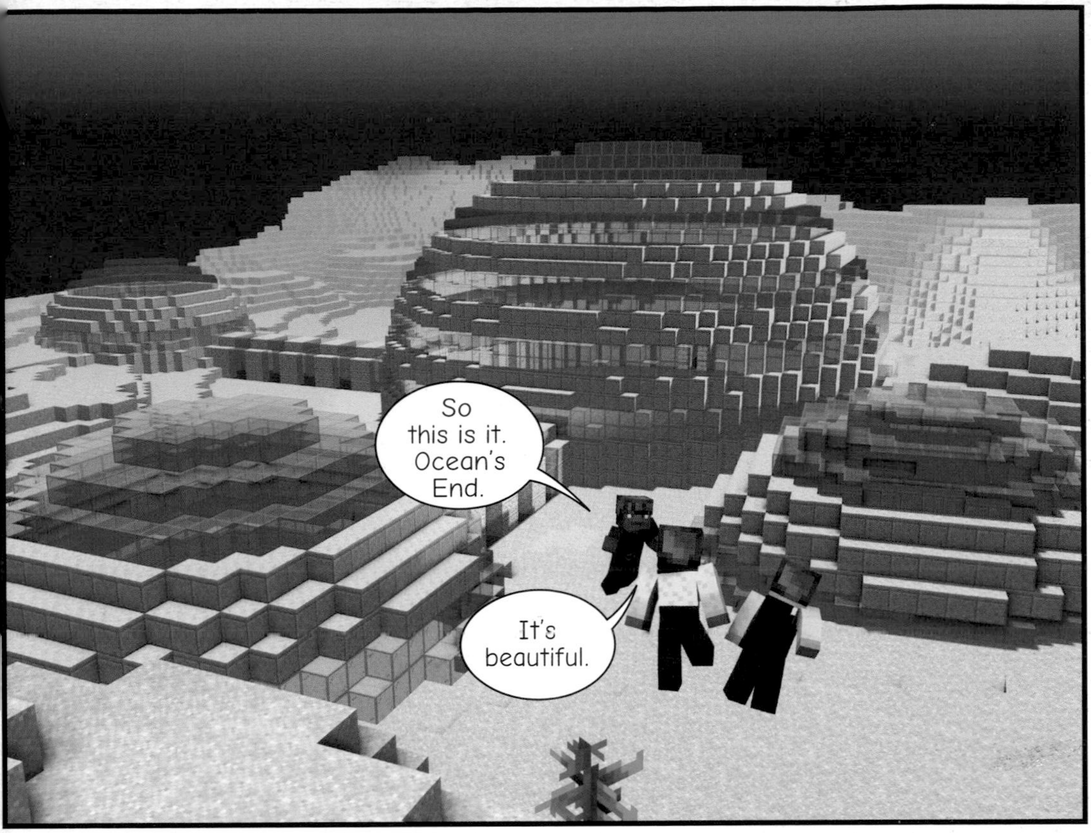
So this is it. Ocean's End.
It's beautiful.

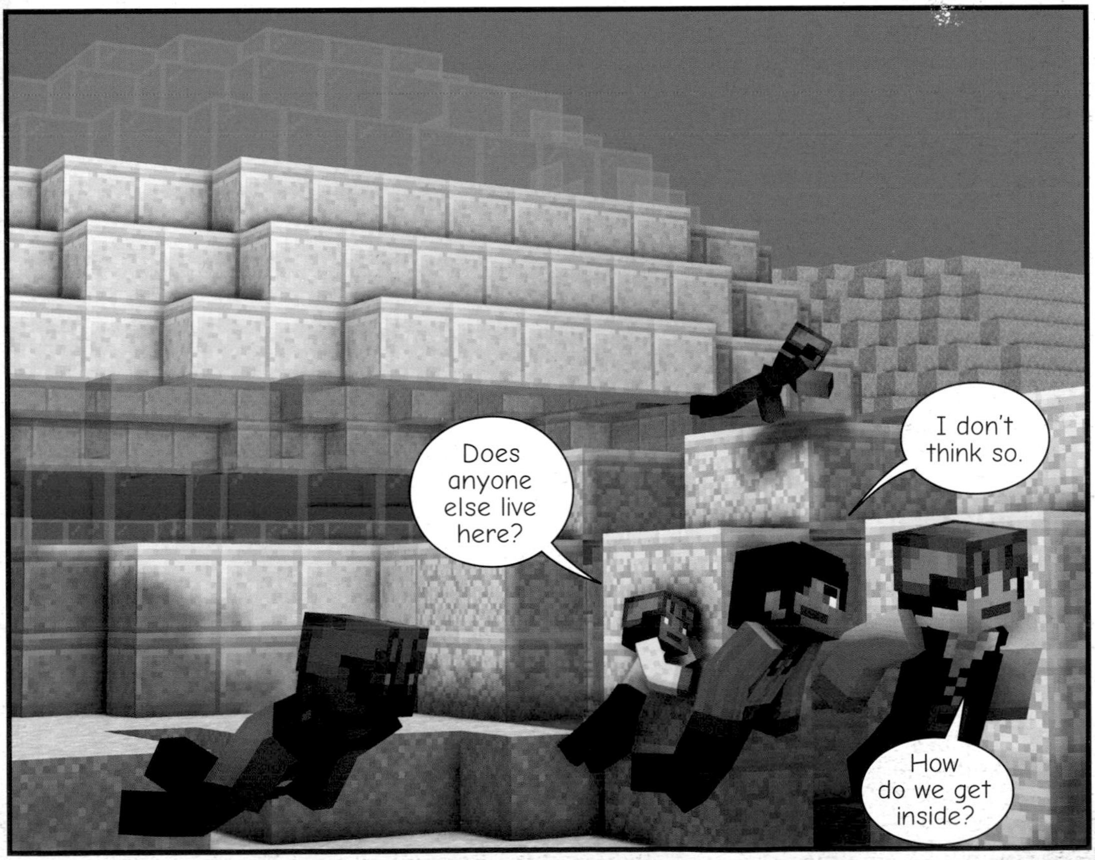
Does anyone else live here?
I don't think so.
How do we get inside?

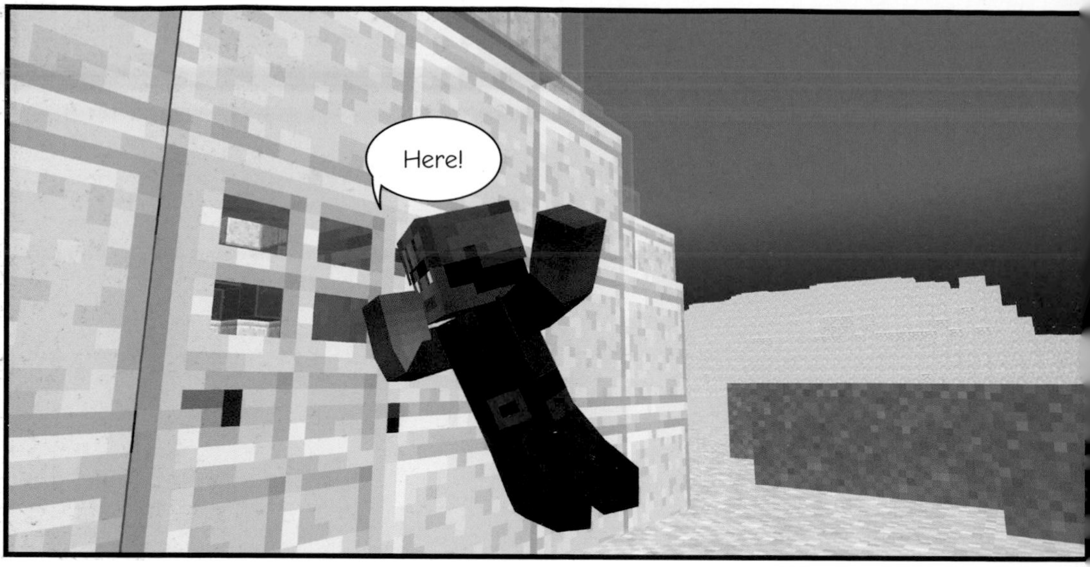
Here!

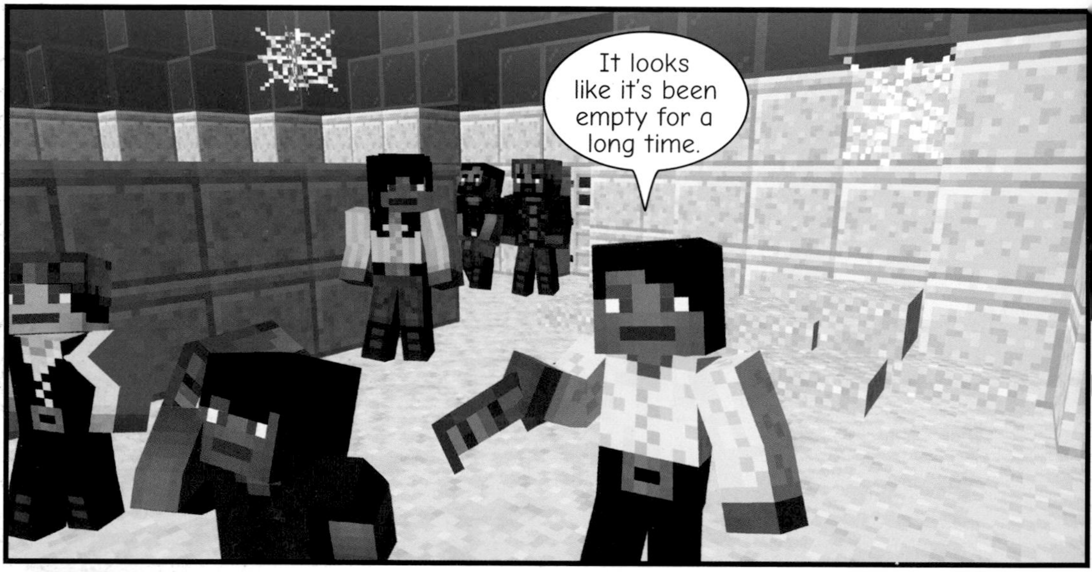
It looks like it's been empty for a long time.

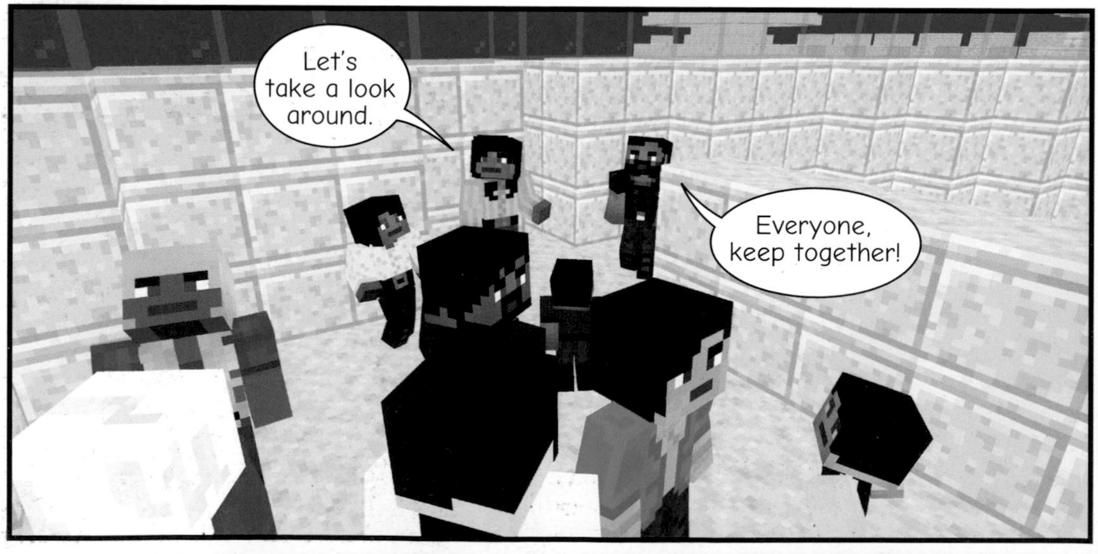
Let's take a look around.
Everyone, keep together!

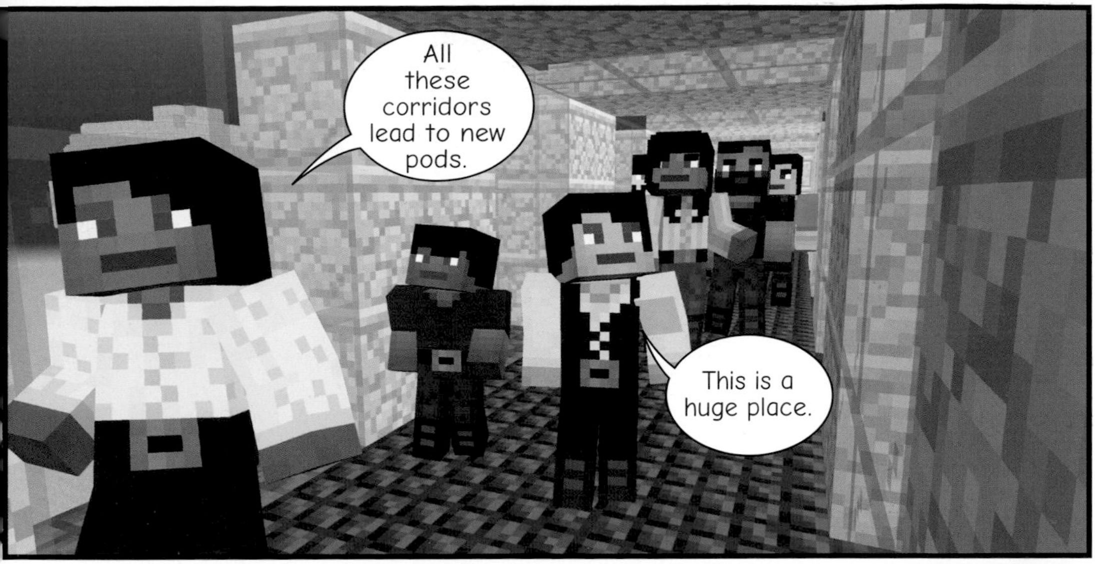
All these corridors lead to new pods.
This is a huge place.

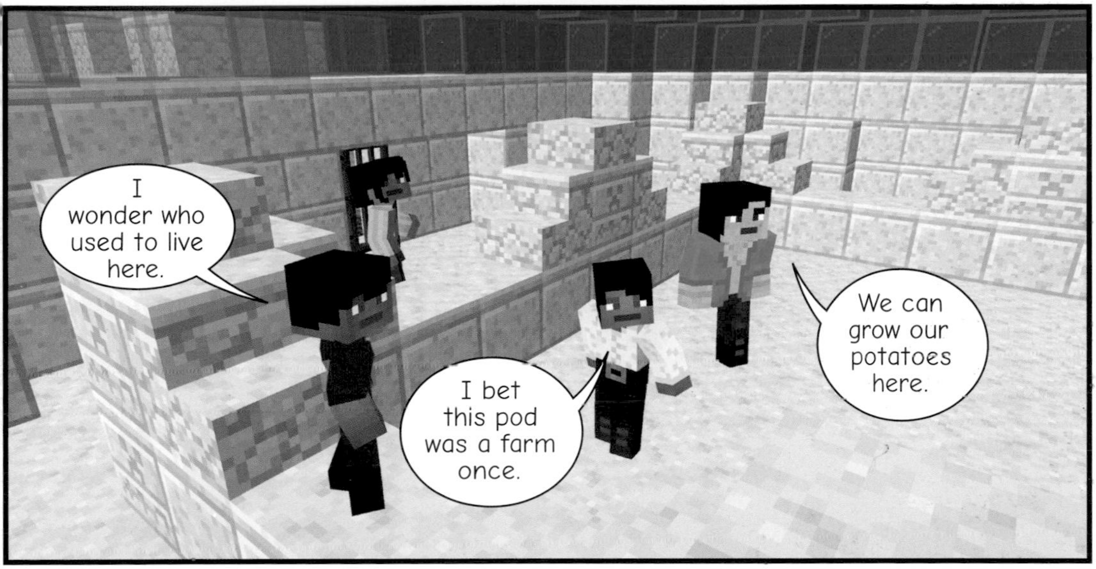
I wonder who used to live here.
I bet this pod was a farm once.
We can grow our potatoes here.

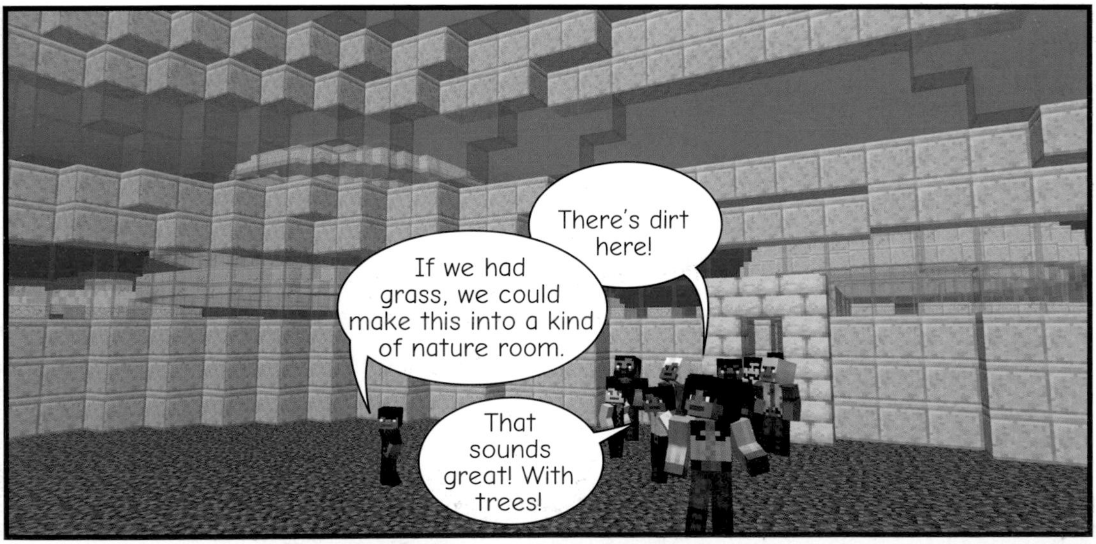
There's dirt here!
If we had grass, we could make this into a kind of nature room.
That sounds great! With trees!

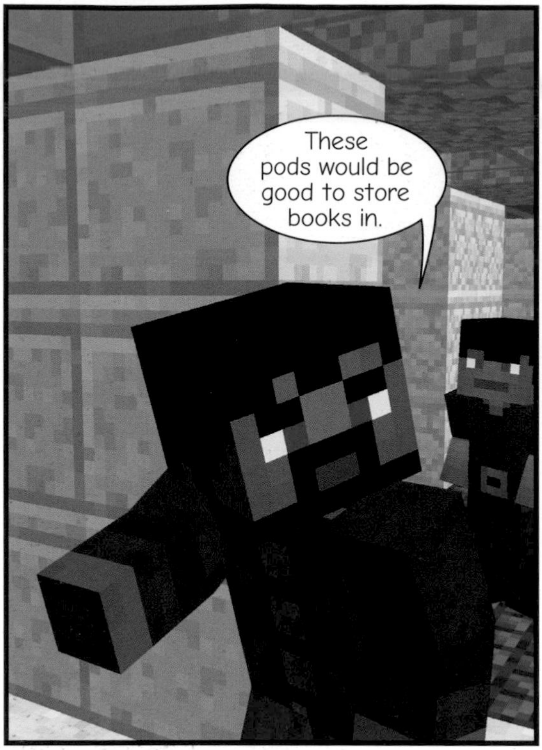
These pods would be good to store books in.

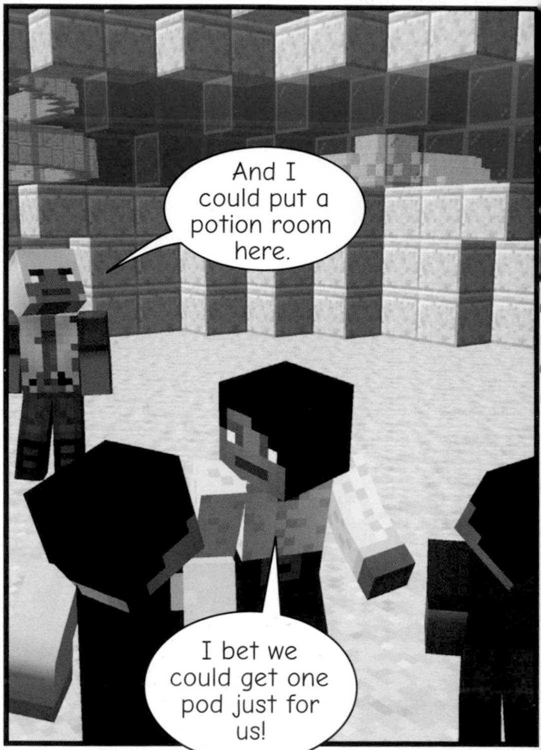
And I could put a potion room here.
I bet we could get one pod just for us!

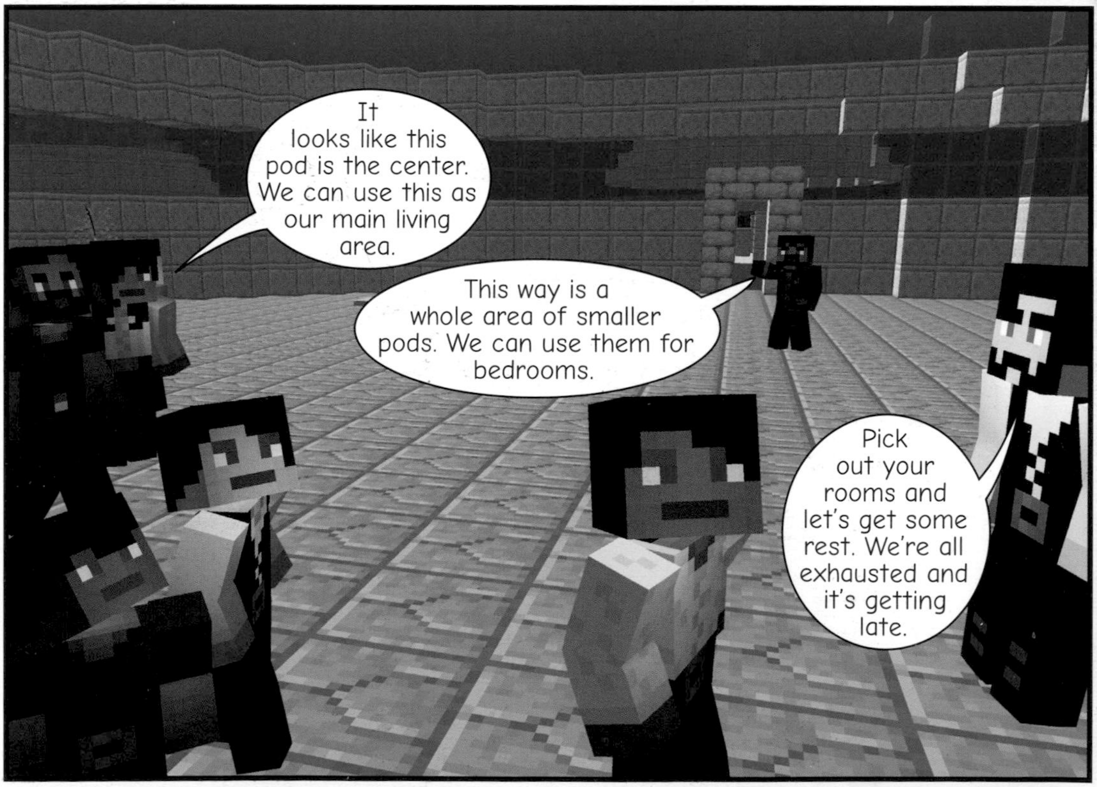
It looks like this pod is the center. We can use this as our main living area.
This way is a whole area of smaller pods. We can use them for bedrooms.
Pick out your rooms and let's get some rest. We're all exhausted and it's getting late.

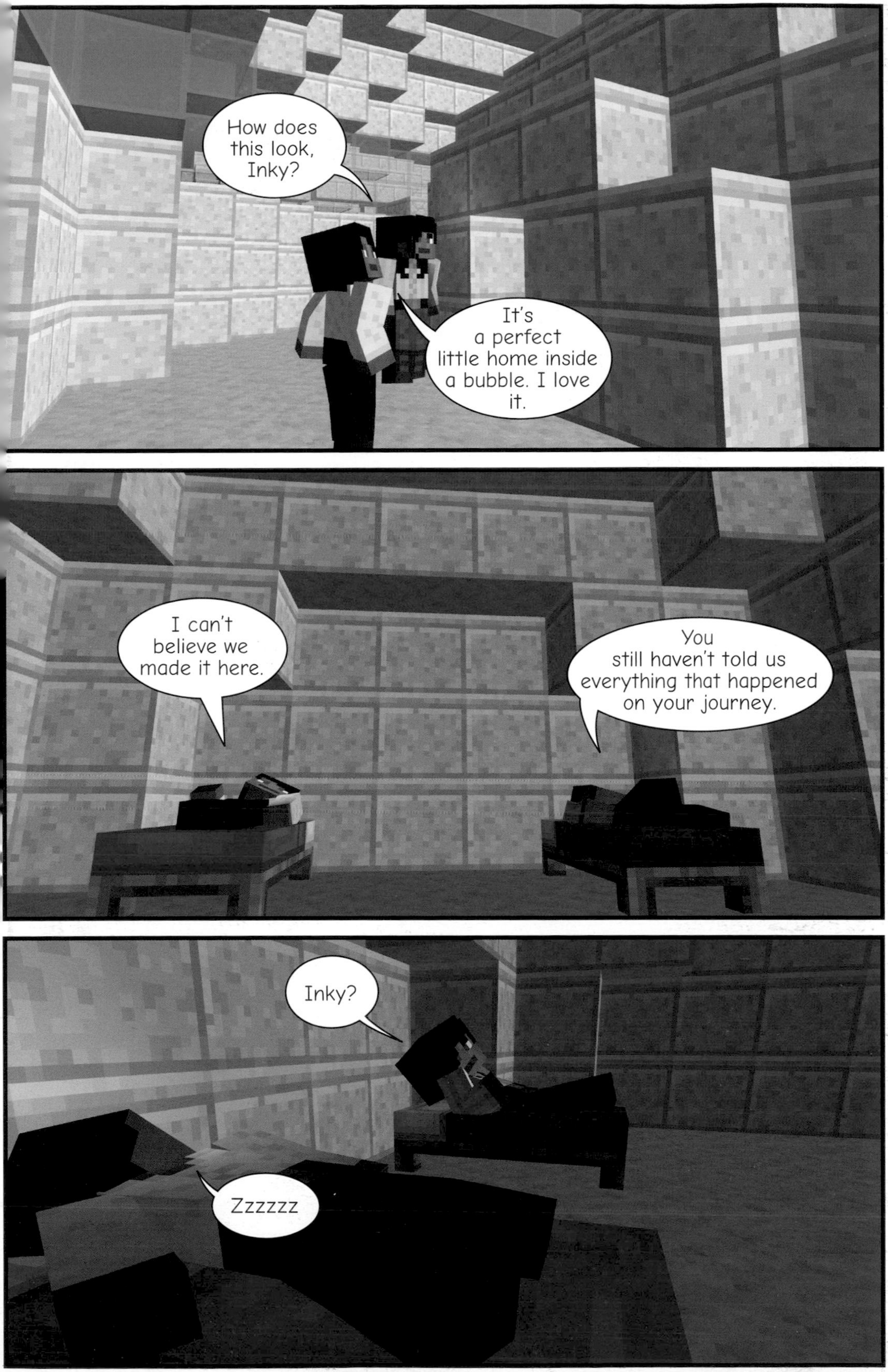
How does this look, Inky?
It's a perfect little home inside a bubble. I love it.
I can't believe we made it here.
You still haven't told us everything that happened on your journey.
Inky?
Zzzzzz

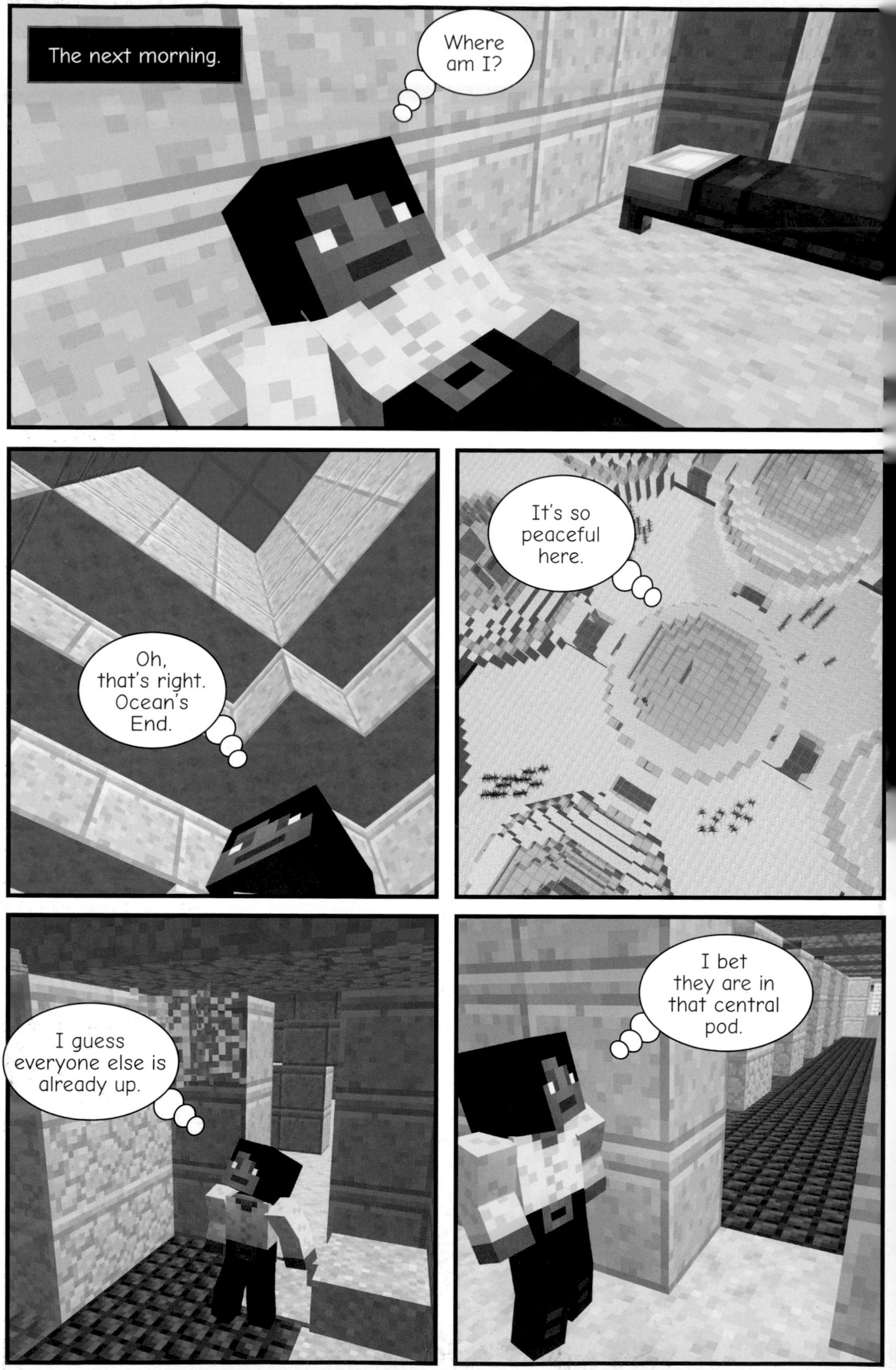
The next morning.
Where am I?
Oh, that's right. Ocean's End.
It's so peaceful here.
I guess everyone else is already up.
I bet they are in that central pod.

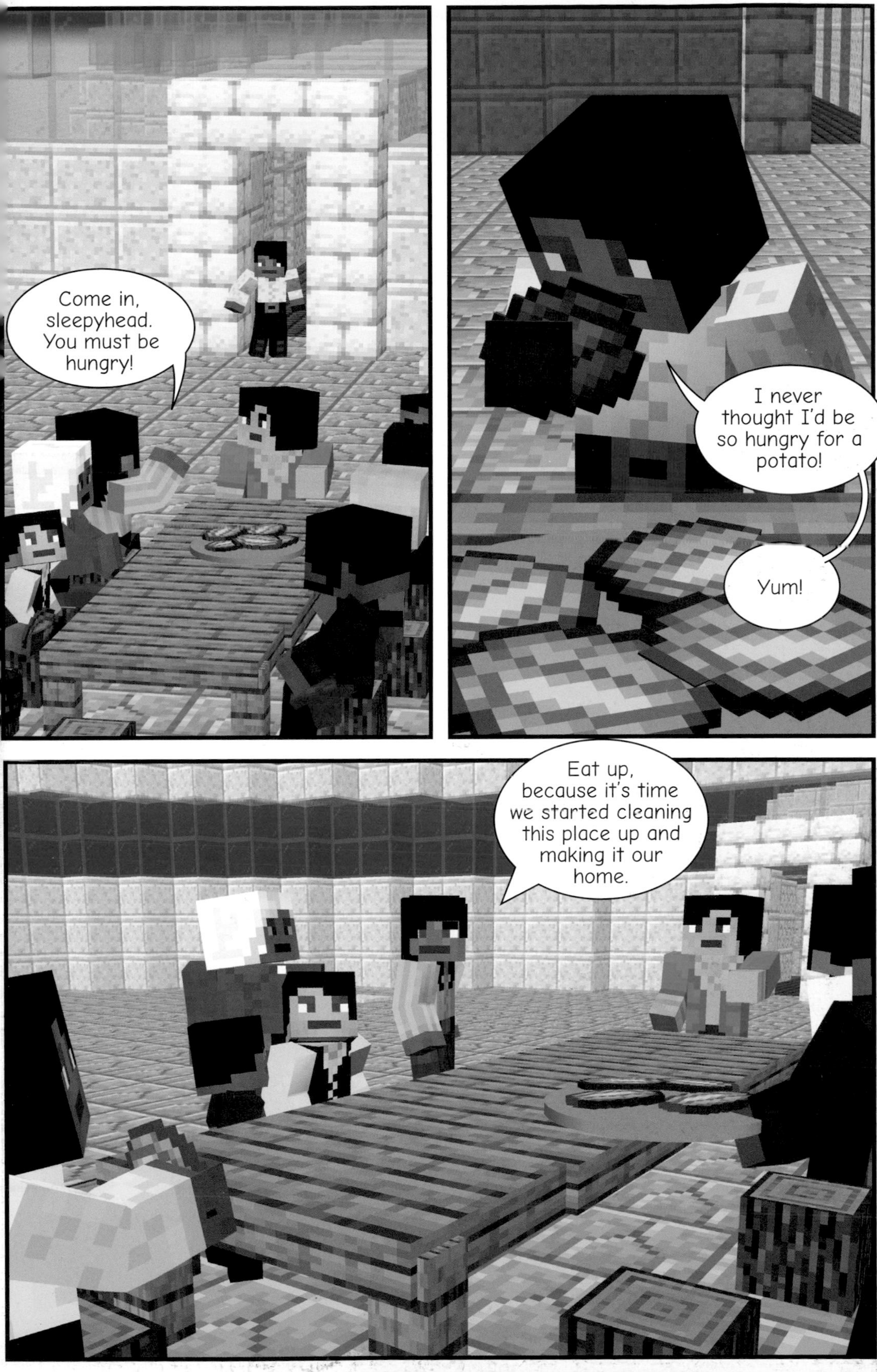
Come in, sleepyhead. You must be hungry!
I never thought I'd be so hungry for a potato!
Yum!
Eat up, because it's time we started cleaning this place up and making it our home.

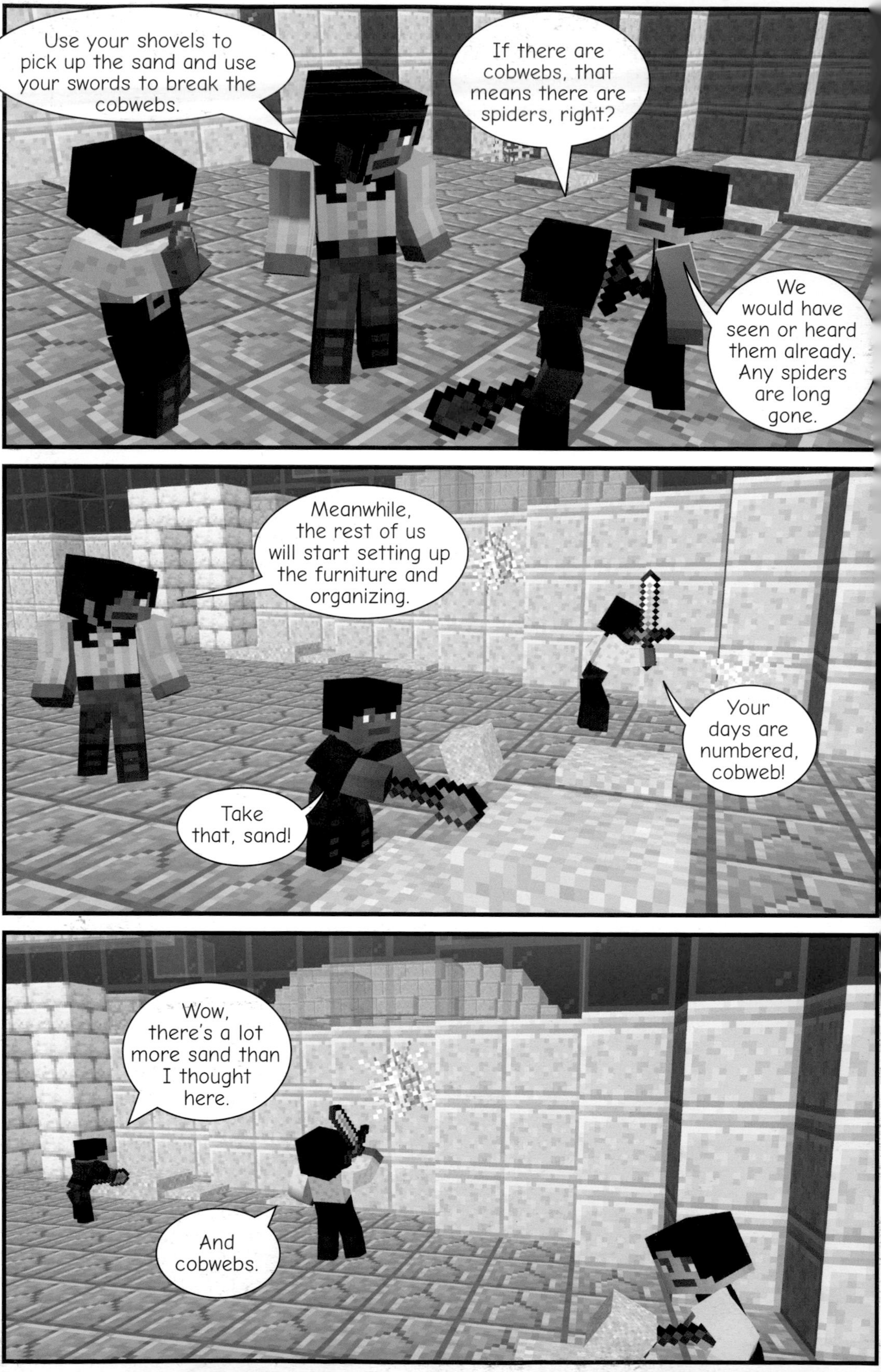

Use your shovels to pick up the sand and use your swords to break the cobwebs.
If there are cobwebs, that means there are spiders, right?
We would have seen or heard them already. Any spiders are long gone.
Meanwhile, the rest of us will start setting up the furniture and organizing.
Your days are numbered, cobweb!
Take that, sand!
Wow, there's a lot more sand than I thought here.
And cobwebs.

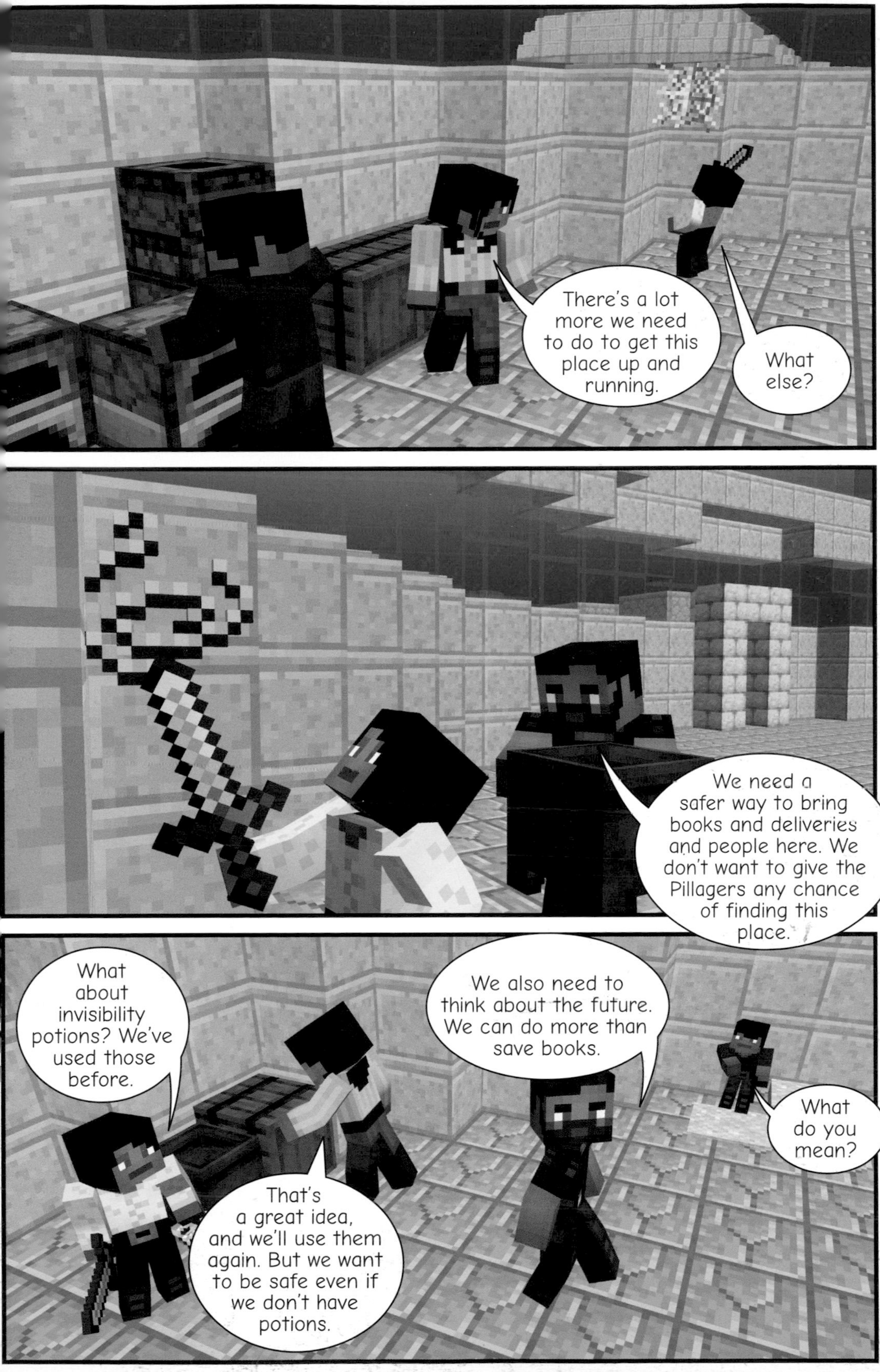
There's a lot more we need to do to get this place up and running.
What else?
We need a safer way to bring books and deliveries and people here. We don't want to give the Pillagers any chance of finding this place.
What about invisibility potions? We've used those before.
That's a great idea, and we'll use them again. But we want to be safe even if we don't have potions.
We also need to think about the future. We can do more than save books.
What do you mean?

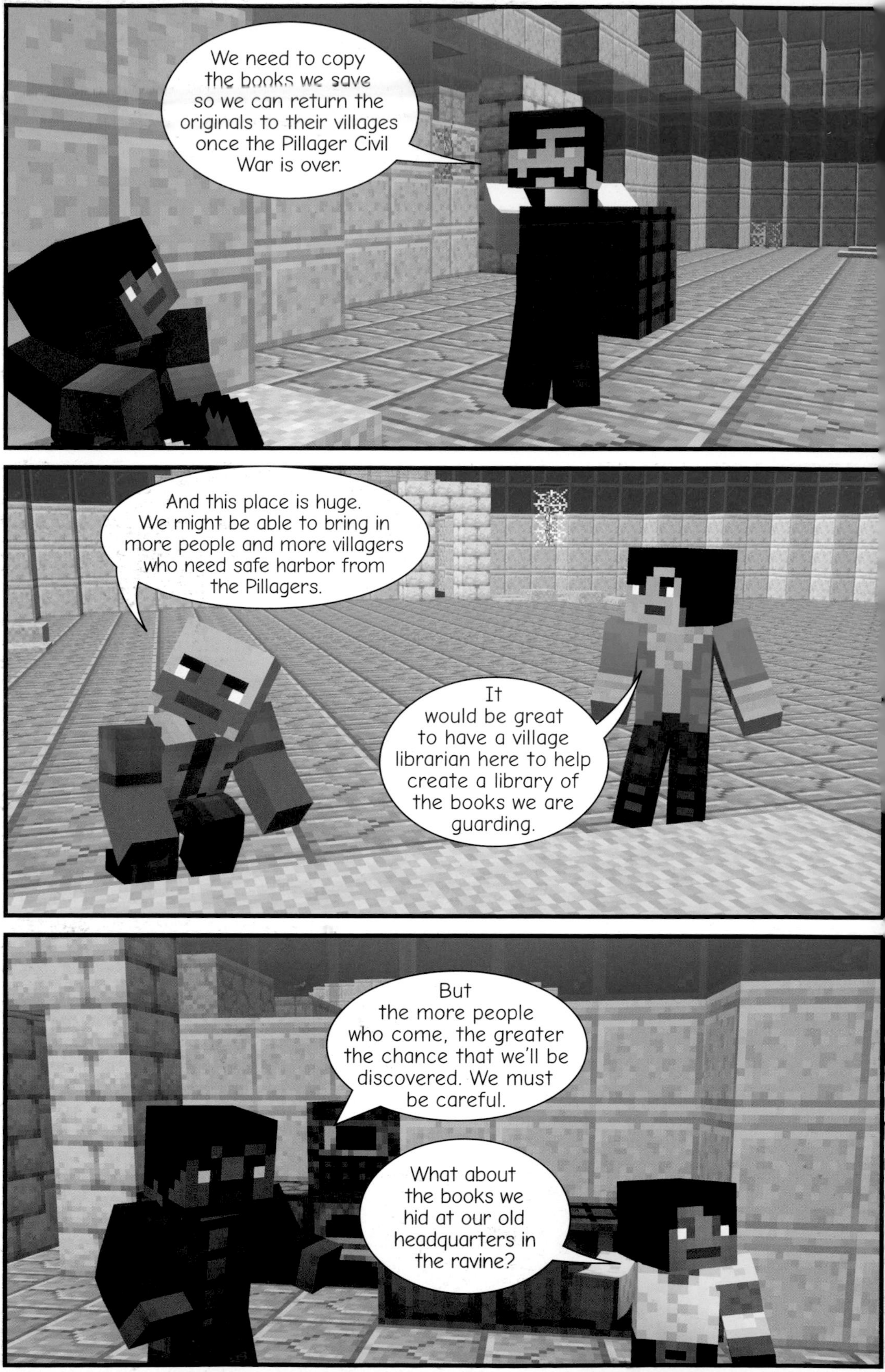
We need to copy the books we save so we can return the originals to their villages once the Pillager Civil War is over.
And this place is huge. We might be able to bring in more people and more villagers who need safe harbor from the Pillagers.
It would be great to have a village librarian here to help create a library of the books we are guarding.
But the more people who come, the greater the chance that we'll be discovered. We must be careful.
What about the books we hid at our old headquarters in the ravine?

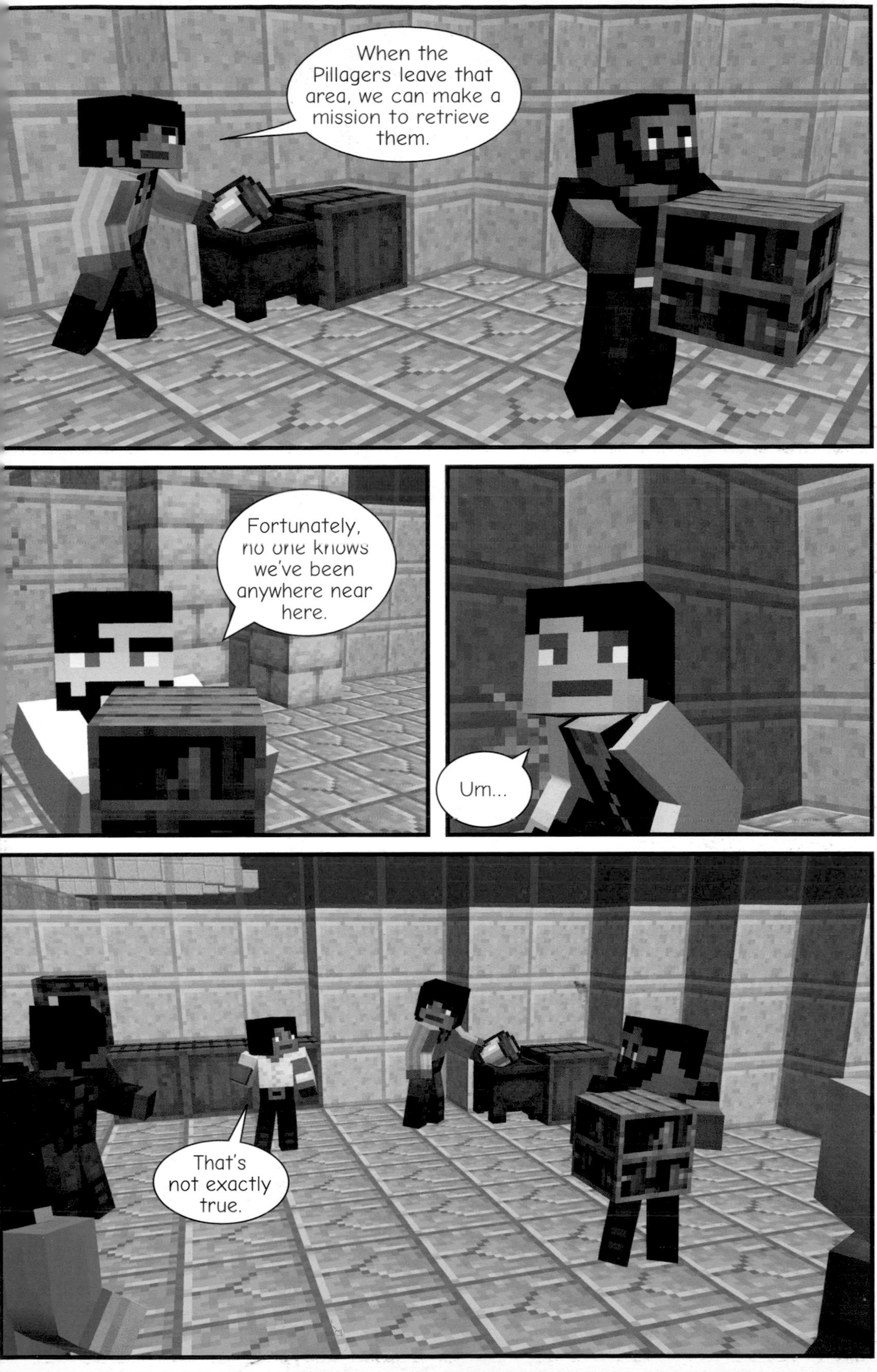
When the Pillagers leave that area, we can make a mission to retrieve them.
Fortunately, no one knows we've been anywhere near here.
Um...
That's not exactly true.

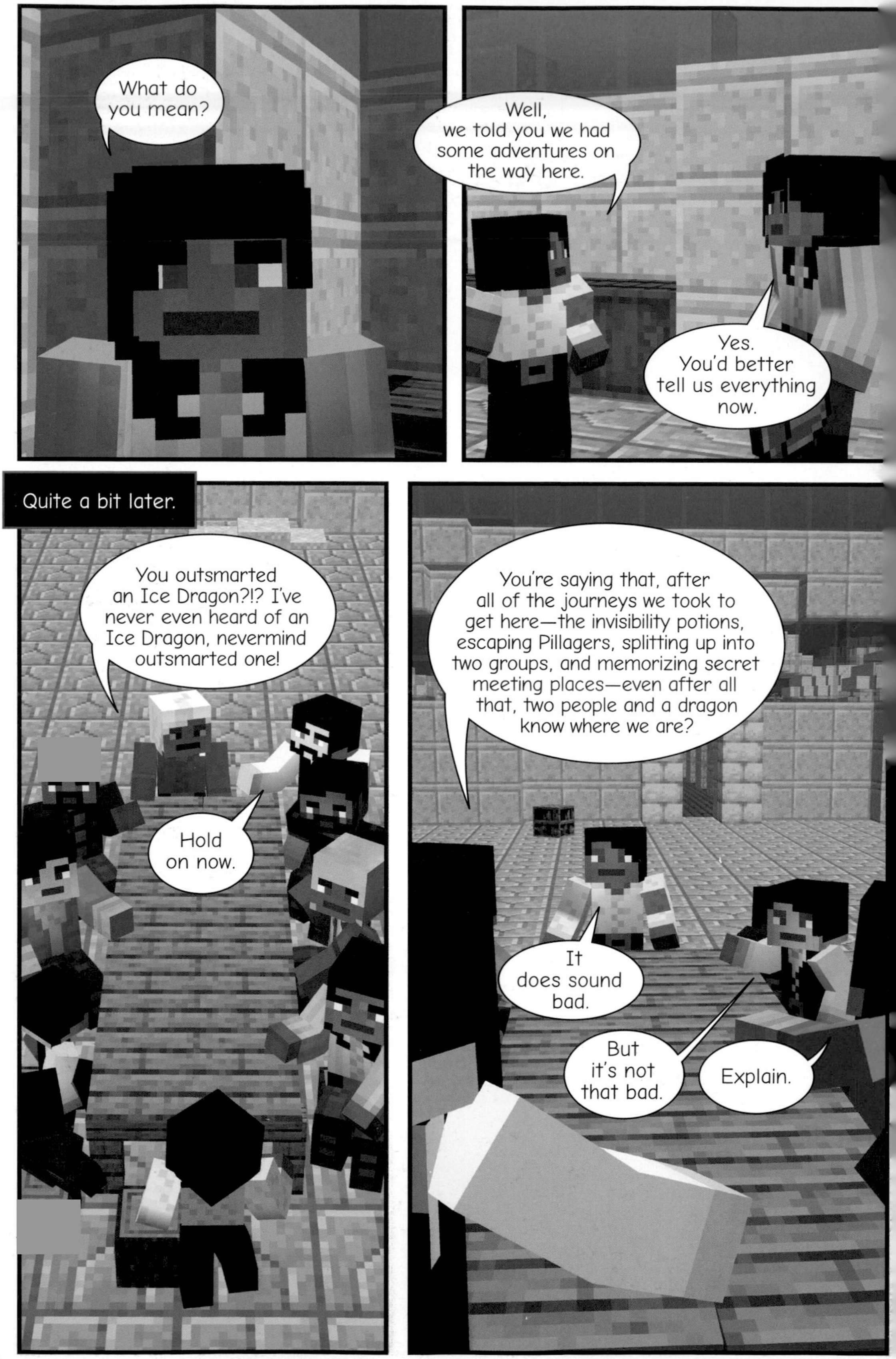

What do you mean?
Well, we told you we had some adventures on the way here.
Yes. You'd better tell us everything now.
Quite a bit later.
You outsmarted an Ice Dragon?!? I've never even heard of an Ice Dragon, nevermind outsmarted one!
Hold on now.
You're saying that, after all of the journeys we took to get here—the invisibility potions, escaping Pillagers, splitting up into two groups, and memorizing secret meeting places—even after all that, two people and a dragon know where we are?
It does sound bad.
But it's not that bad.
Explain.

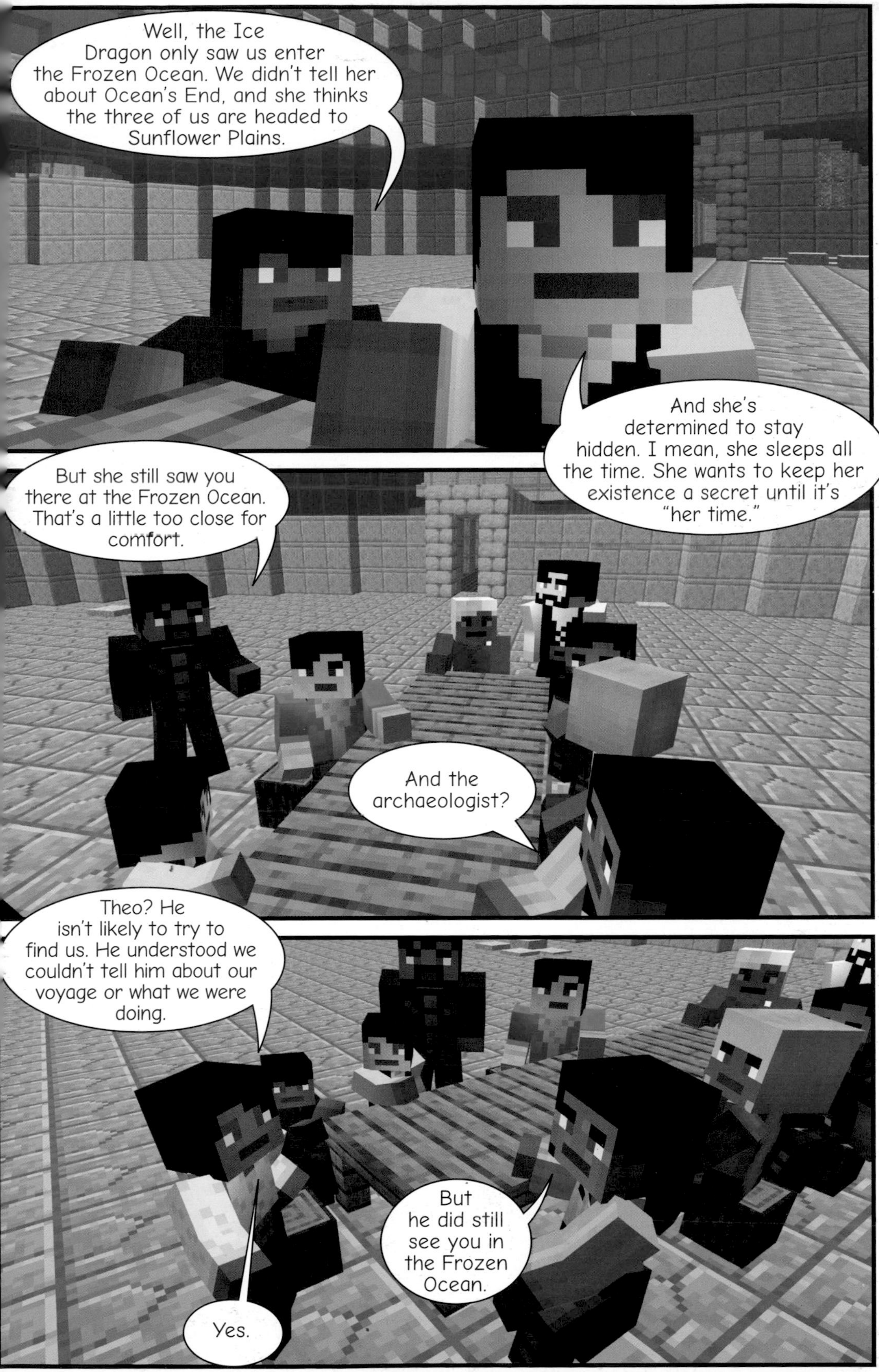
Well, the Ice Dragon only saw us enter the Frozen Ocean. We didn't tell her about Ocean's End, and she thinks the three of us are headed to Sunflower Plains.
And she's determined to stay hidden. I mean, she sleeps all the time. She wants to keep her existence a secret until it's "her time."
But she still saw you there at the Frozen Ocean. That's a little too close for comfort.
And the archaeologist?
Theo? He isn't likely to try to find us. He understood we couldn't tell him about our voyage or what we were doing.
But he did still see you in the Frozen Ocean.
Yes.

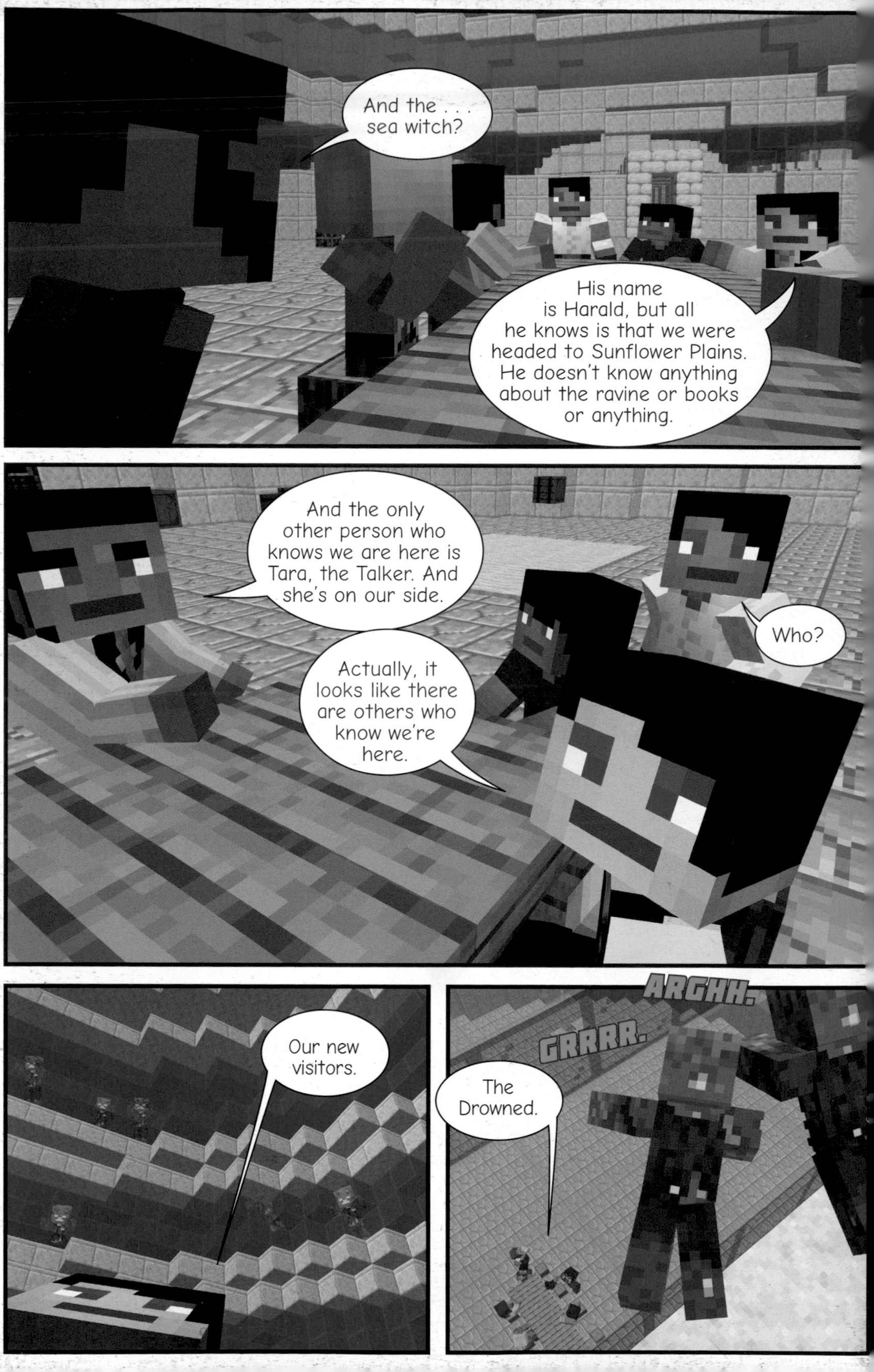
And the . . . sea witch?
His name is Harald, but all he knows is that we were headed to Sunflower Plains. He doesn't know anything about the ravine or books or anything.
And the only other person who knows we are here is Tara, the Talker. And she's on our side.
Who?
Actually, it looks like there are others who know we're here.
Our new visitors.
ARGHH.
GRRRR.
The Drowned.

Chapter 2
Unwelcome
Vistors

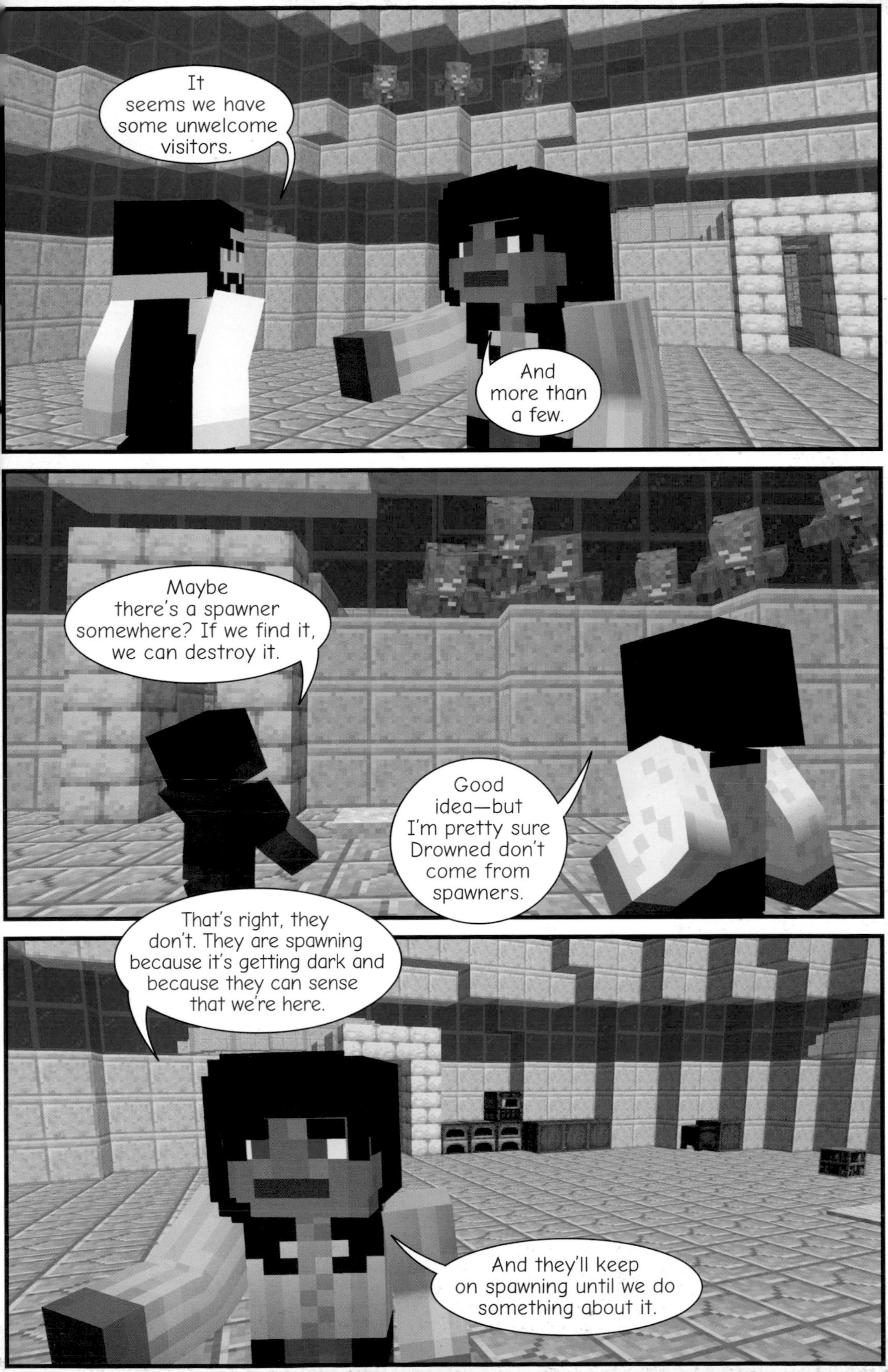
It seems we have some unwelcome visitors.
And more than a few.
Maybe there's a spawner somewhere? If we find it, we can destroy it.
Good idea—but I'm pretty sure Drowned don't come from spawners.
That's right, they don't. They are spawning because it's getting dark and because they can sense that we're here.
And they'll keep on spawning until we do something about it.

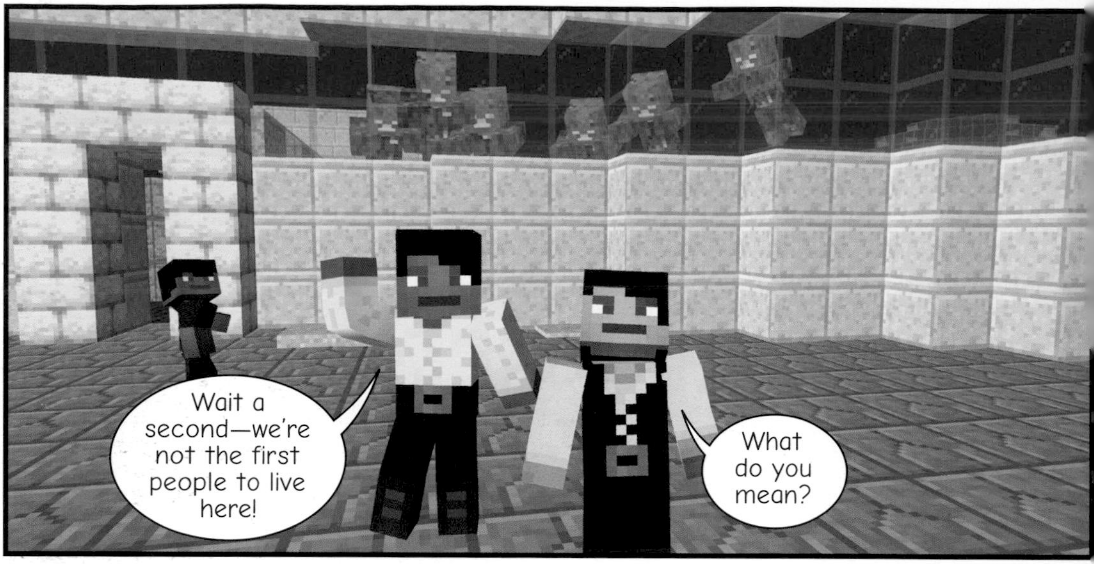
Wait a second—we're not the first people to live here!
What do you mean?

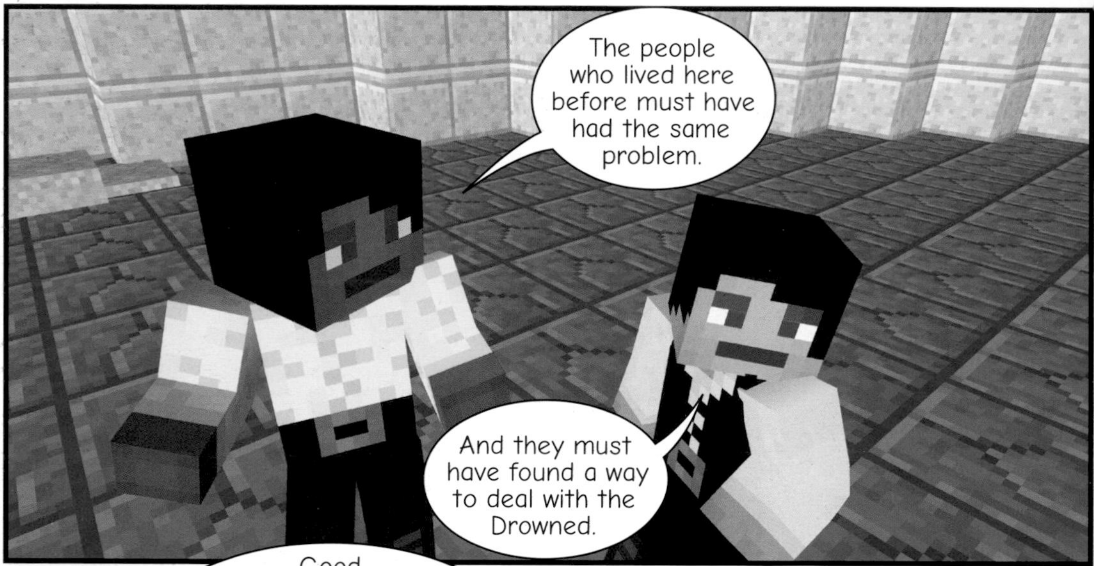
The people who lived here before must have had the same problem.
And they must have found a way to deal with the Drowned.

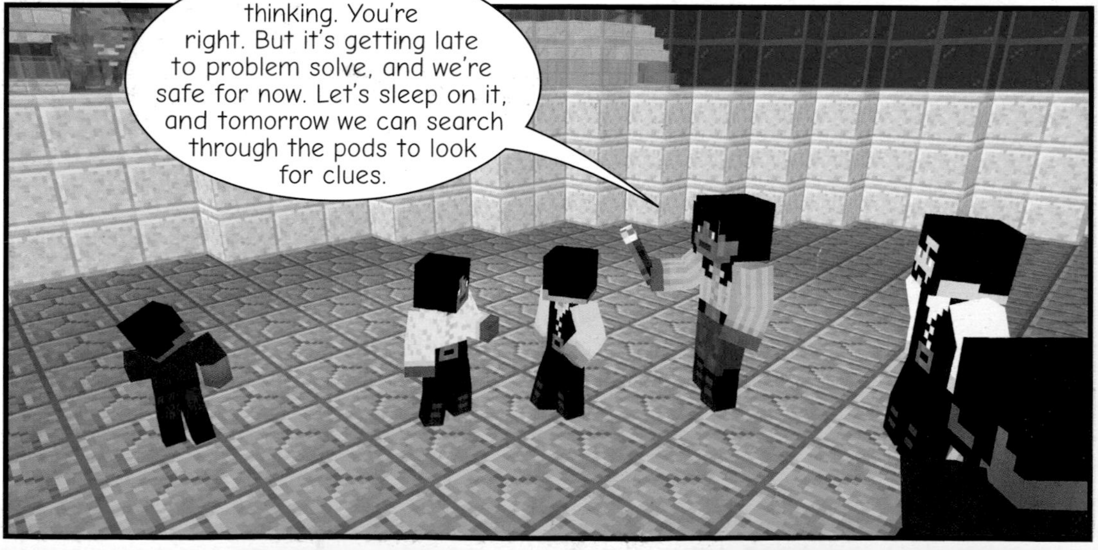
Good thinking. You're right. But it's getting late to problem solve, and we're safe for now. Let's sleep on it, and tomorrow we can search through the pods to look for clues.

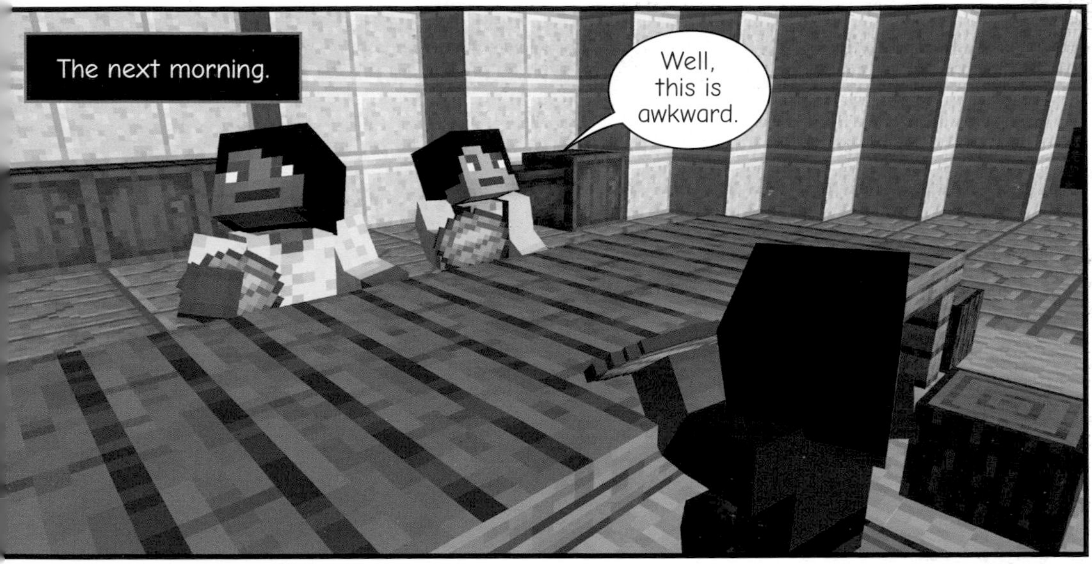
The next morning.
Well, this is awkward.

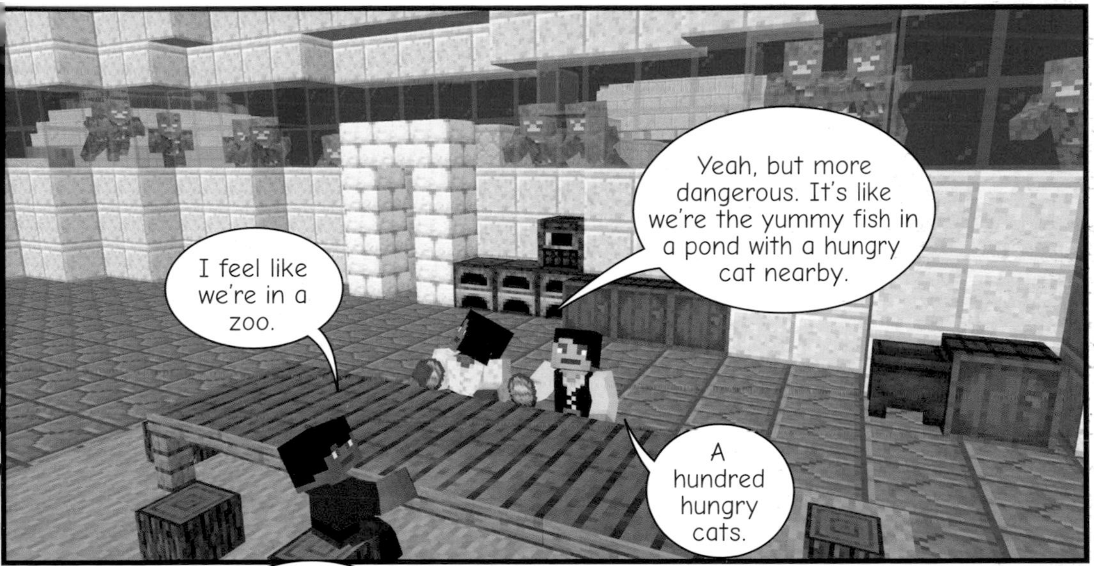
I feel like we're in a zoo.
Yeah, but more dangerous. It's like we're the yummy fish in a pond with a hungry cat nearby.
A hundred hungry cats.

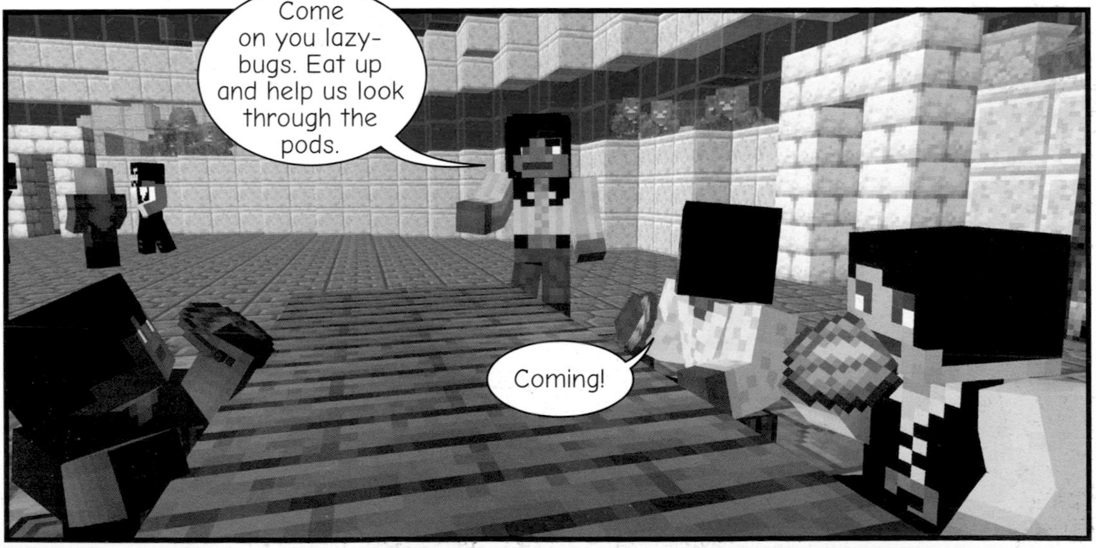
Come on you lazy-bugs. Eat up and help us look through the pods.
Coming!

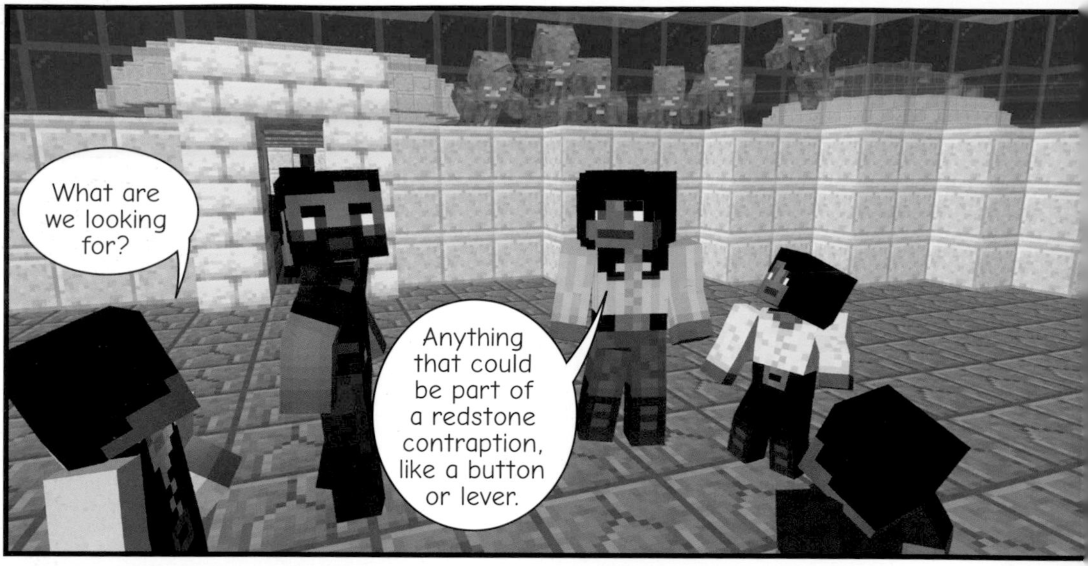
What are we looking for?
Anything that could be part of a redstone contraption, like a button or lever.

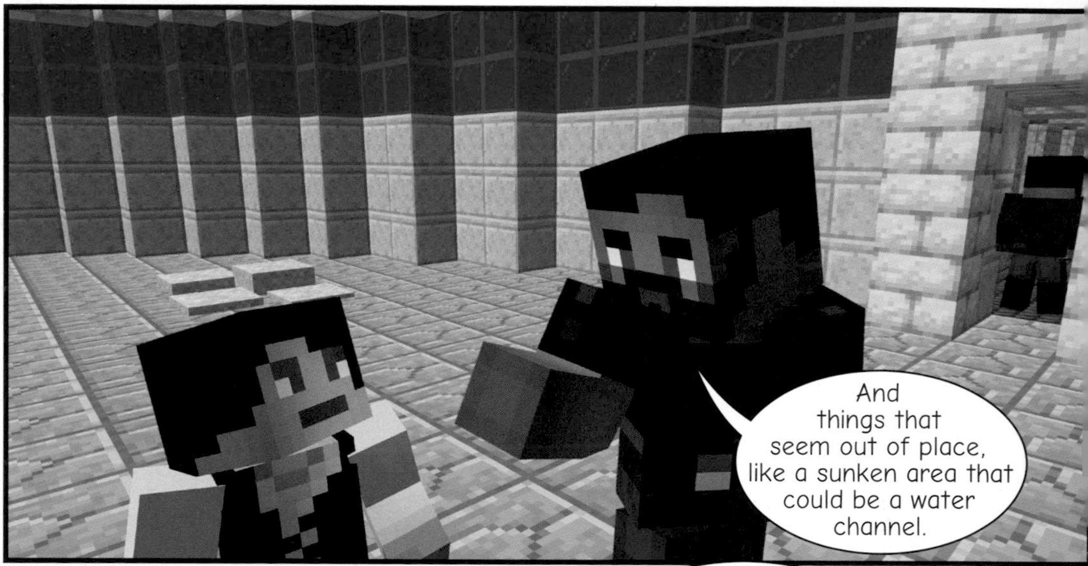
And things that seem out of place, like a sunken area that could be a water channel.

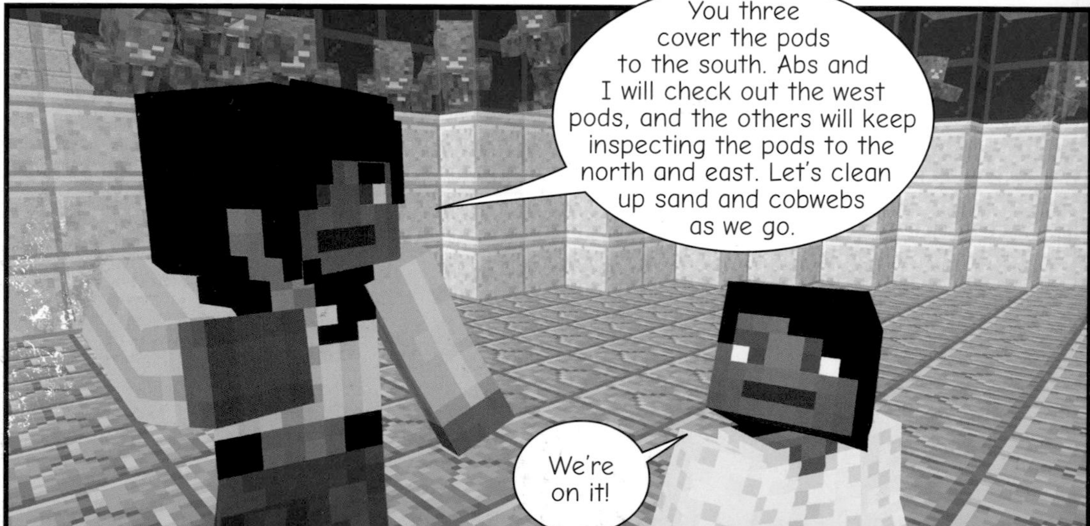
You three cover the pods to the south. Abs and I will check out the west pods, and the others will keep inspecting the pods to the north and east. Let's clean up sand and cobwebs as we go.
We're on it!

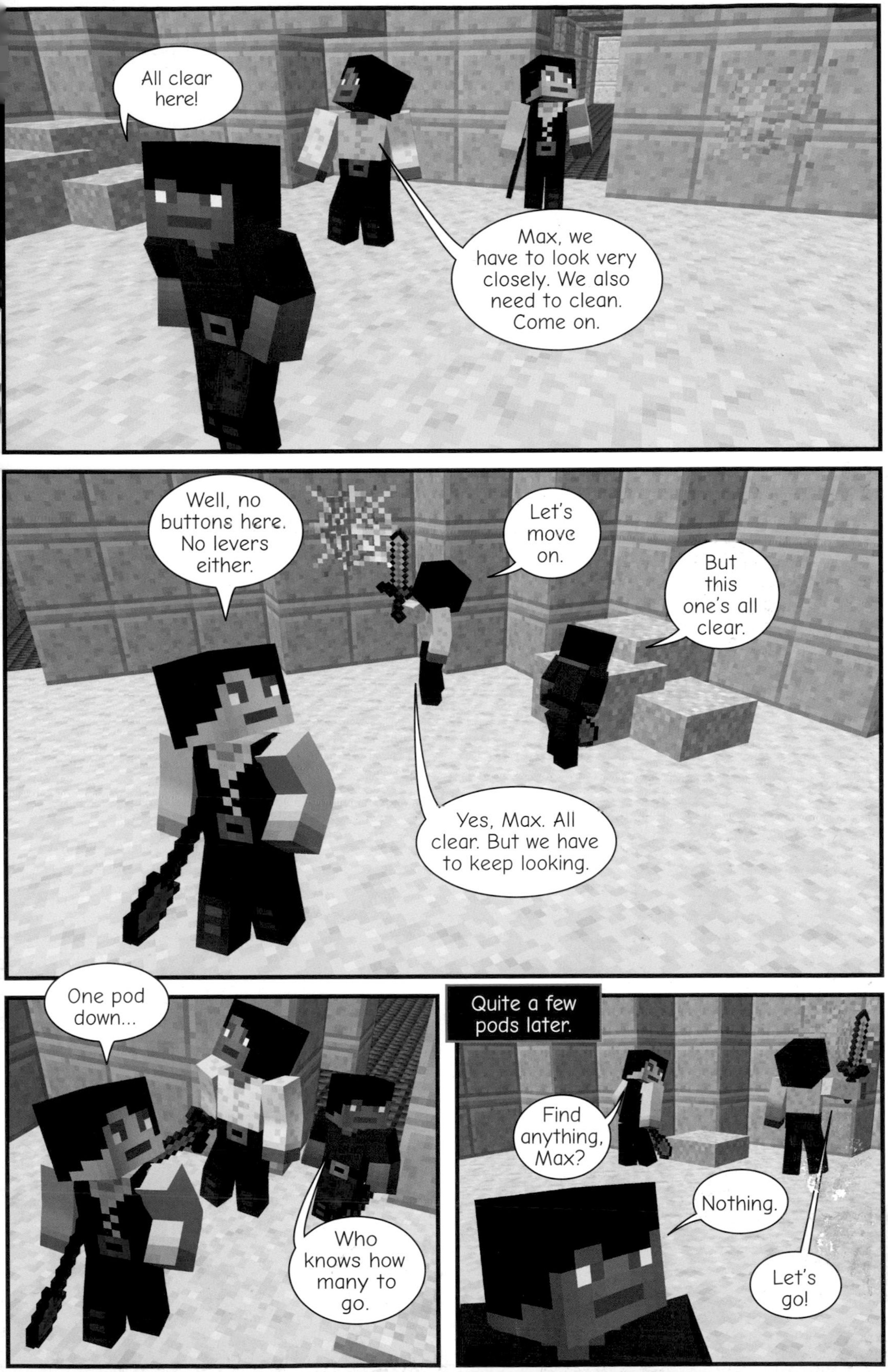
All clear here!
Max, we have to look very closely. We also need to clean. Come on.
Well, no buttons here. No levers either.
Let's move on.
But this one's all clear.
Yes, Max. All clear. But we have to keep looking.
One pod down...
Who knows how many to go.
Quite a few pods later.
Find anything, Max?
Nothing.
Let's go!

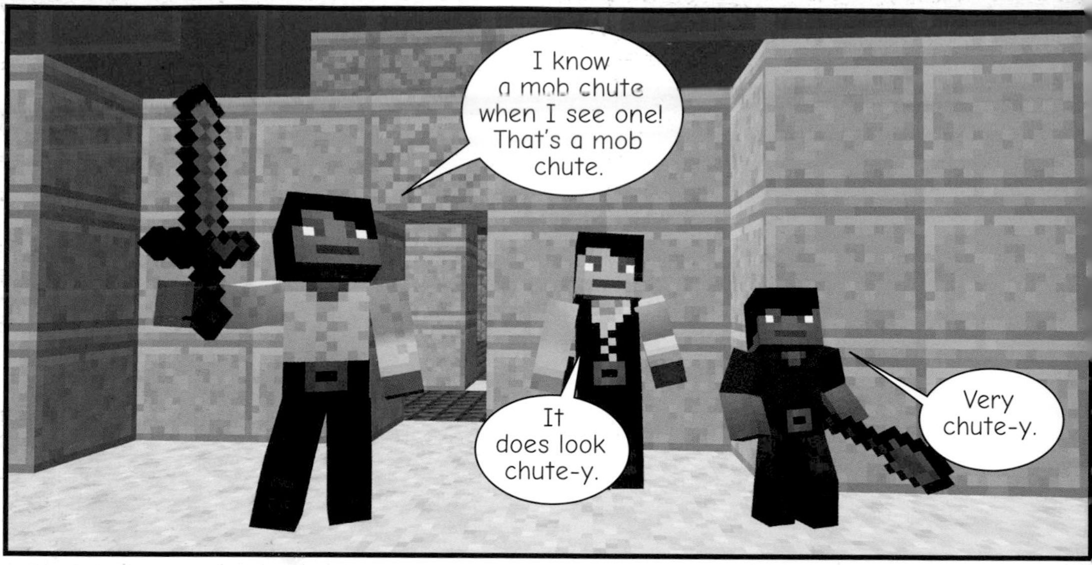
I know a mob chute when I see one! That's a mob chute.
It does look chute-y.
Very chute-y.

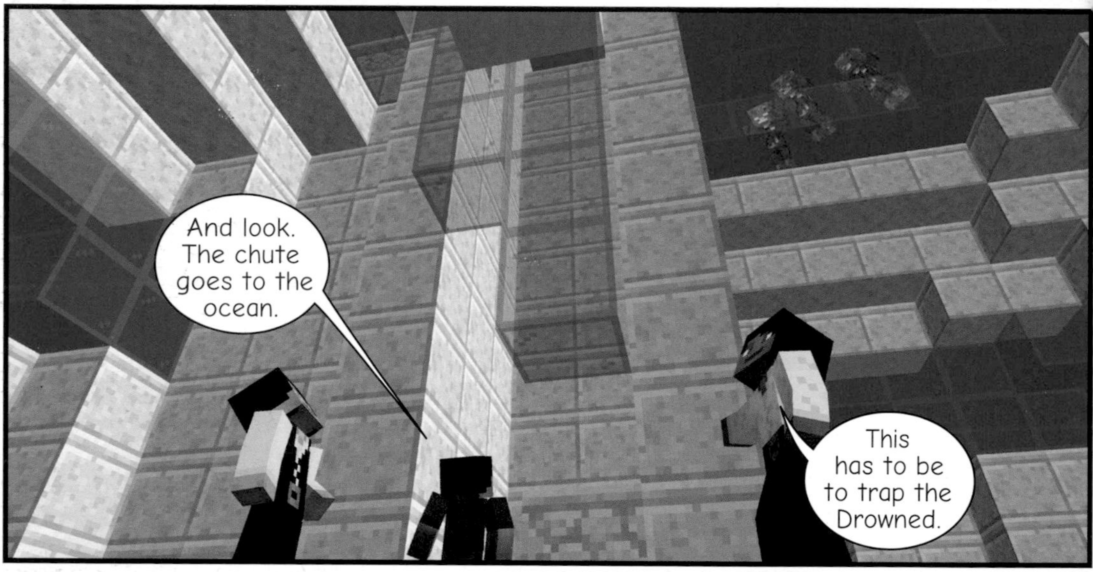
And look. The chute goes to the ocean.
This has to be to trap the Drowned.

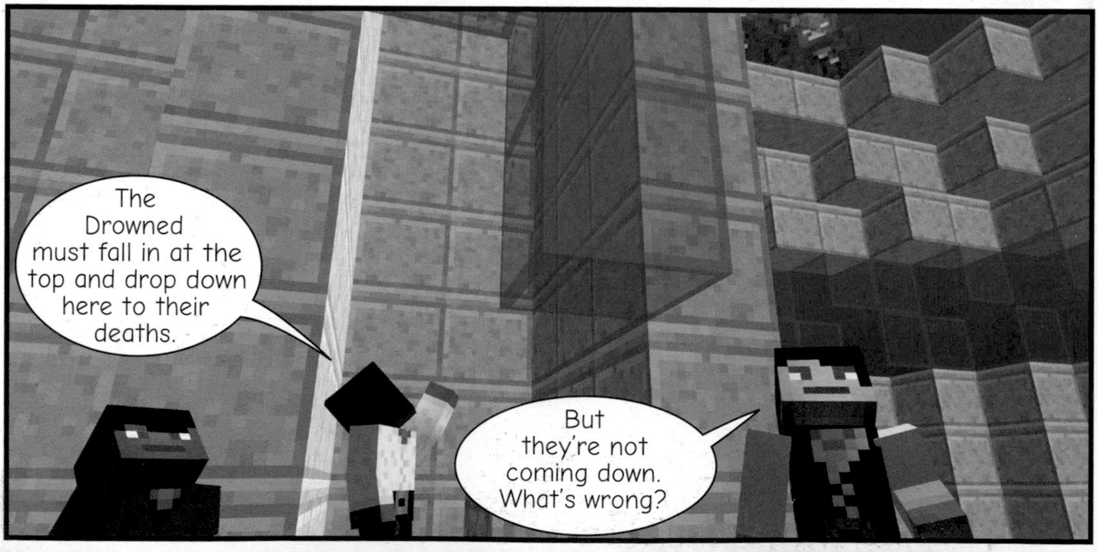
The Drowned must fall in at the top and drop down here to their deaths.
But they're not coming down. What's wrong?

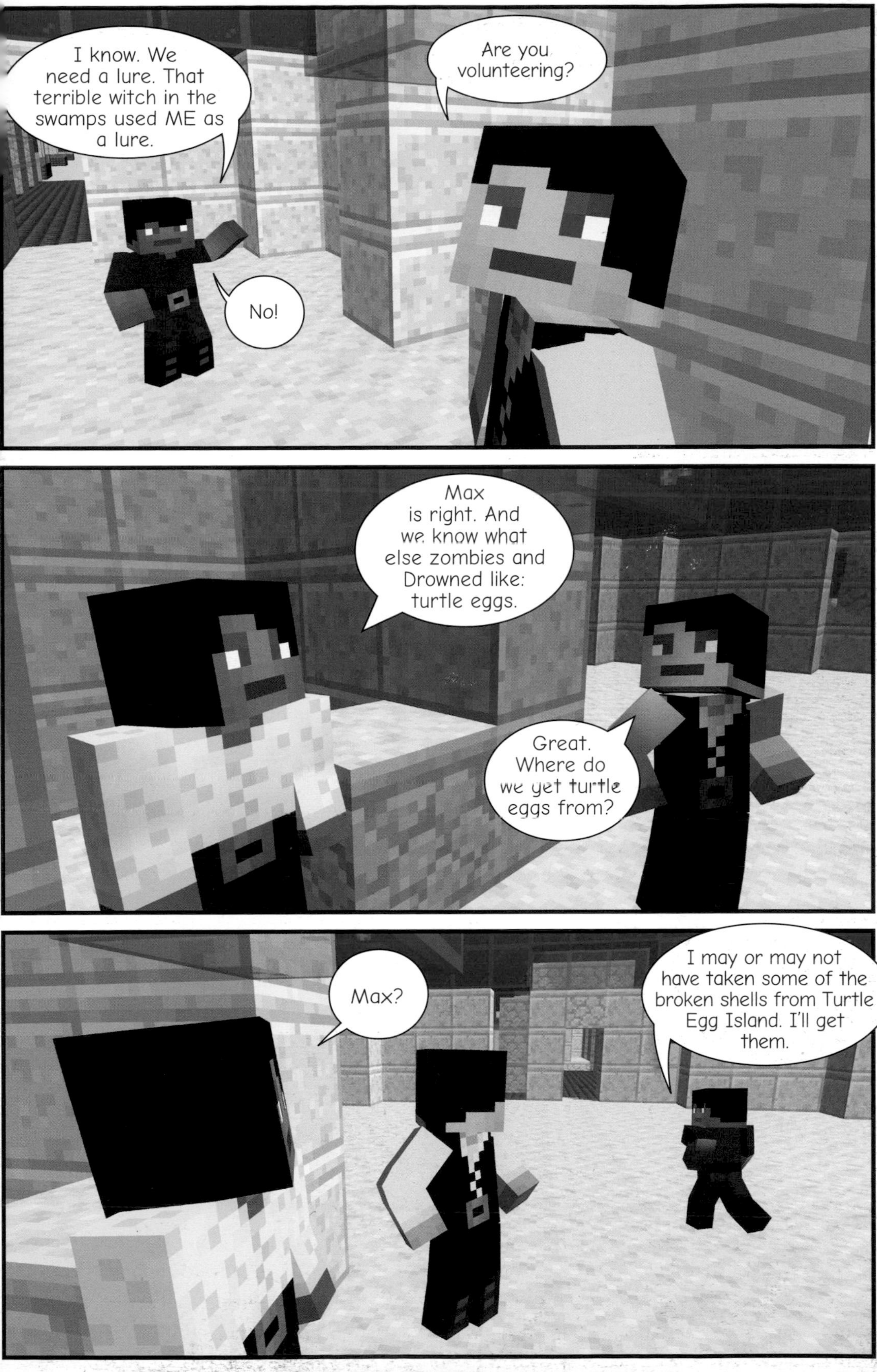
I know. We need a lure. That terrible witch in the swamps used ME as a lure.
Are you volunteering?
No!
Max is right. And we know what else zombies and Drowned like: turtle eggs.
Great. Where do we get turtle eggs from?
Max?
I may or may not have taken some of the broken shells from Turtle Egg Island. I'll get them.

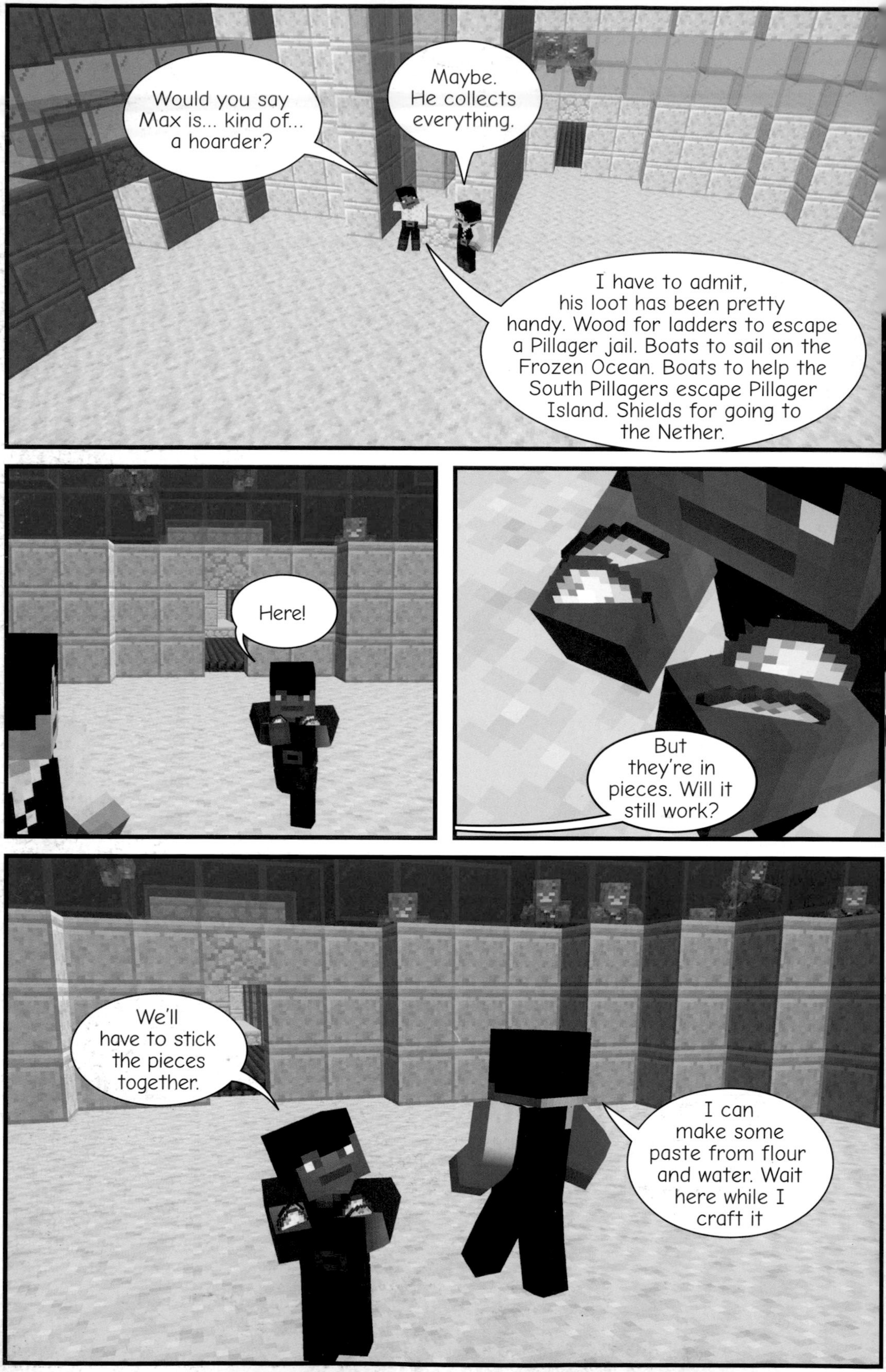
Would you say Max is... kind of... a hoarder?
Maybe. He collects everything.
I have to admit, his loot has been pretty handy. Wood for ladders to escape a Pillager jail. Boats to sail on the Frozen Ocean. Boats to help the South Pillagers escape Pillager Island. Shields for going to the Nether.
Here!
But they're in pieces. Will it still work?
We'll have to stick the pieces together.
I can make some paste from flour and water. Wait here while I craft it

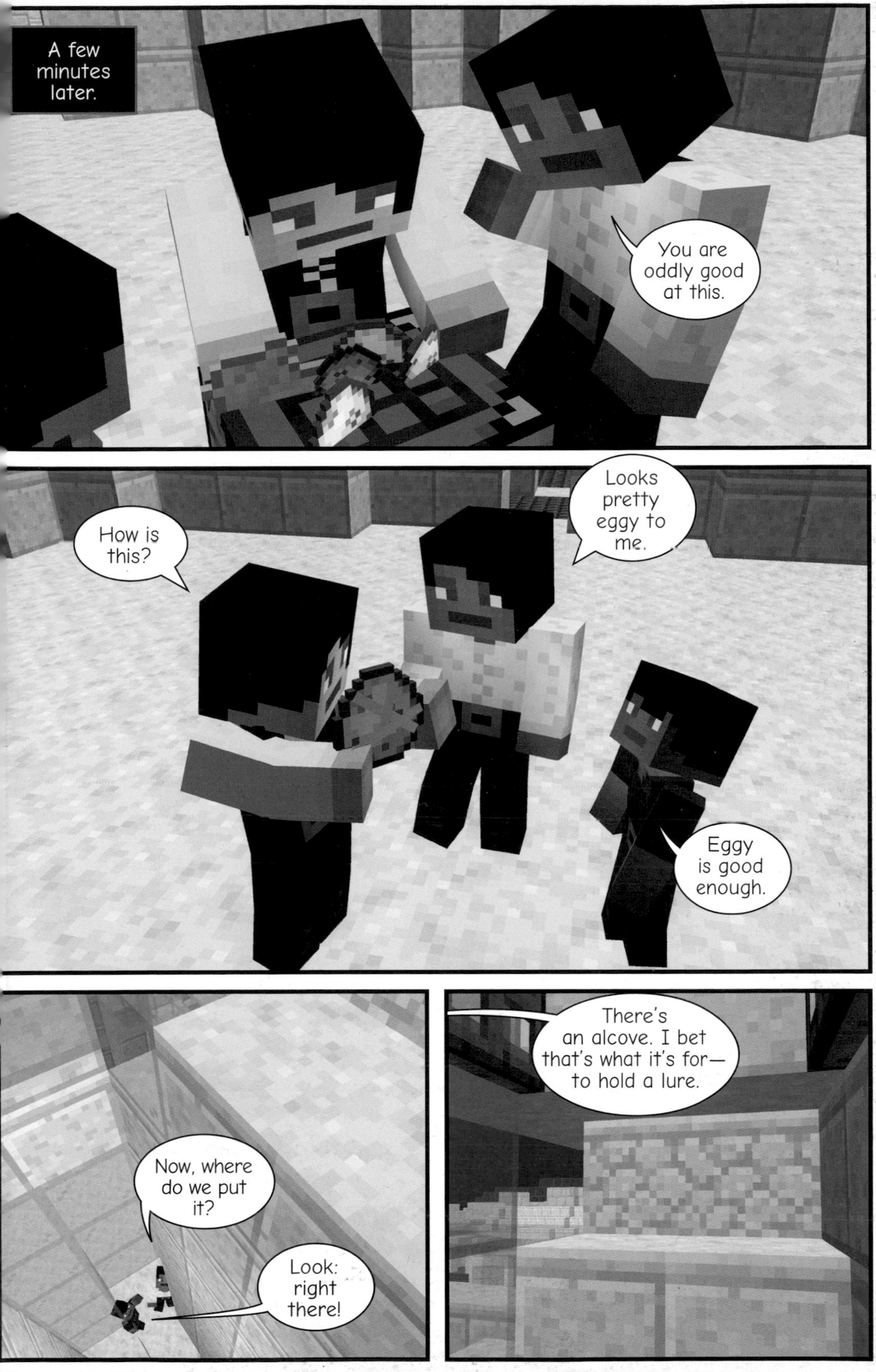
A few minutes later.
You are oddly good at this.
How is this?
Looks pretty eggy to me.
Eggy is good enough.
Now, where do we put it?
Look: right there!
There's an alcove. I bet that's what it's for—to hold a lure.

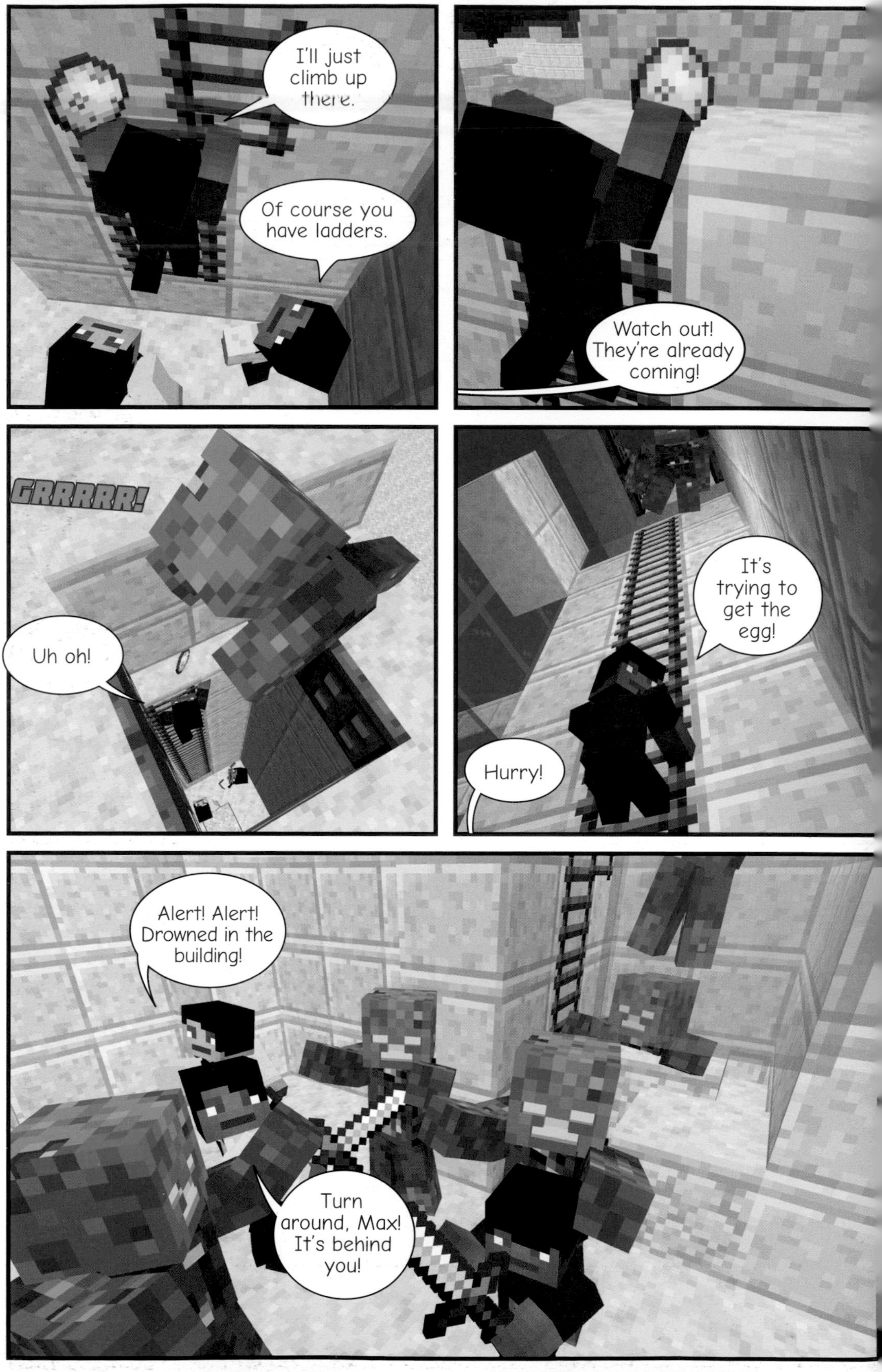
I'll just climb up there.
Of course you have ladders.
Watch out! They're already coming!
GRRRRR!
Uh oh!
It's trying to get the egg!
Hurry!
Alert! Alert! Drowned in the building!
Turn around, Max! It's behind you!

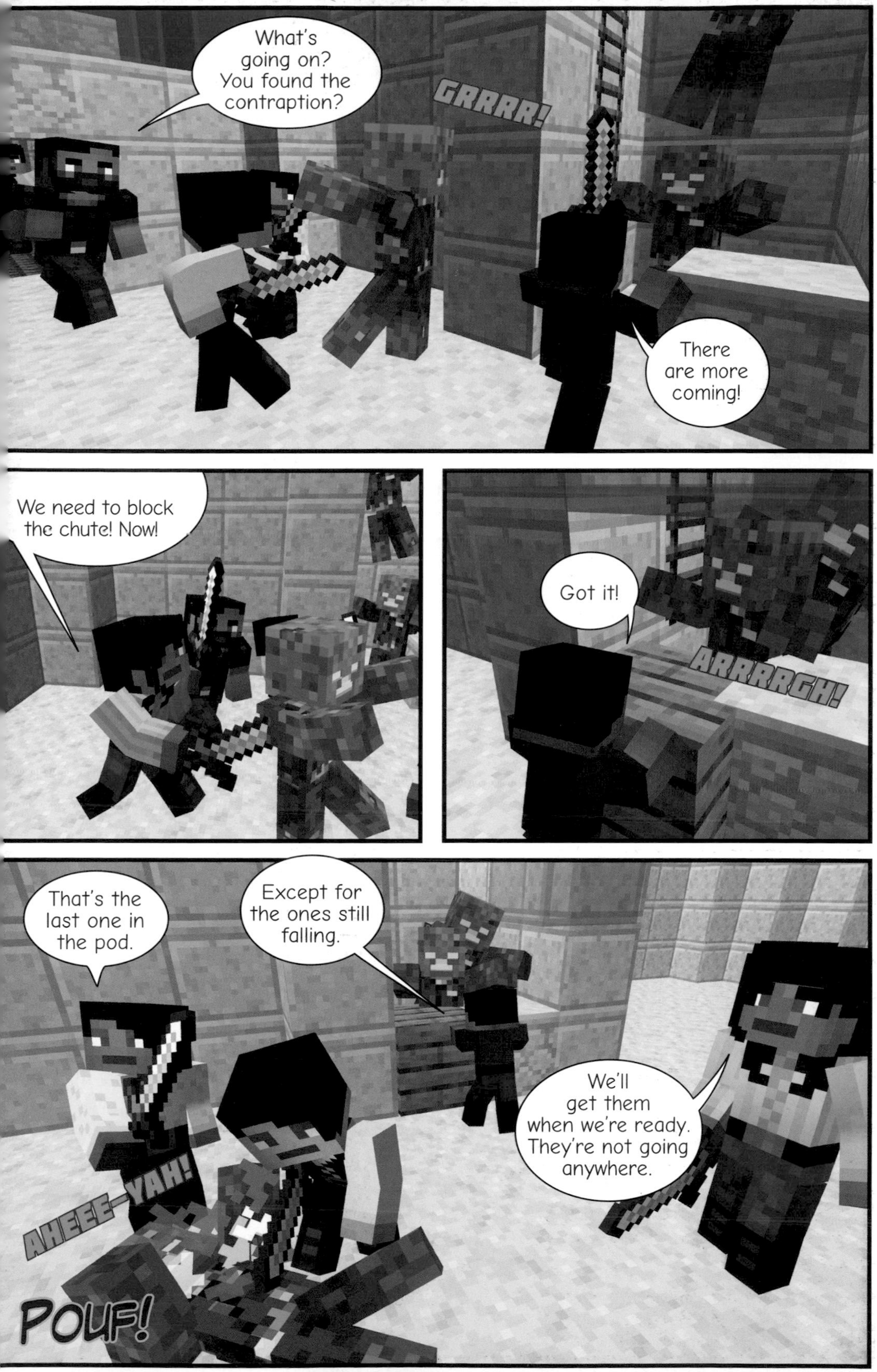
What's going on? You found the contraption?
GRRRR!
There are more coming!
We need to block the chute! Now!
Got it!
ARRRRGH!
That's the last one in the pod.
Except for the ones still falling.
We'll get them when we're ready. They're not going anywhere.
AHEEE-YAH!
POUF!

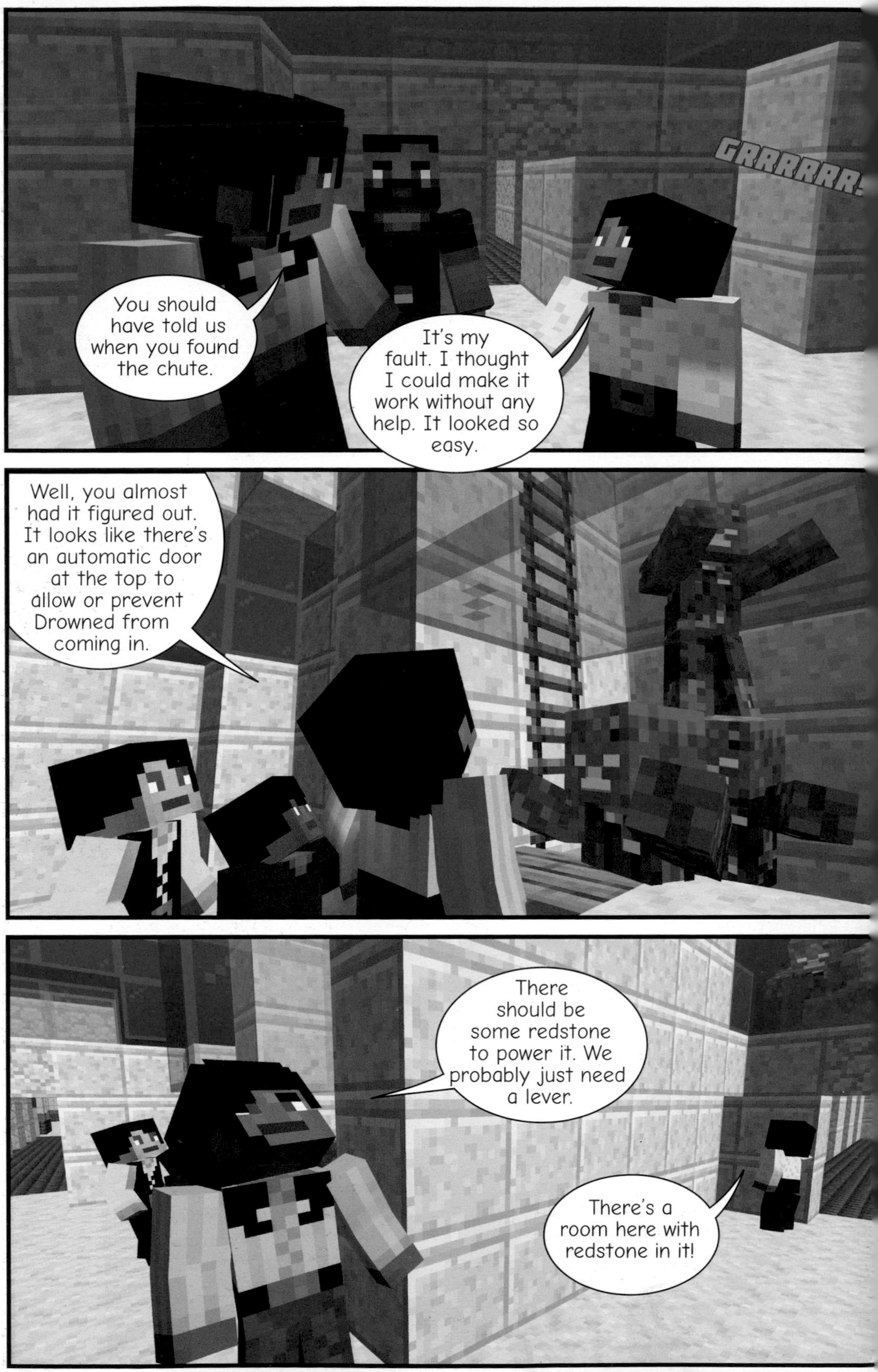
GRRRRRR!
You should have told us when you found the chute.
It's my fault. I thought I could make it work without any help. It looked so easy.
Well, you almost had it figured out. It looks like there's an automatic door at the top to allow or prevent Drowned from coming in.
There should be some redstone to power it. We probably just need a lever.
There's a room here with redstone in it!

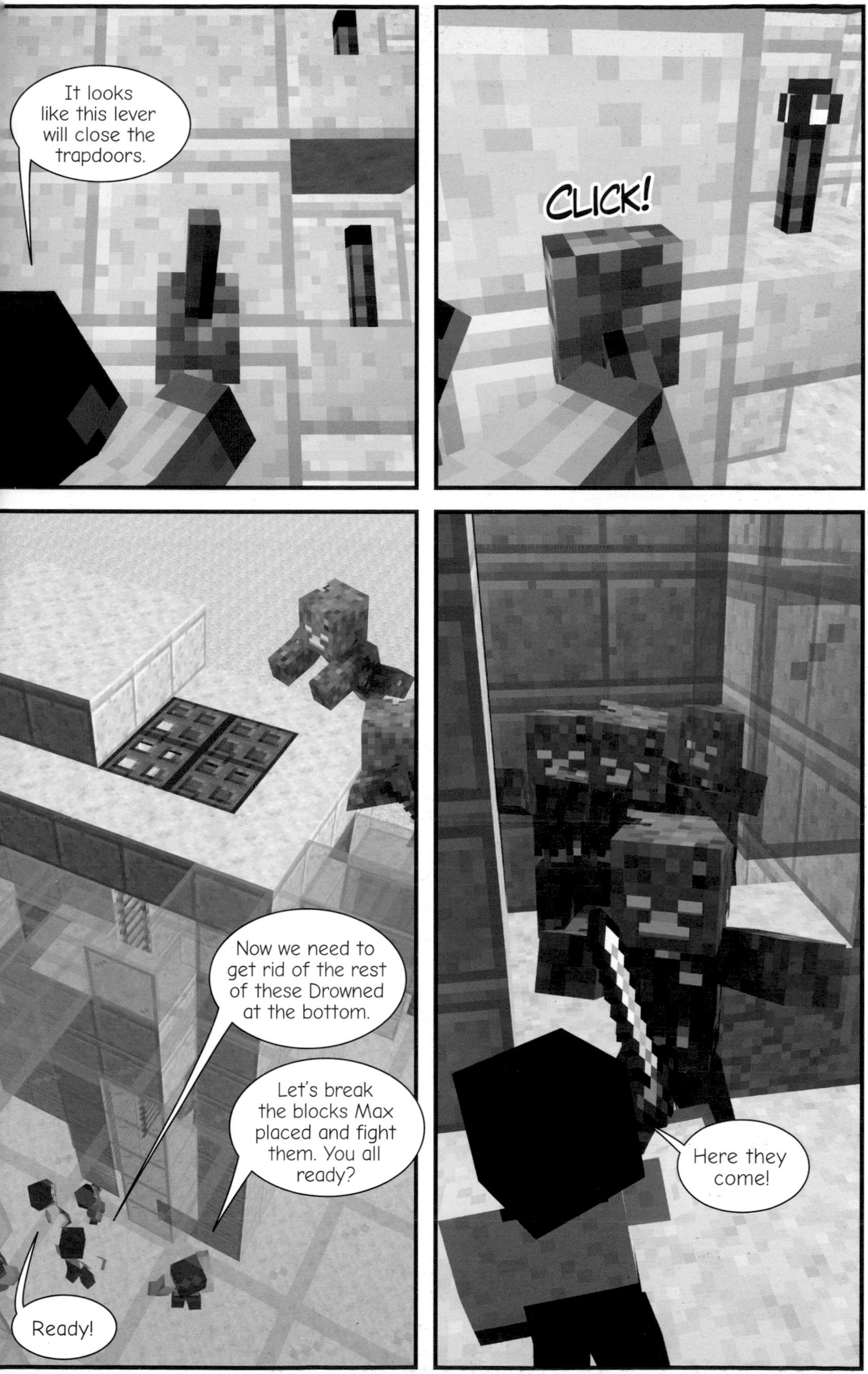
It looks like this lever will close the trapdoors.
CLICK!
Now we need to get rid of the rest of these Drowned at the bottom.
Let's break the blocks Max placed and fight them. You all ready?
Ready!
Here they come!

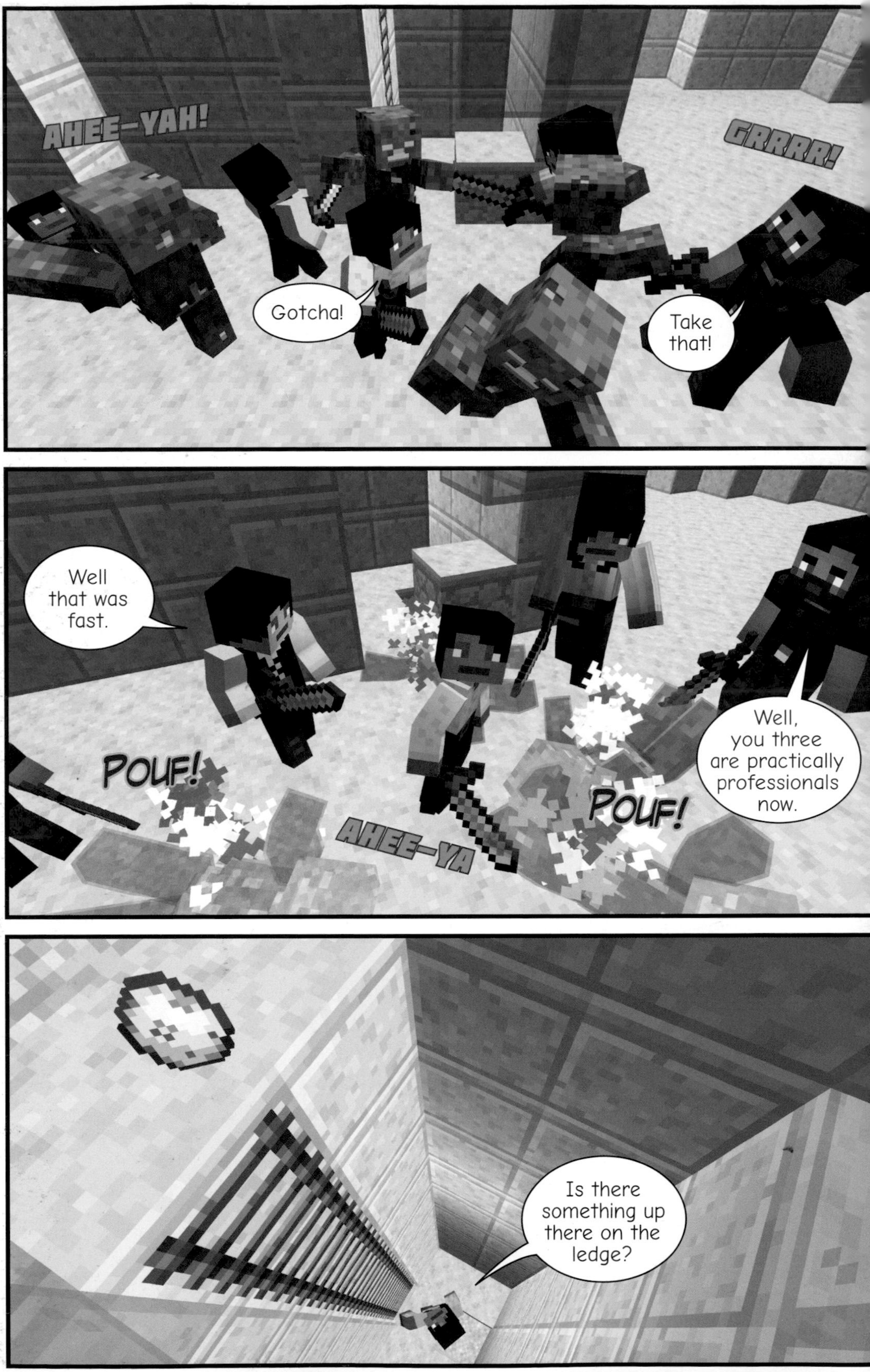
AHEE-YAH!
GRRRR!
Gotcha!
Take that!
Well that was fast.
POUF!
AHEE-YA
POUF!
Well, you three are practically professionals now.
Is there something up there on the ledge?

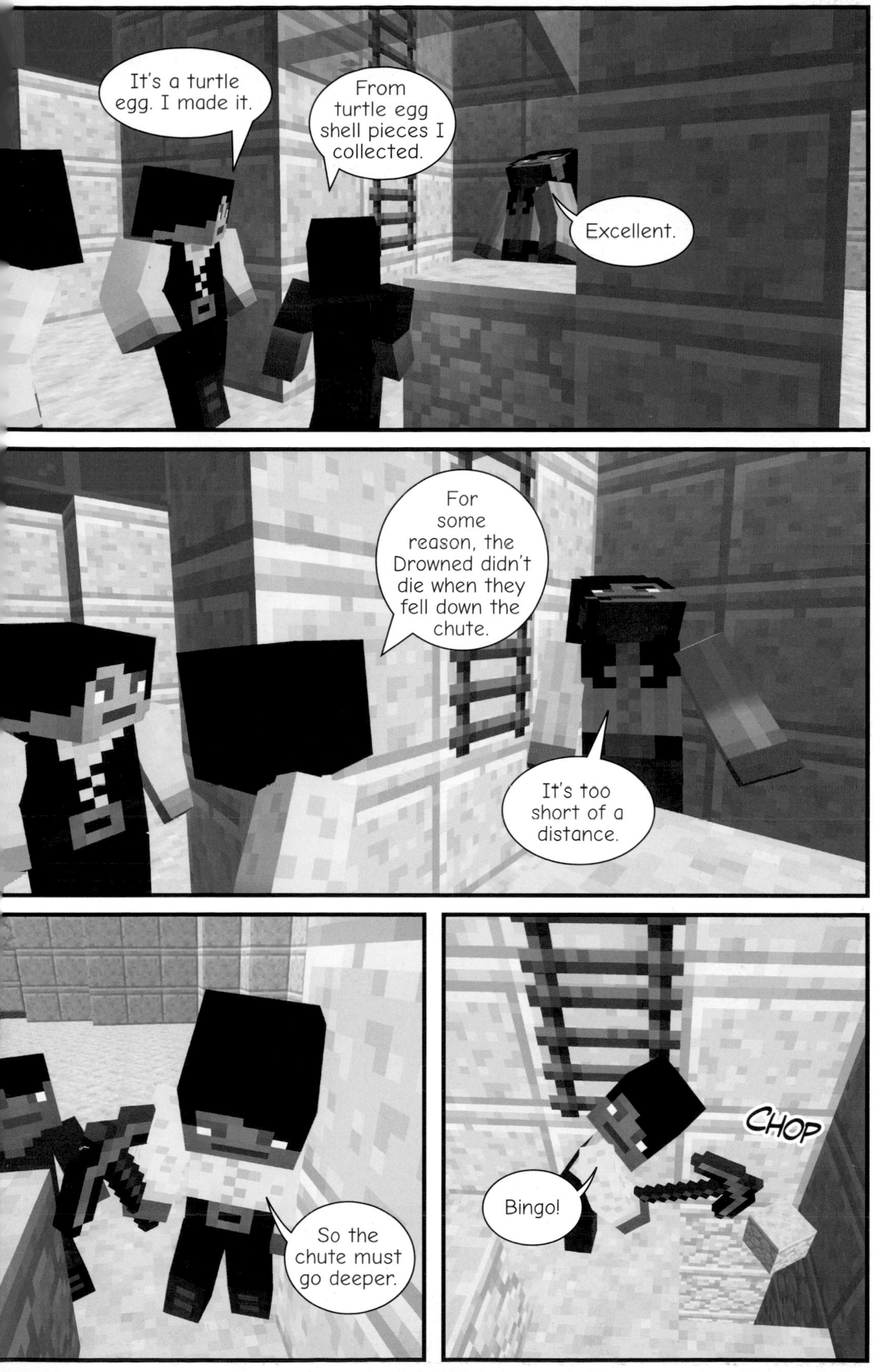
It's a turtle egg. I made it.
From turtle egg shell pieces I collected.
Excellent.
For some reason, the Drowned didn't die when they fell down the chute.
It's too short of a distance.
So the chute must go deeper.
CHOP
Bingo!

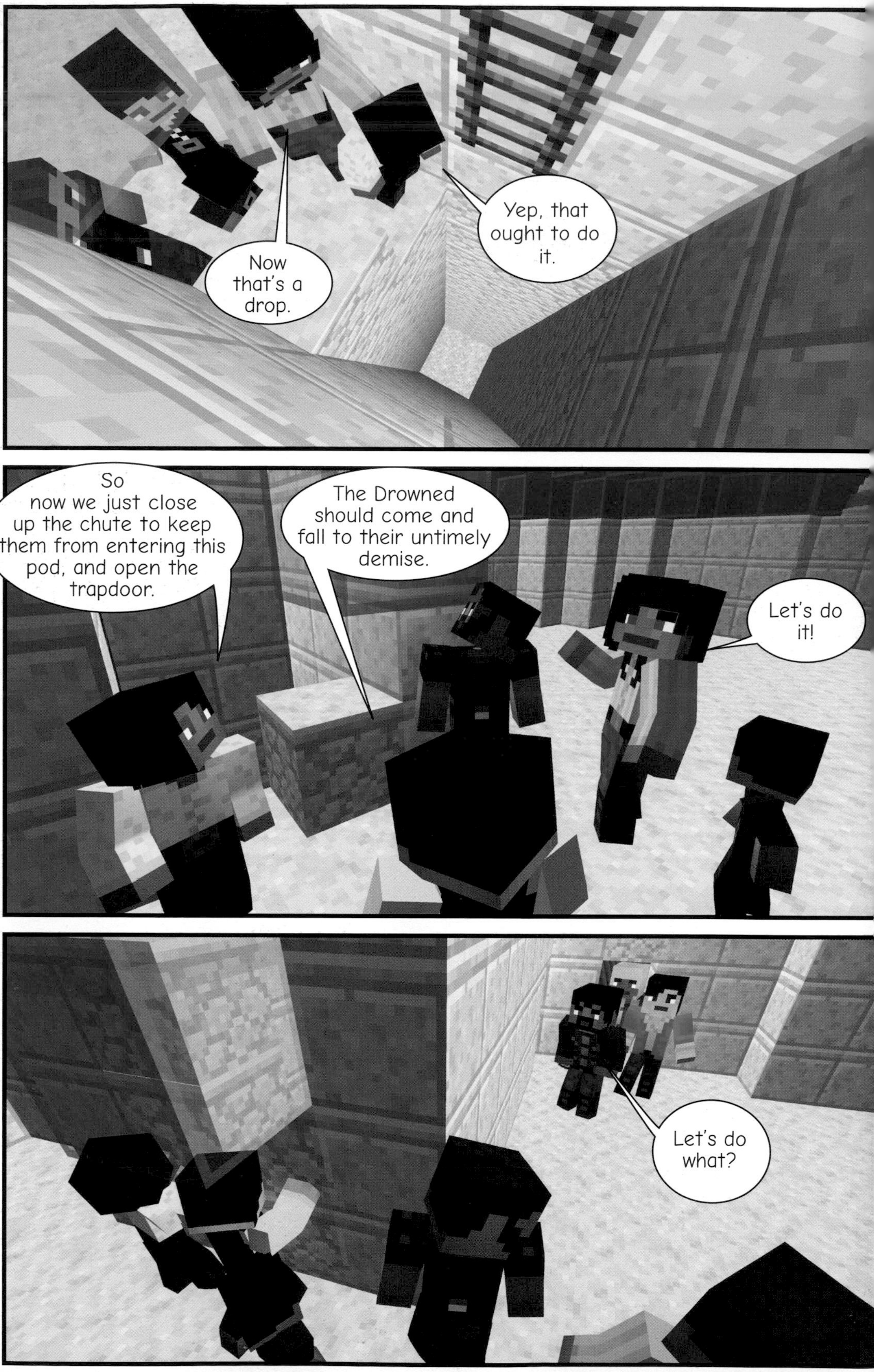
Now that's a drop.
Yep, that ought to do it.
So now we just close up the chute to keep them from entering this pod, and open the trapdoor.
The Drowned should come and fall to their untimely demise.
Let's do it!
Let's do what?

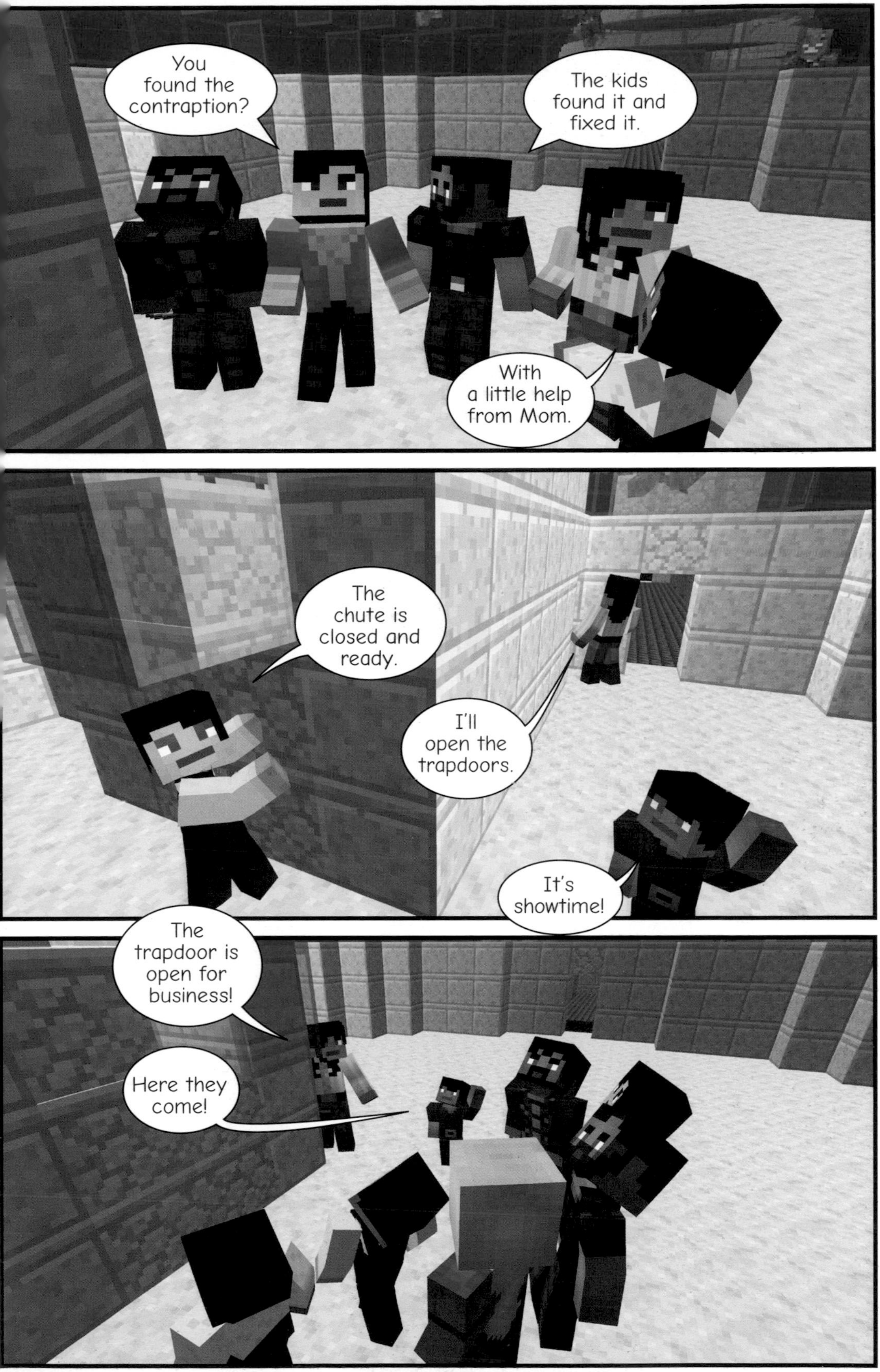

You found the contraption?
The kids found it and fixed it.
With a little help from Mom.
The chute is closed and ready.
I'll open the trapdoors.
It's showtime!
The trapdoor is open for business!
Here they come!

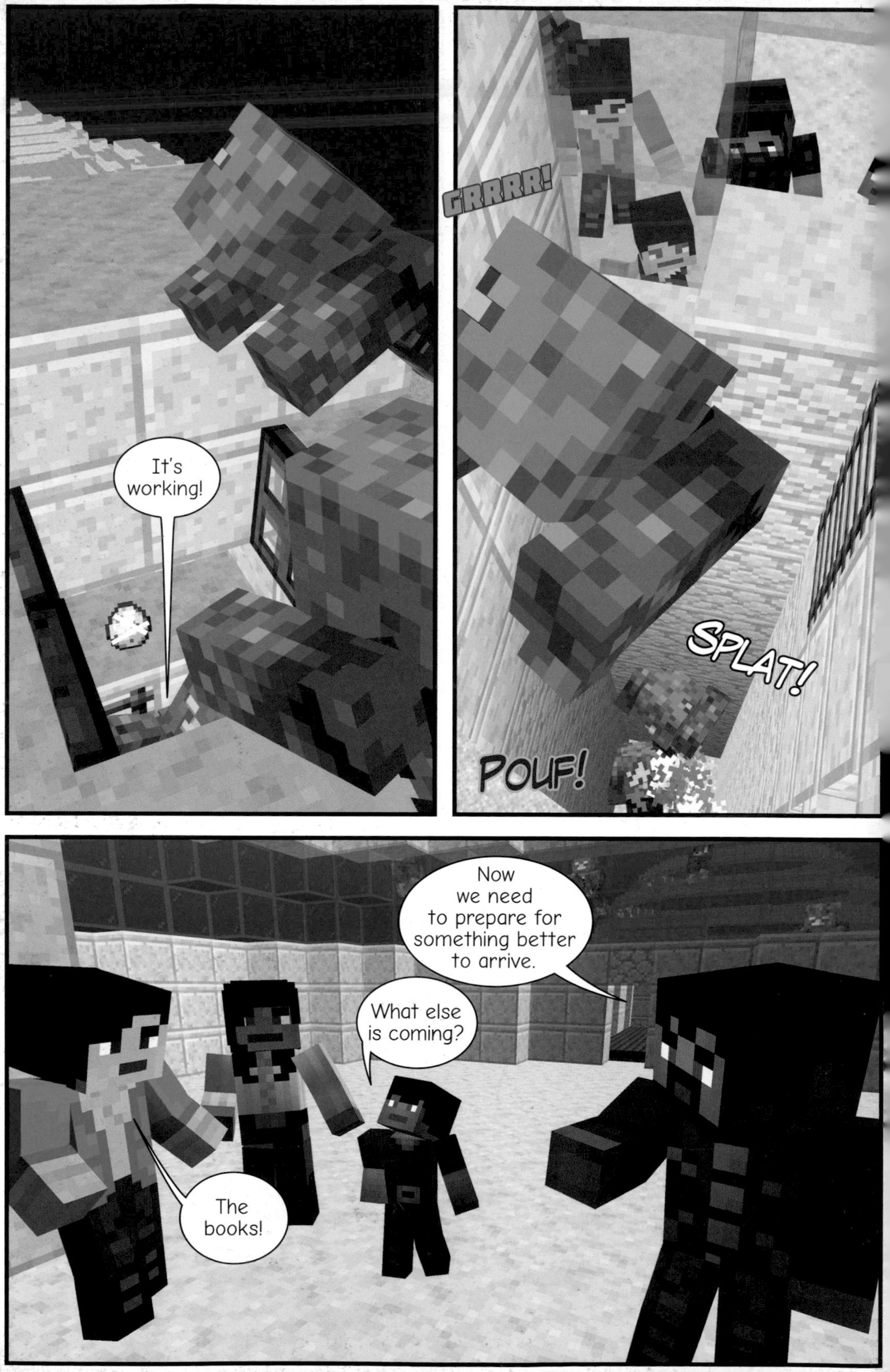
It's working!
GRRRR!
SPLAT!
POUF!
Now we need to prepare for something better to arrive.
What else is coming?
The books!

Chapter 3
A New Life

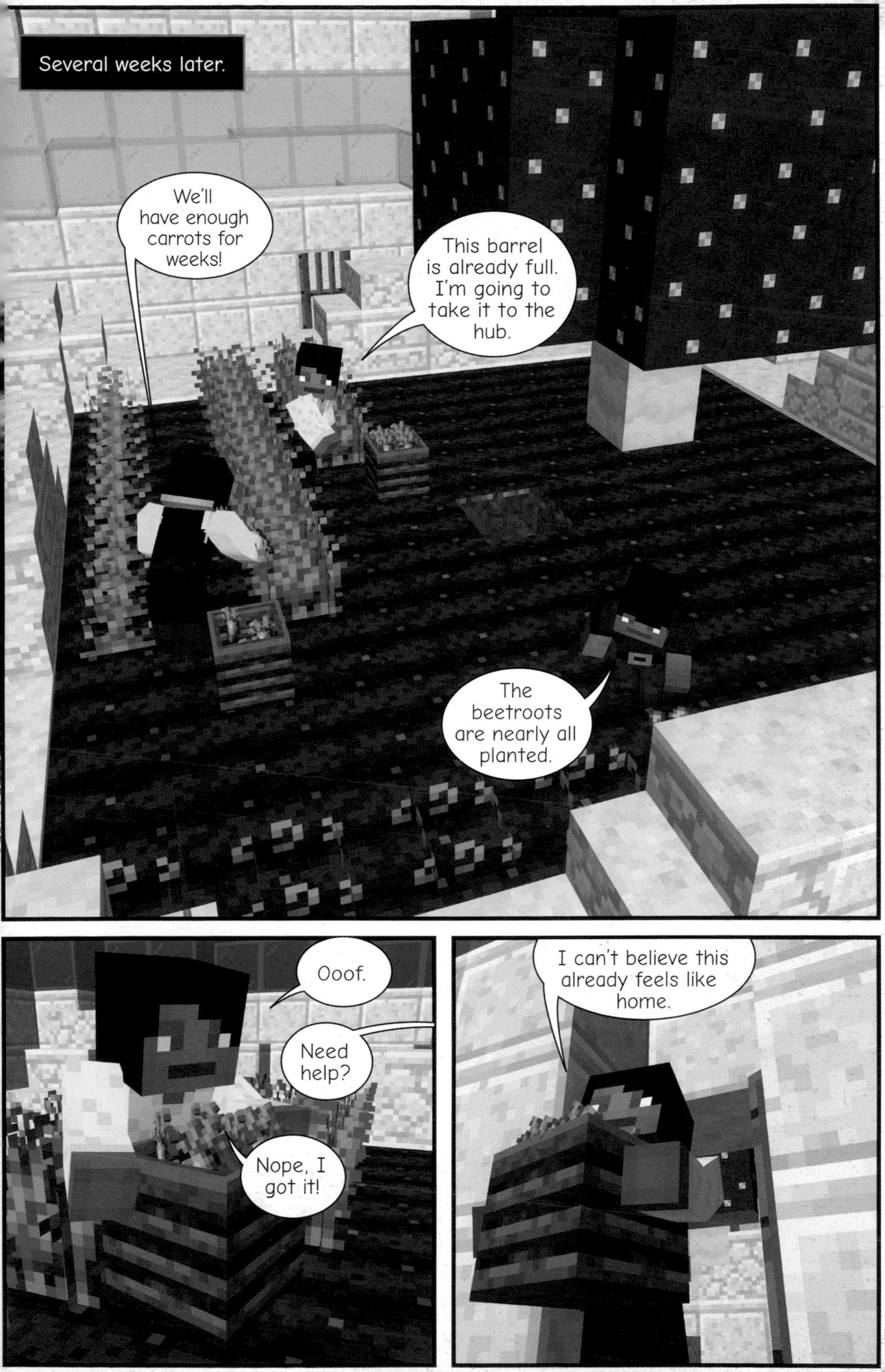

Several weeks later.
We'll have enough carrots for weeks!
This barrel is already full. I'm going to take it to the hub.
The beetroots are nearly all planted.
Ooof.
Need help?
Nope, I got it!
I can't believe this already feels like home.

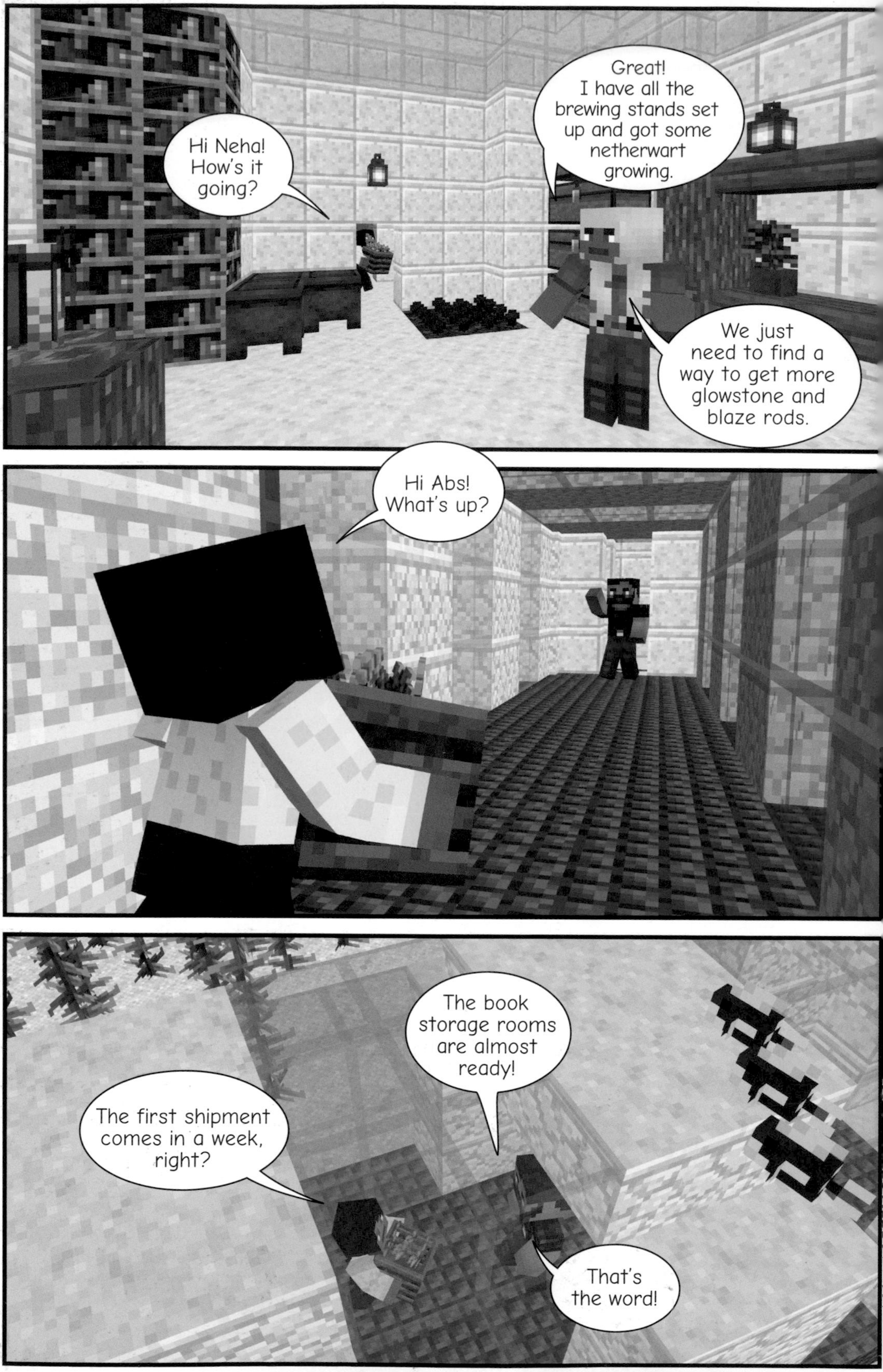
Hi Neha! How's it going?
Great! I have all the brewing stands set up and got some netherwart growing.
We just need to find a way to get more glowstone and blaze rods.
Hi Abs! What's up?
The book storage rooms are almost ready!
The first shipment comes in a week, right?
That's the word!

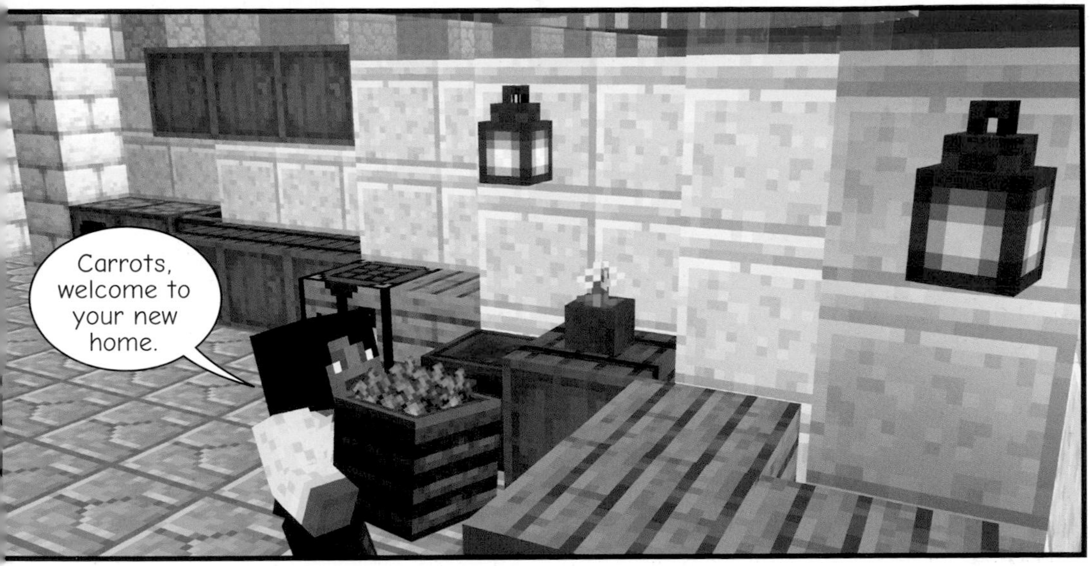
Carrots, welcome to your new home.

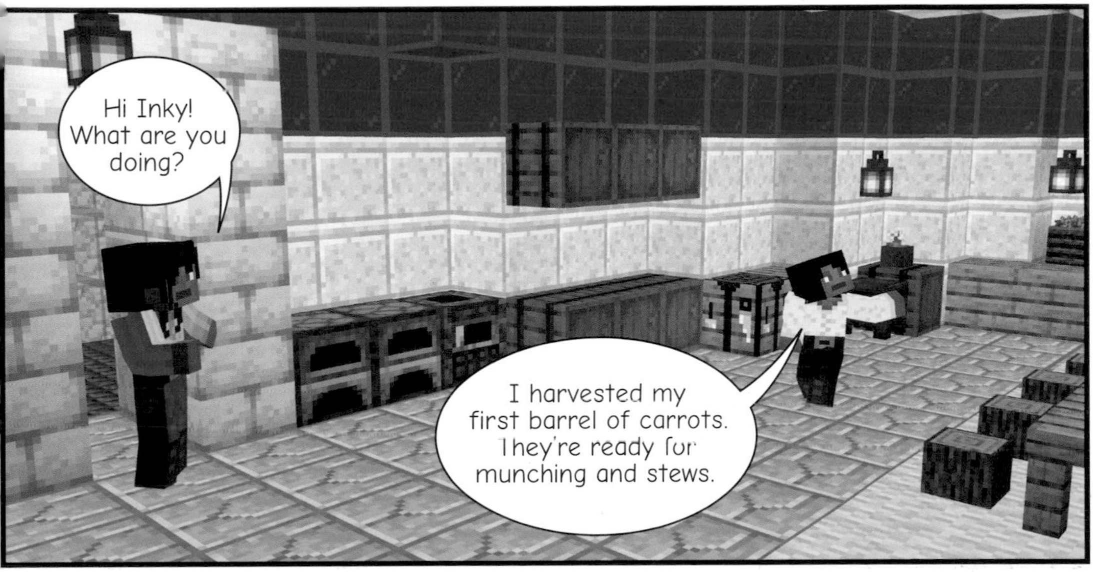
Hi Inky! What are you doing?
I harvested my first barrel of carrots. They're ready for munching and stews.

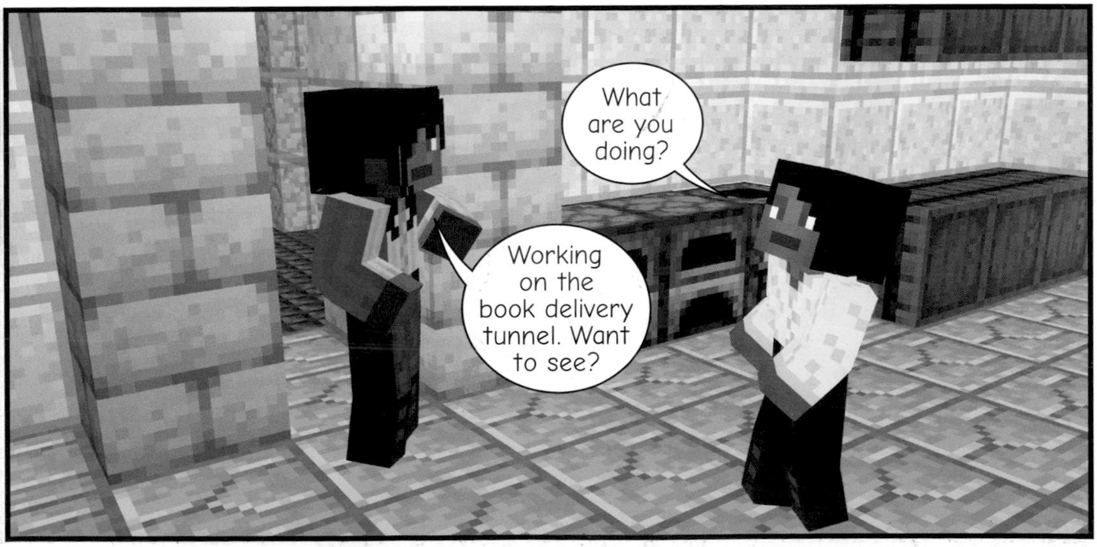
What are you doing?
Working on the book delivery tunnel. Want to see?

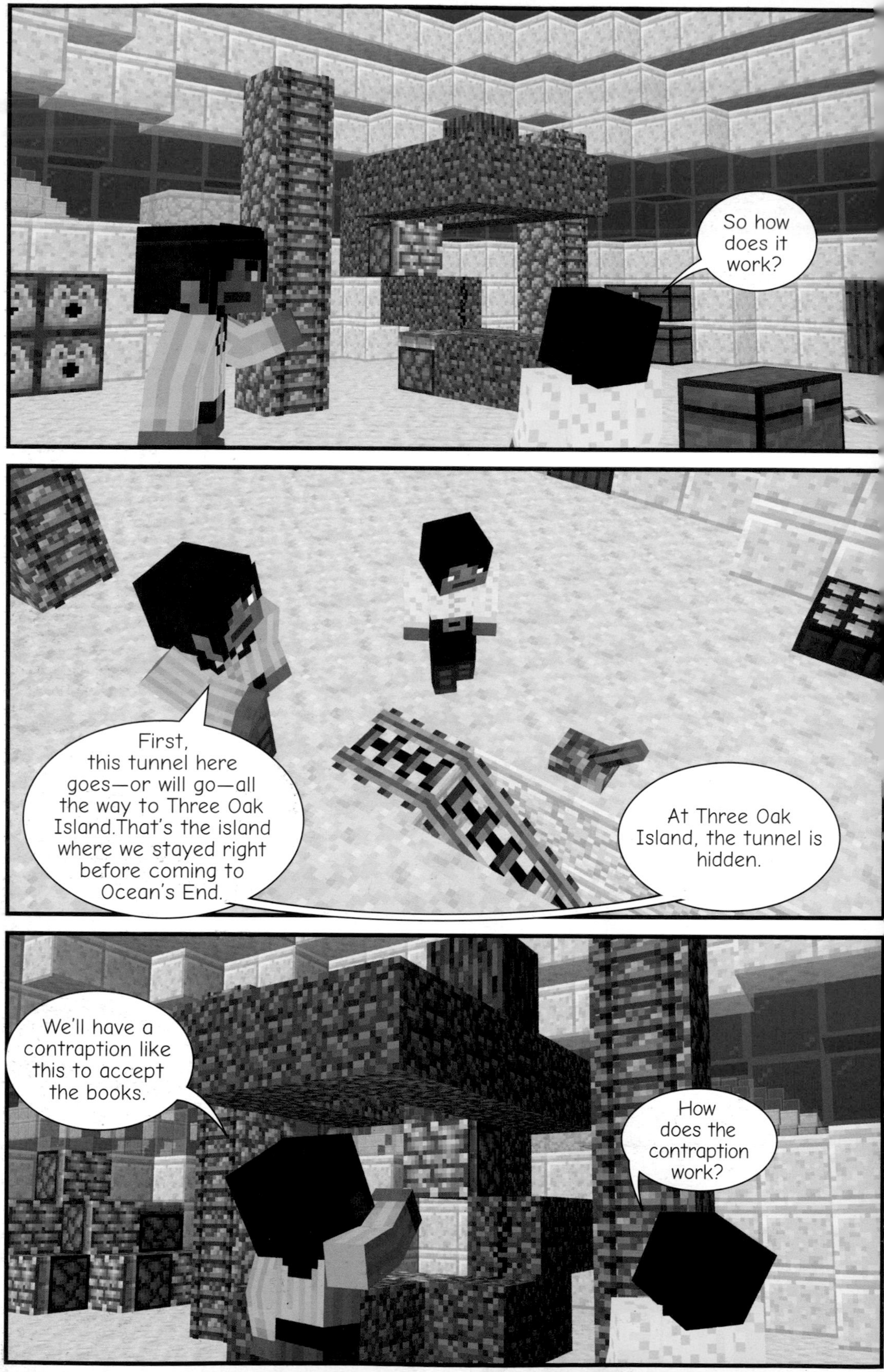

So how does it work?
First, this tunnel here goes—or will go—all the way to Three Oak Island. That's the island where we stayed right before coming to Ocean's End.
At Three Oak Island, the tunnel is hidden.
We'll have a contraption like this to accept the books.
How does the contraption work?

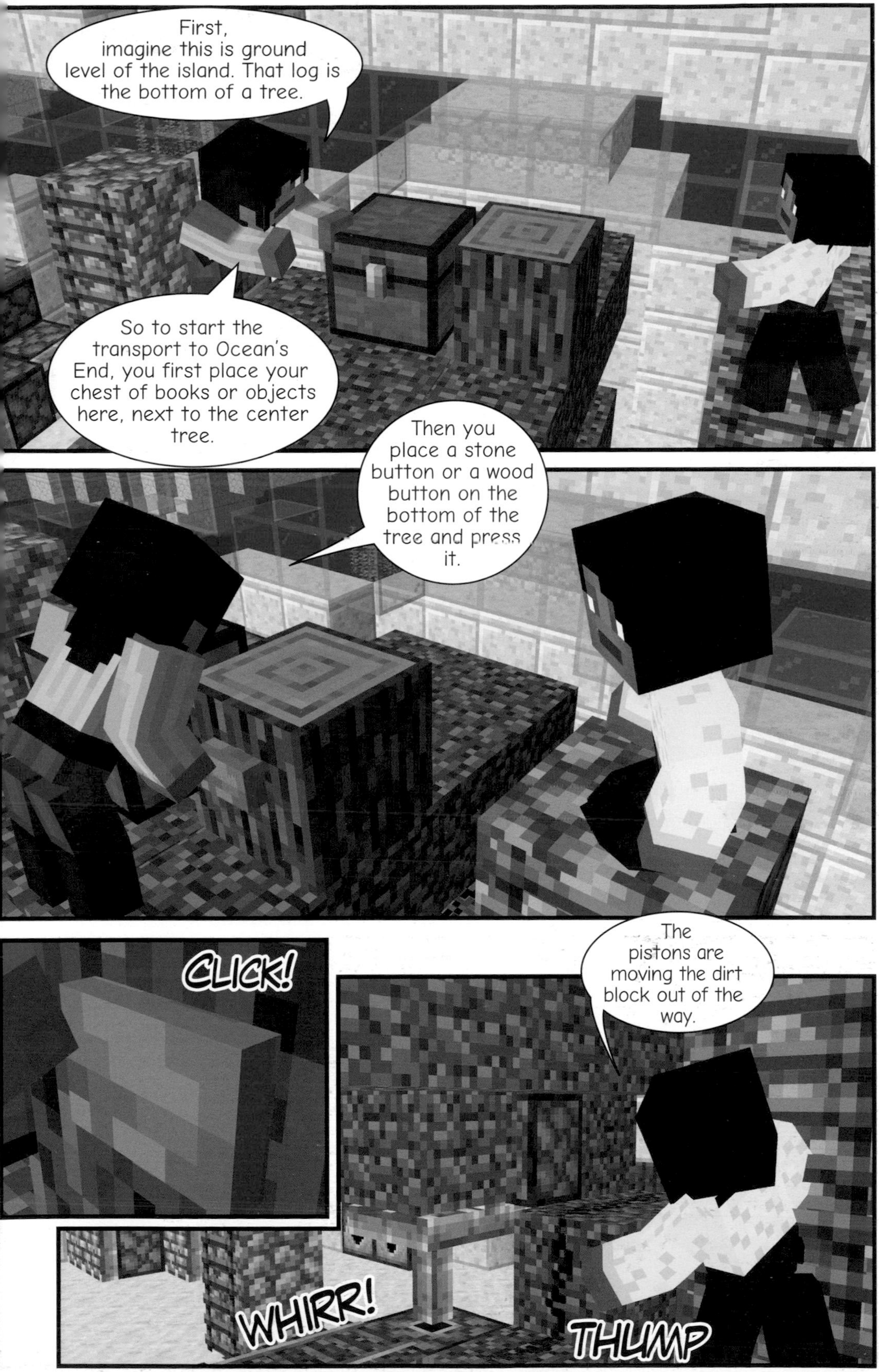
First, imagine this is ground level of the island. That log is the bottom of a tree.
So to start the transport to Ocean's End, you first place your chest of books or objects here, next to the center tree.
Then you place a stone button or a wood button on the bottom of the tree and press it.
CLICK!
The pistons are moving the dirt block out of the way.
WHIRR!
THUMP

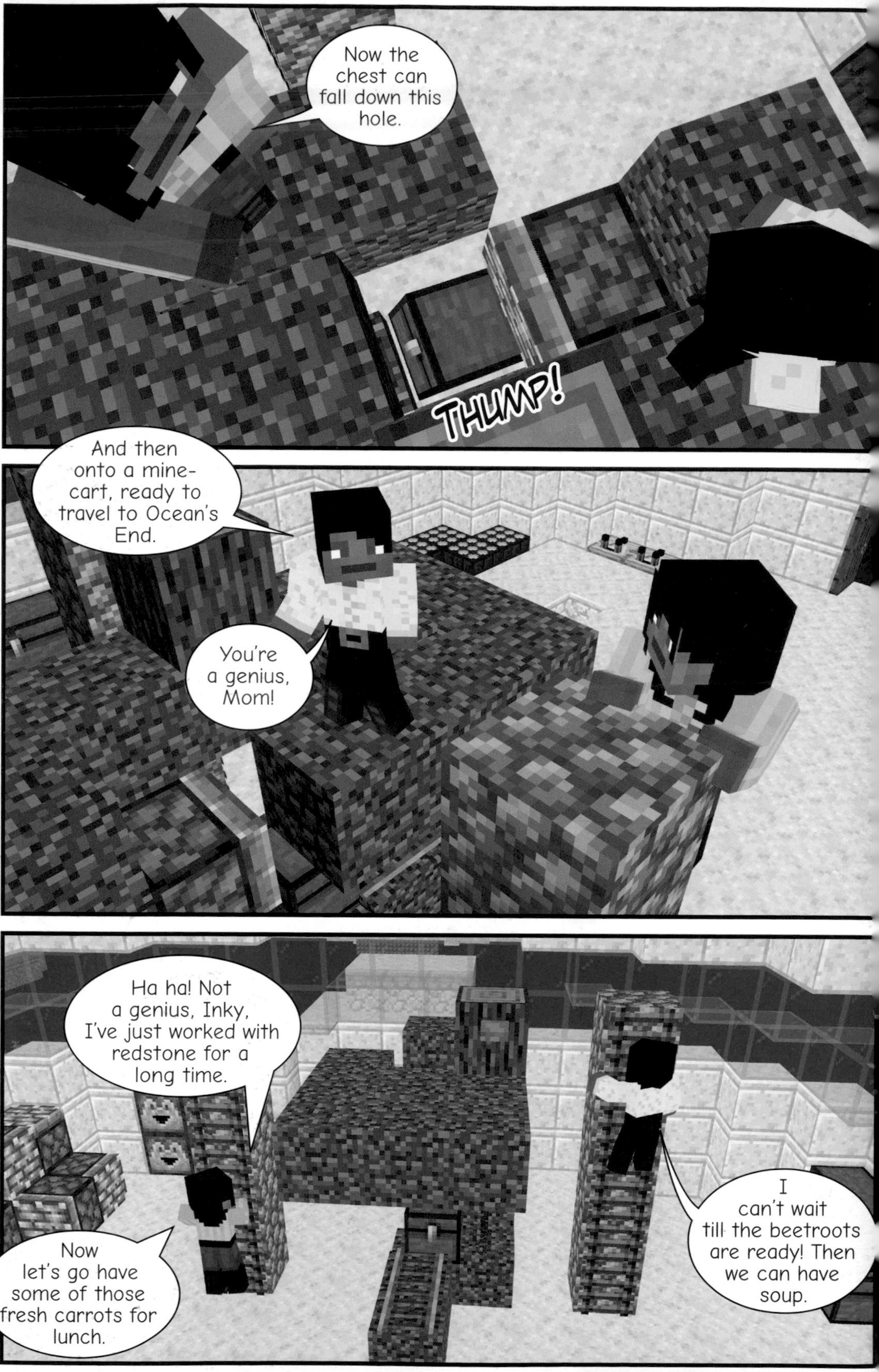
Now the chest can fall down this hole.
THUMP!
And then onto a mine-cart, ready to travel to Ocean's End.
You're a genius, Mom!
Ha ha! Not a genius, Inky, I've just worked with redstone for a long time.
Now let's go have some of those fresh carrots for lunch.
I can't wait till the beetroots are ready! Then we can have soup.

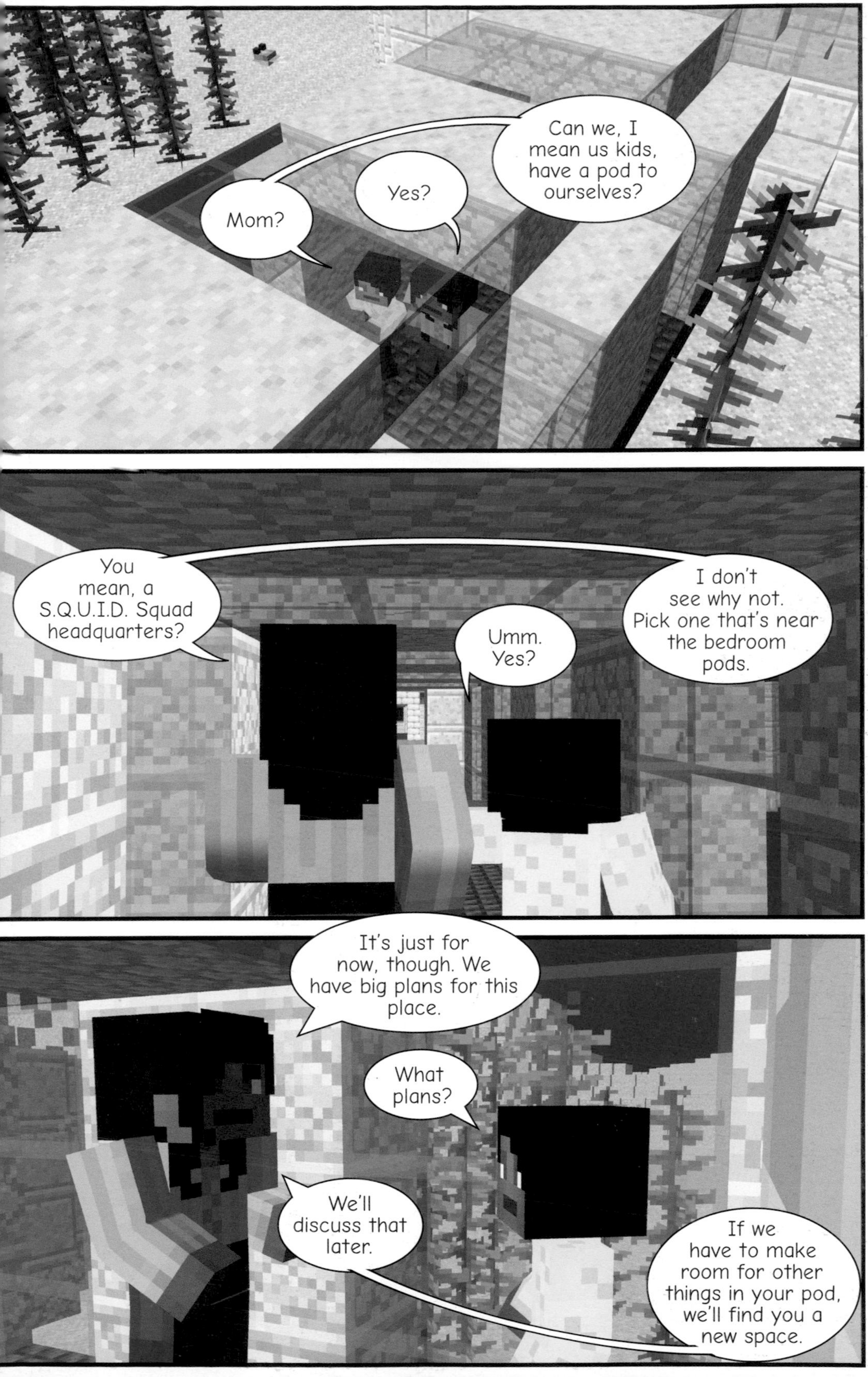
Mom?
Yes?
Can we, I mean us kids, have a pod to ourselves?
You mean, a S.Q.U.I.D. Squad headquarters?
Umm. Yes?
I don't see why not. Pick one that's near the bedroom pods.
It's just for now, though. We have big plans for this place.
What plans?
We'll discuss that later.
If we have to make room for other things in your pod, we'll find you a new space.

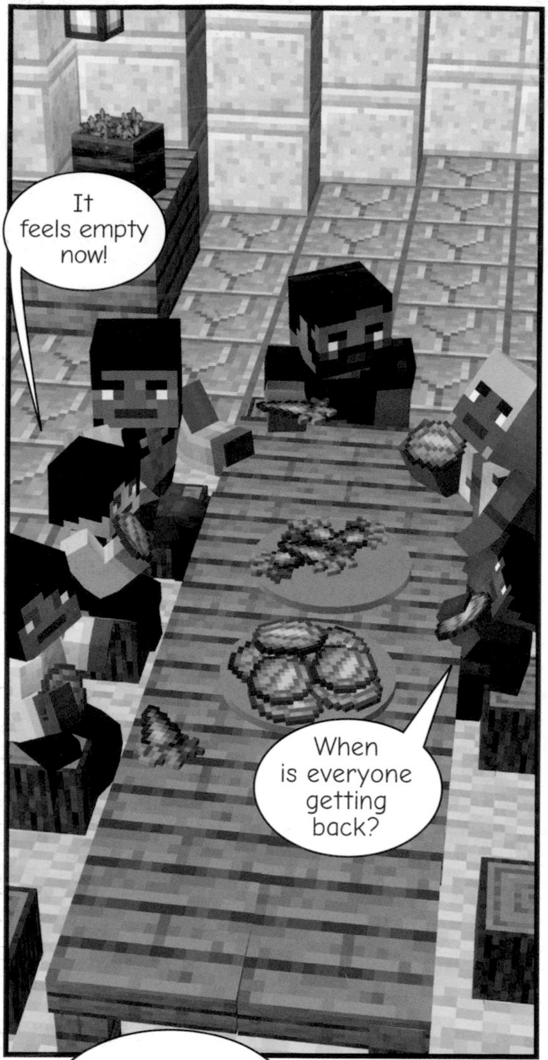
It feels empty now!
When is everyone getting back?
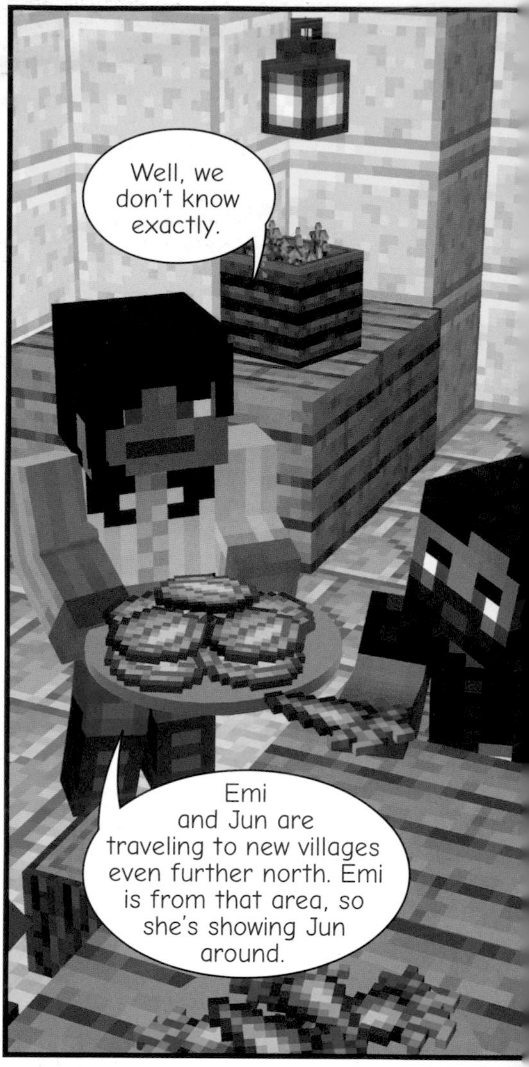
Well, we don't know exactly.
Emi and Jun are traveling to new villages even further north. Emi is from that area, so she's showing Jun around.
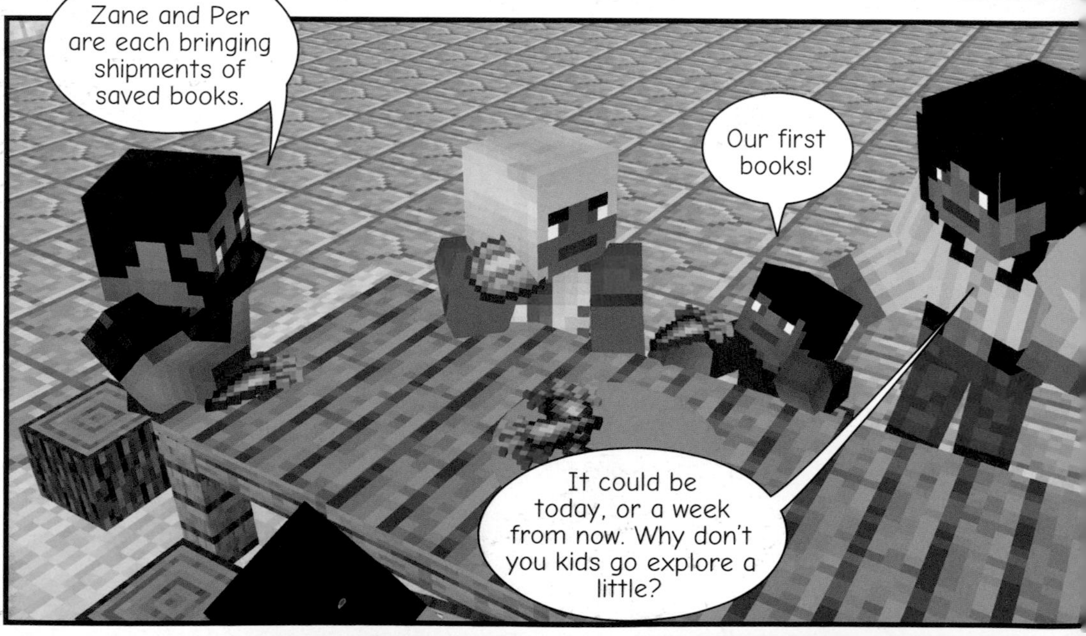
Zane and Per are each bringing shipments of saved books.
Our first books!
It could be today, or a week from now. Why don't you kids go explore a little?

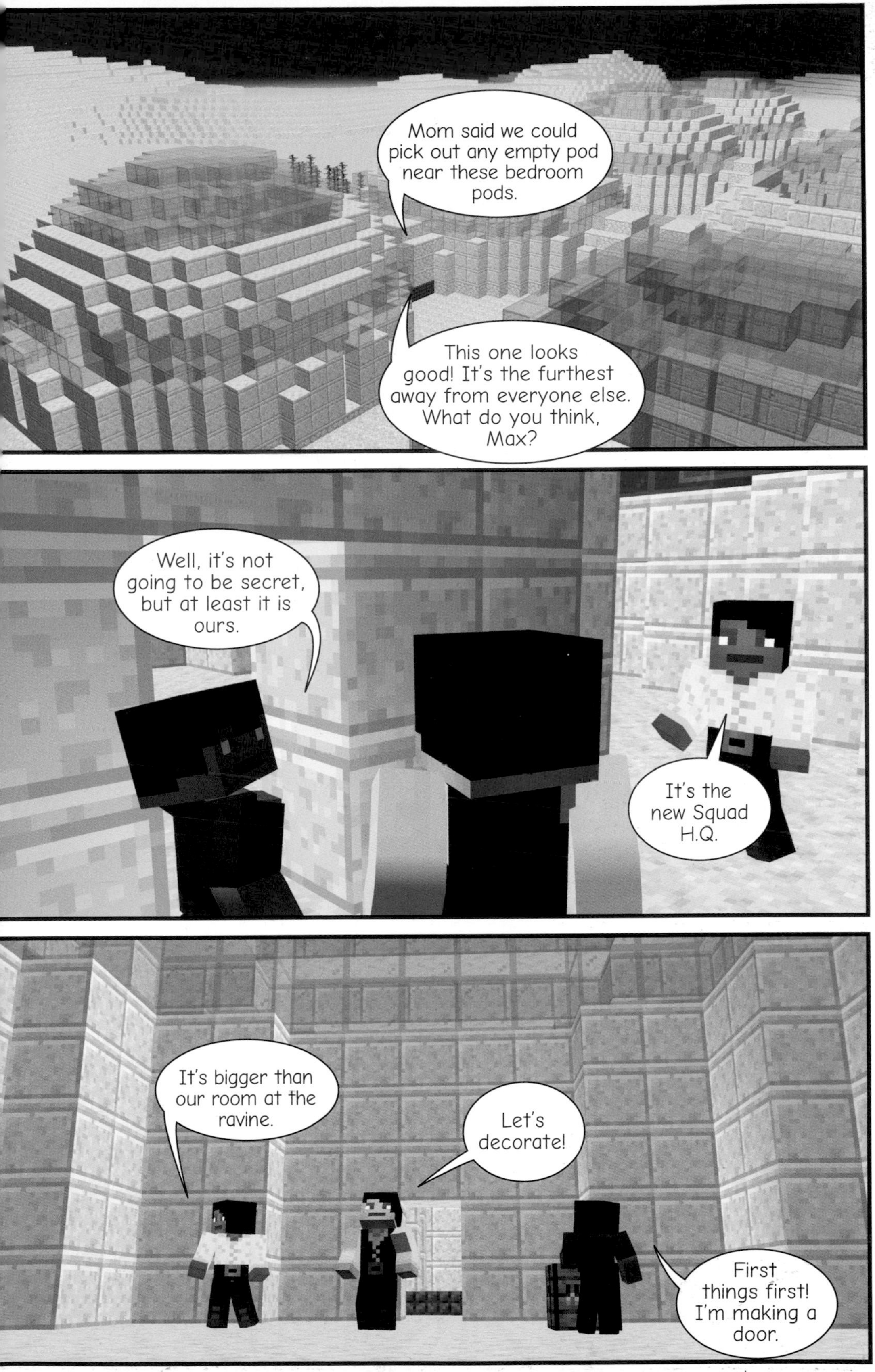
Mom said we could pick out any empty pod near these bedroom pods.
This one looks good! It's the furthest away from everyone else. What do you think, Max?
Well, it's not going to be secret, but at least it is ours.
It's the new Squad H.Q.
It's bigger than our room at the ravine.
Let's decorate!
First things first! I'm making a door.

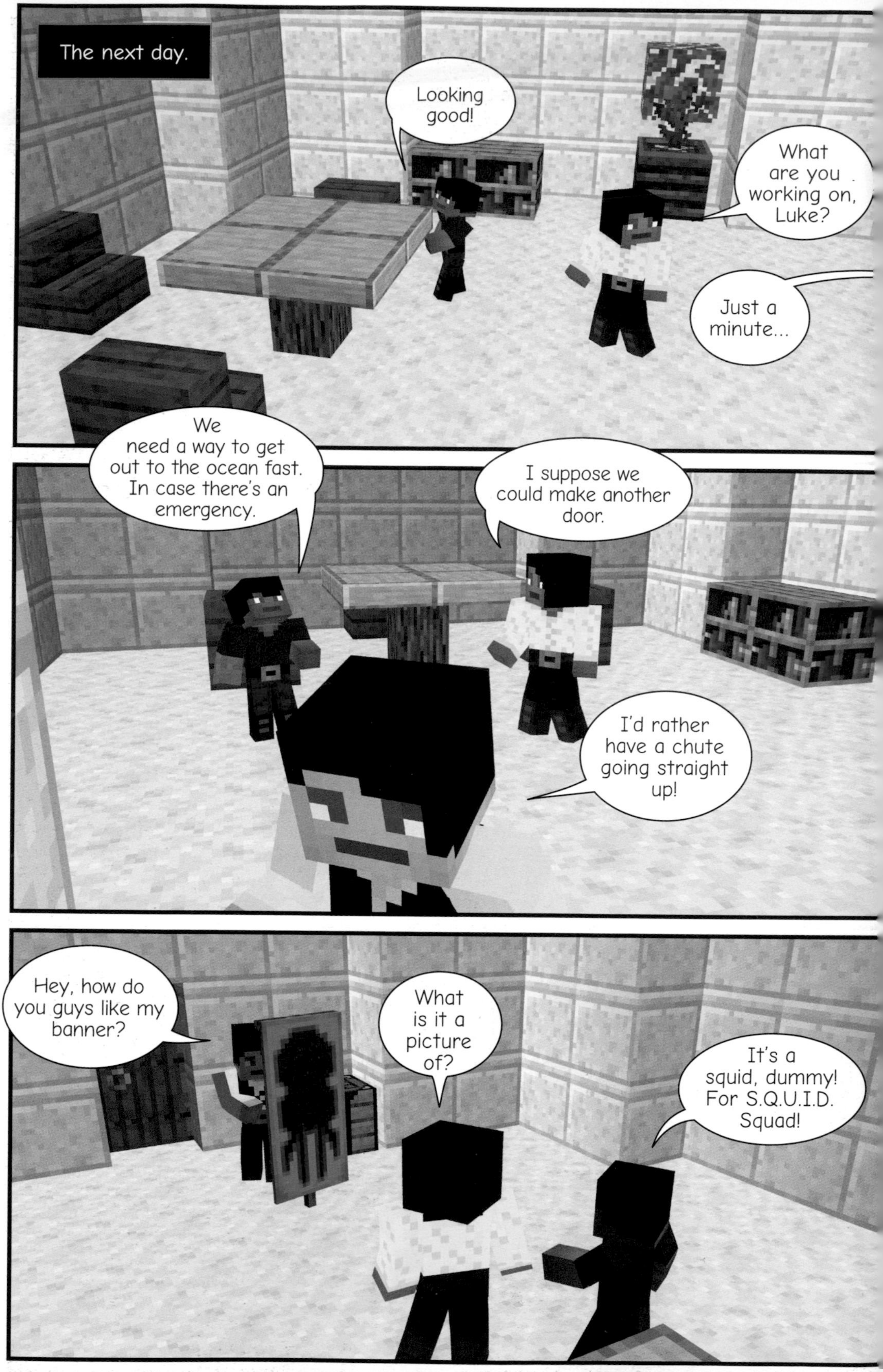
The next day.
Looking good!
What are you working on, Luke?
Just a minute...
We need a way to get out to the ocean fast. In case there's an emergency.
I suppose we could make another door.
I'd rather have a chute going straight up!
Hey, how do you guys like my banner?
What is it a picture of?
It's a squid, dummy! For S.Q.U.I.D. Squad!

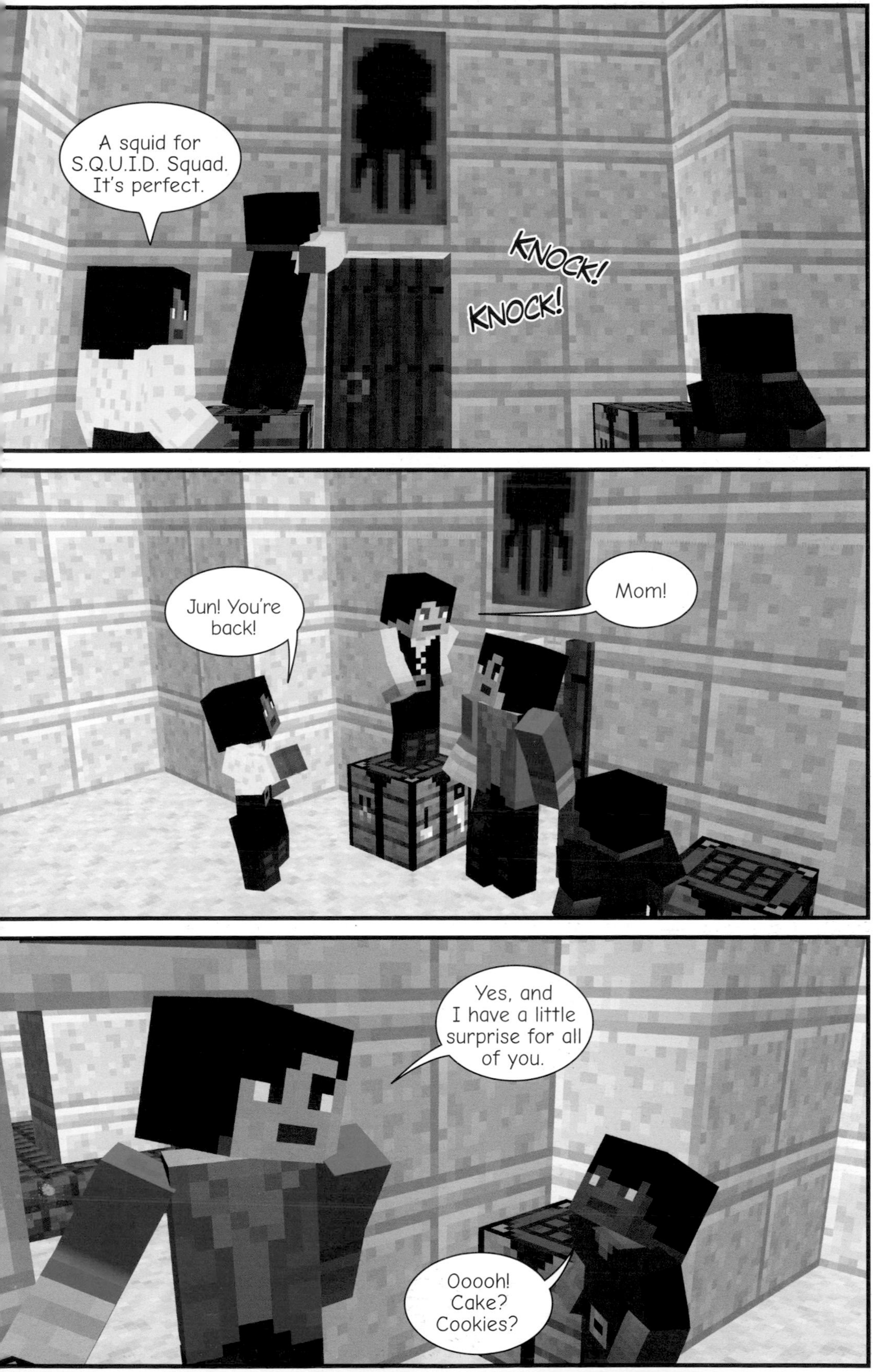
A squid for S.Q.U.I.D. Squad. It's perfect.
KNOCK!
KNOCK!
Jun! You're back!
Mom!
Yes, and I have a little surprise for all of you.
Ooooh! Cake? Cookies?

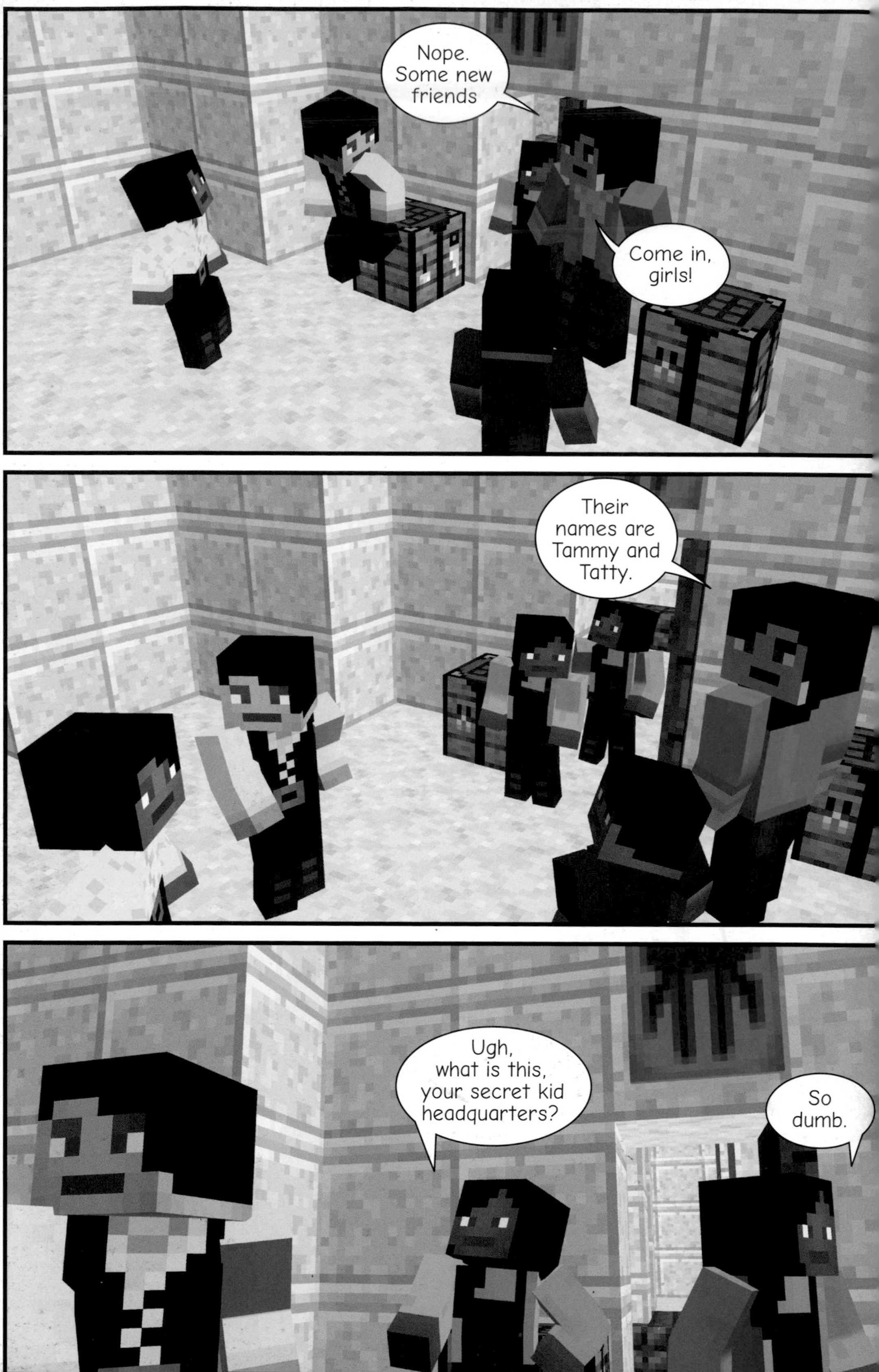
Nope. Some new friends
Come in, girls!
Their names are Tammy and Tatty.
Ugh, what is this, your secret kid headquarters?
So dumb.

Chapter 4
Hide-and-Seek

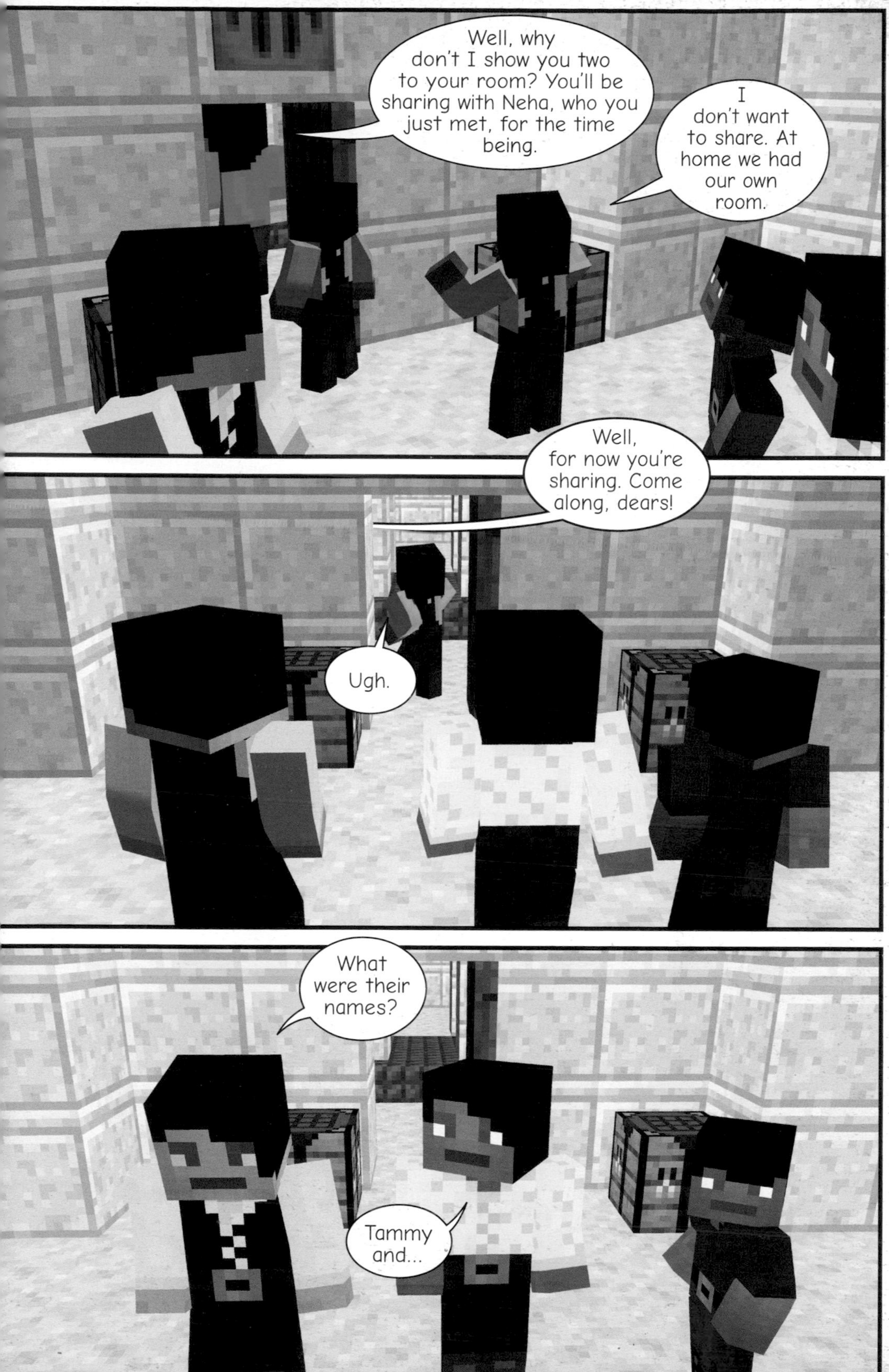
Well, why don't I show you two to your room? You'll be sharing with Neha, who you just met, for the time being.
I don't want to share. At home we had our own room.
Well, for now you're sharing. Come along, dears!
Ugh.
What were their names?
Tammy and...

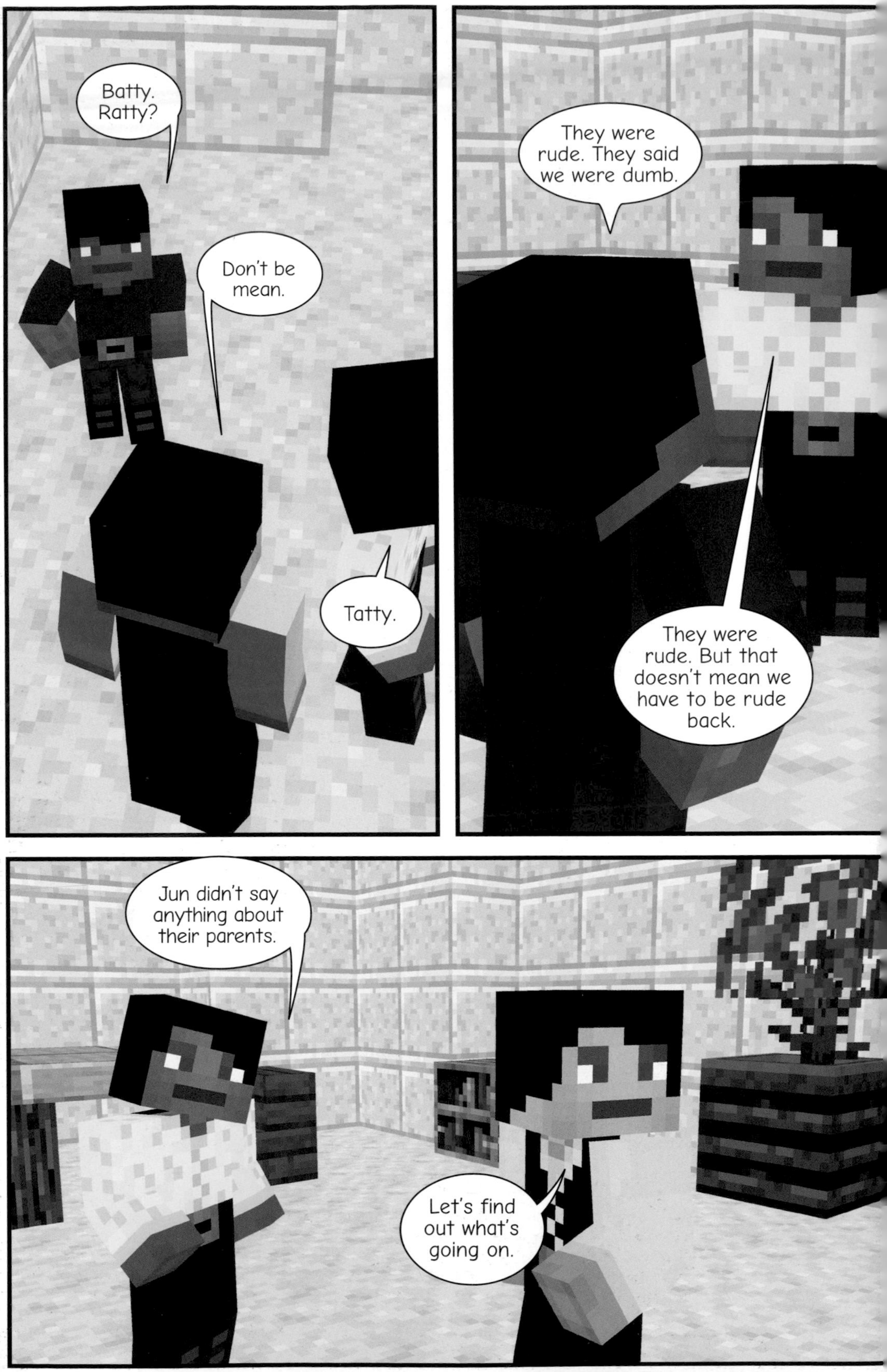
Batty. Ratty?
Don't be mean.
Tatty.
They were rude. They said we were dumb.
They were rude. But that doesn't mean we have to be rude back.
Jun didn't say anything about their parents.
Let's find out what's going on.

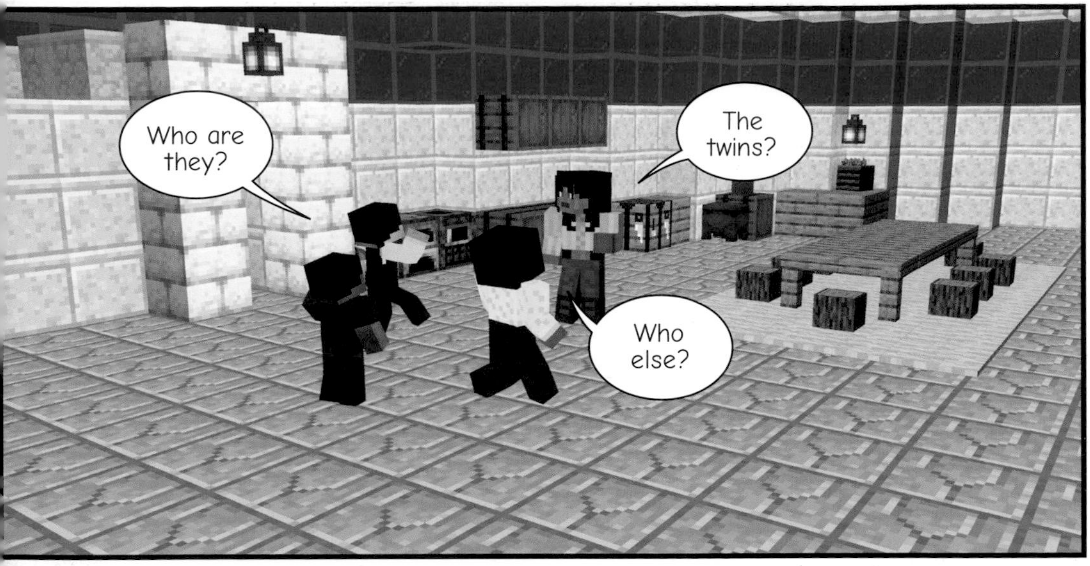
Who are they?
The twins?
Who else?

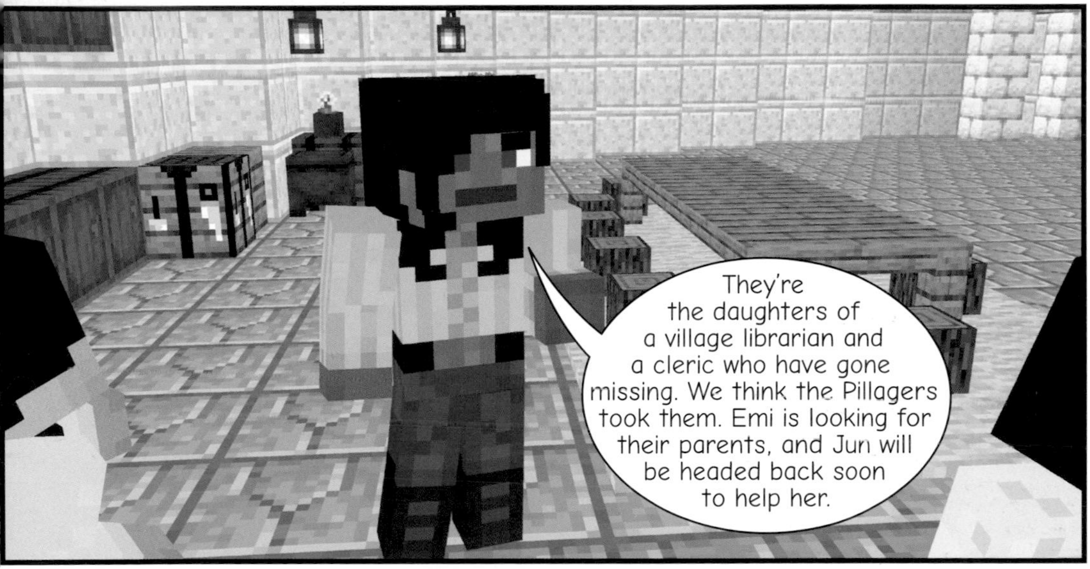
They're the daughters of a village librarian and a cleric who have gone missing. We think the Pillagers took them. Emi is looking for their parents, and Jun will be headed back soon to help her.

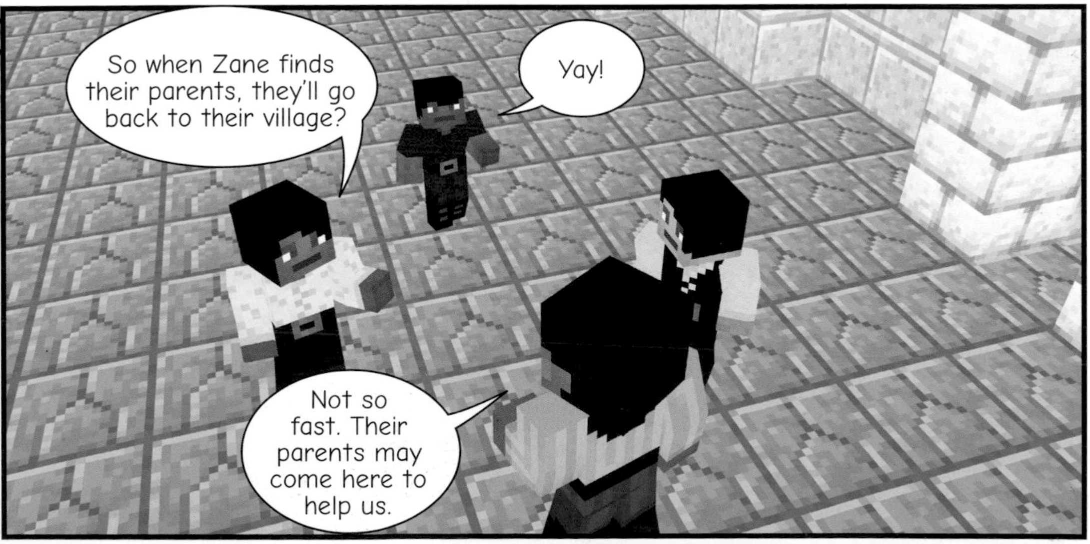
So when Zane finds their parents, they'll go back to their village?
Yay!
Not so fast. Their parents may come here to help us.

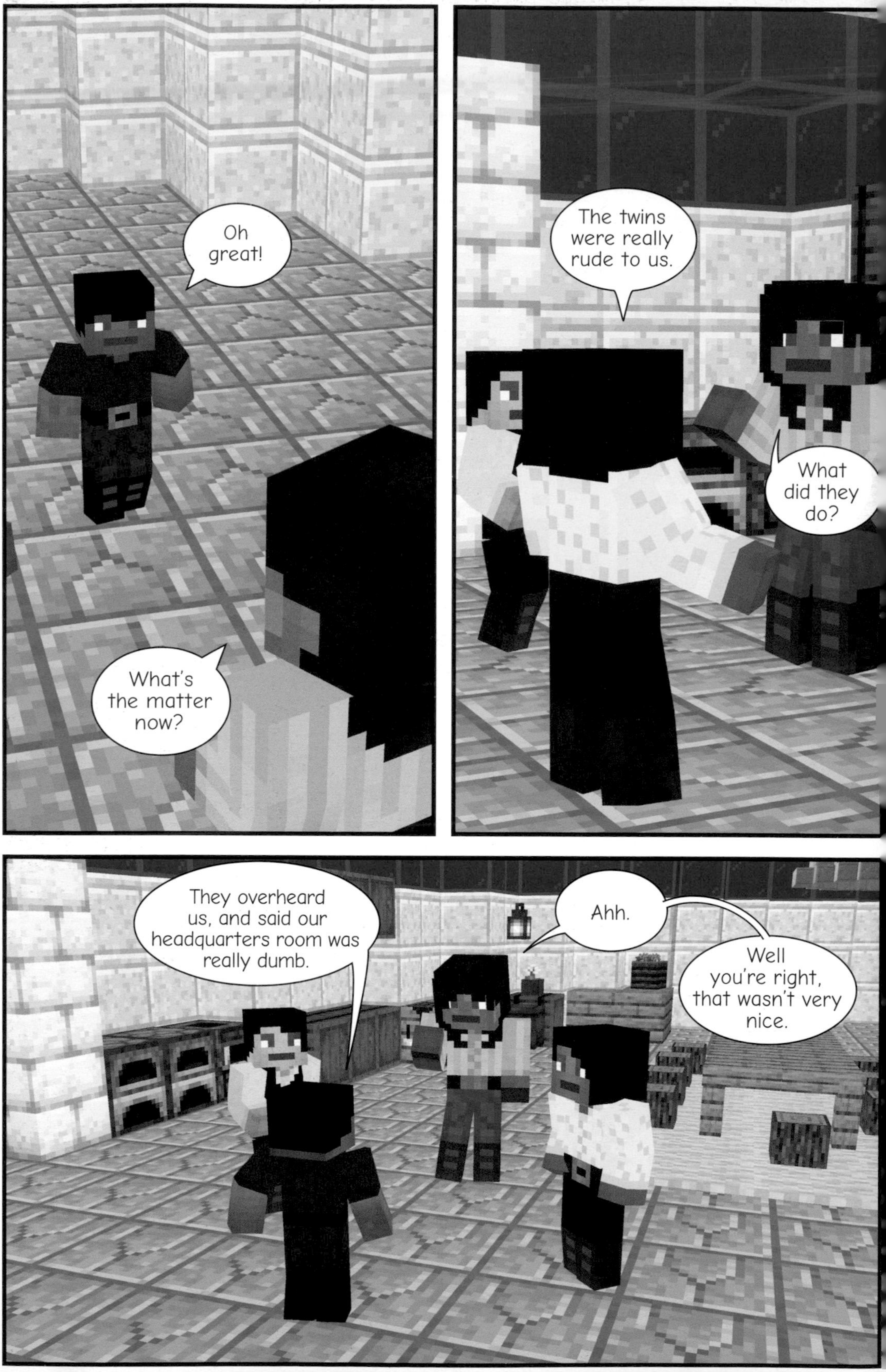
Oh great!
What's the matter now?
The twins were really rude to us.
What did they do?
They overheard us, and said our headquarters room was really dumb.
Ahh.
Well you're right, that wasn't very nice.

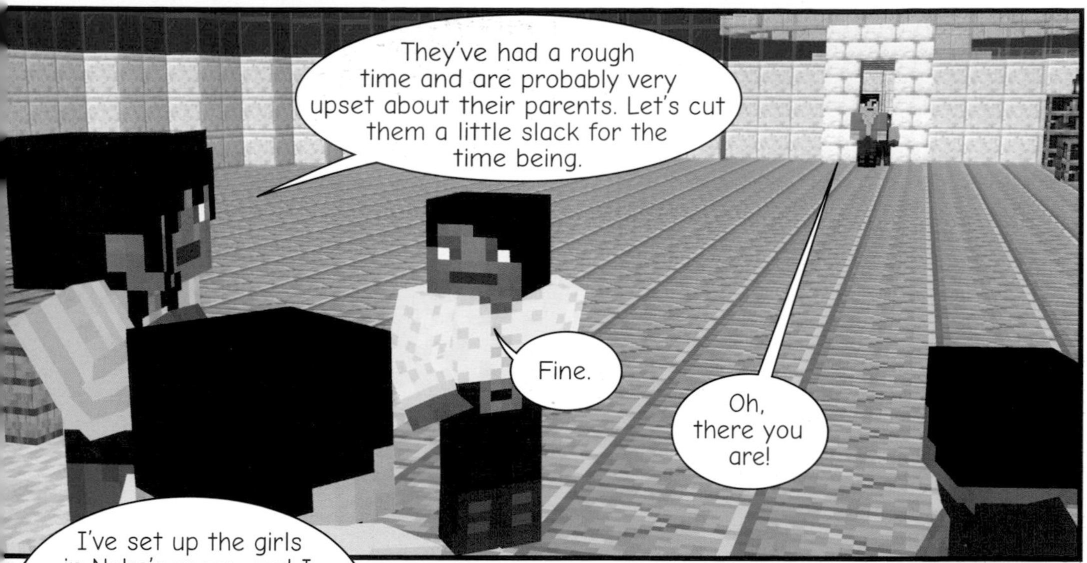
They've had a rough time and are probably very upset about their parents. Let's cut them a little slack for the time being.
Fine.
Oh, there you are!

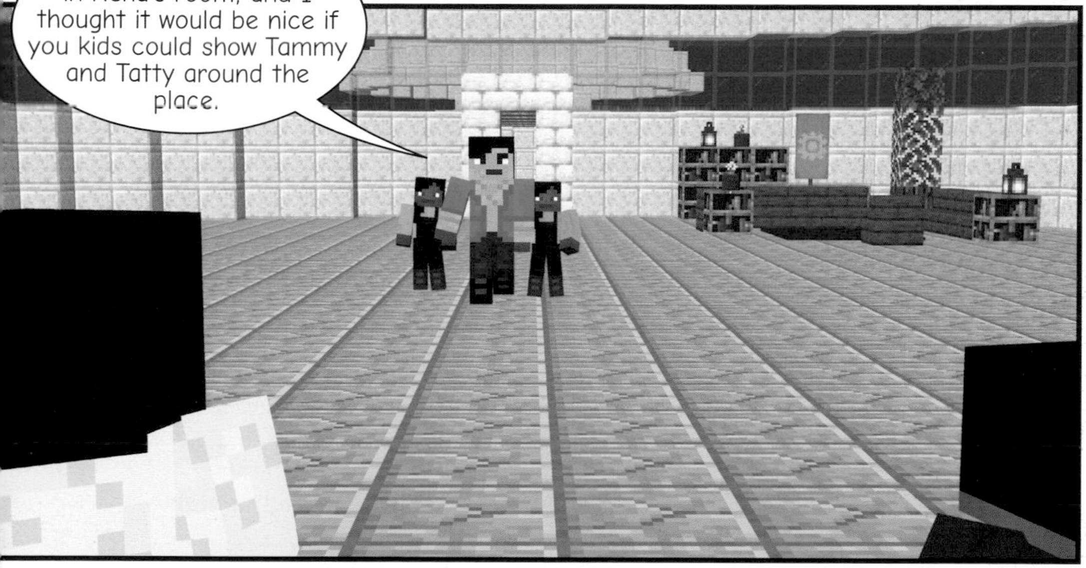
I've set up the girls in Neha's room, and I thought it would be nice if you kids could show Tammy and Tatty around the place.

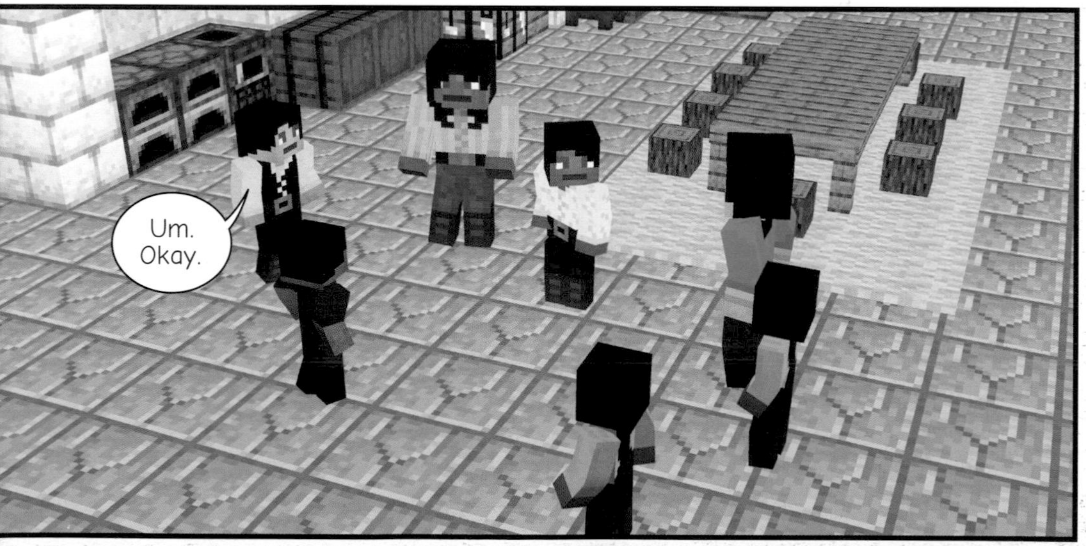
Um. Okay.

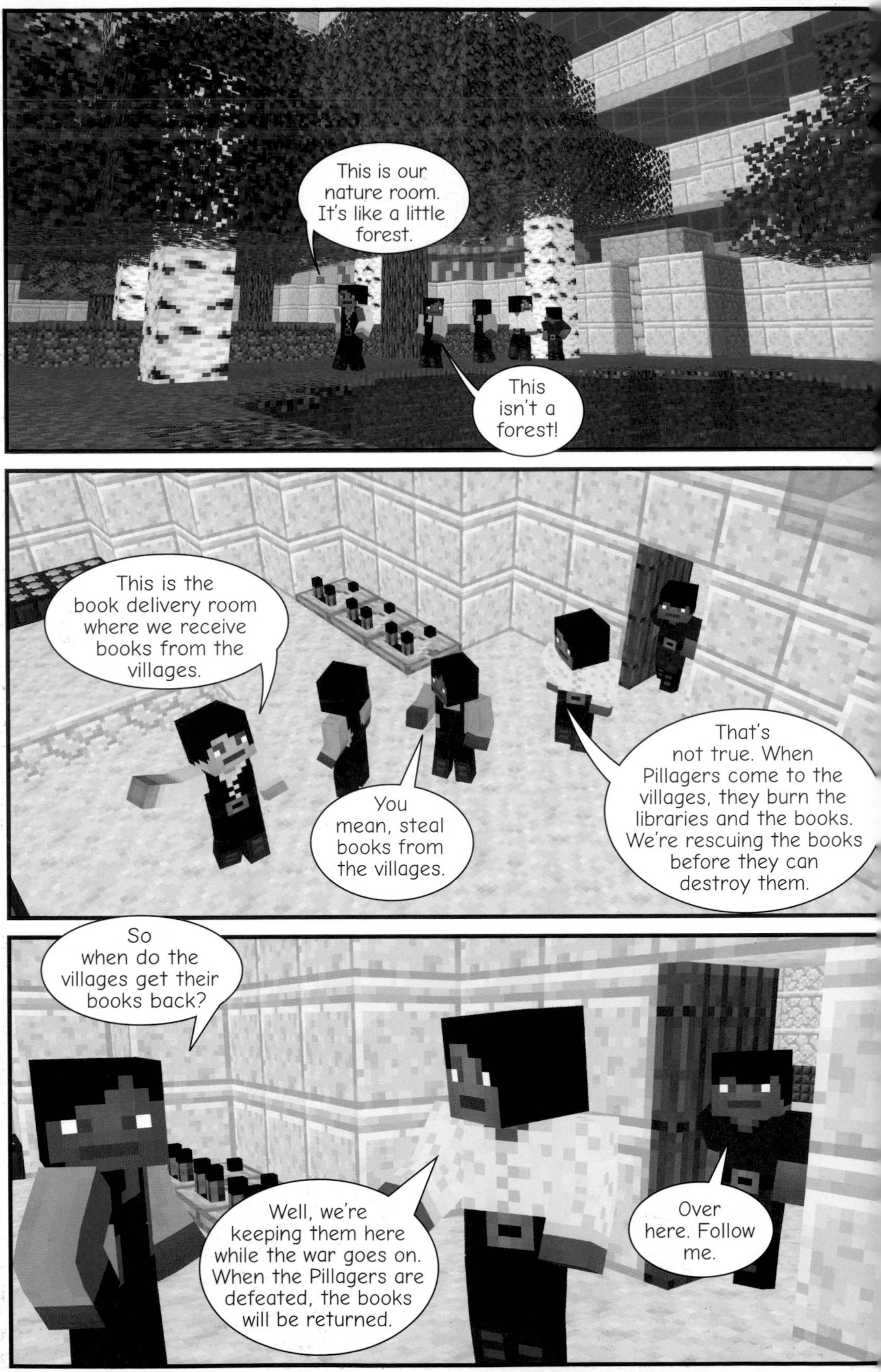
This is our nature room. It's like a little forest.
This isn't a forest!
This is the book delivery room where we receive books from the villages.
You mean, steal books from the villages.
That's not true. When Pillagers come to the villages, they burn the libraries and the books. We're rescuing the books before they can destroy them.
So when do the villages get their books back?
Well, we're keeping them here while the war goes on. When the Pillagers are defeated, the books will be returned.
Over here. Follow me.

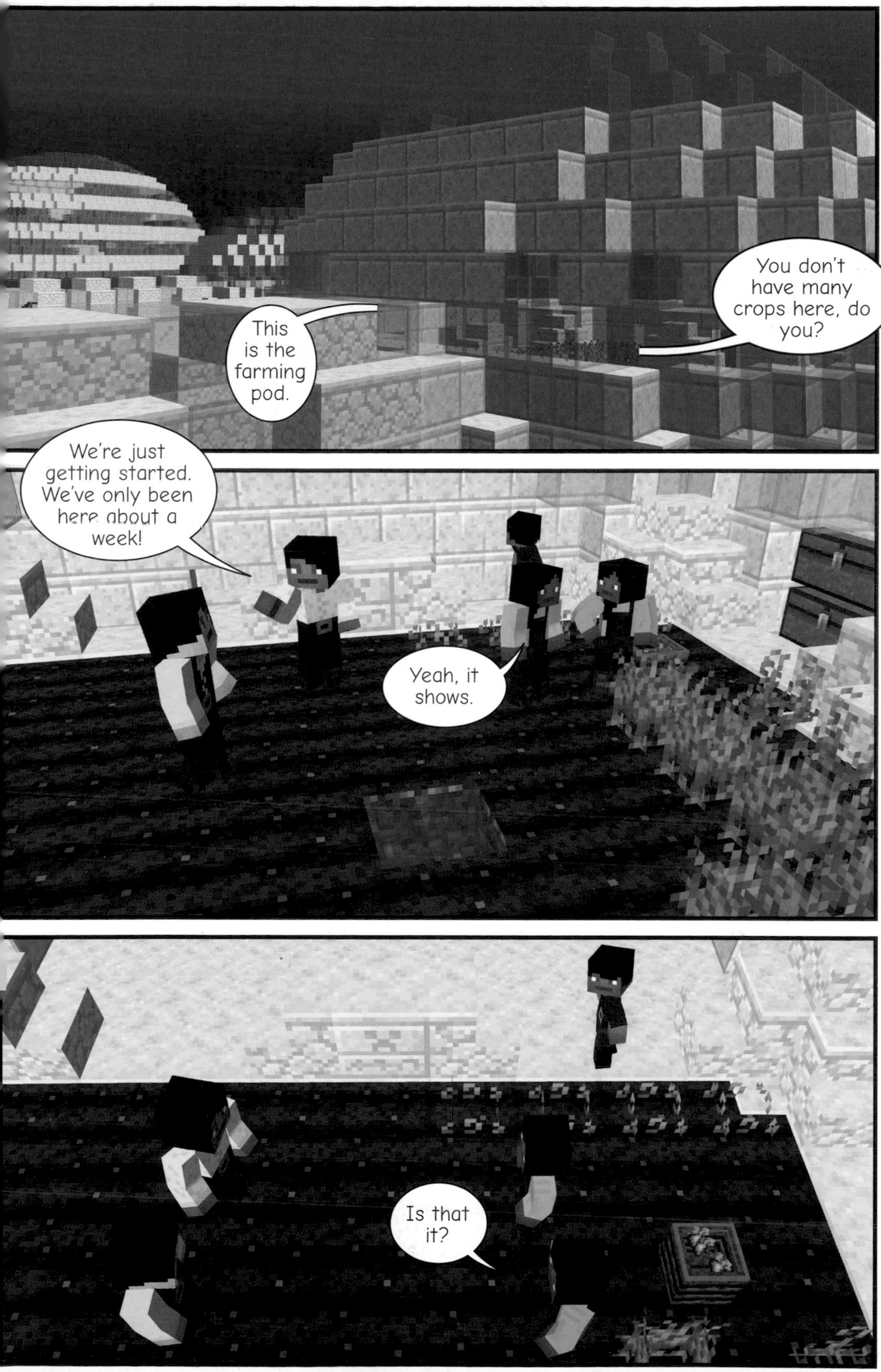
This is the farming pod.
You don't have many crops here, do you?
We're just getting started. We've only been here about a week!
Yeah, it shows.
Is that it?

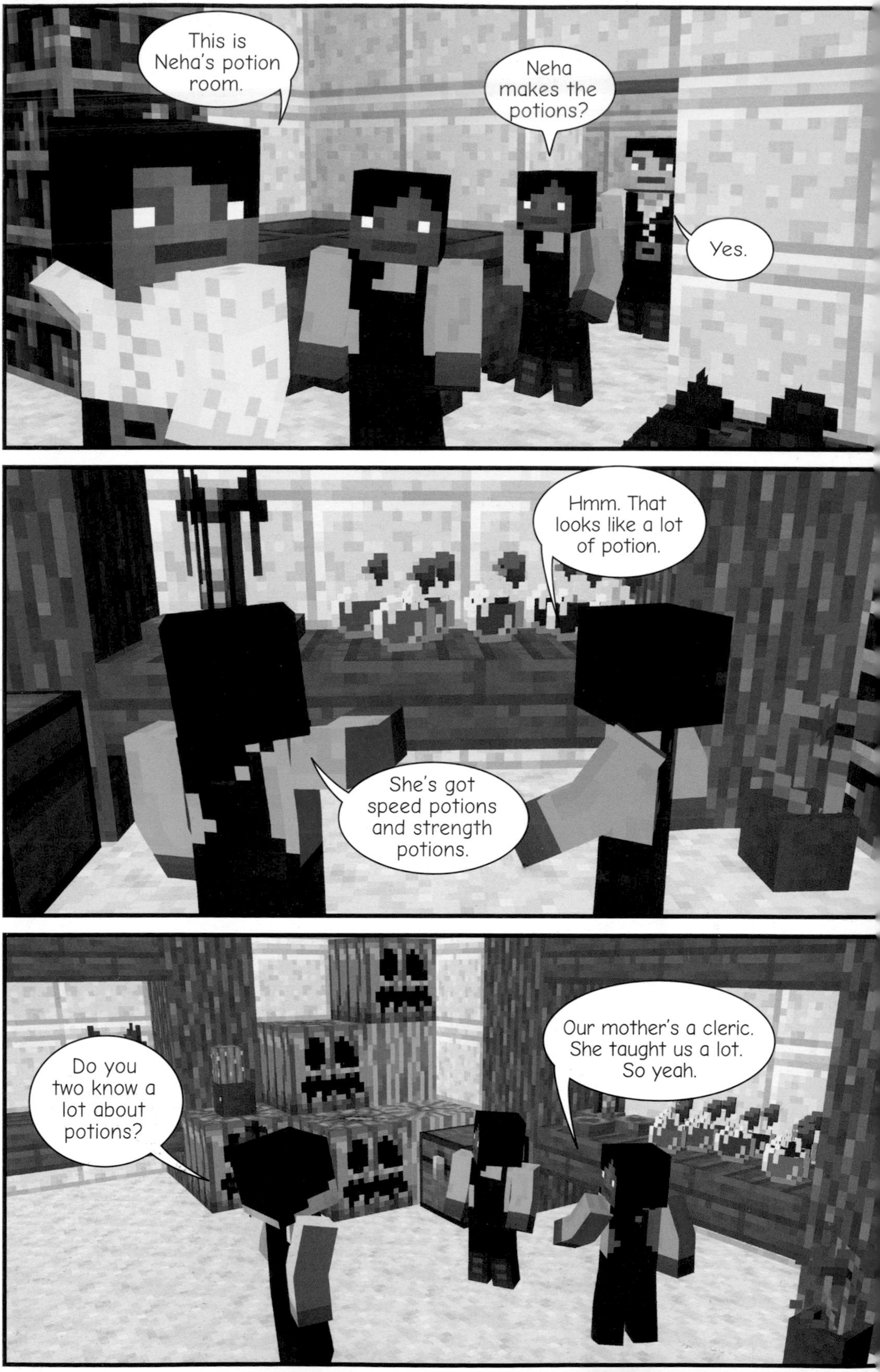
This is Neha's potion room.
Neha makes the potions?
Yes.
Hmm. That looks like a lot of potion.
She's got speed potions and strength potions.
Do you two know a lot about potions?
Our mother's a cleric. She taught us a lot. So yeah.

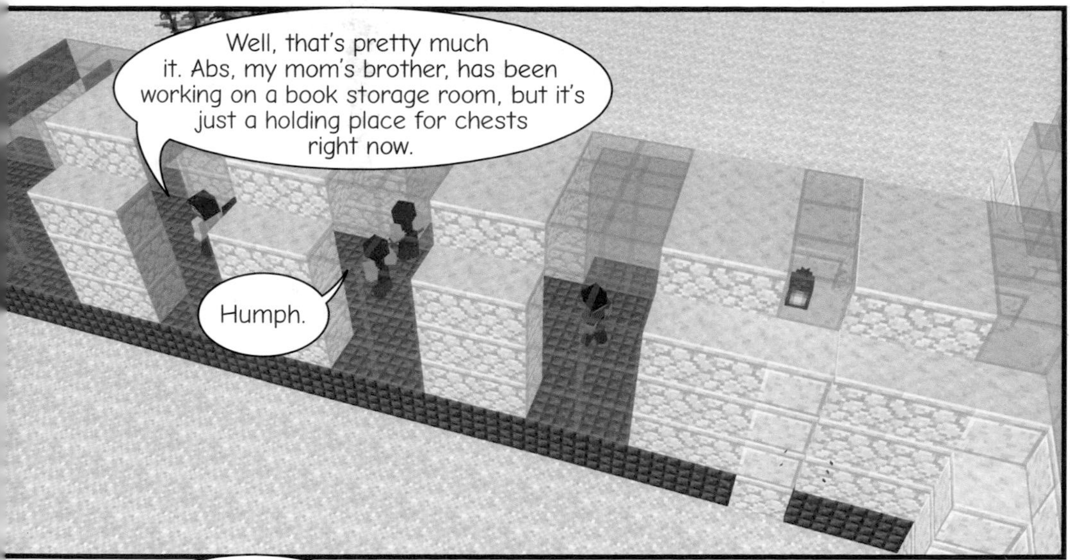
Well, that's pretty much it. Abs, my mom's brother, has been working on a book storage room, but it's just a holding place for chests right now.
Humph.

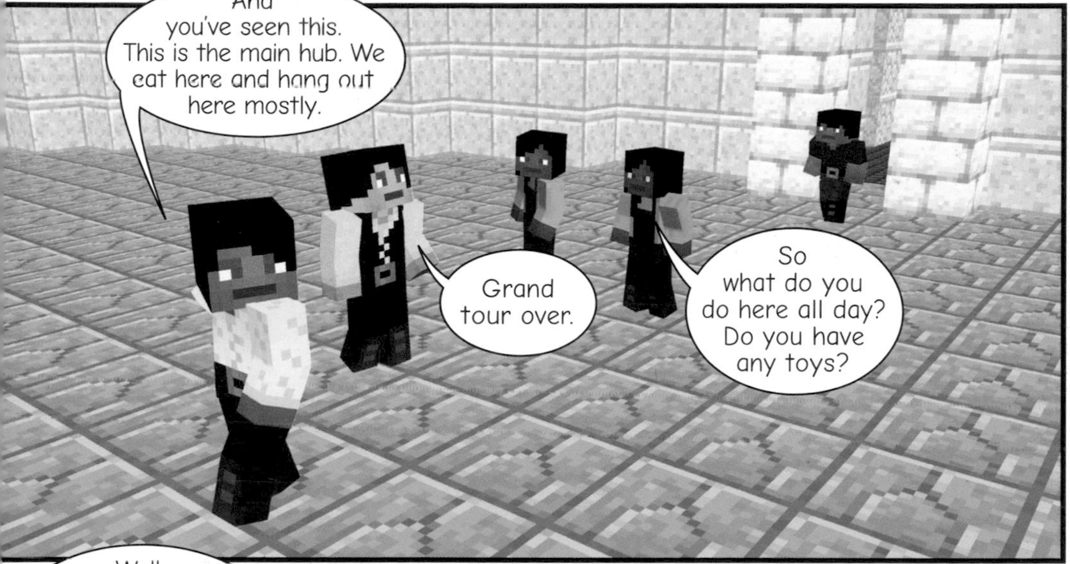
And you've seen this. This is the main hub. We eat here and hang out here mostly.
Grand tour over.
So what do you do here all day? Do you have any toys?

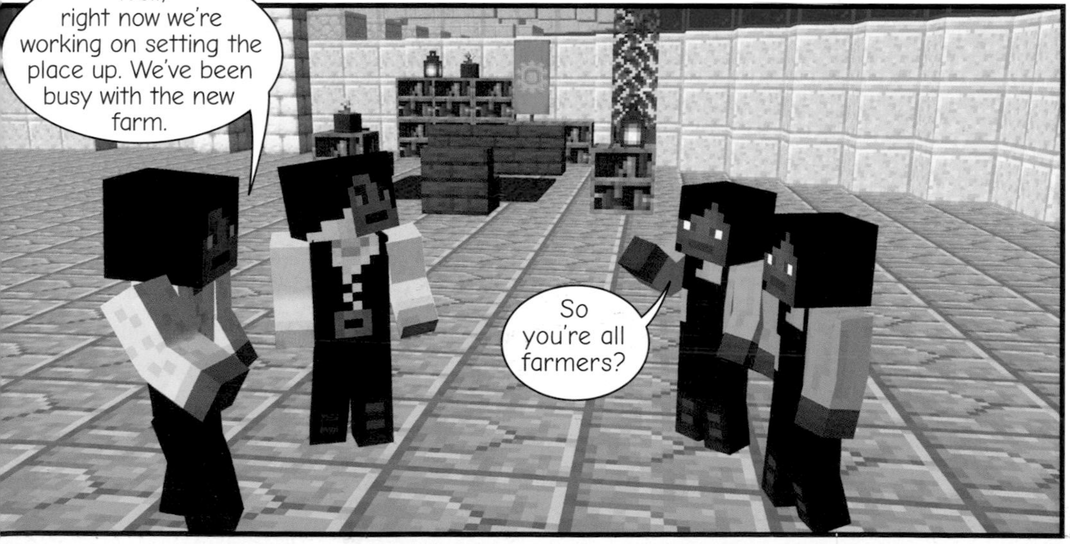
Well, right now we're working on setting the place up. We've been busy with the new farm.
So you're all farmers?

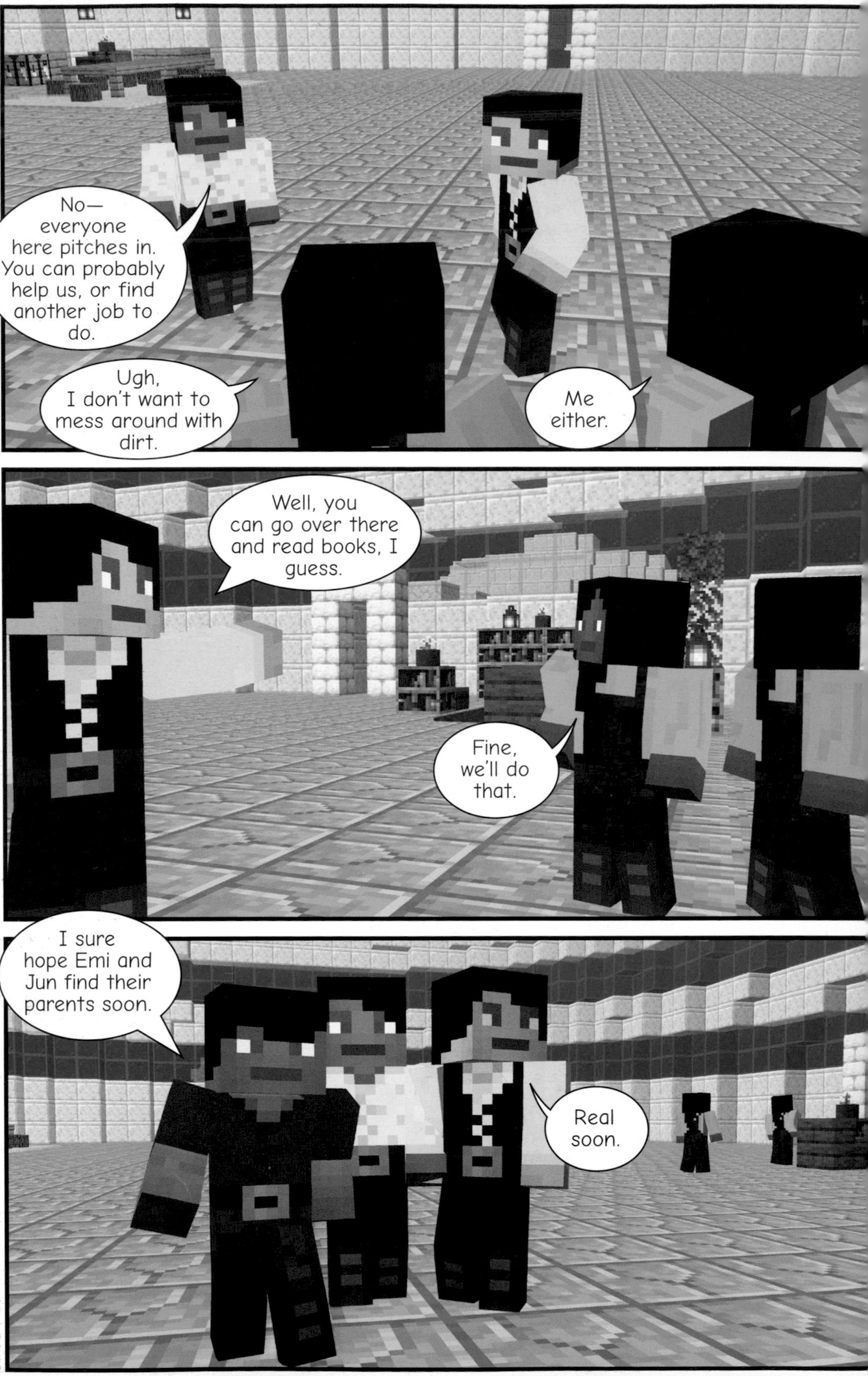
No—everyone here pitches in. You can probably help us, or find another job to do.
Ugh, I don't want to mess around with dirt.
Me either.
Well, you can go over there and read books, I guess.
Fine, we'll do that.
I sure hope Emi and Jun find their parents soon.
Real soon.

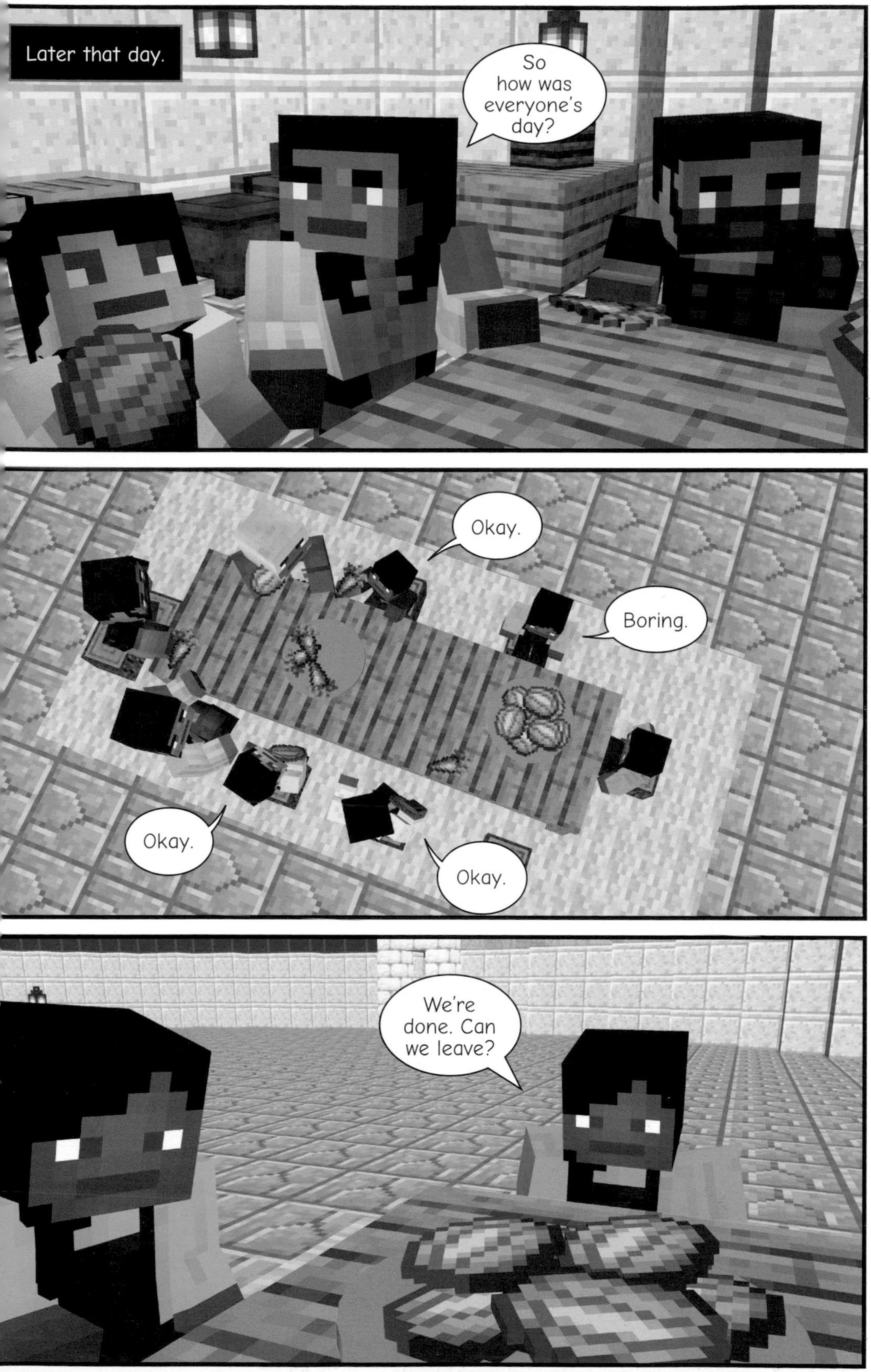
Later that day.
So how was everyone's day?
Okay.
Boring.
Okay.
Okay.
We're done. Can we leave?

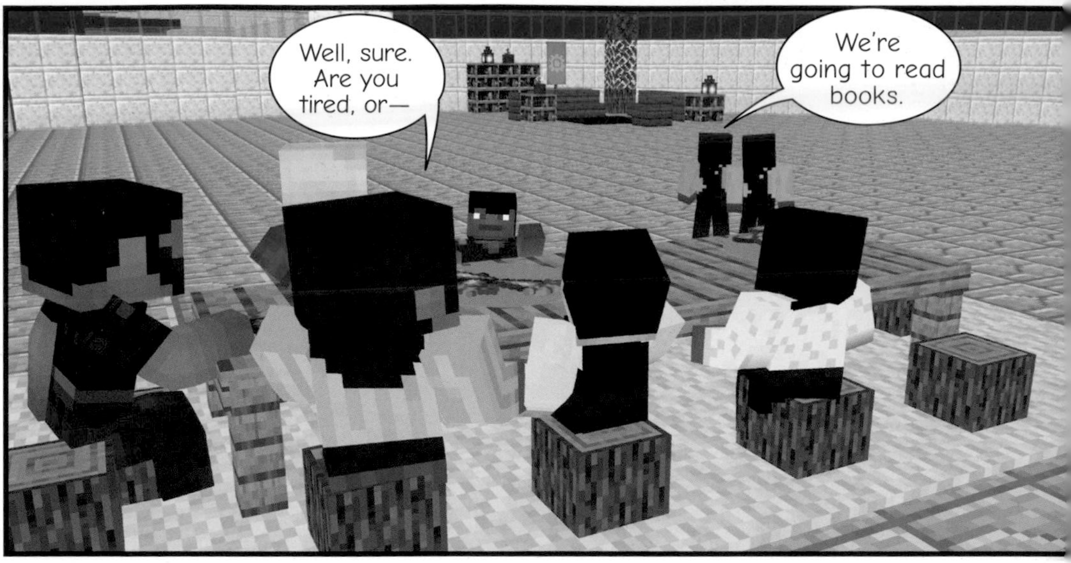
Well, sure. Are you tired, or—
We're going to read books.
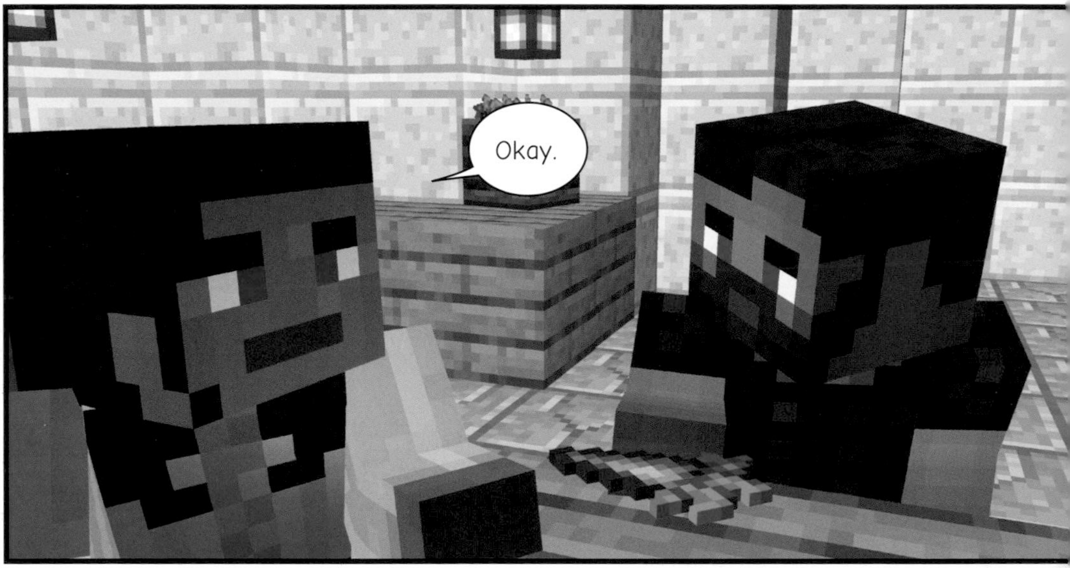
Okay.
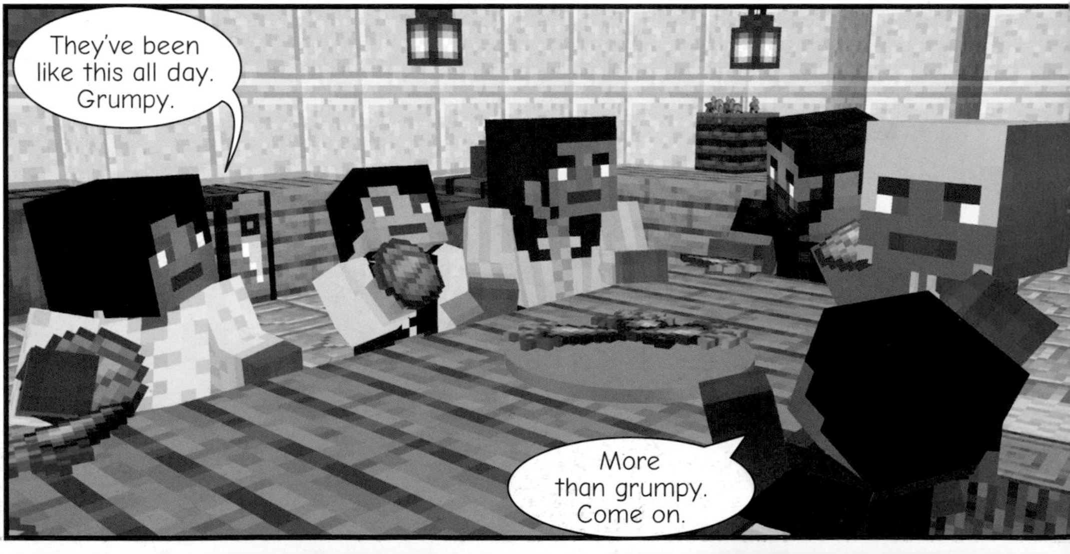
They've been like this all day. Grumpy.
More than grumpy. Come on.

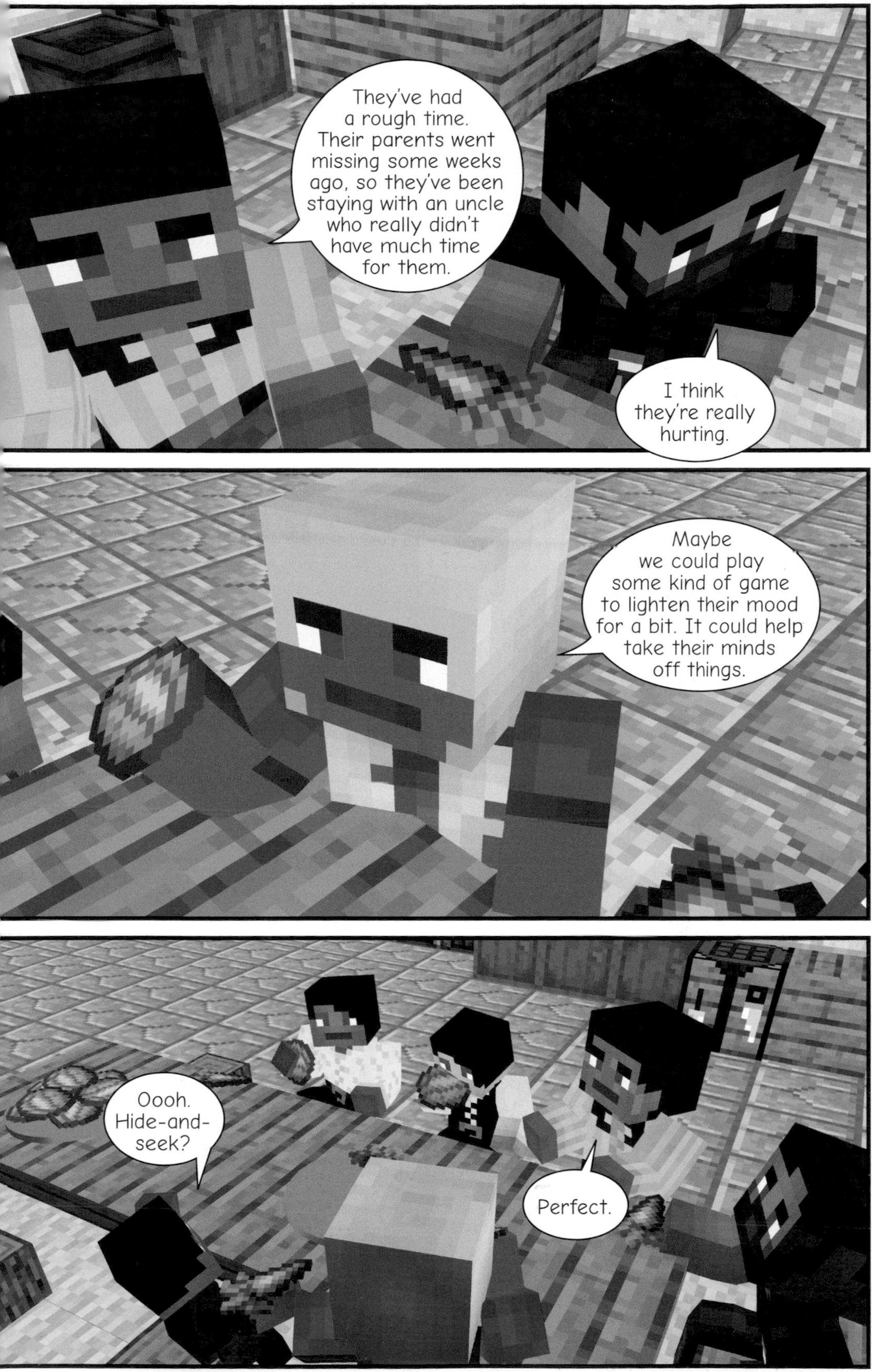
They've had a rough time. Their parents went missing some weeks ago, so they've been staying with an uncle who really didn't have much time for them.
I think they're really hurting.
Maybe we could play some kind of game to lighten their mood for a bit. It could help take their minds off things.
Oooh. Hide-and-seek?
Perfect.

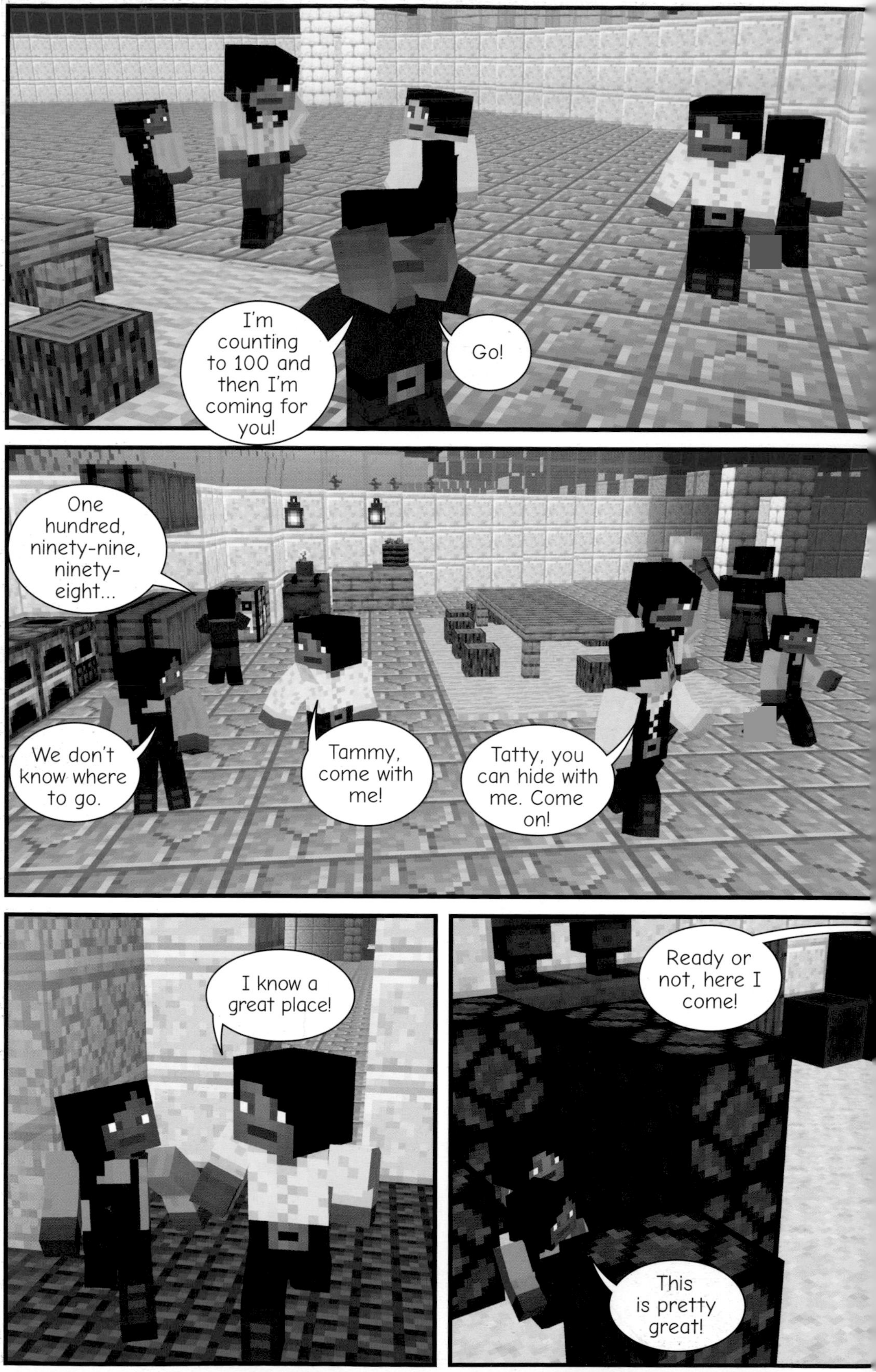
I'm counting to 100 and then I'm coming for you!
Go!
One hundred, ninety-nine, ninety-eight...
We don't know where to go.
Tammy, come with me!
Tatty, you can hide with me. Come on!
I know a great place!
Ready or not, here I come!
This is pretty great!

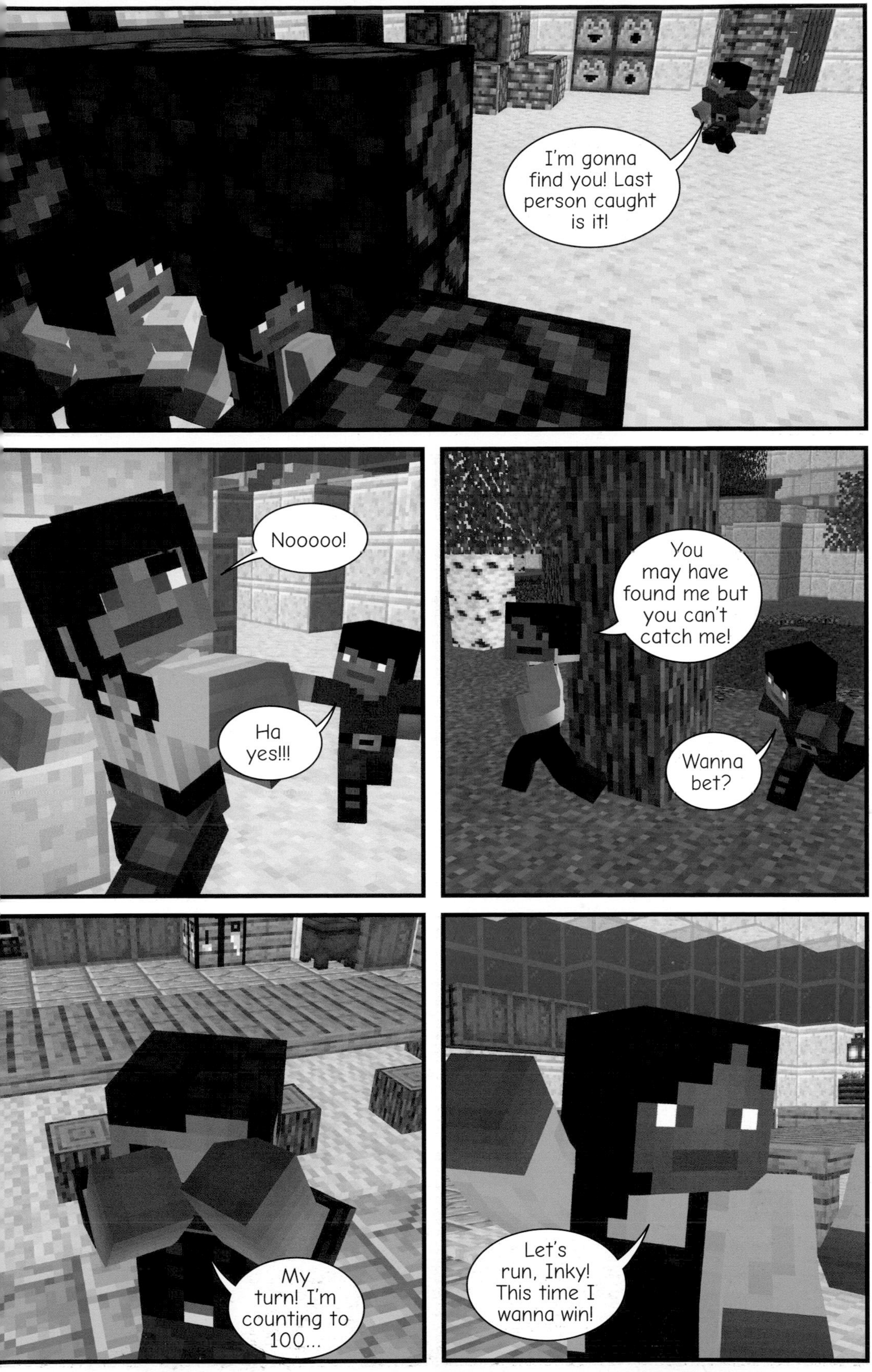

I'm gonna find you! Last person caught is it!
Nooooo!
Ha yes!!!
You may have found me but you can't catch me!
Wanna bet?
My turn! I'm counting to 100...
Let's run, Inky! This time I wanna win!

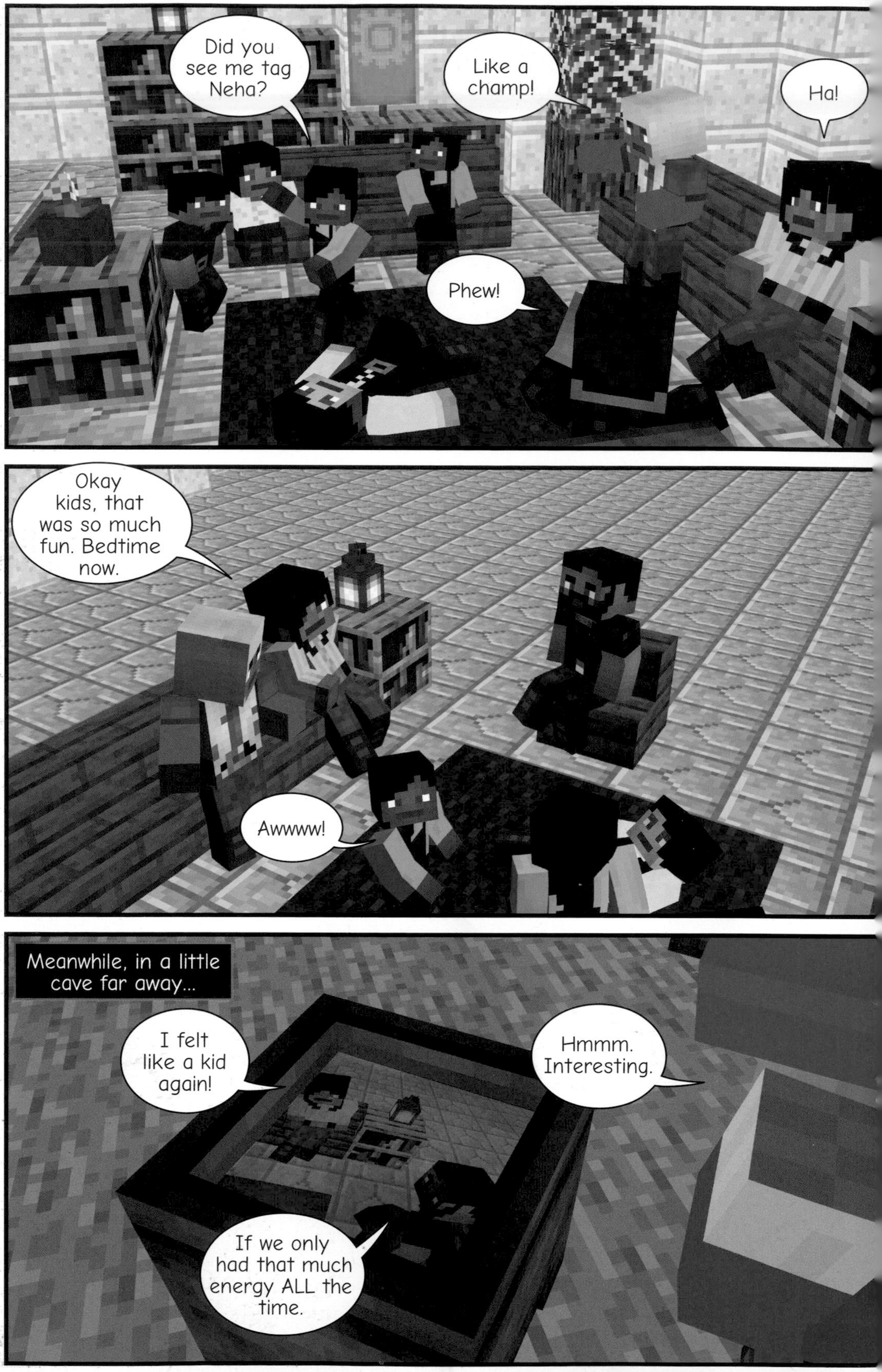
Did you see me tag Neha?
Like a champ!
Ha!
Phew!
Okay kids, that was so much fun. Bedtime now.
Awwww!
Meanwhile, in a little cave far away...
I felt like a kid again!
Hmmm. Interesting.
If we only had that much energy ALL the time.

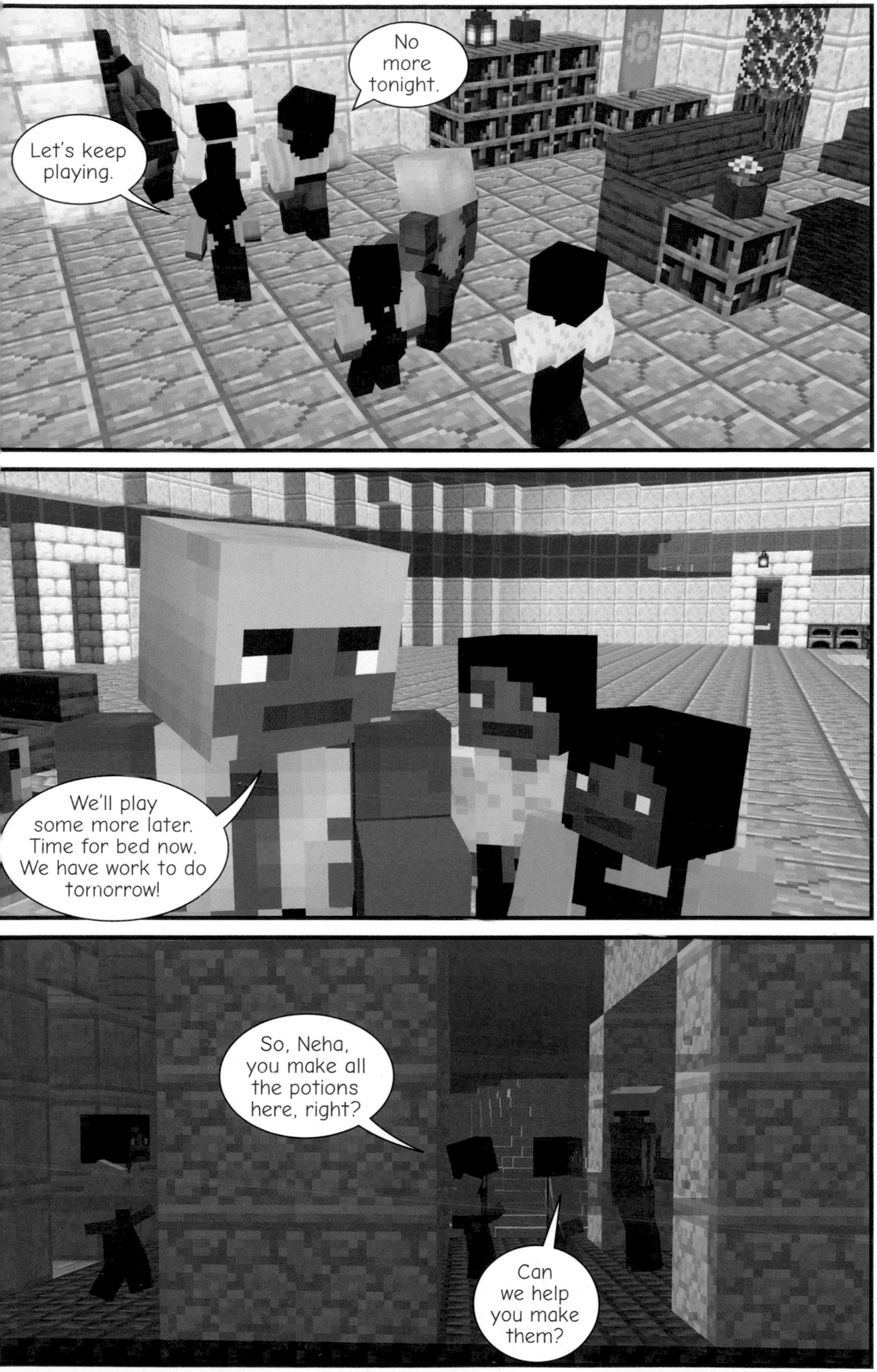
Let's keep playing.
No more tonight.
We'll play some more later. Time for bed now. We have work to do tomorrow!
So, Neha, you make all the potions here, right?
Can we help you make them?

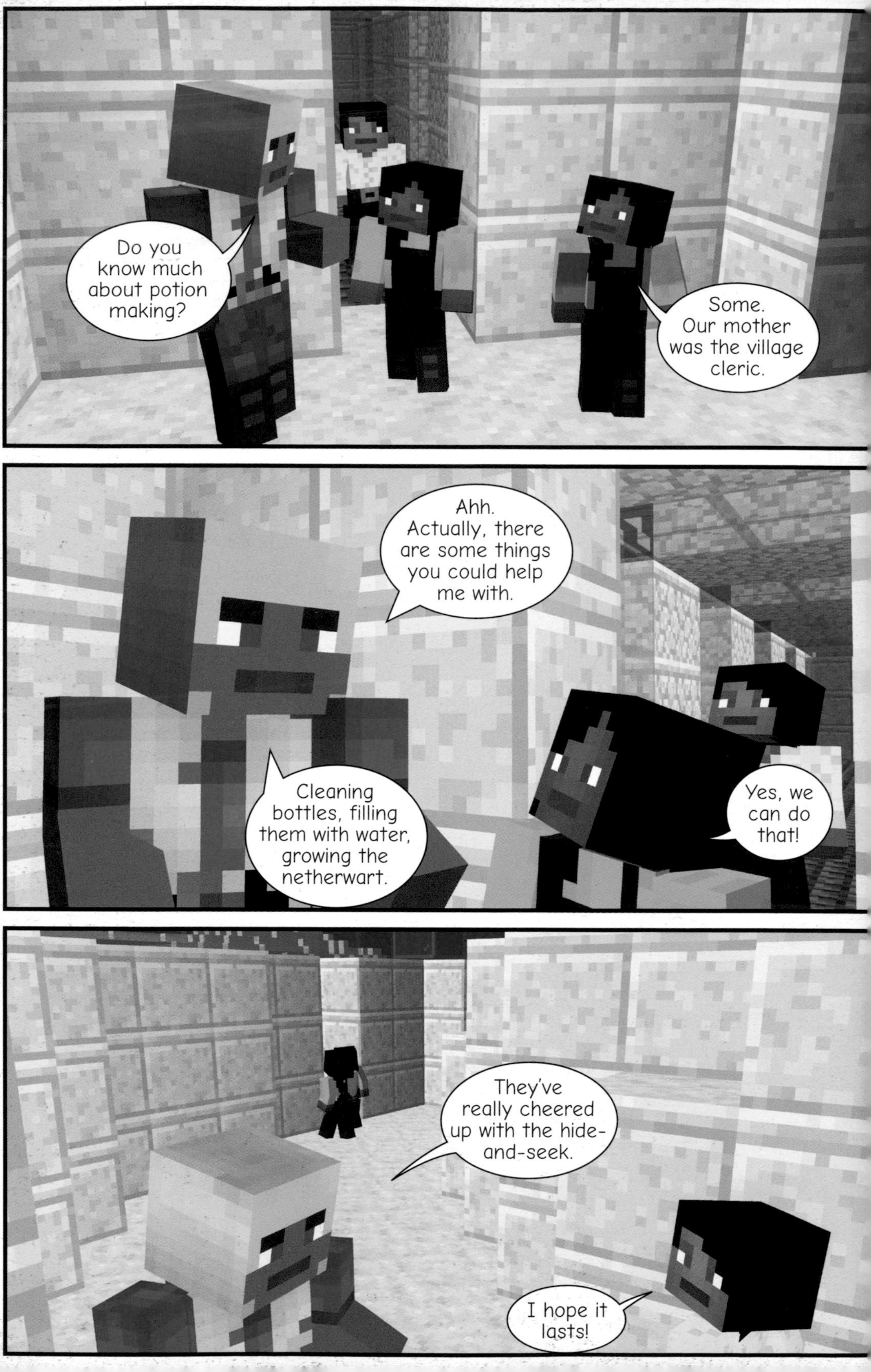
Do you know much about potion making?
Some. Our mother was the village cleric.
Ahh. Actually, there are some things you could help me with.
Cleaning bottles, filling them with water, growing the netherwart.
Yes, we can do that!
They've really cheered up with the hide-and-seek.
I hope it lasts!

Chapter 5
All Play and No Work

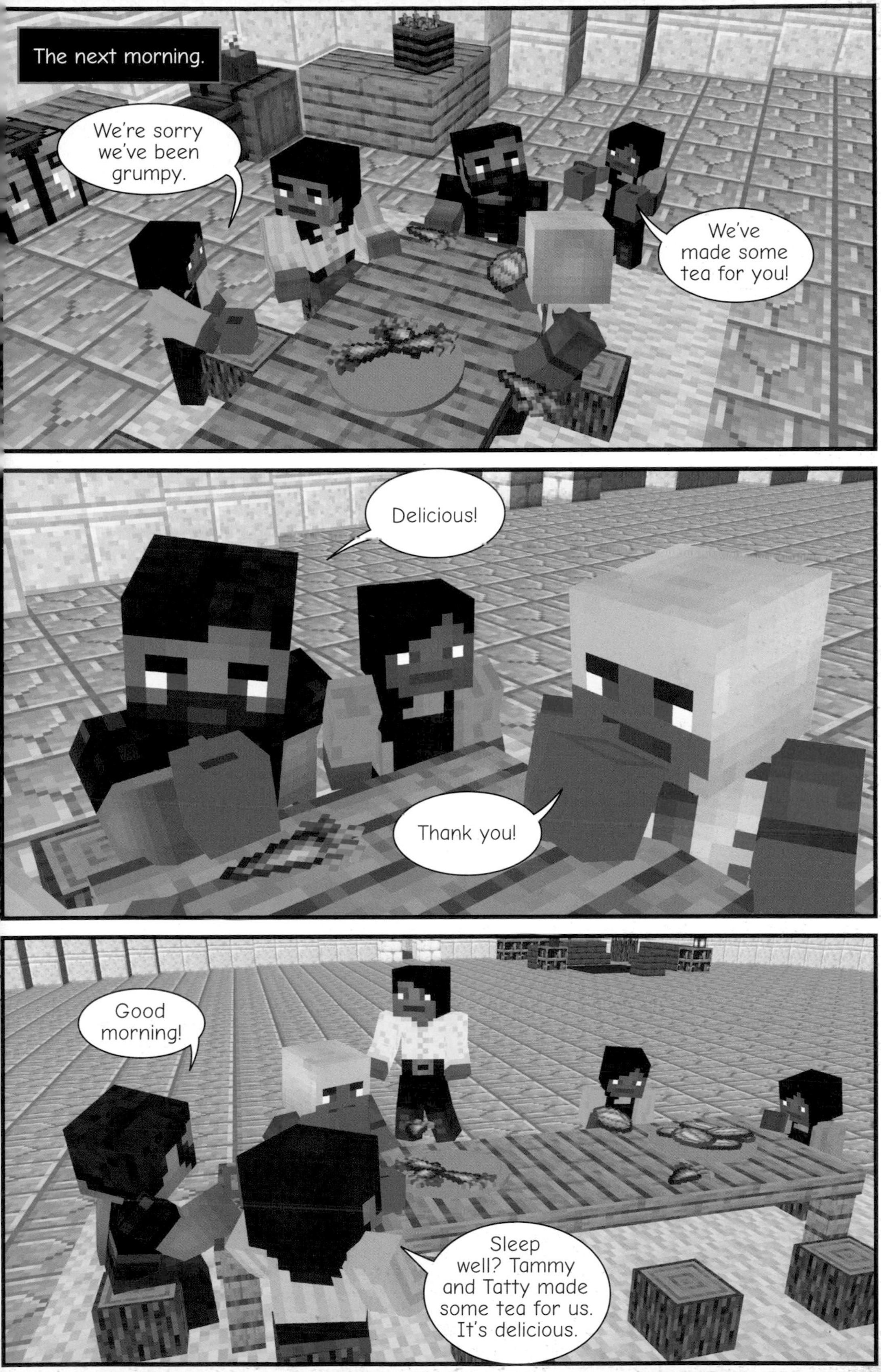
The next morning.
We're sorry we've been grumpy.
We've made some tea for you!
Delicious!
Thank you!
Good morning!
Sleep well? Tammy and Tatty made some tea for us. It's delicious.

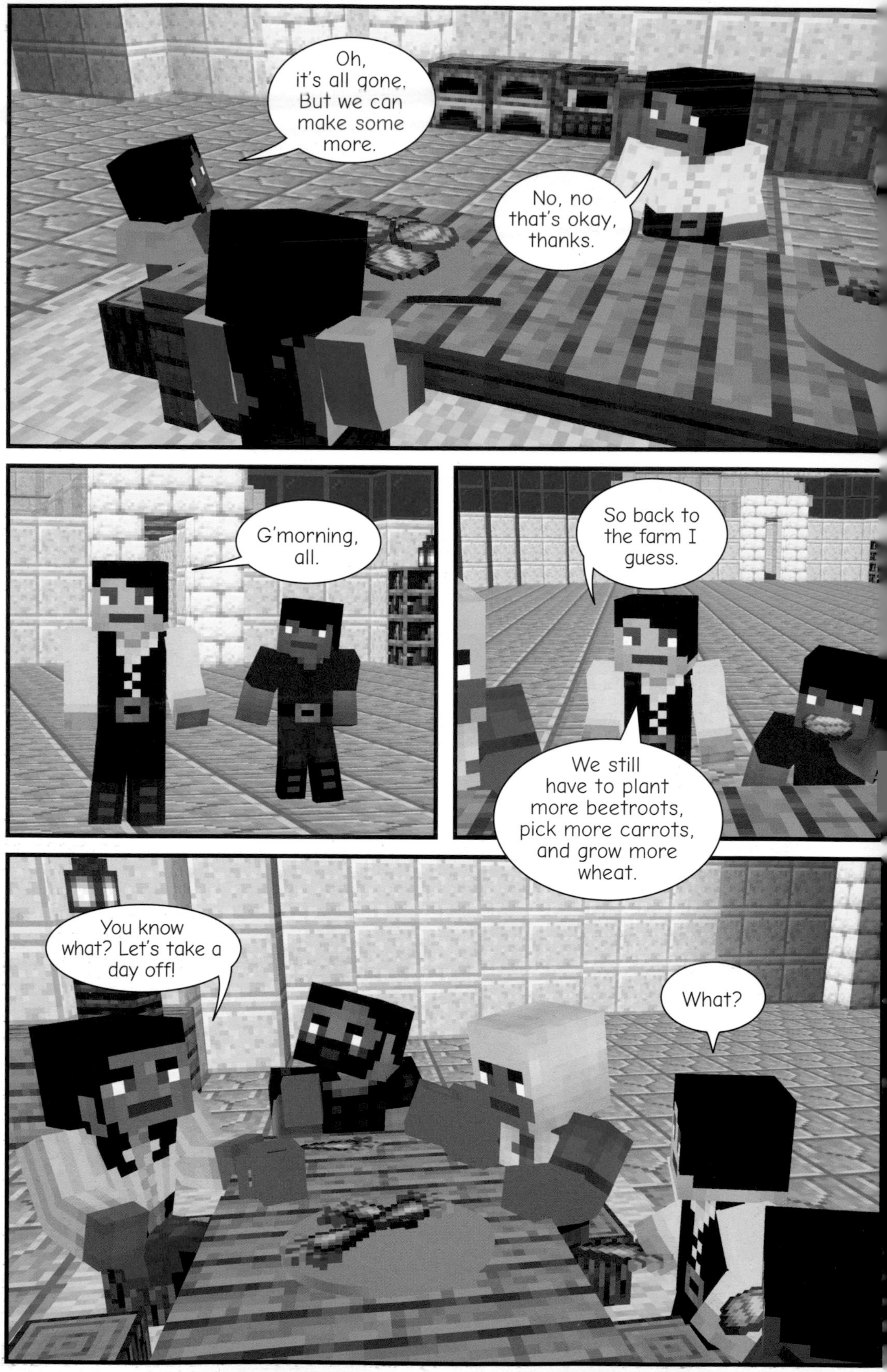
Oh, it's all gone, But we can make some more.
No, no that's okay, thanks.
G'morning, all.
So back to the farm I guess.
We still have to plant more beetroots, pick more carrots, and grow more wheat.
You know what? Let's take a day off!
What?

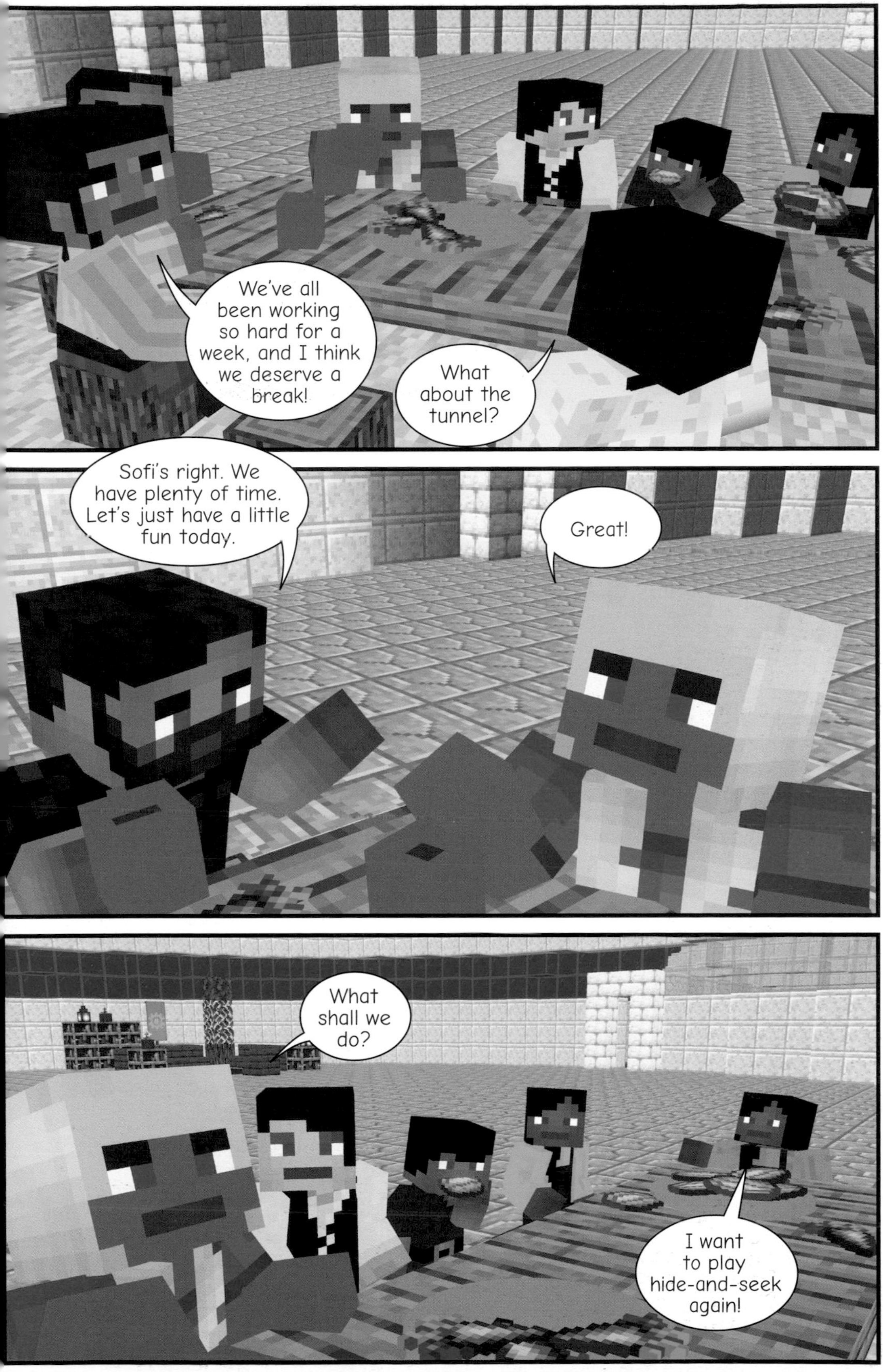
We've all been working so hard for a week, and I think we deserve a break!
What about the tunnel?
Sofi's right. We have plenty of time. Let's just have a little fun today.
Great!
What shall we do?
I want to play hide-and-seek again!

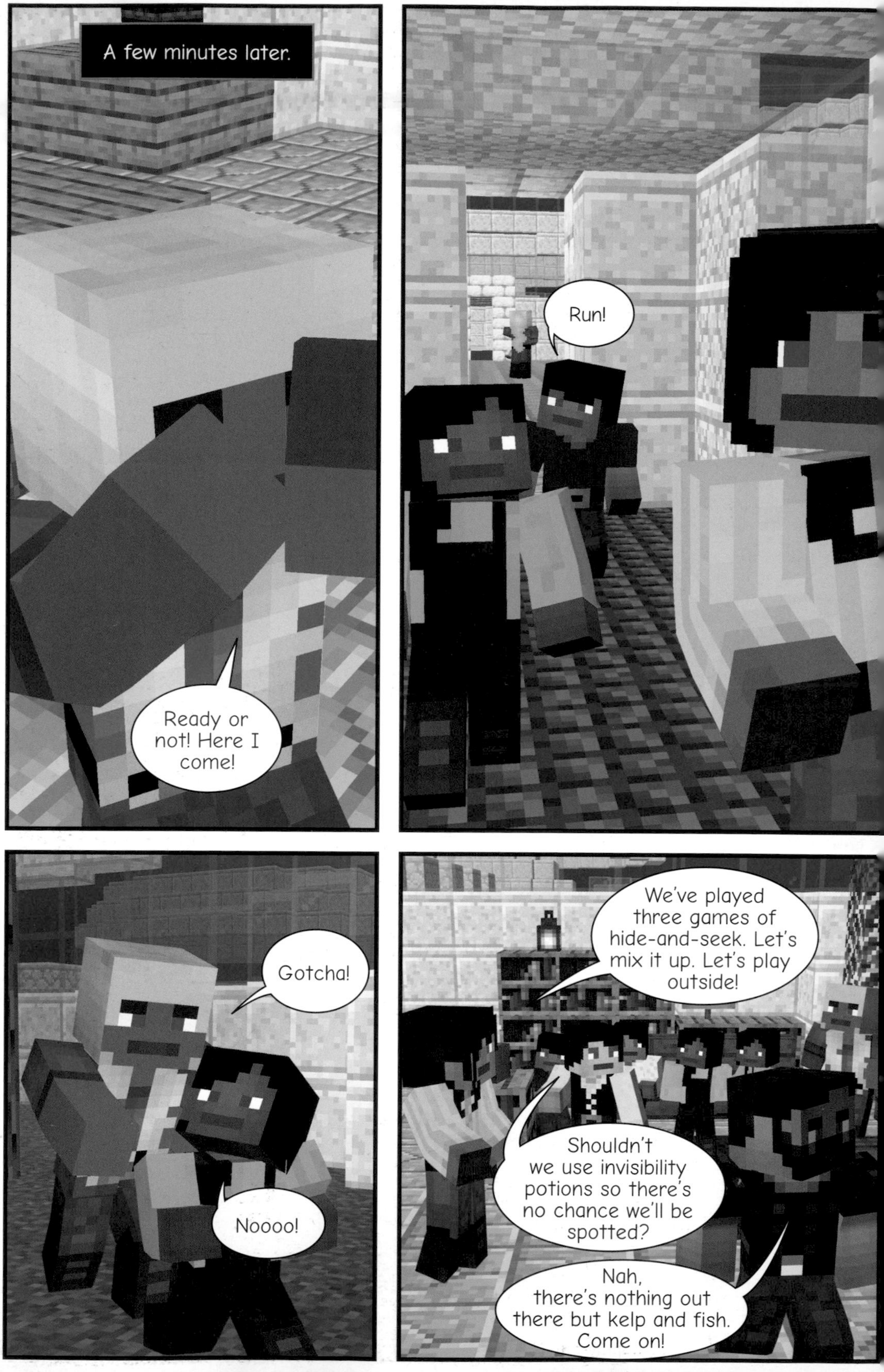
A few minutes later.
Ready or not! Here I come!
Run!
Gotcha!
Noooo!
We've played three games of hide-and-seek. Let's mix it up. Let's play outside!
Shouldn't we use invisibility potions so there's no chance we'll be spotted?
Nah, there's nothing out there but kelp and fish. Come on!

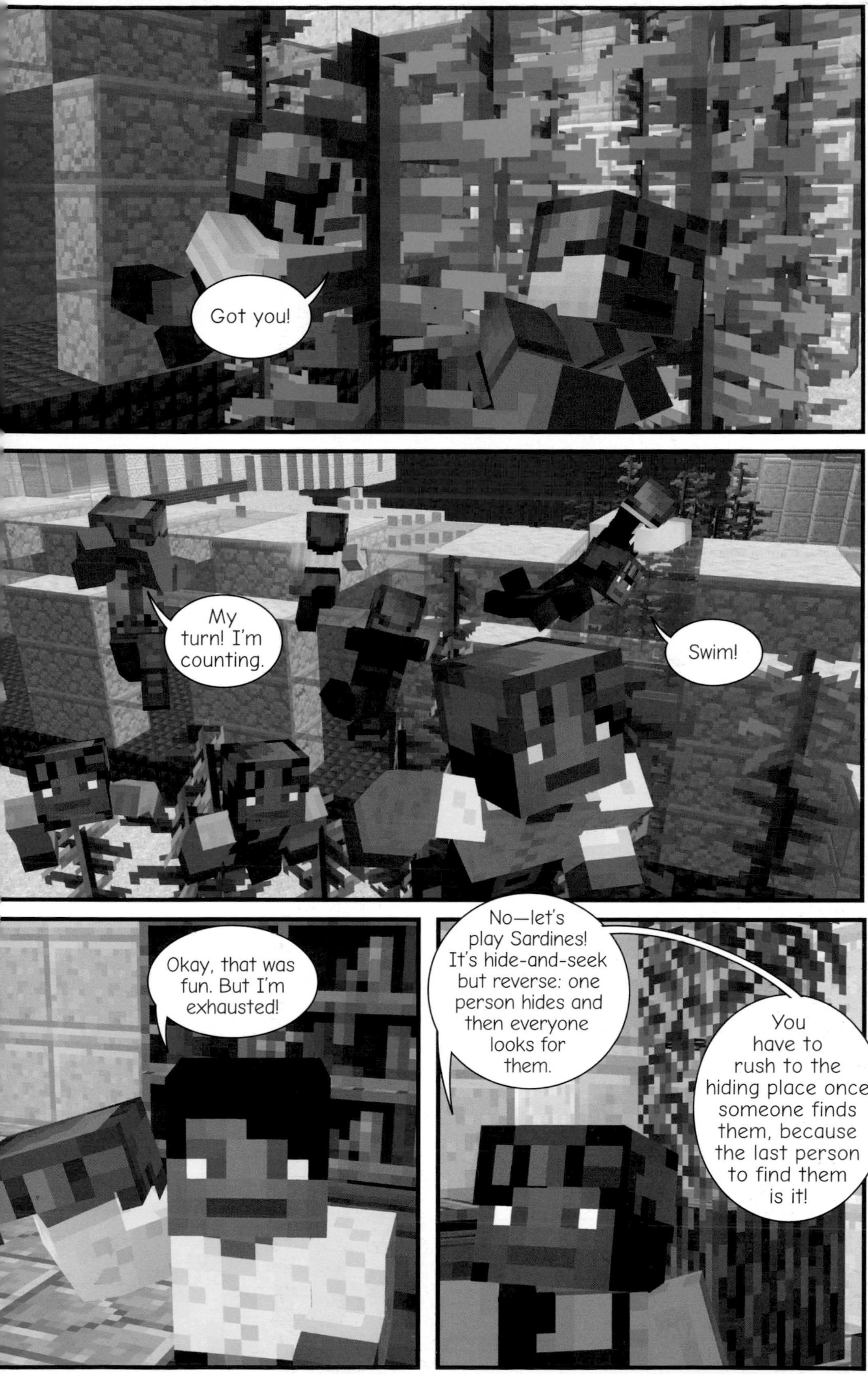
Got you!
My turn! I'm counting.
Swim!
Okay, that was fun. But I'm exhausted!
No—let's play Sardines! It's hide-and-seek but reverse: one person hides and then everyone looks for them.
You have to rush to the hiding place once someone finds them, because the last person to find them is it!

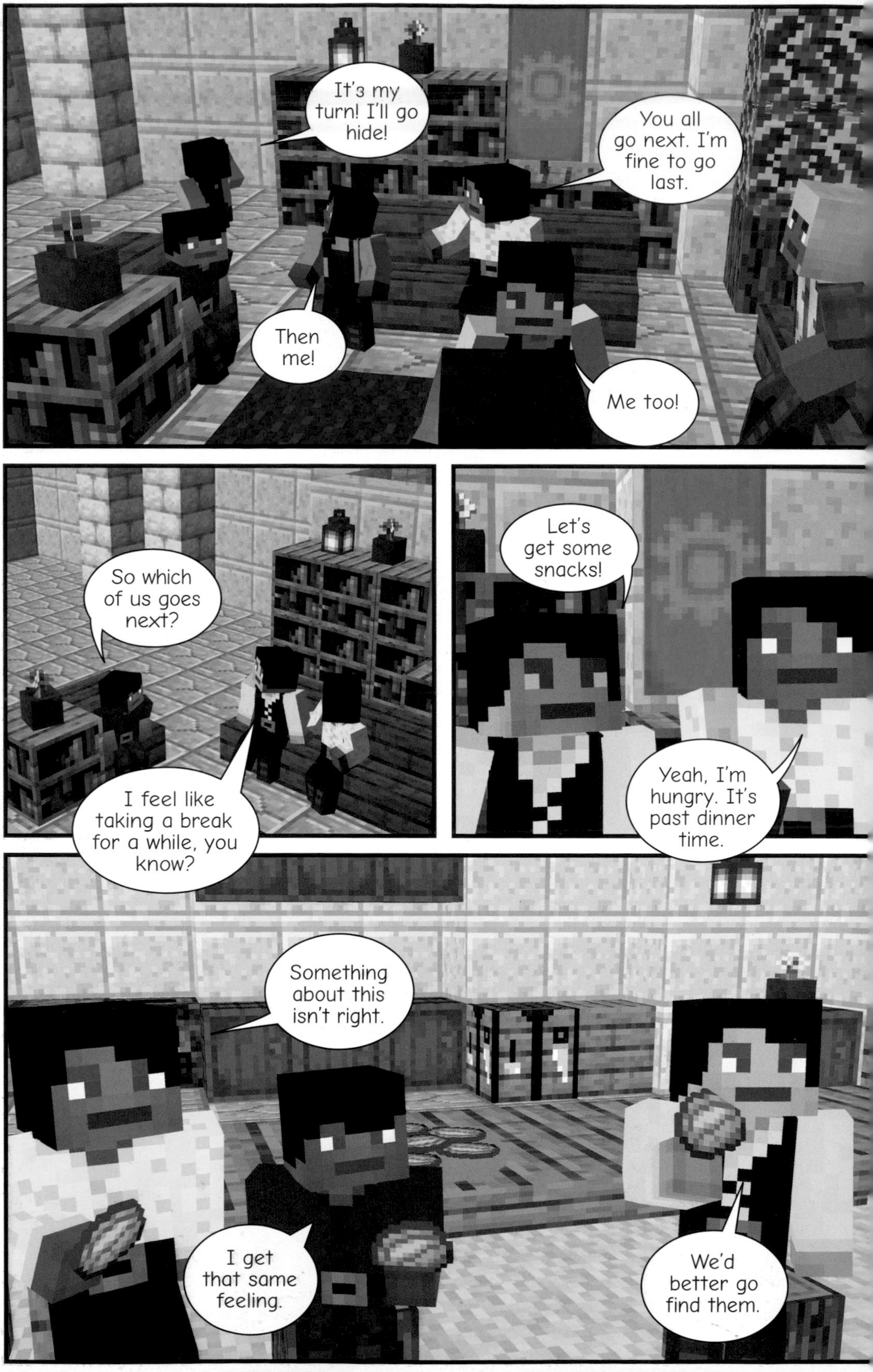
It's my turn! I'll go hide!
You all go next. I'm fine to go last.
Then me!
Me too!
So which of us goes next?
I feel like taking a break for a while, you know?
Let's get some snacks!
Yeah, I'm hungry. It's past dinner time.
Something about this isn't right.
I get that same feeling.
We'd better go find them.

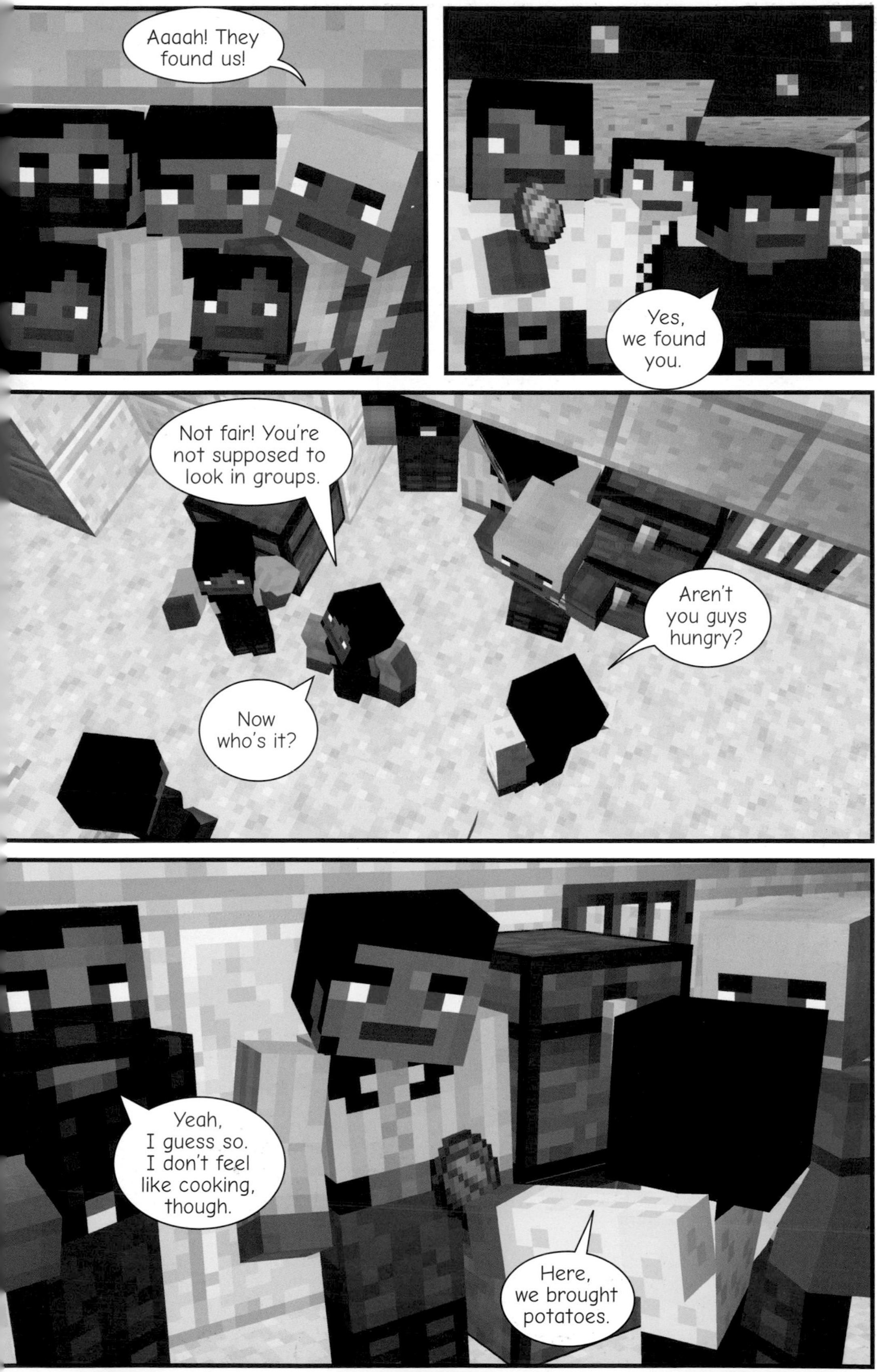
Aaaah! They found us!
Yes, we found you.
Not fair! You're not supposed to look in groups.
Aren't you guys hungry?
Now who's it?
Yeah, I guess so. I don't feel like cooking, though.
Here, we brought potatoes.

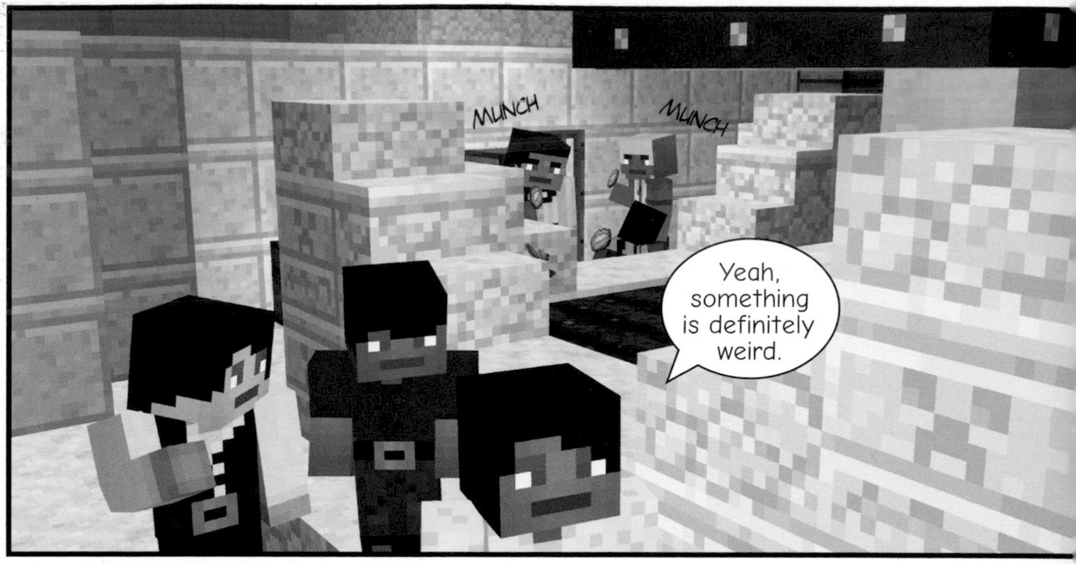
MUNCH
MUNCH
Yeah, something is definitely weird.

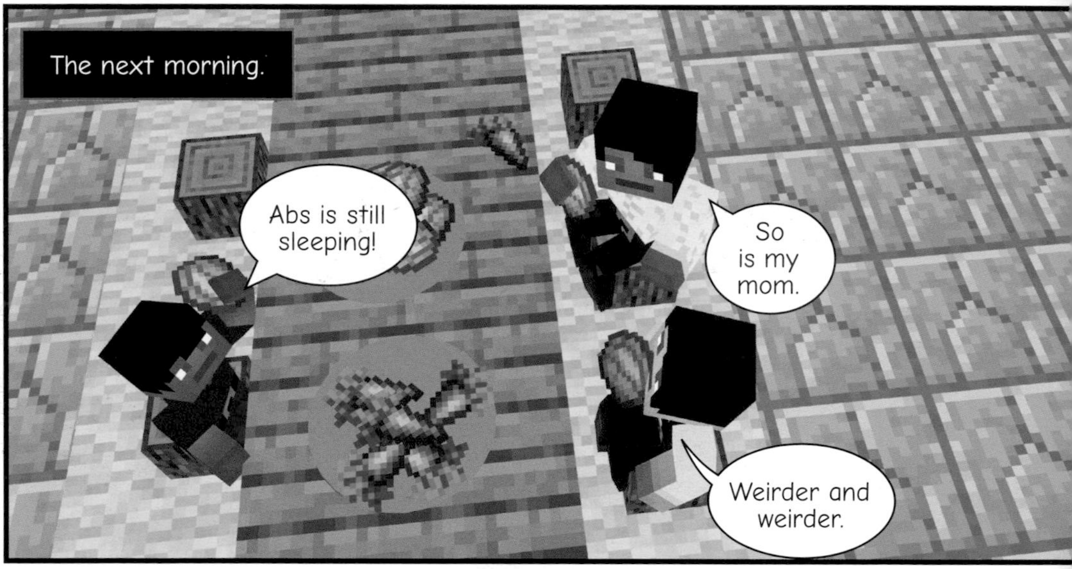
The next morning.
Abs is still sleeping!
So is my mom.
Weirder and weirder.

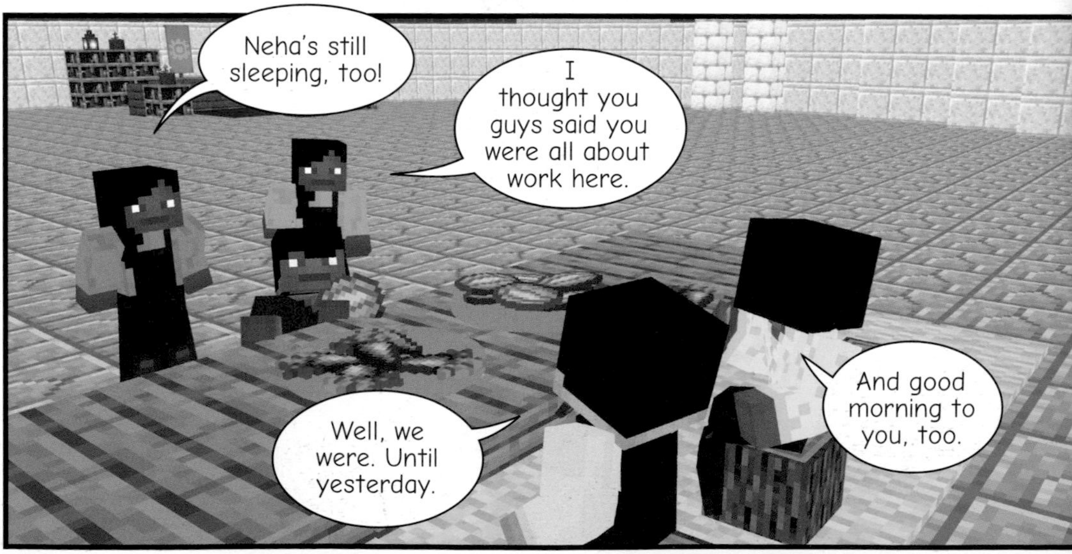
Neha's still sleeping, too!
I thought you guys said you were all about work here.
Well, we were. Until yesterday.
And good morning to you, too.

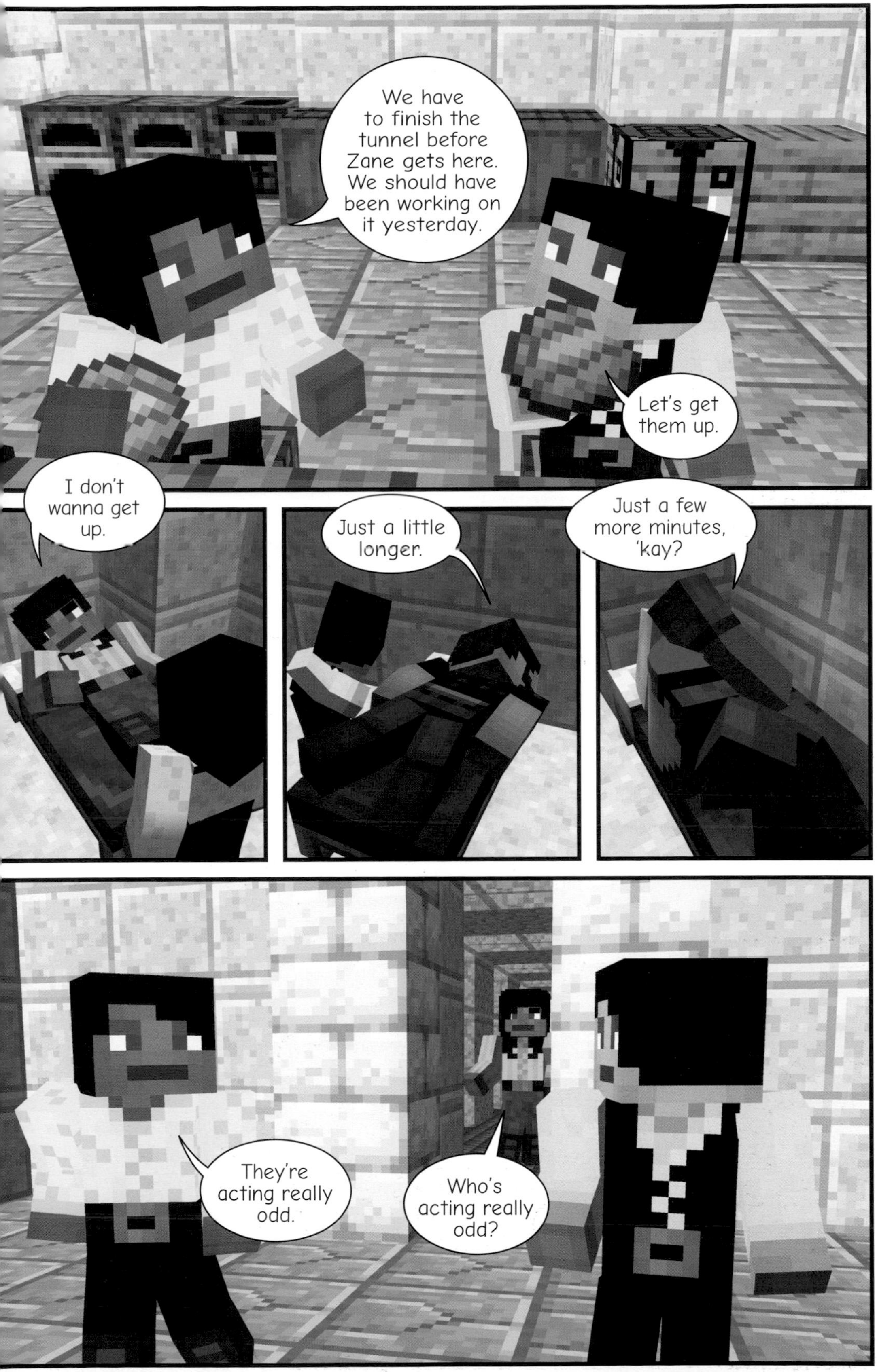
We have to finish the tunnel before Zane gets here. We should have been working on it yesterday.
Let's get them up.
I don't wanna get up.
Just a little longer.
Just a few more minutes, 'kay?
They're acting really odd.
Who's acting really odd?

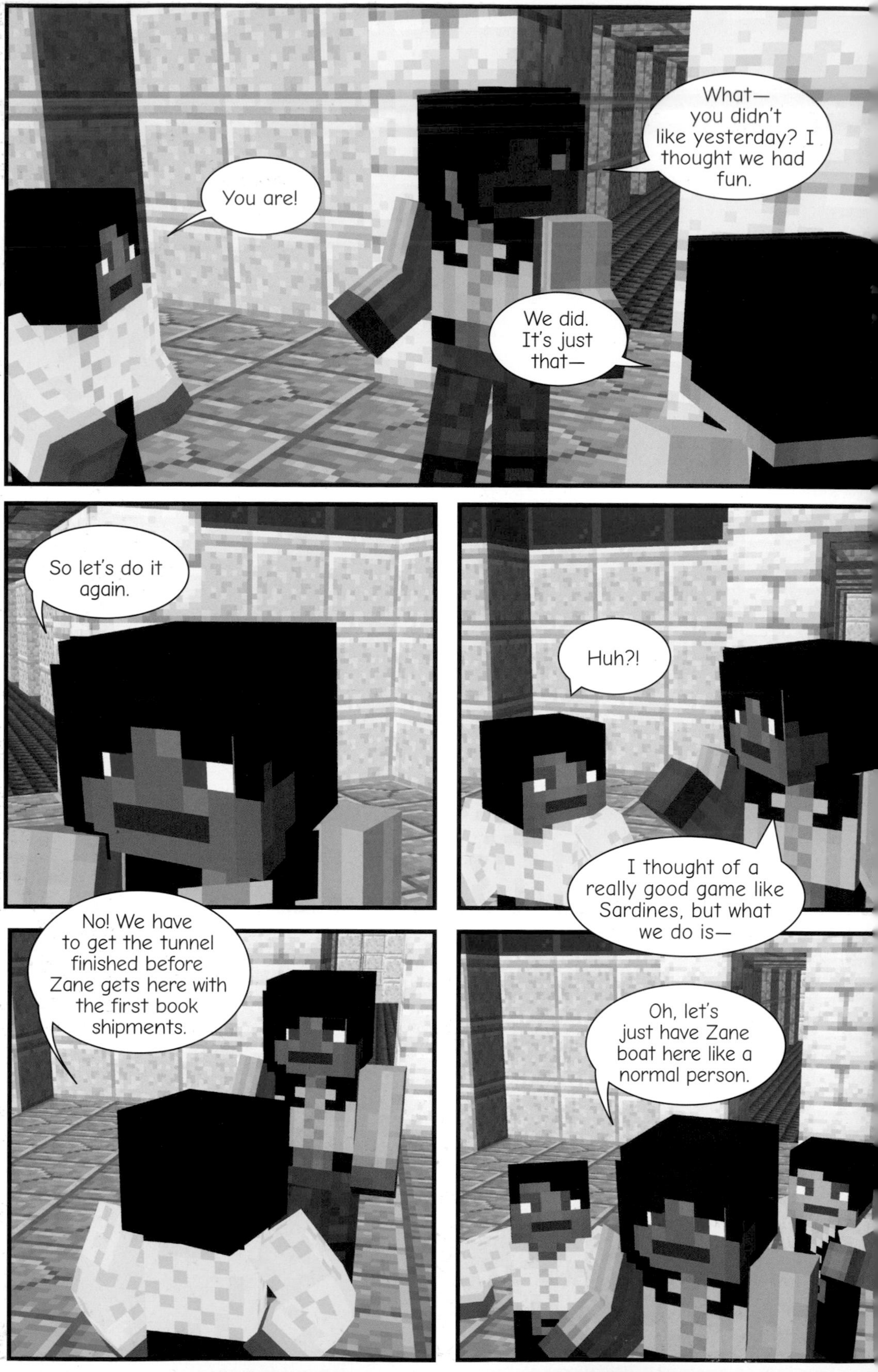
You are!
What— you didn't like yesterday? I thought we had fun.
We did. It's just that—
So let's do it again.
Huh?!
I thought of a really good game like Sardines, but what we do is—
No! We have to get the tunnel finished before Zane gets here with the first book shipments.
Oh, let's just have Zane boat here like a normal person.

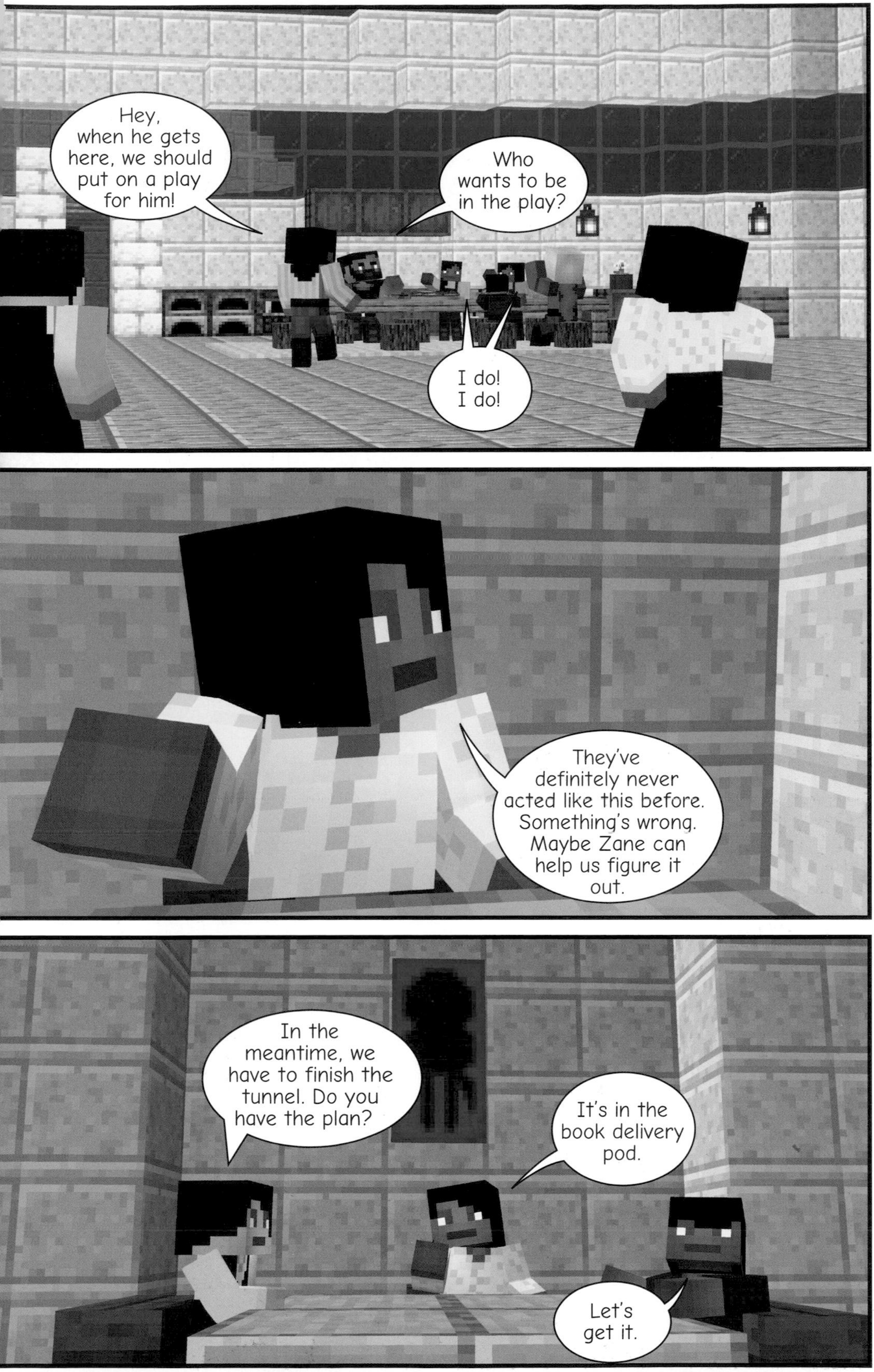
Hey, when he gets here, we should put on a play for him!
Who wants to be in the play?
I do! I do!
They've definitely never acted like this before. Something's wrong. Maybe Zane can help us figure it out.
In the meantime, we have to finish the tunnel. Do you have the plan?
It's in the book delivery pod.
Let's get it.

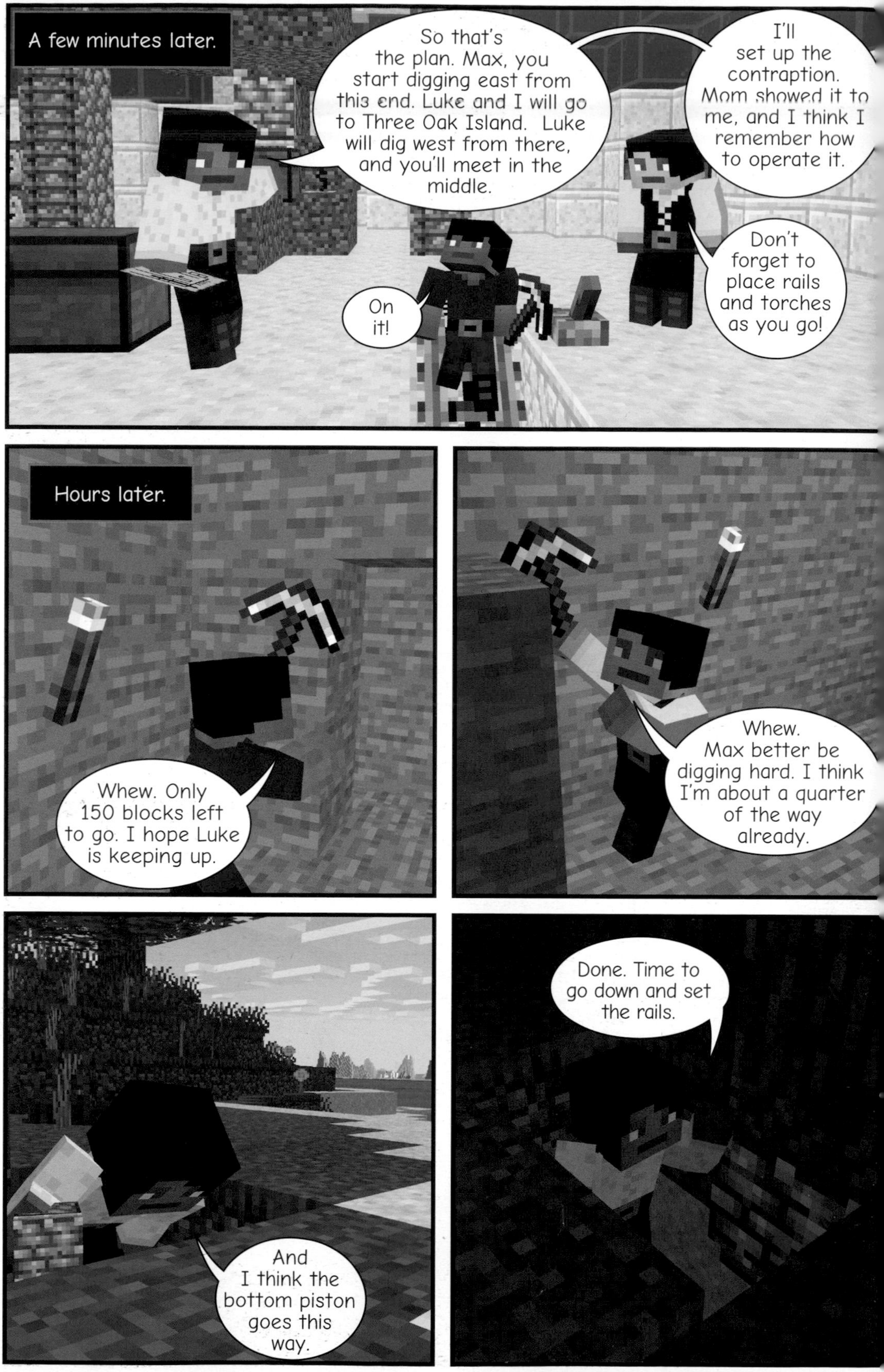
A few minutes later.
So that's the plan. Max, you start digging east from this end. Luke and I will go to Three Oak Island. Luke will dig west from there, and you'll meet in the middle.
I'll set up the contraption. Mom showed it to me, and I think I remember how to operate it.
On it!
Don't forget to place rails and torches as you go!
Hours later.
Whew. Only 150 blocks left to go. I hope Luke is keeping up.
Whew. Max better be digging hard. I think I'm about a quarter of the way already.
And I think the bottom piston goes this way.
Done. Time to go down and set the rails.

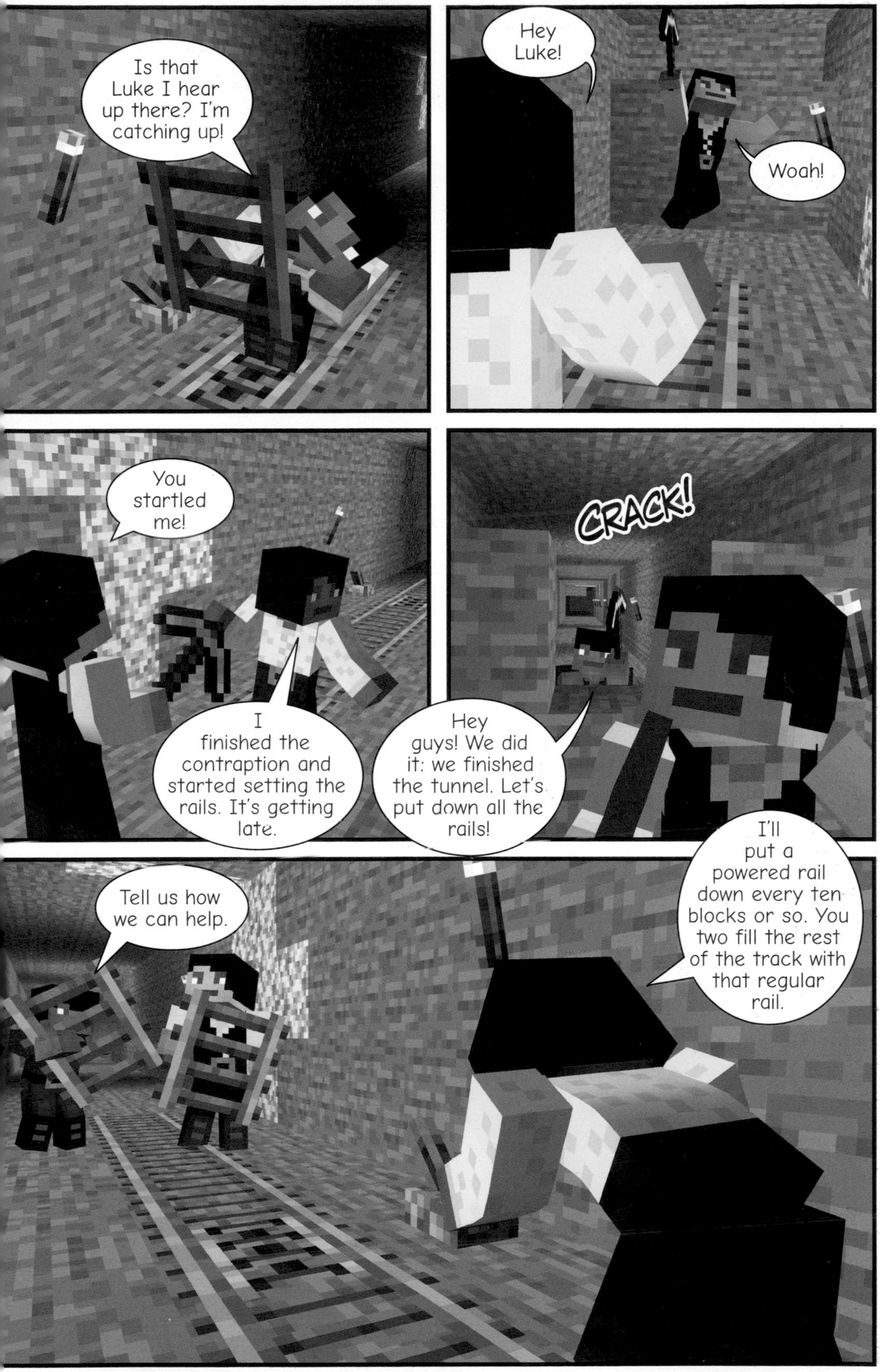
Is that Luke I hear up there? I'm catching up!
Hey Luke!
Woah!
You startled me!
I finished the contraption and started setting the rails. It's getting late.
CRACK!
Hey guys! We did it: we finished the tunnel. Let's put down all the rails!
Tell us how we can help.
I'll put a powered rail down every ten blocks or so. You two fill the rest of the track with that regular rail.

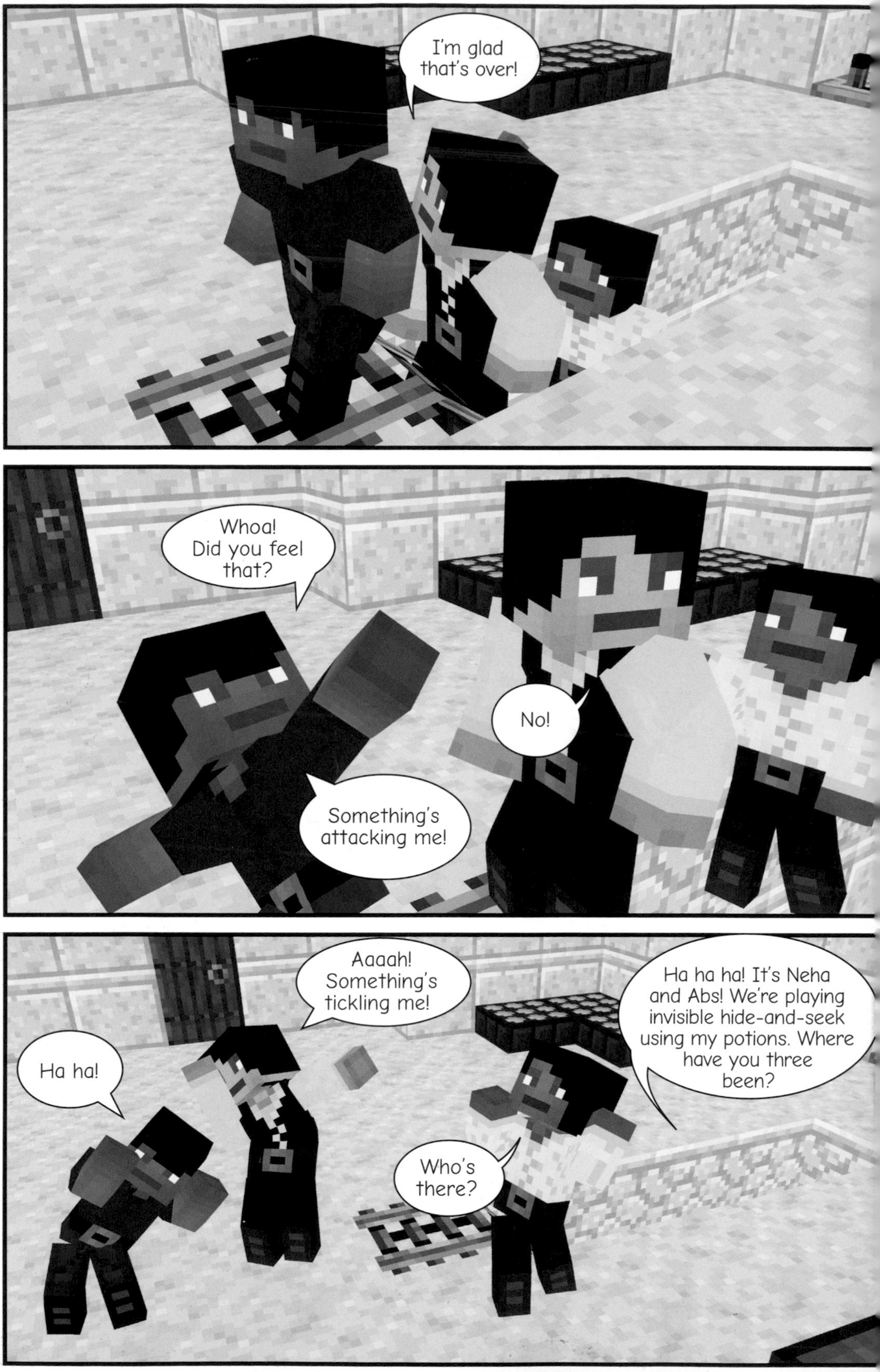

I'm glad that's over!
Whoa! Did you feel that?
No!
Something's attacking me!
Aaaah! Something's tickling me!
Ha ha!
Ha ha ha! It's Neha and Abs! We're playing invisible hide-and-seek using my potions. Where have you three been?
Who's there?

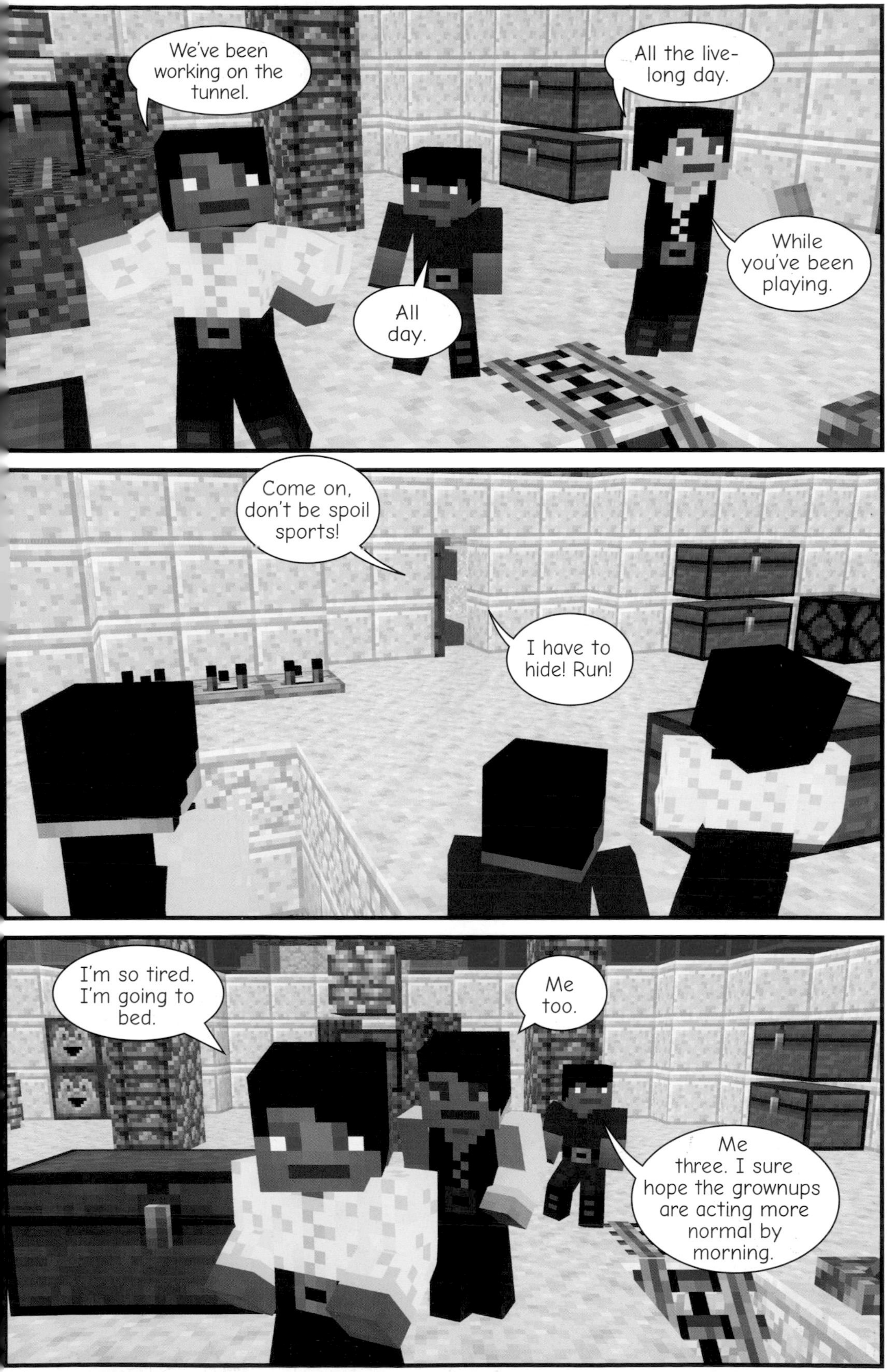
We've been working on the tunnel.
All day.
All the live-long day.
While you've been playing.
Come on, don't be spoil sports!
I have to hide! Run!
I'm so tired. I'm going to bed.
Me too.
Me three. I sure hope the grownups are acting more normal by morning.

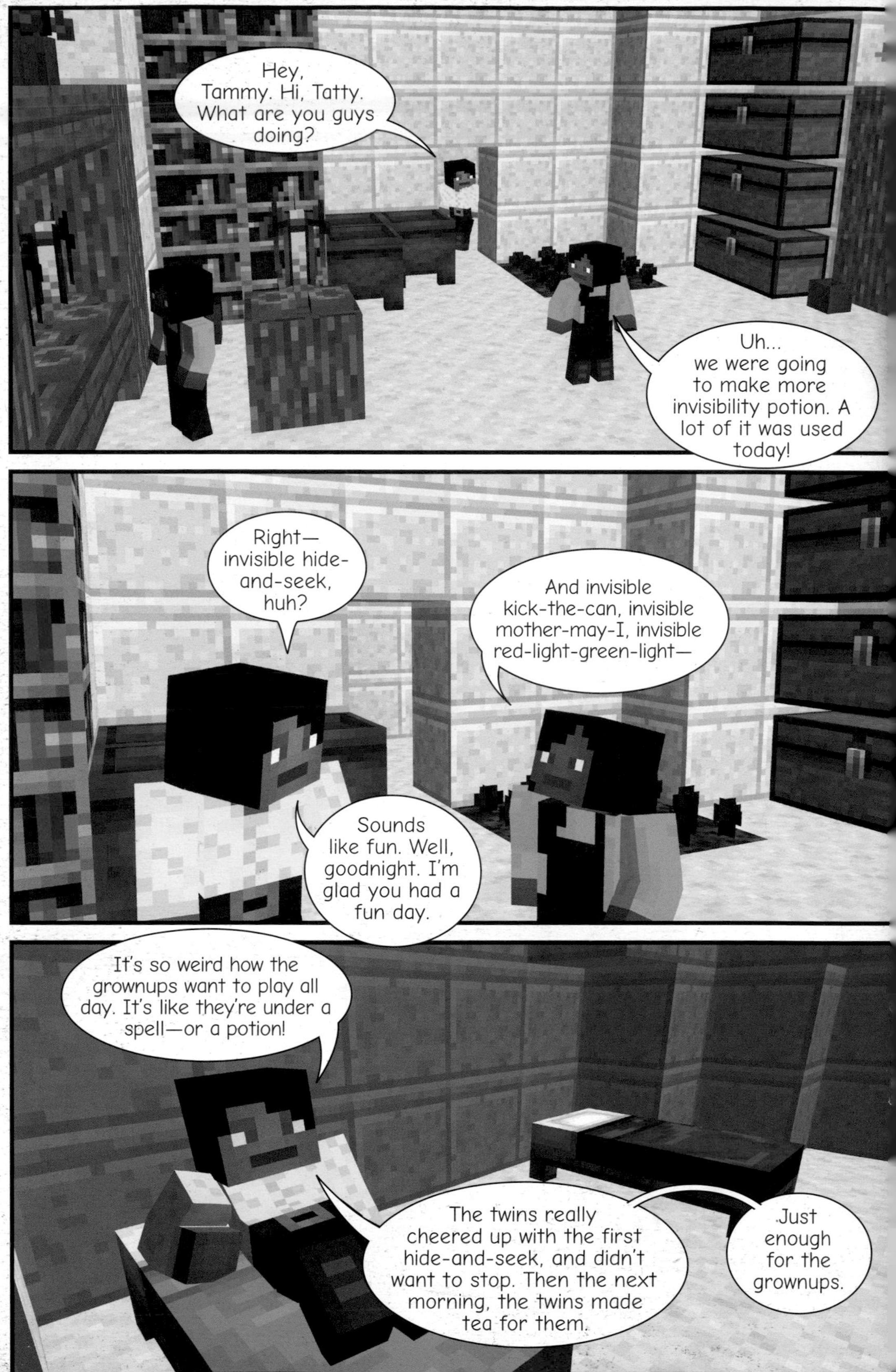
Hey, Tammy. Hi, Tatty. What are you guys doing?
Uh... we were going to make more invisibility potion. A lot of it was used today!
Right—invisible hide-and-seek, huh?
And invisible kick-the-can, invisible mother-may-I, invisible red-light-green-light—
Sounds like fun. Well, goodnight. I'm glad you had a fun day.
It's so weird how the grownups want to play all day. It's like they're under a spell—or a potion!
The twins really cheered up with the first hide-and-seek, and didn't want to stop. Then the next morning, the twins made tea for them.
Just enough for the grownups.

Chapter 6
Work and More Work

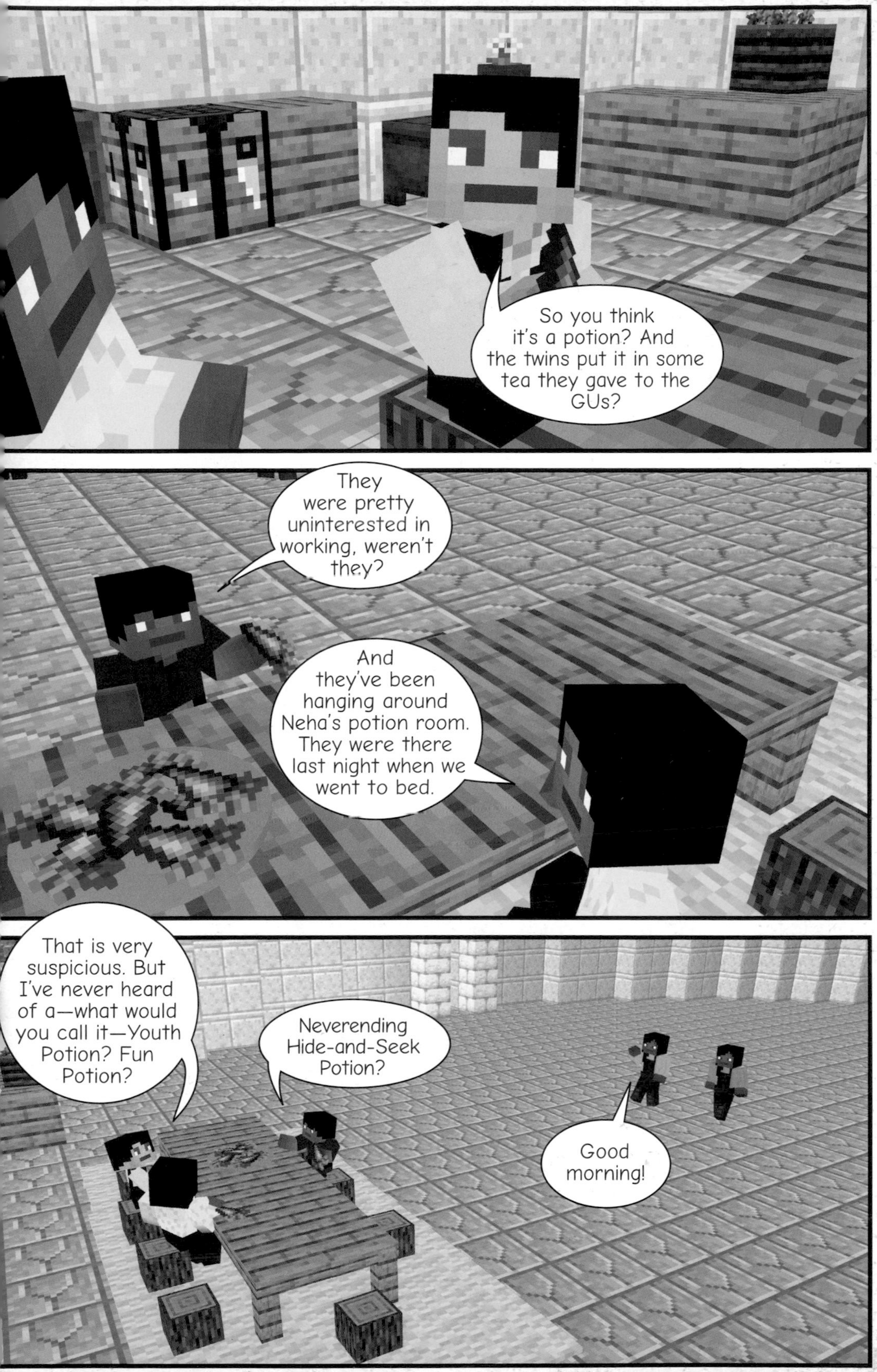

So you think it's a potion? And the twins put it in some tea they gave to the GUs?
They were pretty uninterested in working, weren't they?
And they've been hanging around Neha's potion room. They were there last night when we went to bed.
That is very suspicious. But I've never heard of a—what would you call it—Youth Potion? Fun Potion?
Neverending Hide-and-Seek Potion?
Good morning!

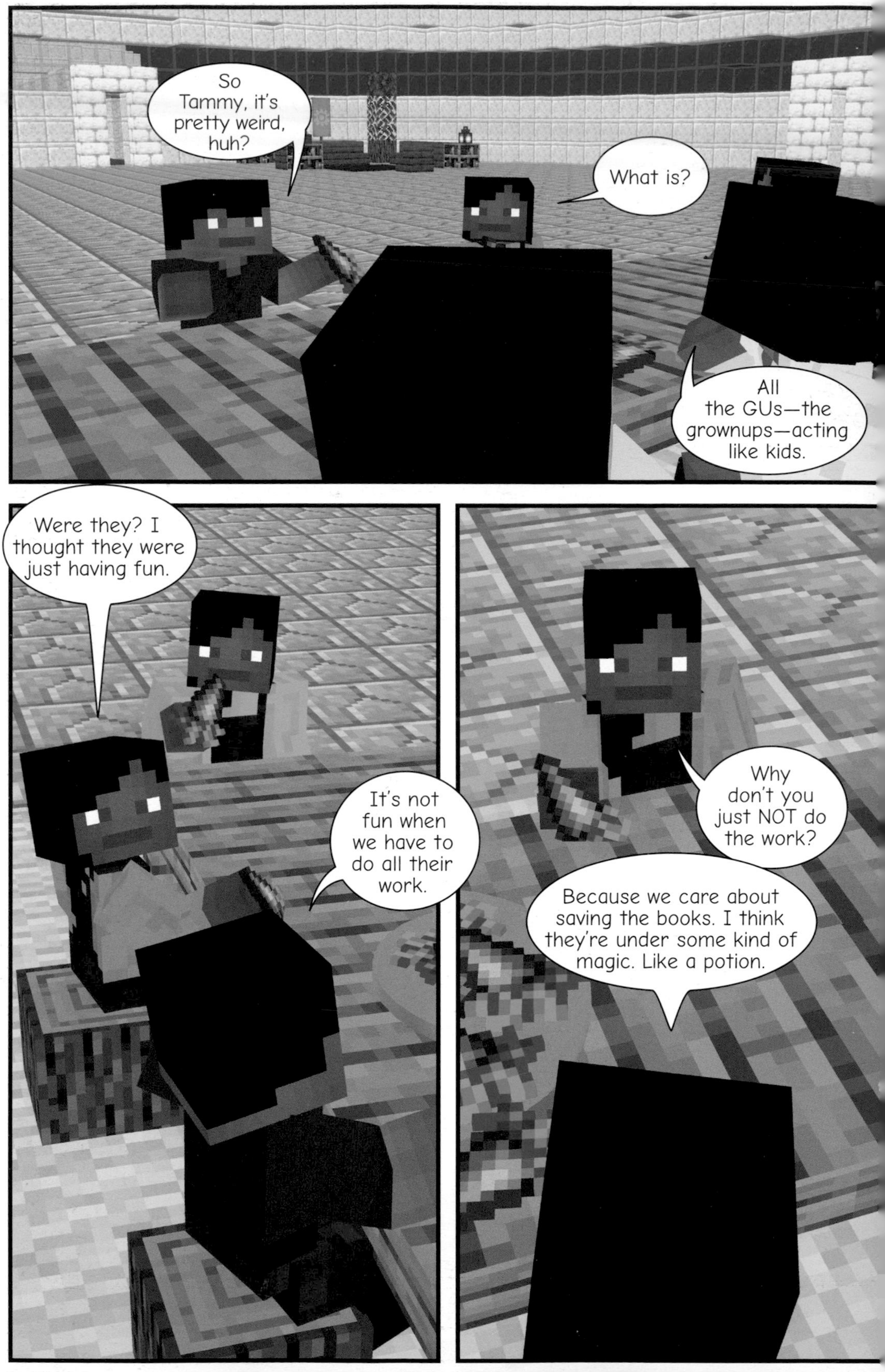
So Tammy, it's pretty weird, huh?
What is?
All the GUs—the grownups—acting like kids.
Were they? I thought they were just having fun.
It's not fun when we have to do all their work.
Why don't you just NOT do the work?
Because we care about saving the books. I think they're under some kind of magic. Like a potion.

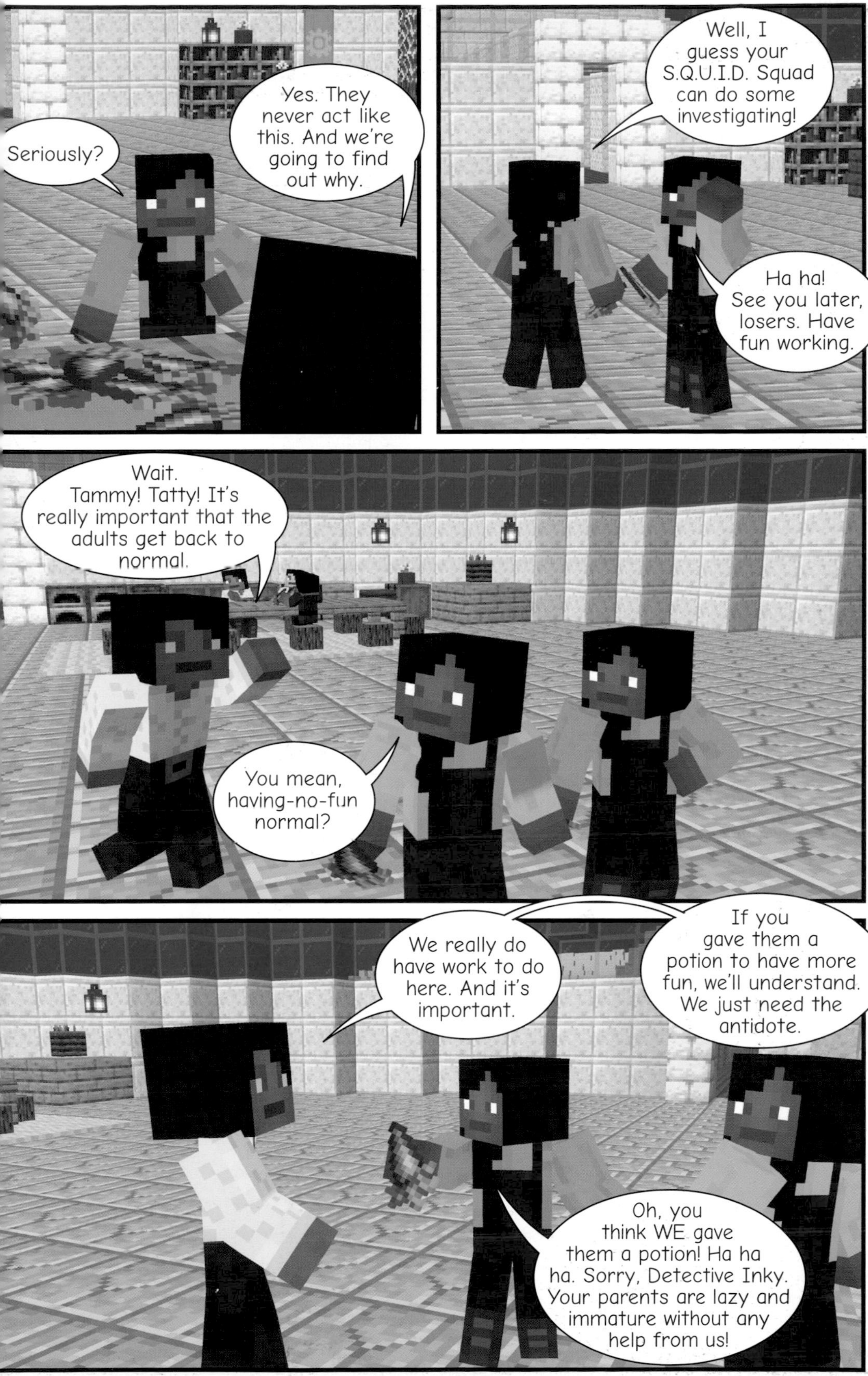
Seriously?
Yes. They never act like this. And we're going to find out why.
Well, I guess your S.Q.U.I.D. Squad can do some investigating!
Ha ha! See you later, losers. Have fun working.
Wait. Tammy! Tatty! It's really important that the adults get back to normal.
You mean, having-no-fun normal?
We really do have work to do here. And it's important.
If you gave them a potion to have more fun, we'll understand. We just need the antidote.
Oh, you think WE gave them a potion! Ha ha ha. Sorry, Detective Inky. Your parents are lazy and immature without any help from us!

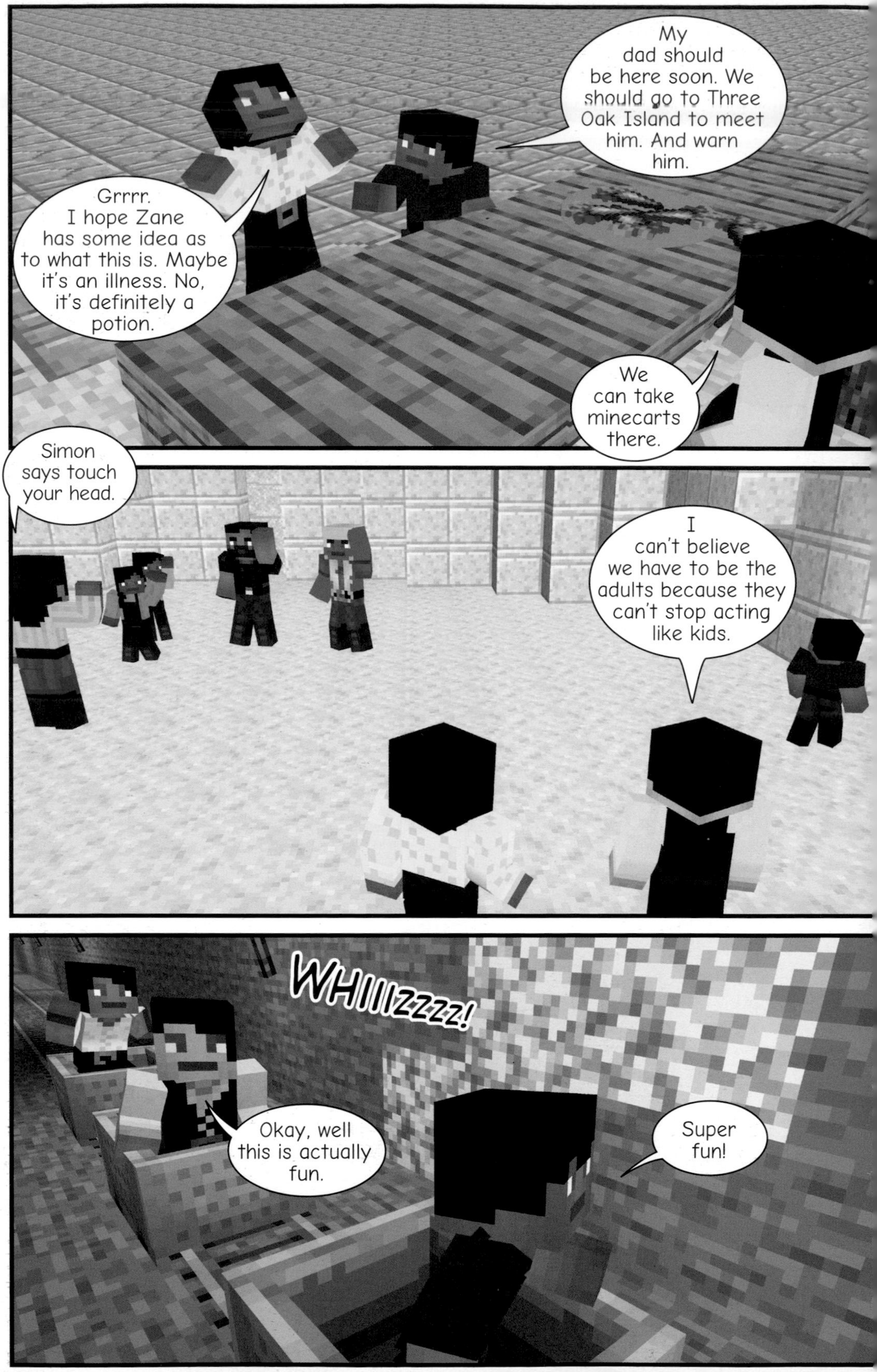
My dad should be here soon. We should go to Three Oak Island to meet him. And warn him.
Grrrr. I hope Zane has some idea as to what this is. Maybe it's an illness. No, it's definitely a potion.
We can take minecarts there.
Simon says touch your head.
I can't believe we have to be the adults because they can't stop acting like kids.
WHIIIIZZZZ!
Okay, well this is actually fun.
Super fun!

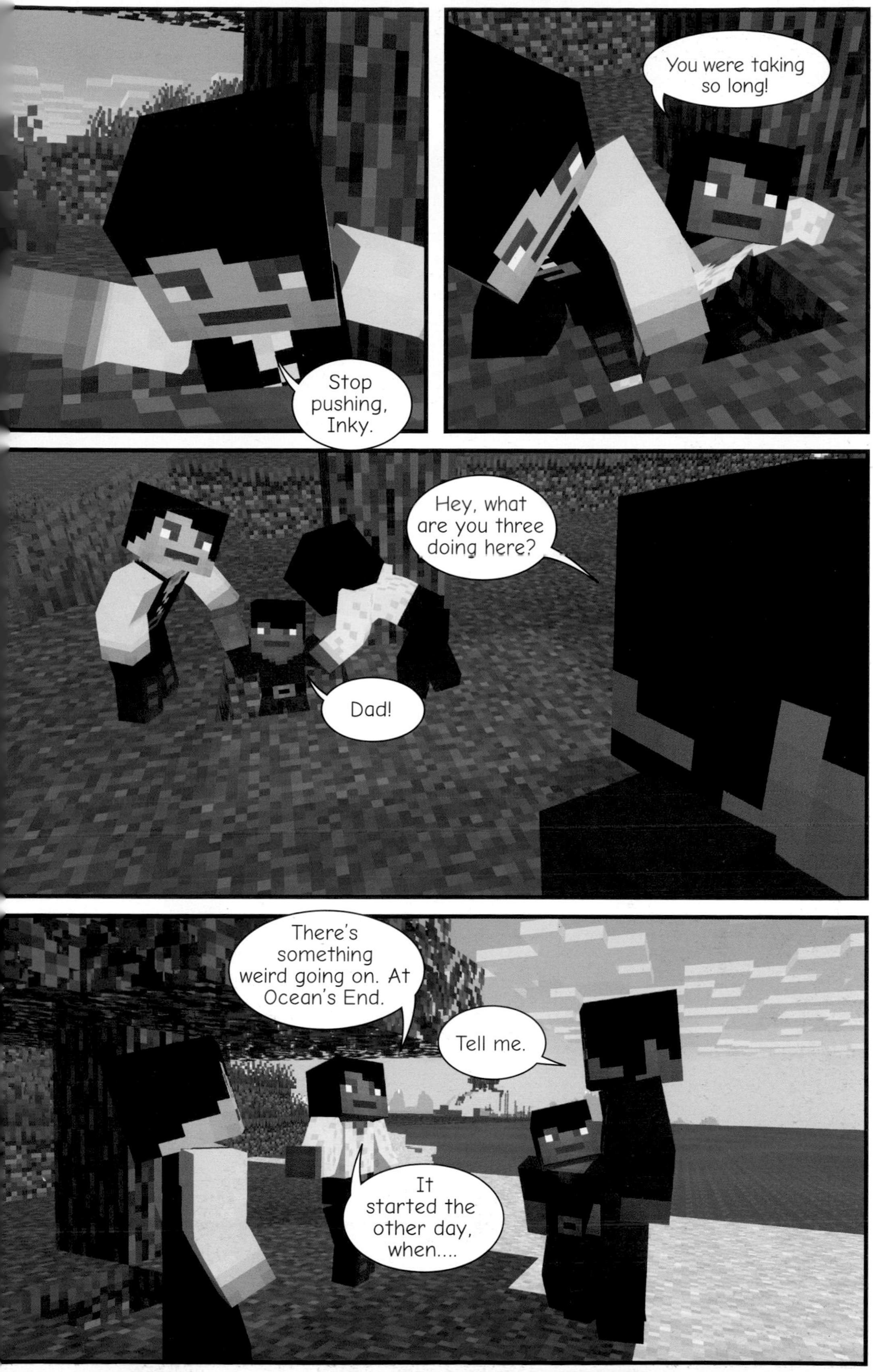
Stop pushing, Inky.
You were taking so long!
Hey, what are you three doing here?
Dad!
There's something weird going on. At Ocean's End.
Tell me.
It started the other day, when....

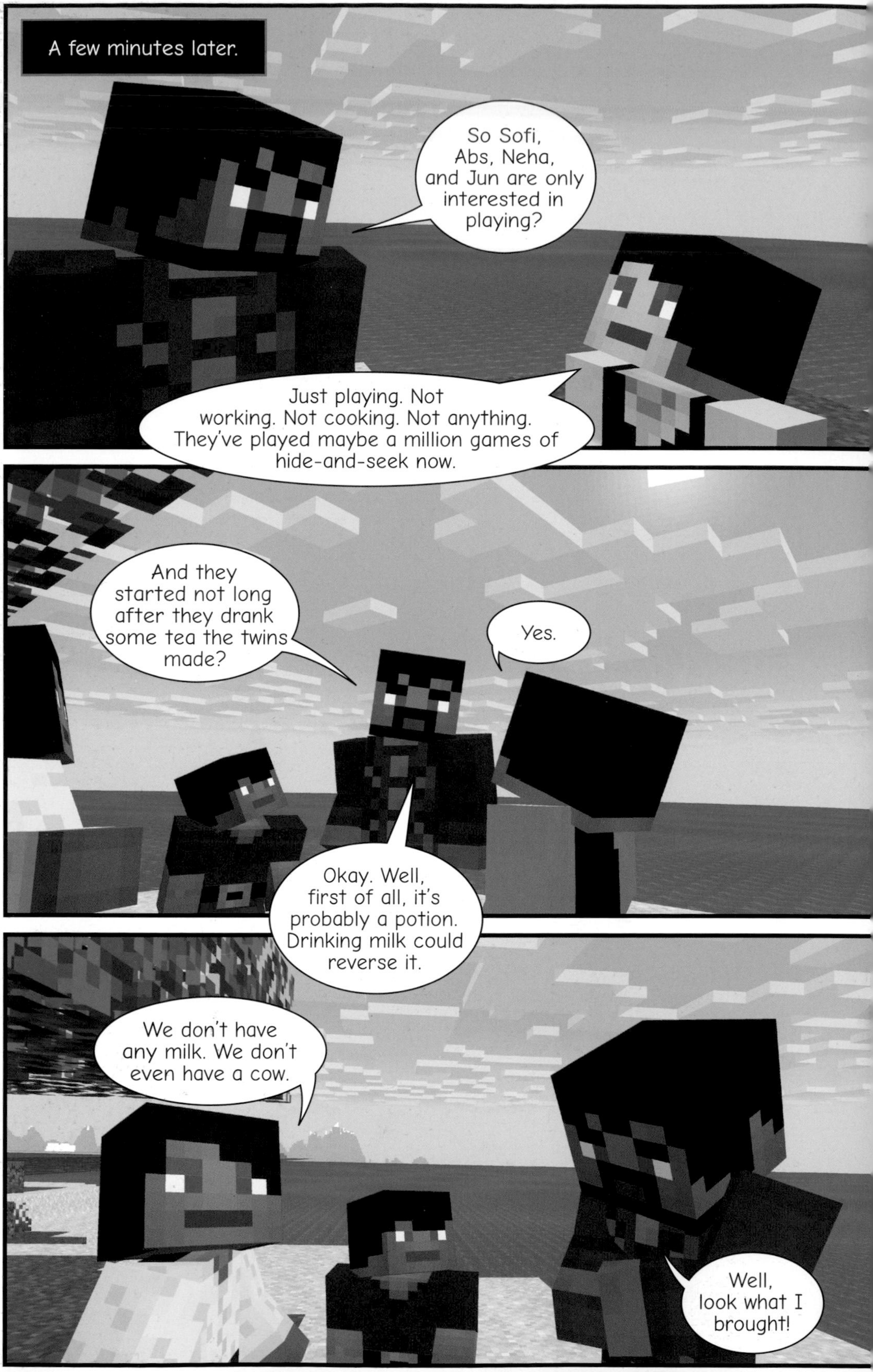
A few minutes later.
So Sofi, Abs, Neha, and Jun are only interested in playing?
Just playing. Not working. Not cooking. Not anything. They've played maybe a million games of hide-and-seek now.
And they started not long after they drank some tea the twins made?
Yes.
Okay. Well, first of all, it's probably a potion. Drinking milk could reverse it.
We don't have any milk. We don't even have a cow.
Well, look what I brought!

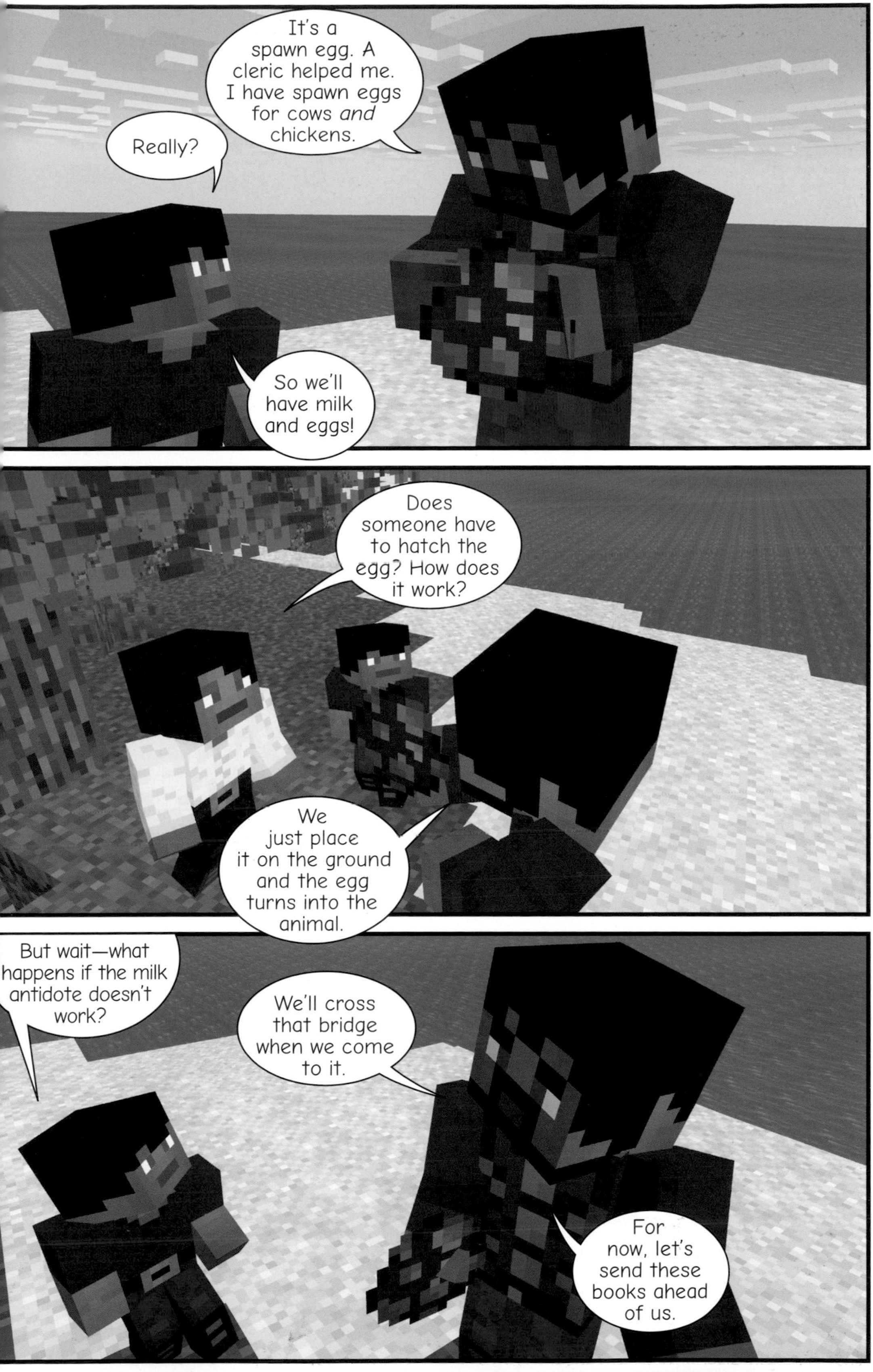

Really?
It's a spawn egg. A cleric helped me. I have spawn eggs for cows *and* chickens.
So we'll have milk and eggs!
Does someone have to hatch the egg? How does it work?
We just place it on the ground and the egg turns into the animal.
But wait—what happens if the milk antidote doesn't work?
We'll cross that bridge when we come to it.
For now, let's send these books ahead of us.

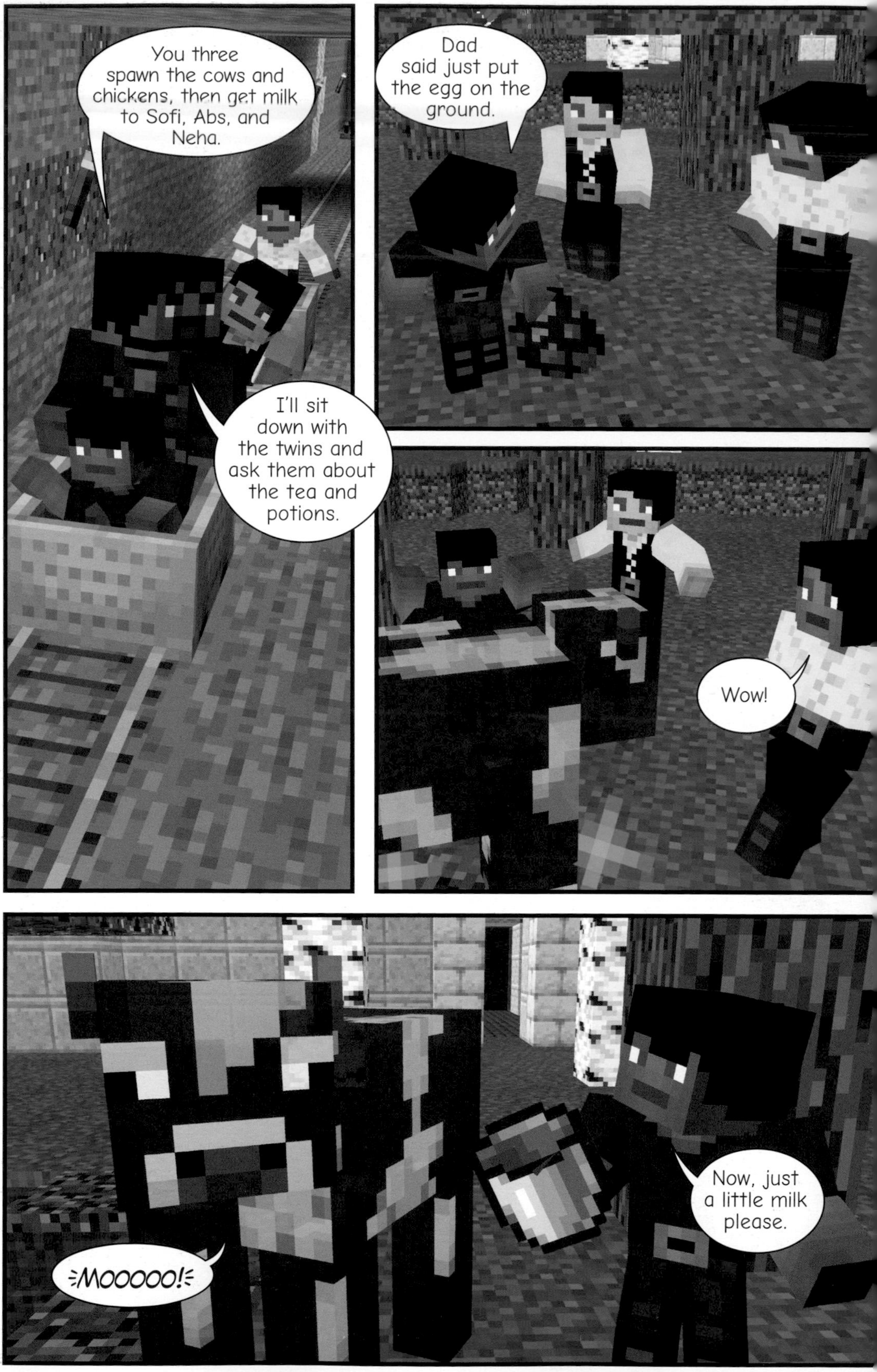
You three spawn the cows and chickens, then get milk to Sofi, Abs, and Neha.
I'll sit down with the twins and ask them about the tea and potions.
Dad said just put the egg on the ground.
Wow!
MOOOOO!
Now, just a little milk please.

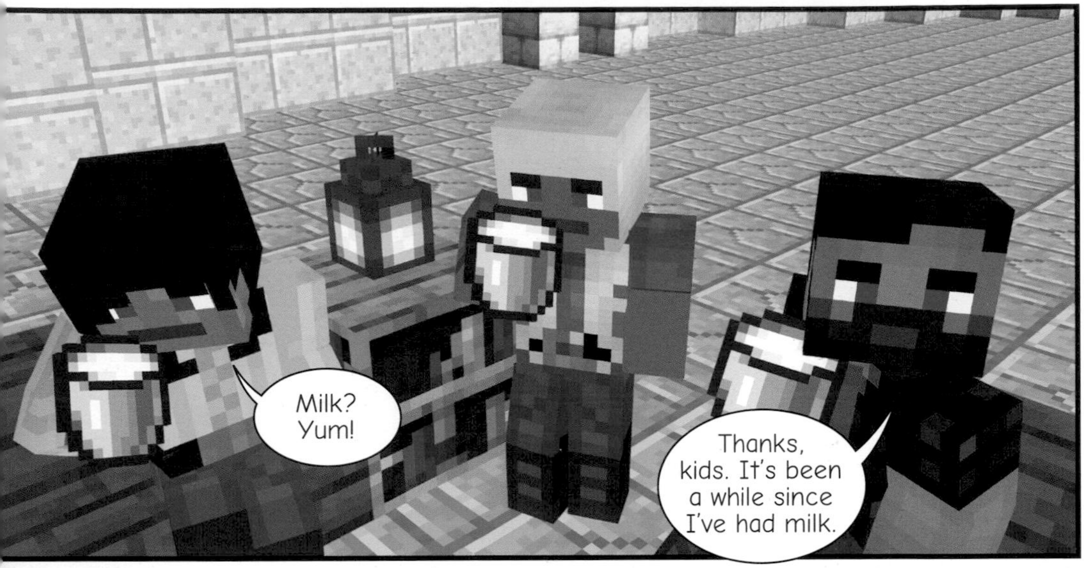
Milk?
Yum!
Thanks, kids. It's been a while since I've had milk.
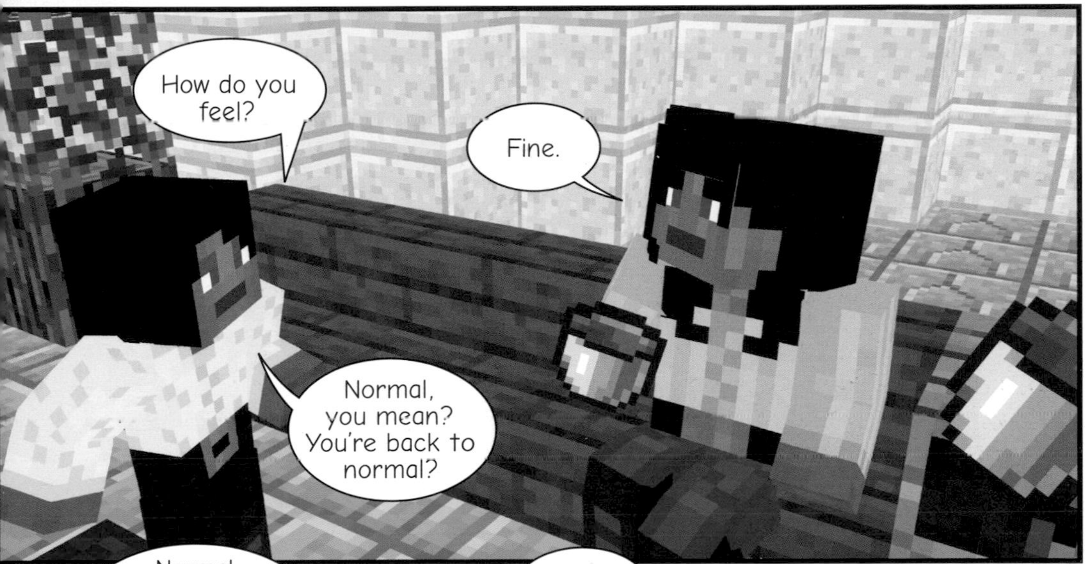
How do you feel?
Fine.
Normal, you mean? You're back to normal?
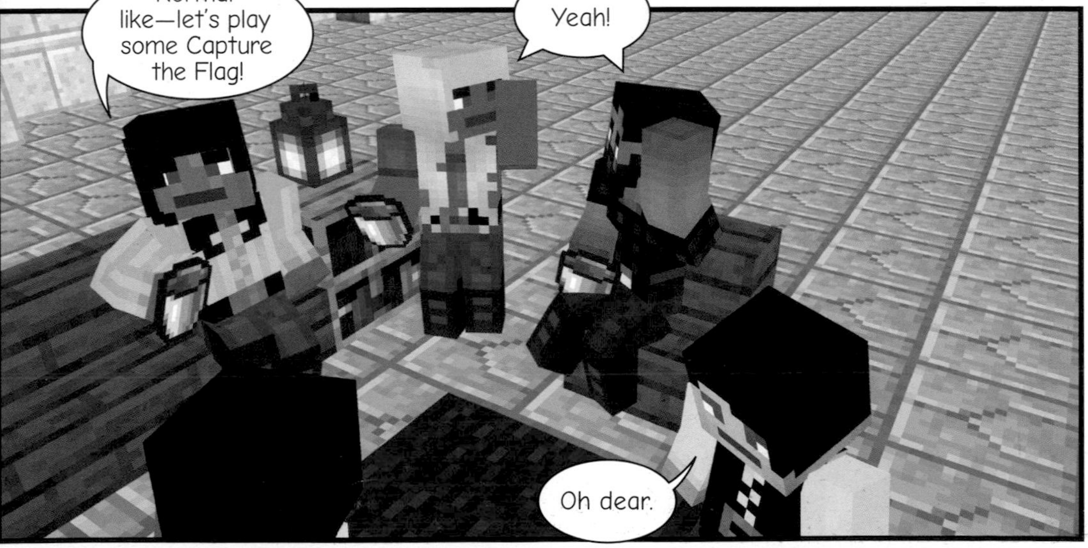
Normal like—let's play some Capture the Flag!
Yeah!
Oh dear.

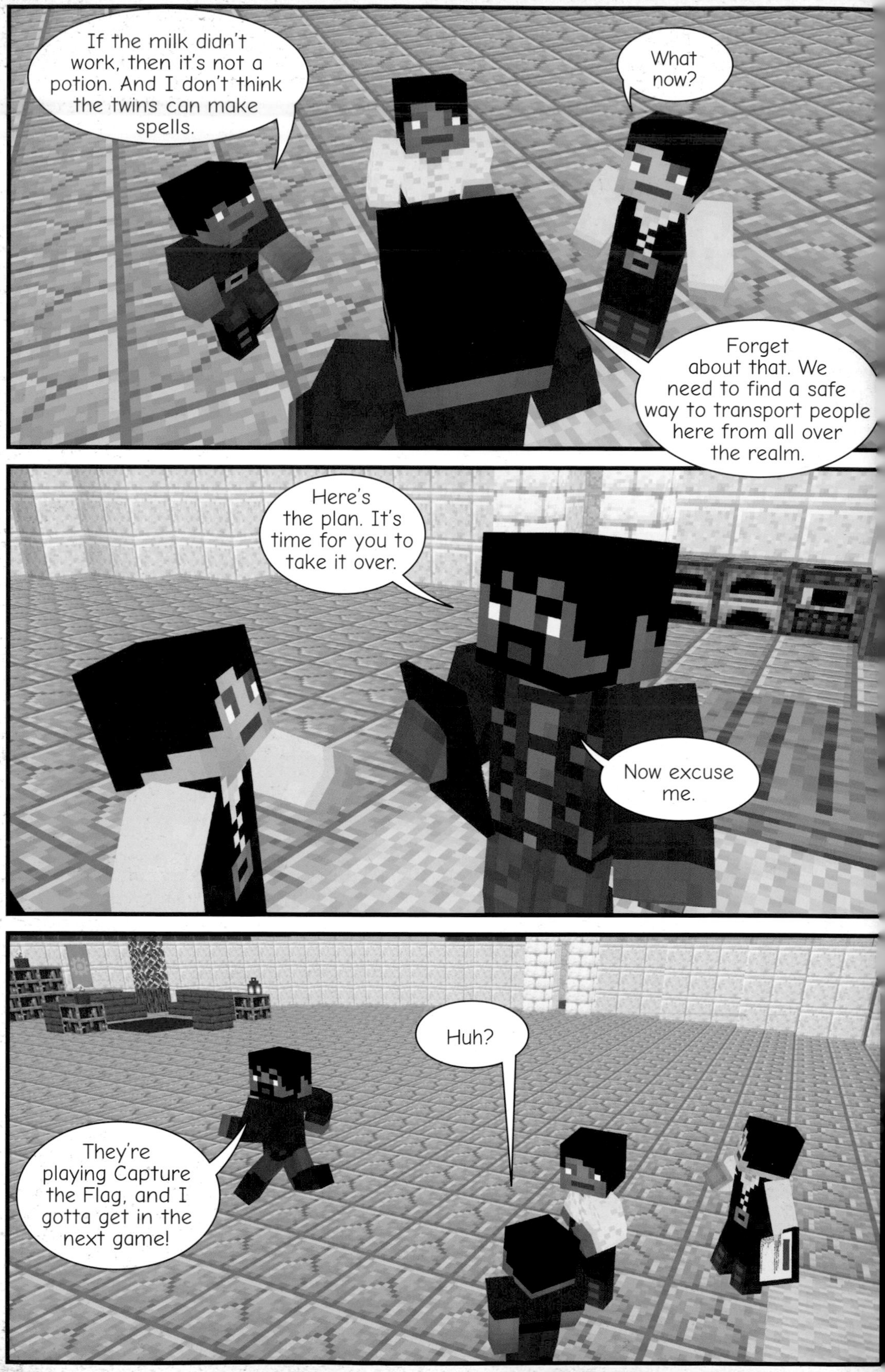
If the milk didn't work, then it's not a potion. And I don't think the twins can make spells.
What now?
Forget about that. We need to find a safe way to transport people here from all over the realm.
Here's the plan. It's time for you to take it over.
Now excuse me.
Huh?
They're playing Capture the Flag, and I gotta get in the next game!

Chapter 7
Nether
Say Nether

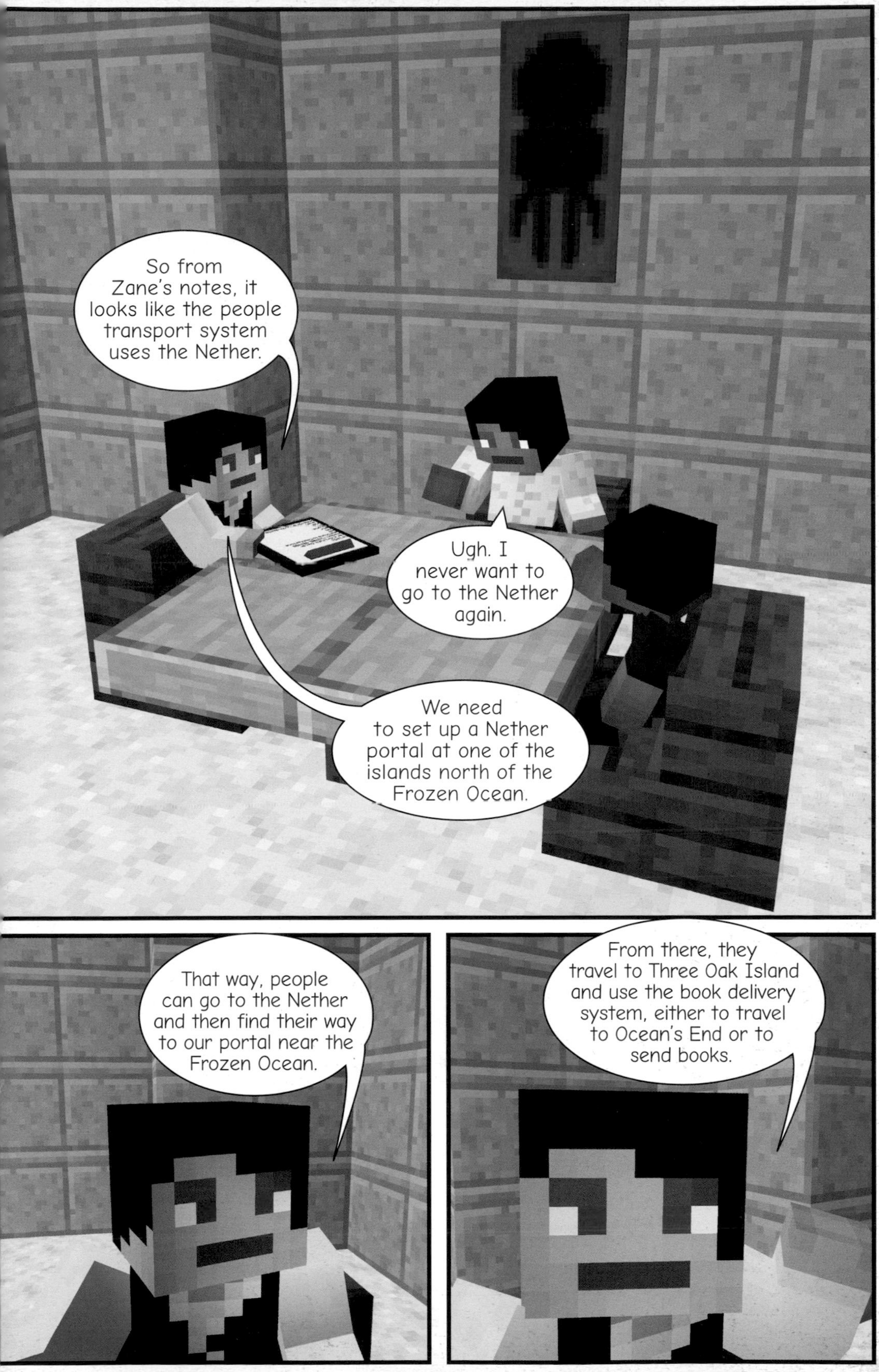
So from Zane's notes, it looks like the people transport system uses the Nether.
Ugh. I never want to go to the Nether again.
We need to set up a Nether portal at one of the islands north of the Frozen Ocean.
That way, people can go to the Nether and then find their way to our portal near the Frozen Ocean.
From there, they travel to Three Oak Island and use the book delivery system, either to travel to Ocean's End or to send books.

But how do they find our portal in the Nether?

And how do they get from the first island to Three Oak Island?

With lodestone compasses and lodestones.

Compasses don't work in the Nether.

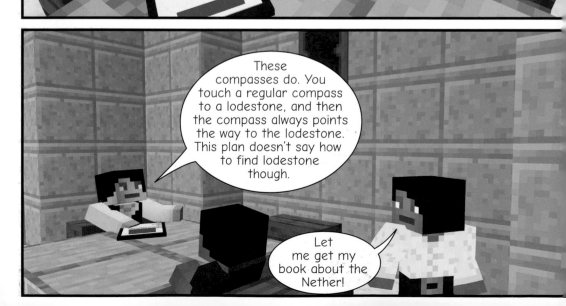

These compasses do. You touch a regular compass to a lodestone, and then the compass always points the way to the lodestone. This plan doesn't say how to find lodestone though.

Let me get my book about the Nether!

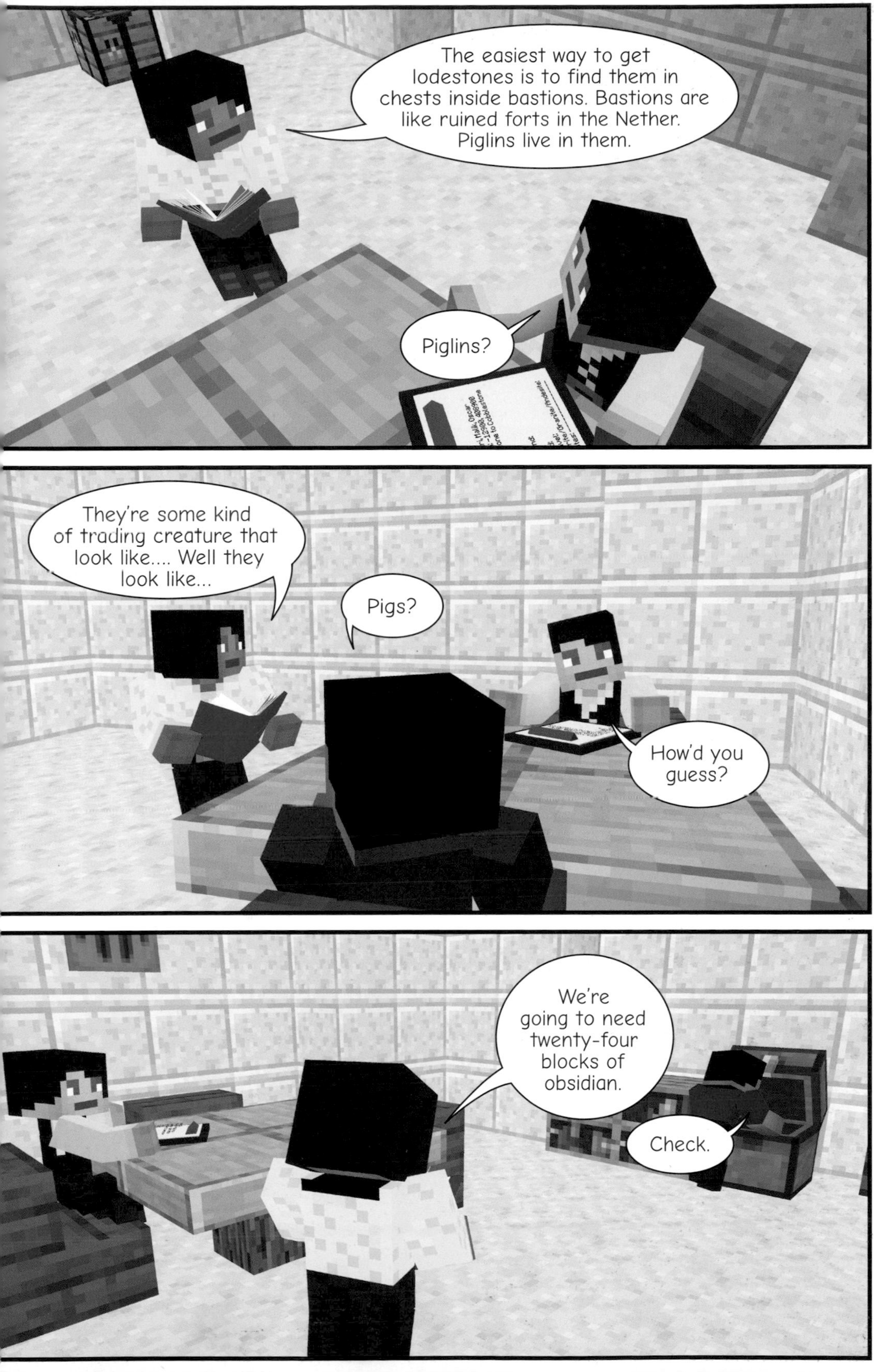
The easiest way to get lodestones is to find them in chests inside bastions. Bastions are like ruined forts in the Nether. Piglins live in them.
Piglins?
They're some kind of trading creature that look like.... Well they look like...
Pigs?
How'd you guess?
We're going to need twenty-four blocks of obsidian.
Check.

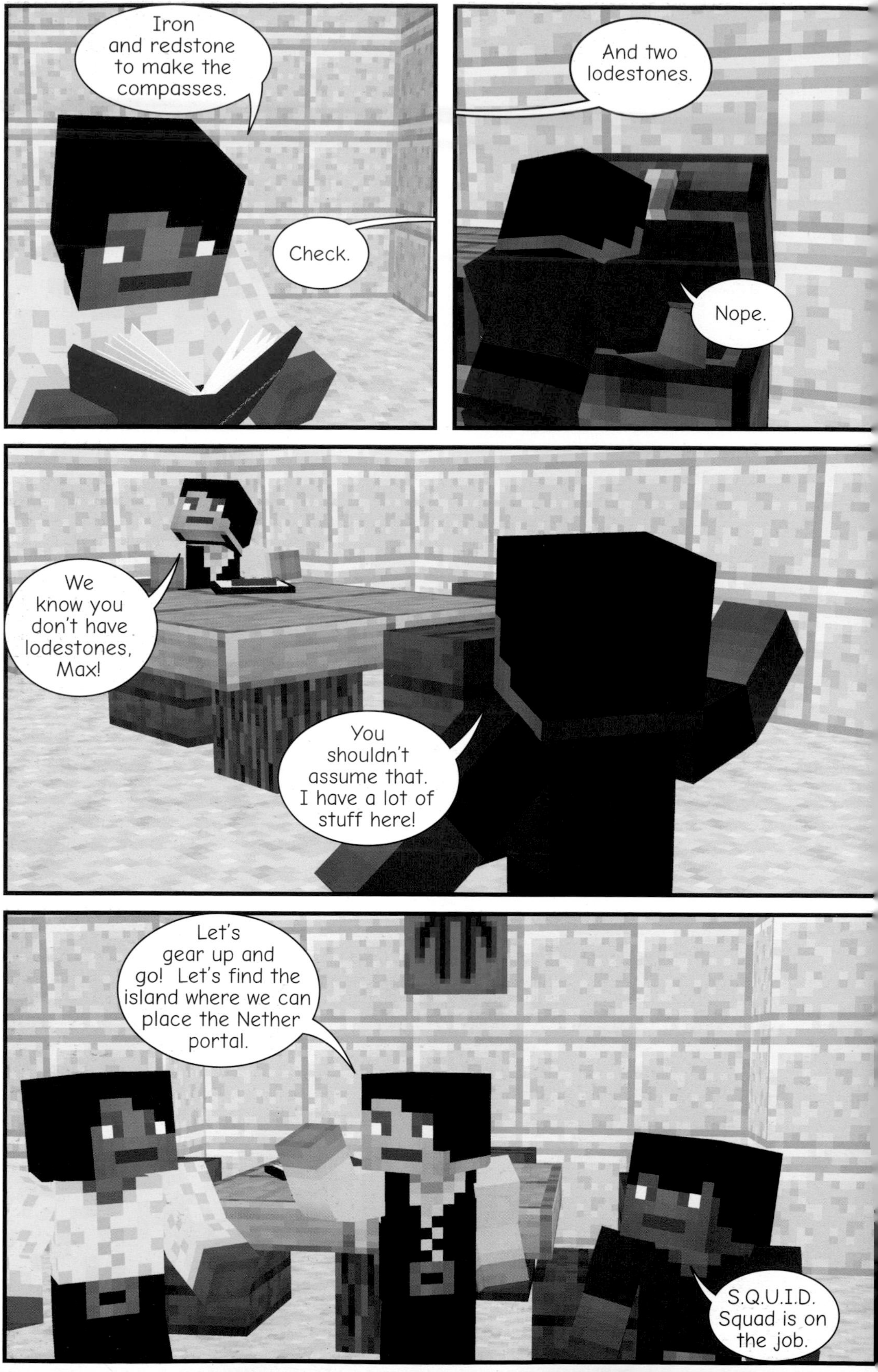
Iron and redstone to make the compasses.
Check.
And two lodestones.
Nope.
We know you don't have lodestones, Max!
You shouldn't assume that. I have a lot of stuff here!
Let's gear up and go! Let's find the island where we can place the Nether portal.
S.Q.U.I.D. Squad is on the job.

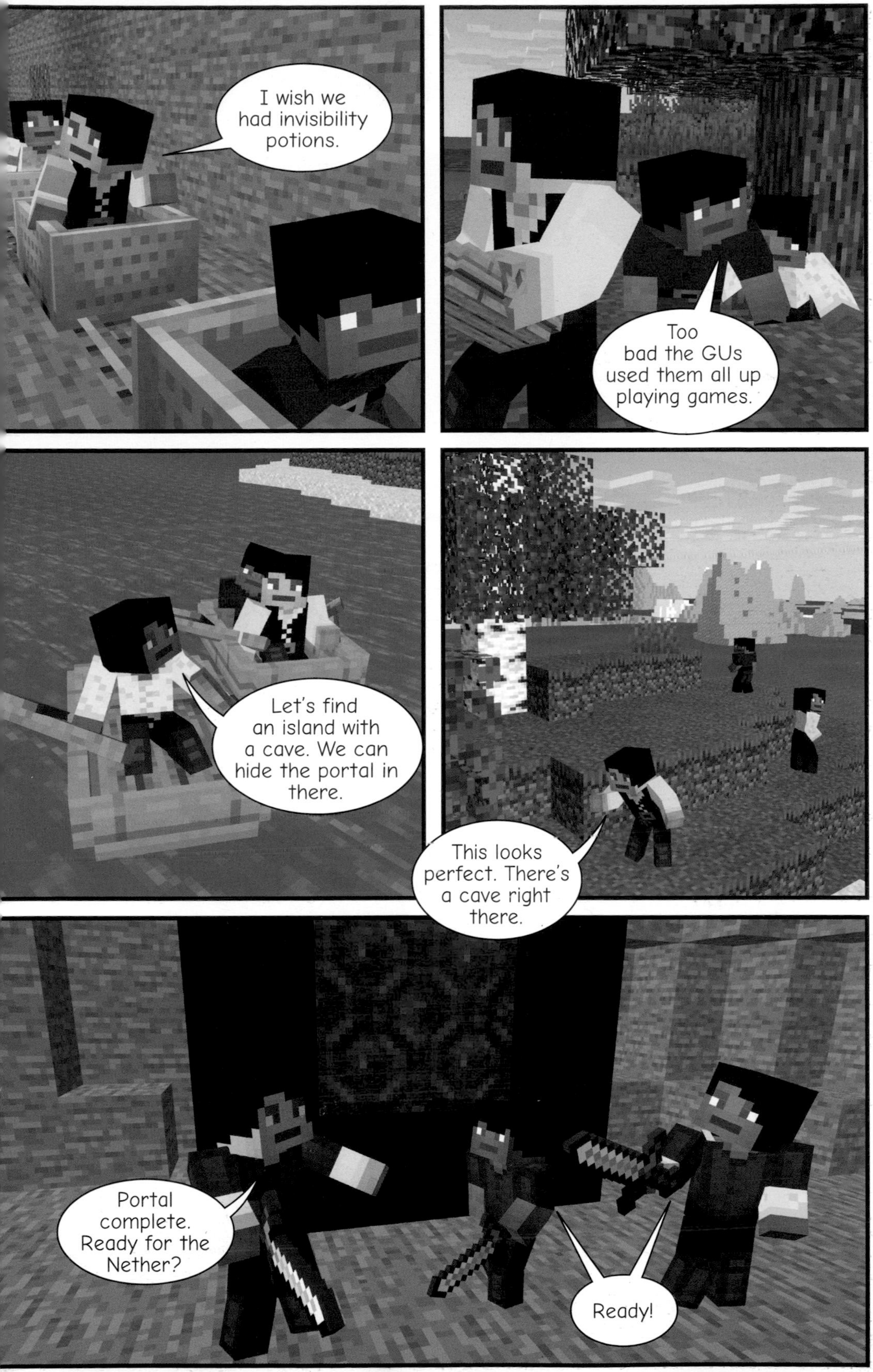
I wish we had invisibility potions.
Too bad the GUs used them all up playing games.
Let's find an island with a cave. We can hide the portal in there.
This looks perfect. There's a cave right there.
Portal complete. Ready for the Nether?
Ready!

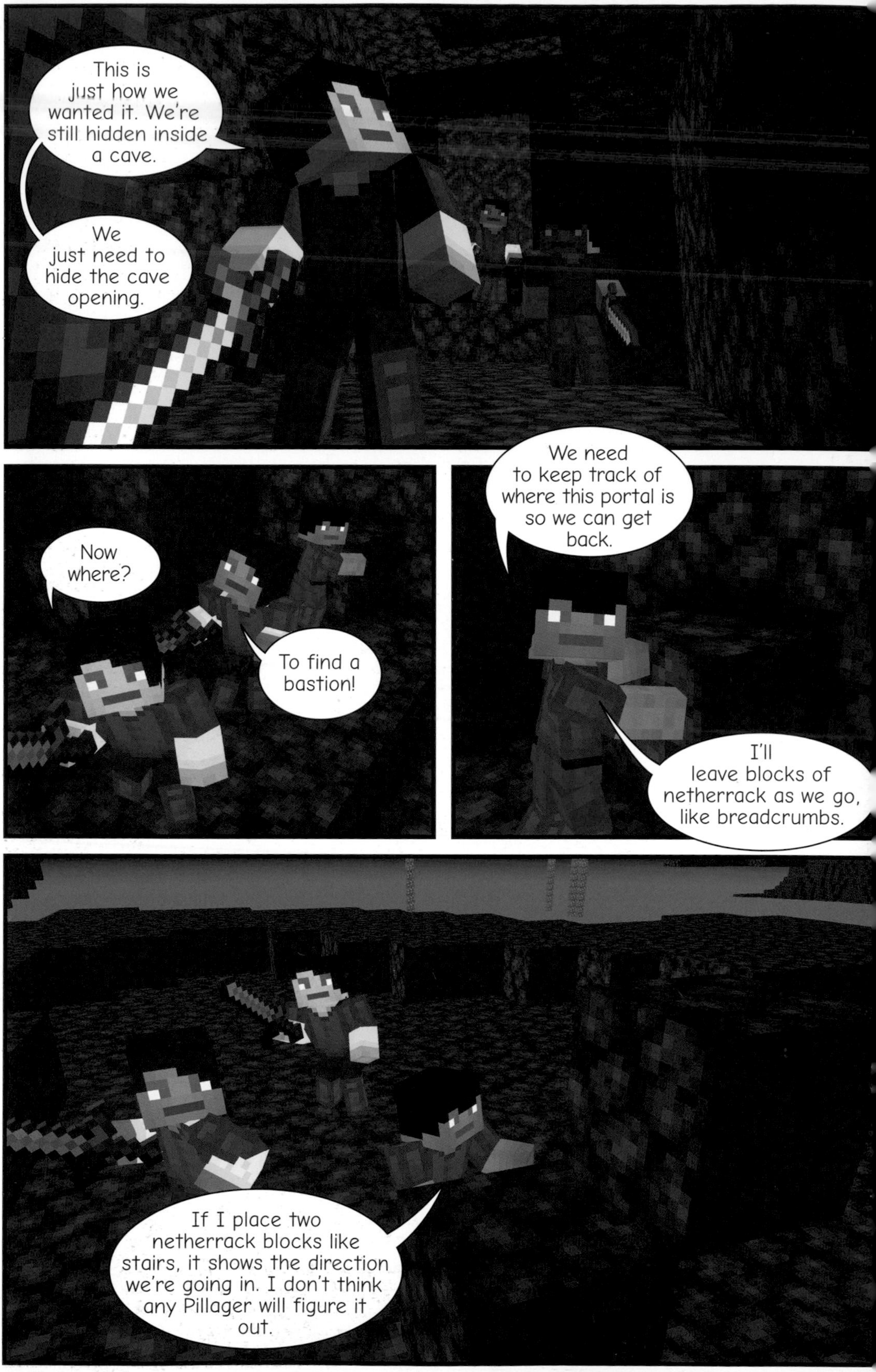
This is just how we wanted it. We're still hidden inside a cave.
We just need to hide the cave opening.
Now where?
To find a bastion!
We need to keep track of where this portal is so we can get back.
I'll leave blocks of netherrack as we go, like breadcrumbs.
If I place two netherrack blocks like stairs, it shows the direction we're going in. I don't think any Pillager will figure it out.

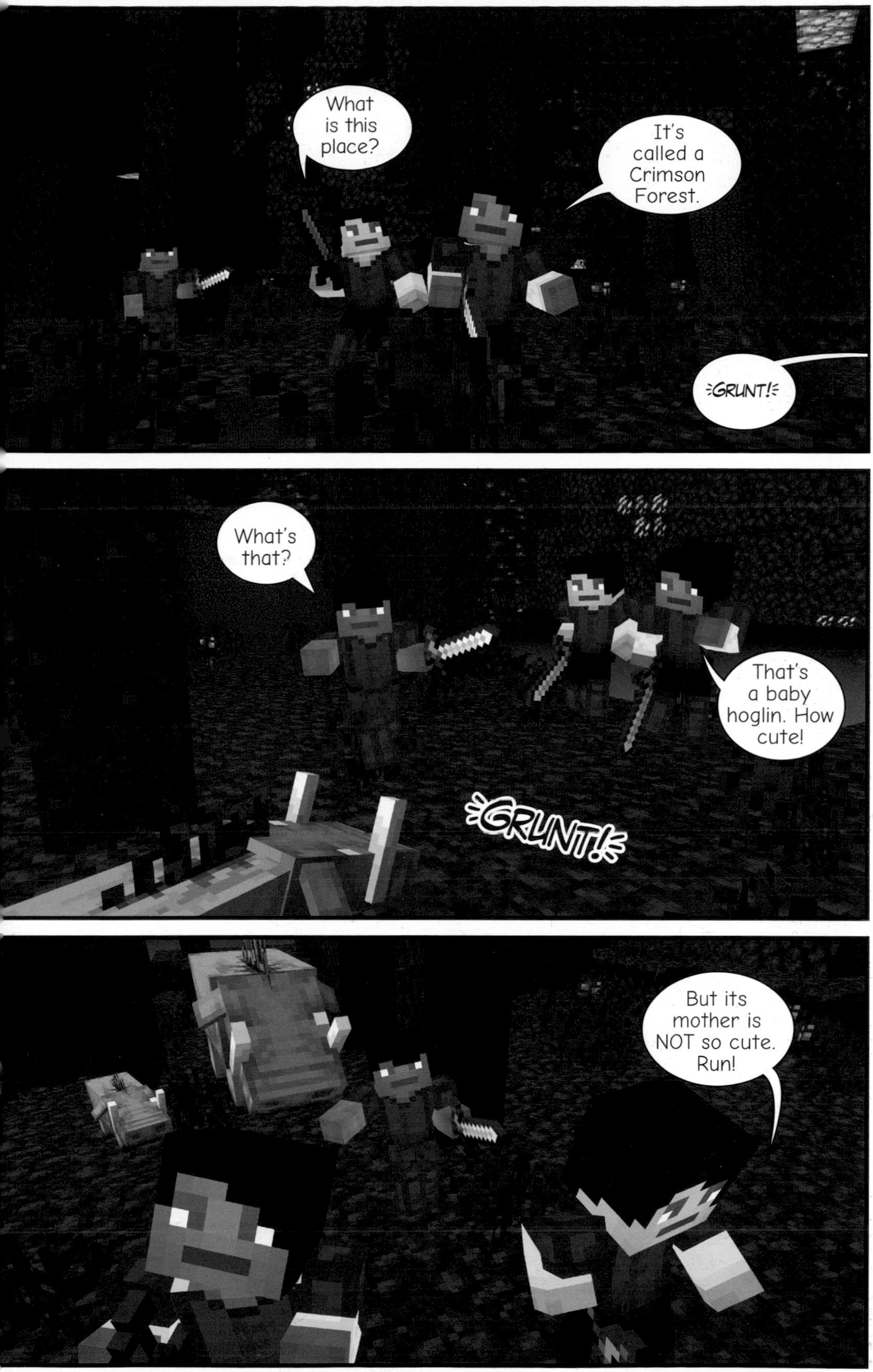
What is this place?
It's called a Crimson Forest.
GRUNT!
What's that?
That's a baby hoglin. How cute!
GRUNT!
But its mother is NOT so cute. Run!

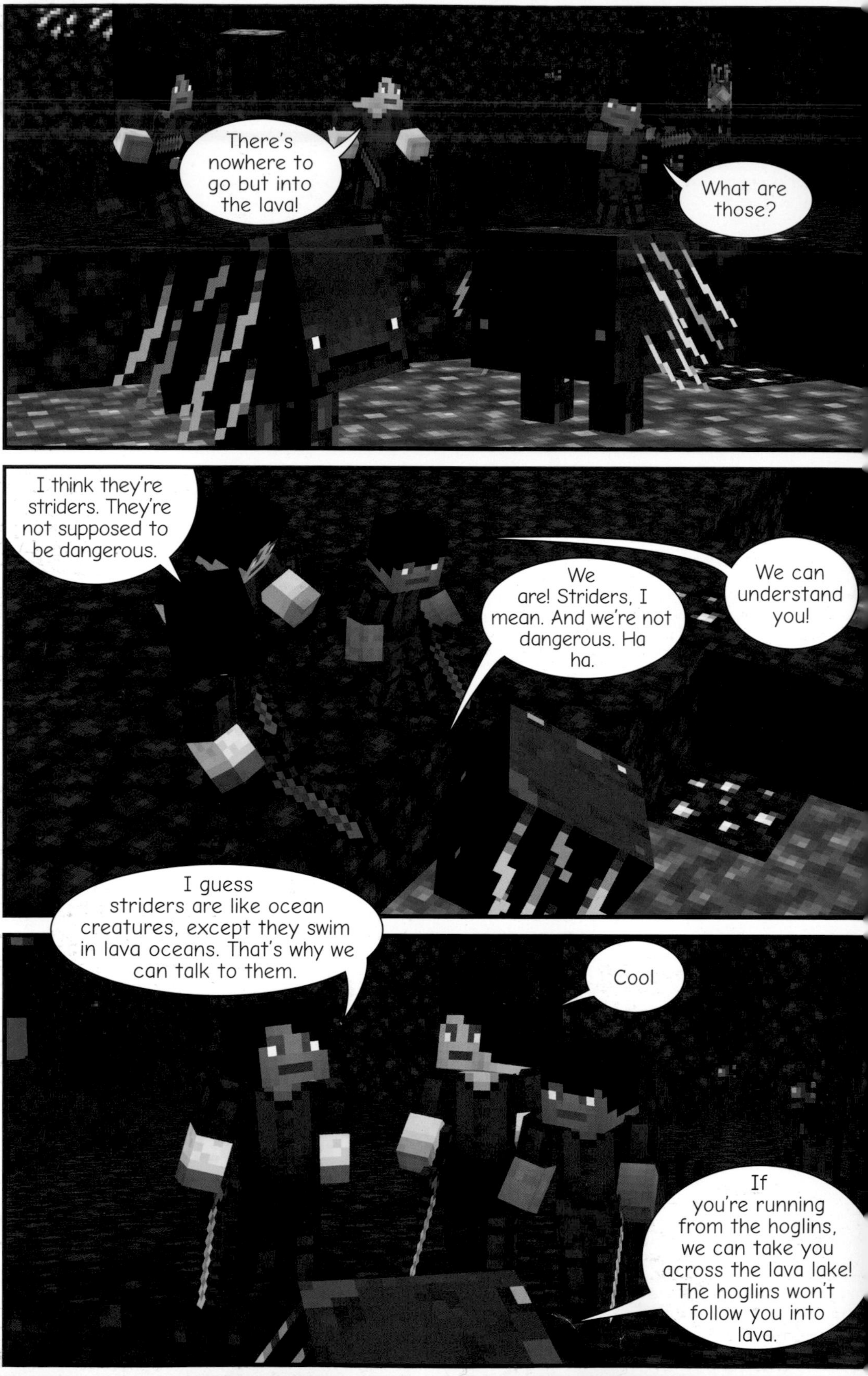
There's nowhere to go but into the lava!
What are those?
I think they're striders. They're not supposed to be dangerous.
We can understand you!
We are! Striders, I mean. And we're not dangerous. Ha ha.
I guess striders are like ocean creatures, except they swim in lava oceans. That's why we can talk to them.
Cool
If you're running from the hoglins, we can take you across the lava lake! The hoglins won't follow you into lava.

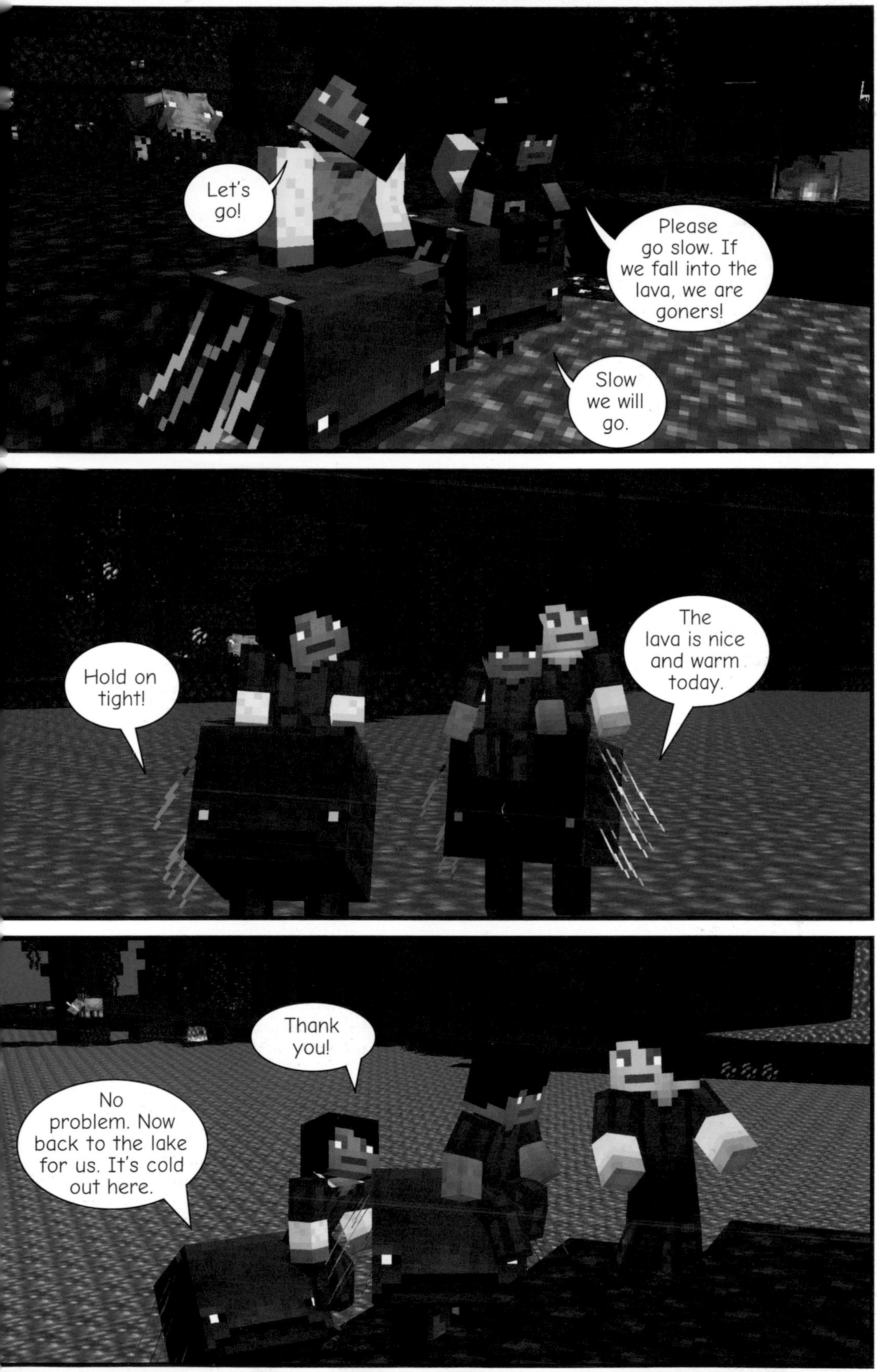
Let's go!
Please go slow. If we fall into the lava, we are goners!
Slow we will go.
Hold on tight!
The lava is nice and warm today.
Thank you!
No problem. Now back to the lake for us. It's cold out here.

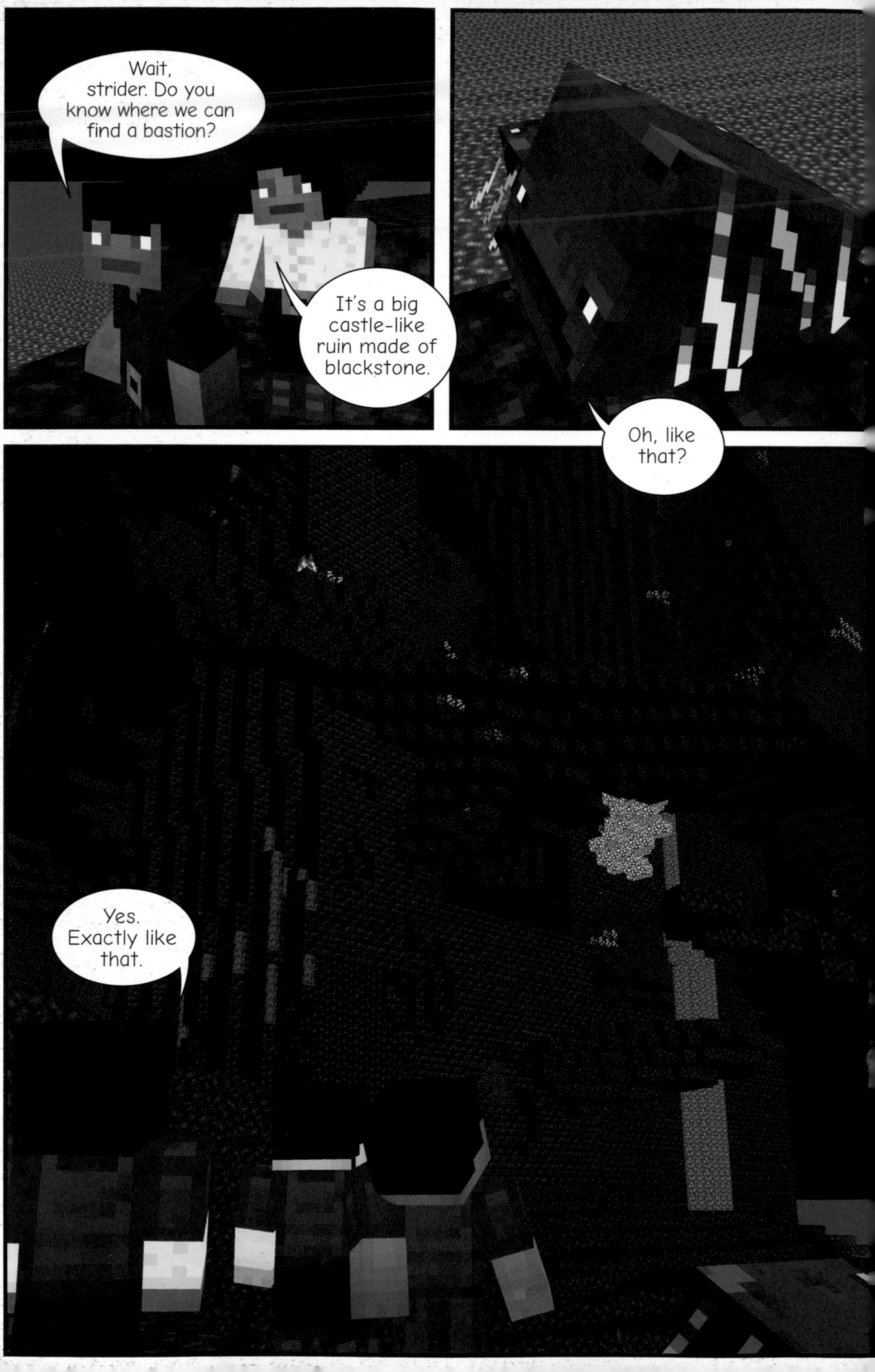
Wait, strider. Do you know where we can find a bastion?
It's a big castle-like ruin made of blackstone.
Oh, like that?
Yes. Exactly like that.

Chapter 8
The Bastion

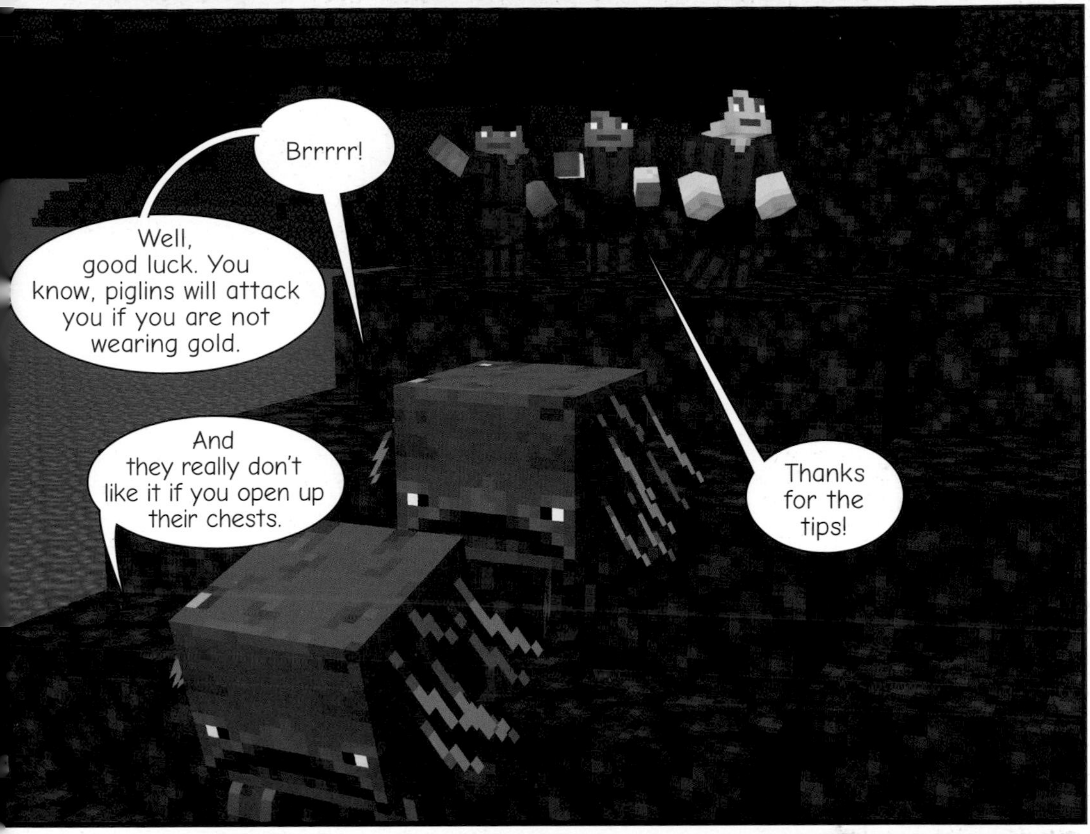
Brrrrr!
Well, good luck. You know, piglins will attack you if you are not wearing gold.
And they really don't like it if you open up their chests.
Thanks for the tips!

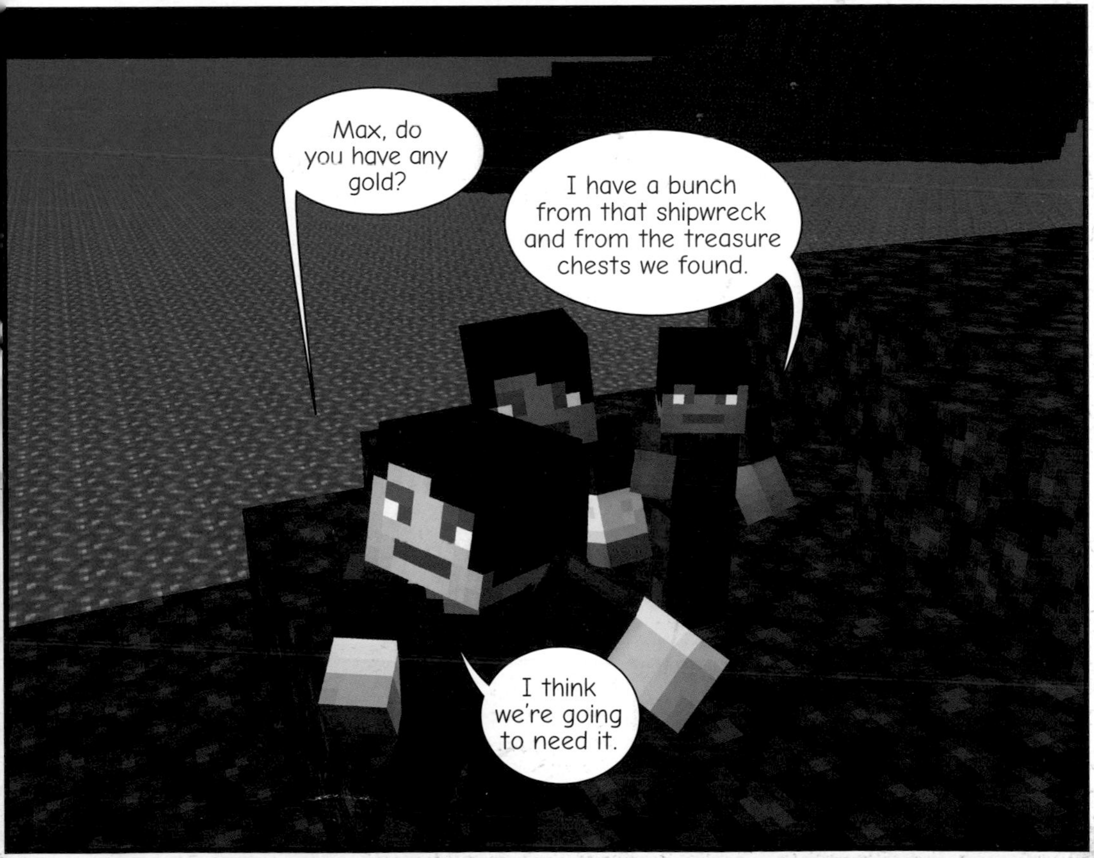
Max, do you have any gold?
I have a bunch from that shipwreck and from the treasure chests we found.
I think we're going to need it.

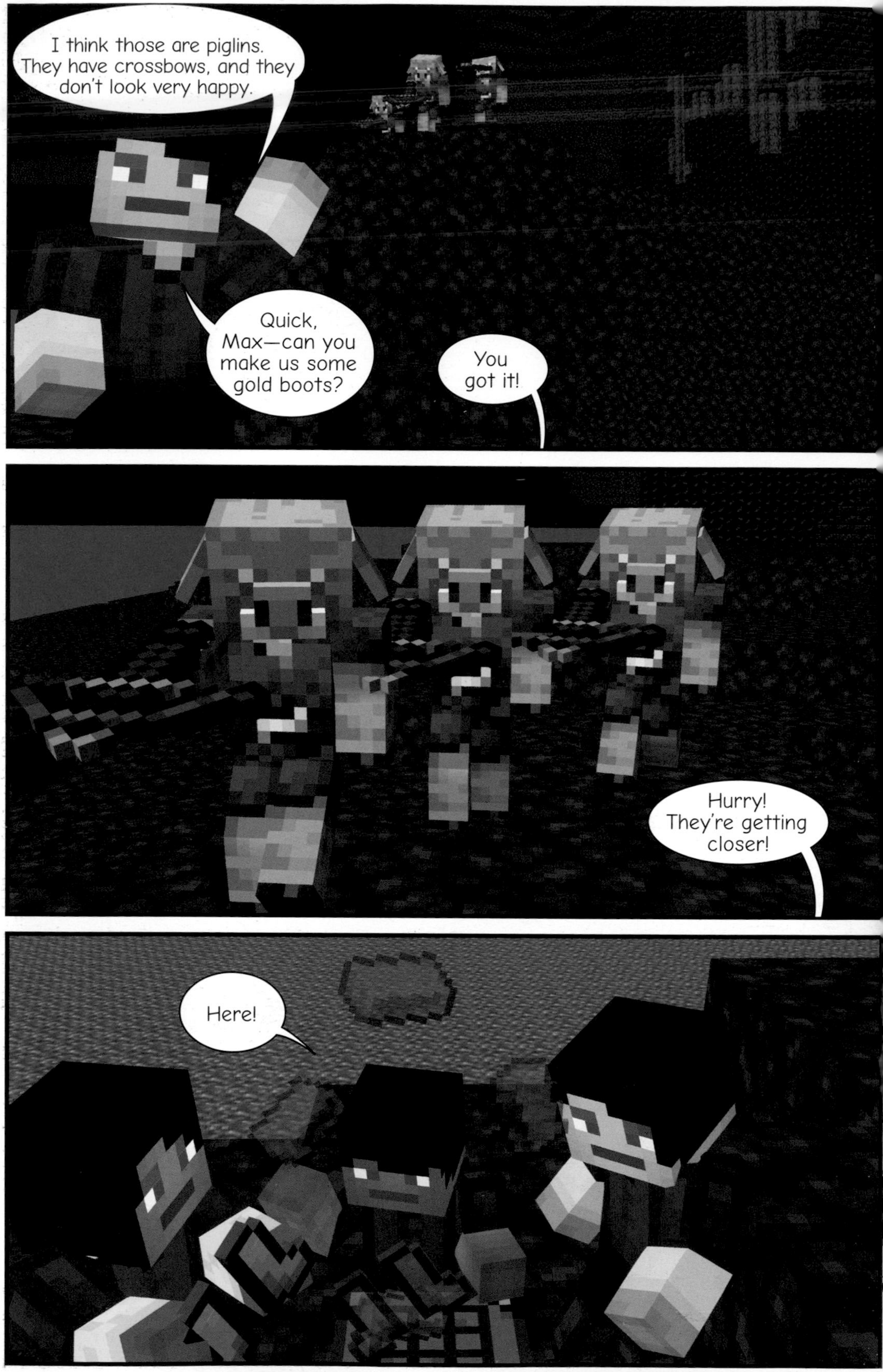
I think those are piglins. They have crossbows, and they don't look very happy.
Quick, Max—can you make us some gold boots?
You got it!
Hurry! They're getting closer!
Here!

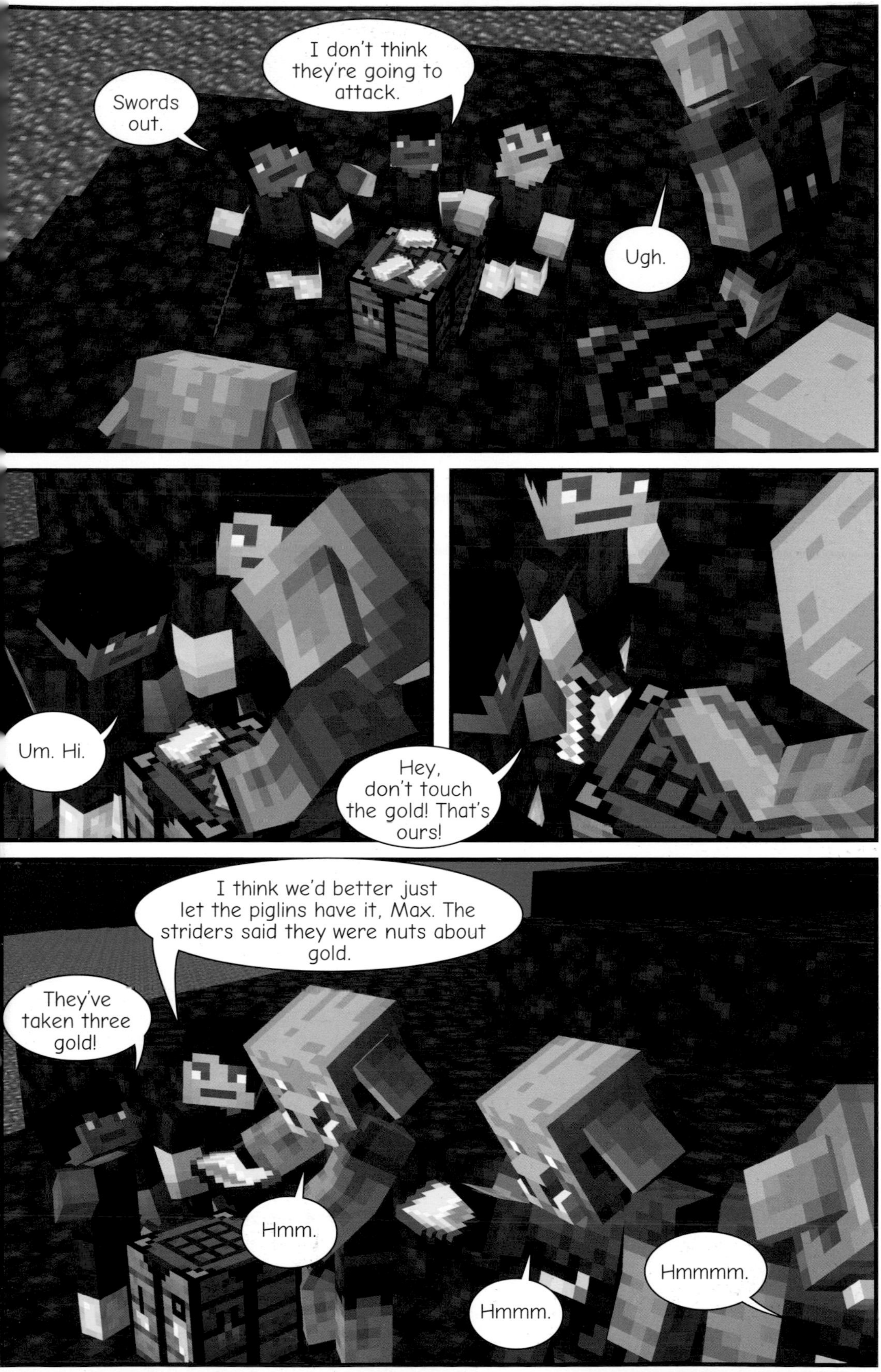
Swords out.
I don't think they're going to attack.
Ugh.
Um. Hi.
Hey, don't touch the gold! That's ours!
They've taken three gold!
I think we'd better just let the piglins have it, Max. The striders said they were nuts about gold.
Hmm.
Hmmm.
Hmmmm.

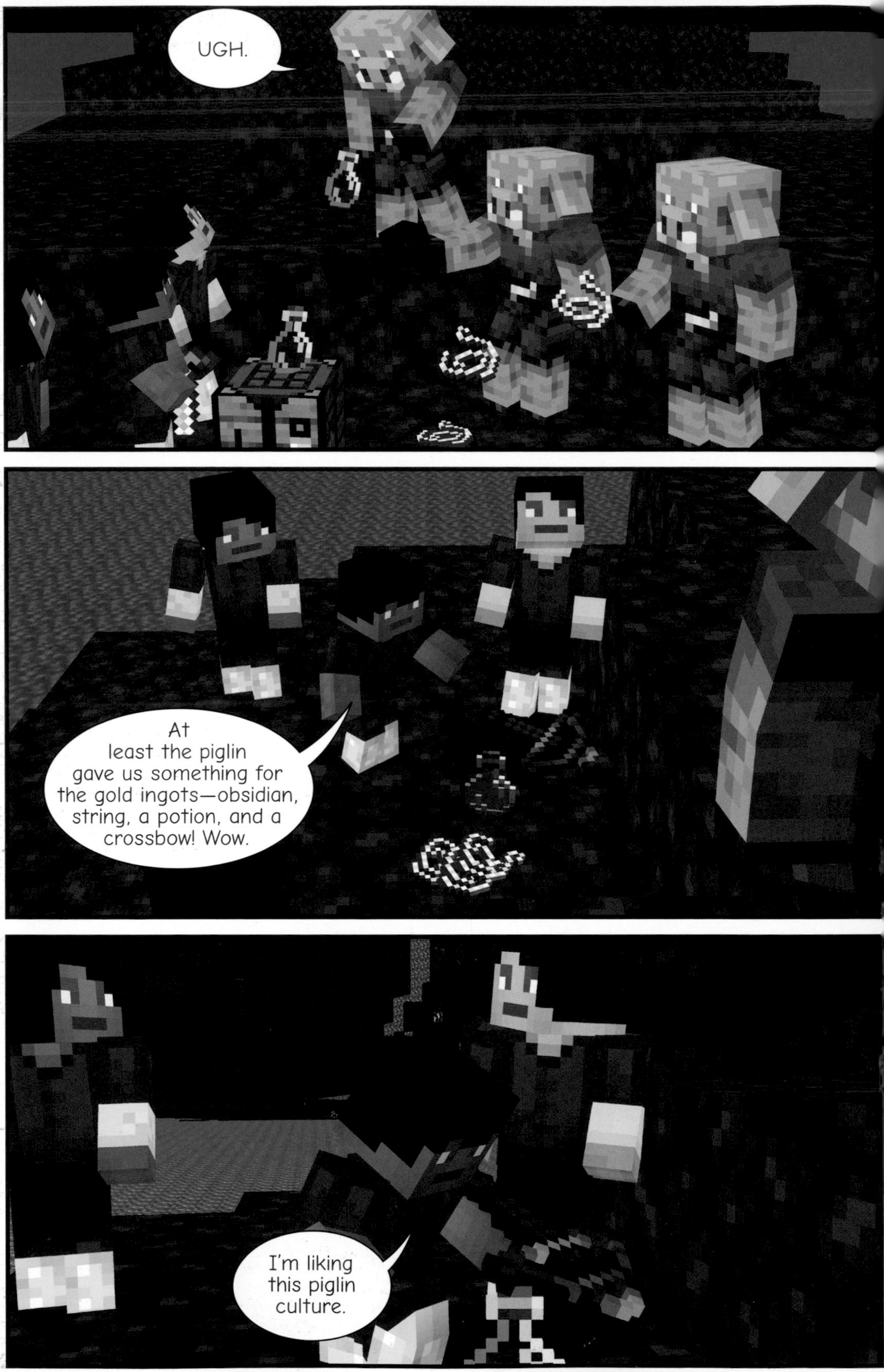
UGH.
At least the piglin gave us something for the gold ingots—obsidian, string, a potion, and a crossbow! Wow.
I'm liking this piglin culture.

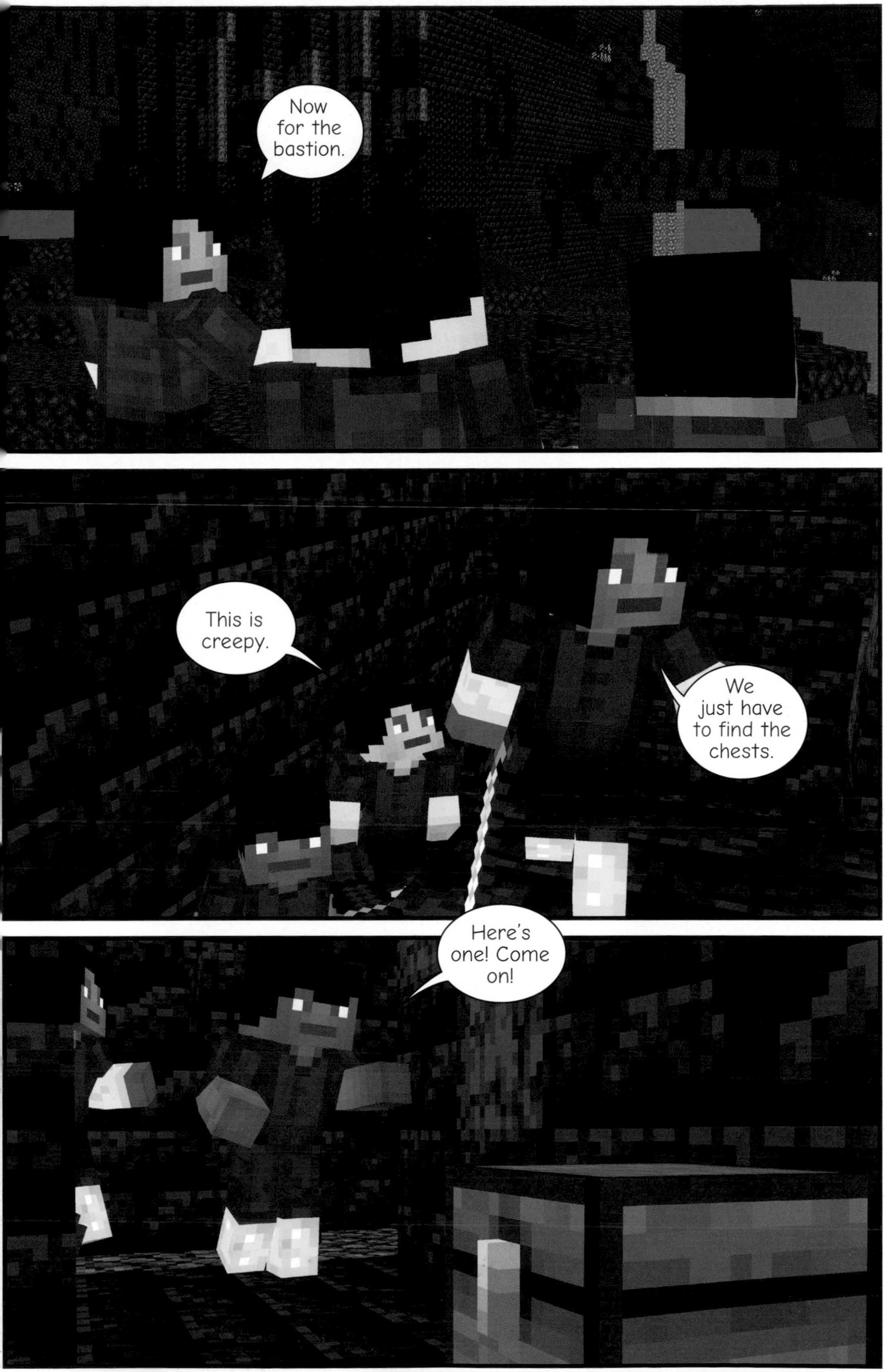
Now for the bastion.
This is creepy.
We just have to find the chests.
Here's one! Come on!

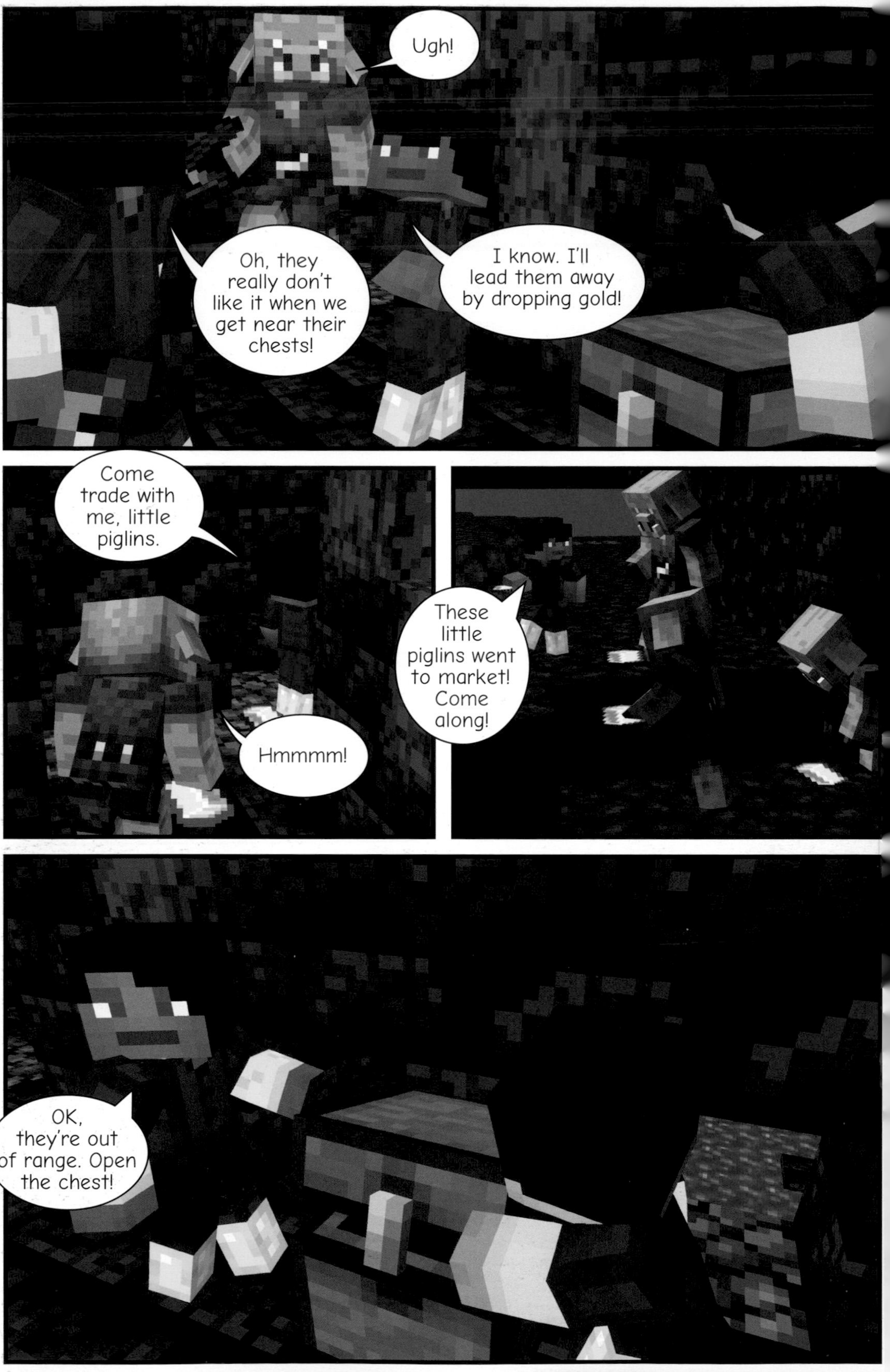
Ugh!
Oh, they really don't like it when we get near their chests!
I know. I'll lead them away by dropping gold!
Come trade with me, little piglins.
Hmmmm!
These little piglins went to market! Come along!
OK, they're out of range. Open the chest!

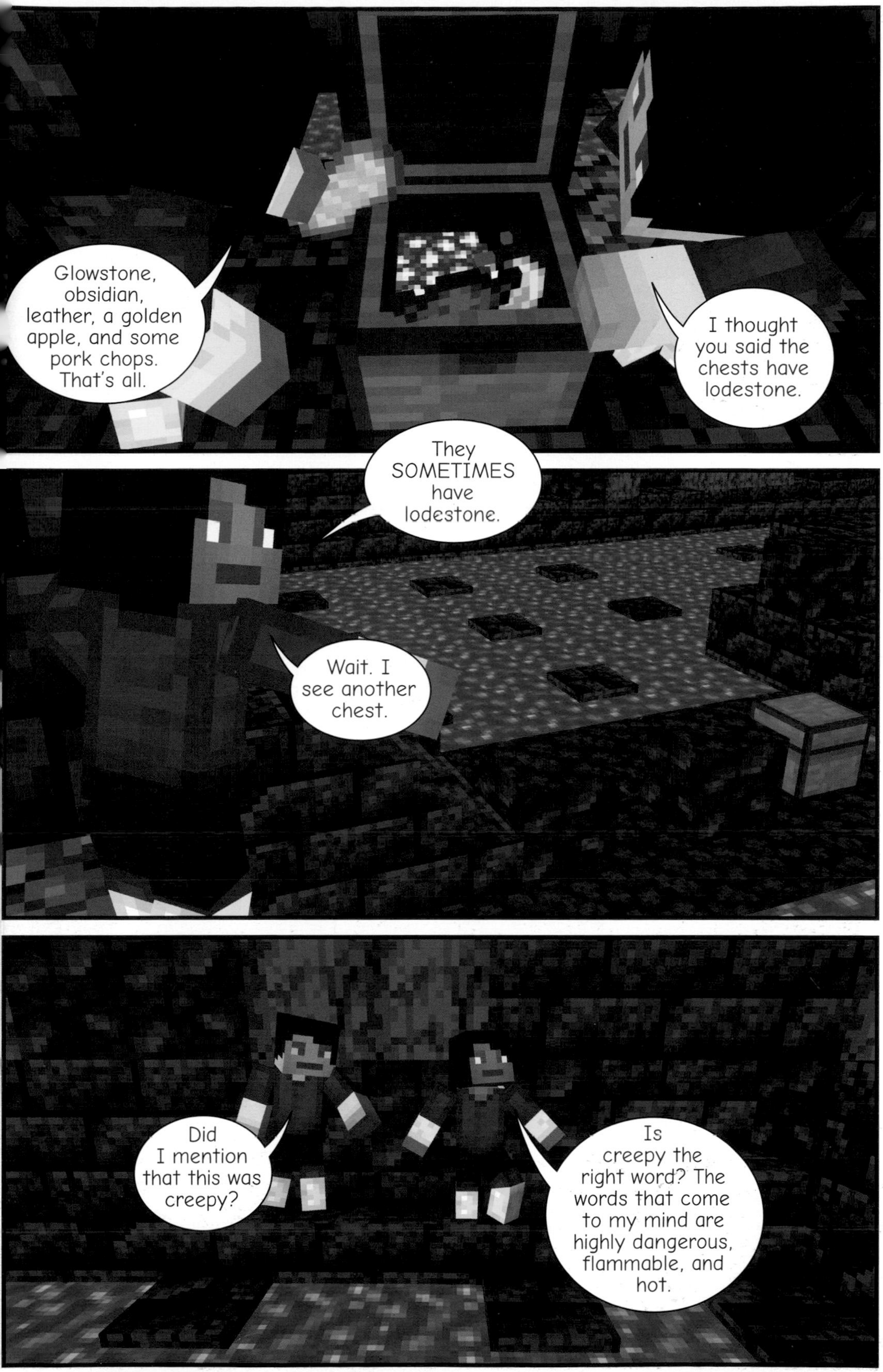
Glowstone, obsidian, leather, a golden apple, and some pork chops. That's all.
I thought you said the chests have lodestone.
They SOMETIMES have lodestone.
Wait. I see another chest.
Did I mention that this was creepy?
Is creepy the right word? The words that come to my mind are highly dangerous, flammable, and hot.

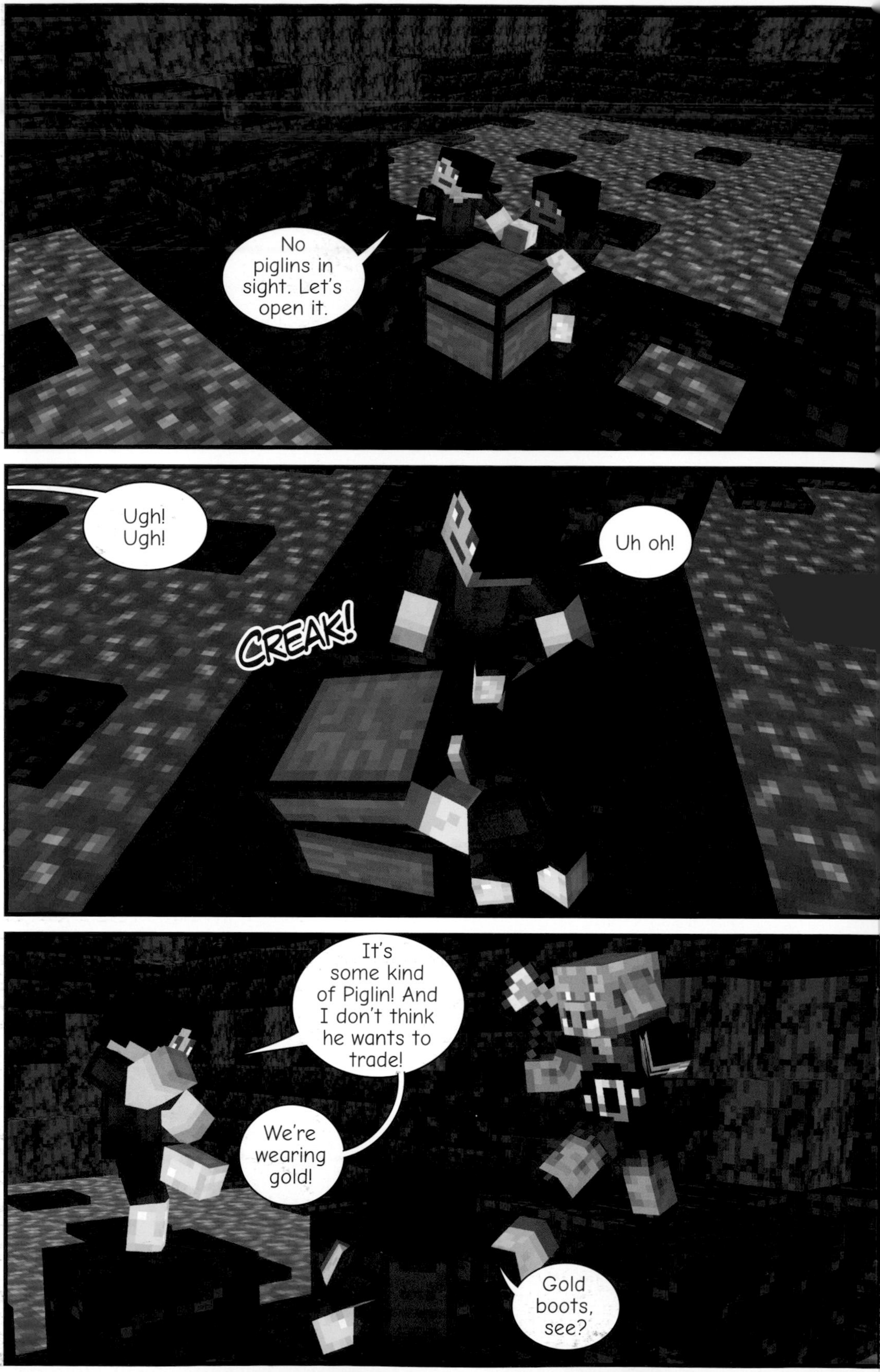
No piglins in sight. Let's open it.
Ugh! Ugh!
CREAK!
Uh oh!
It's some kind of Piglin! And I don't think he wants to trade!
We're wearing gold!
Gold boots, see?

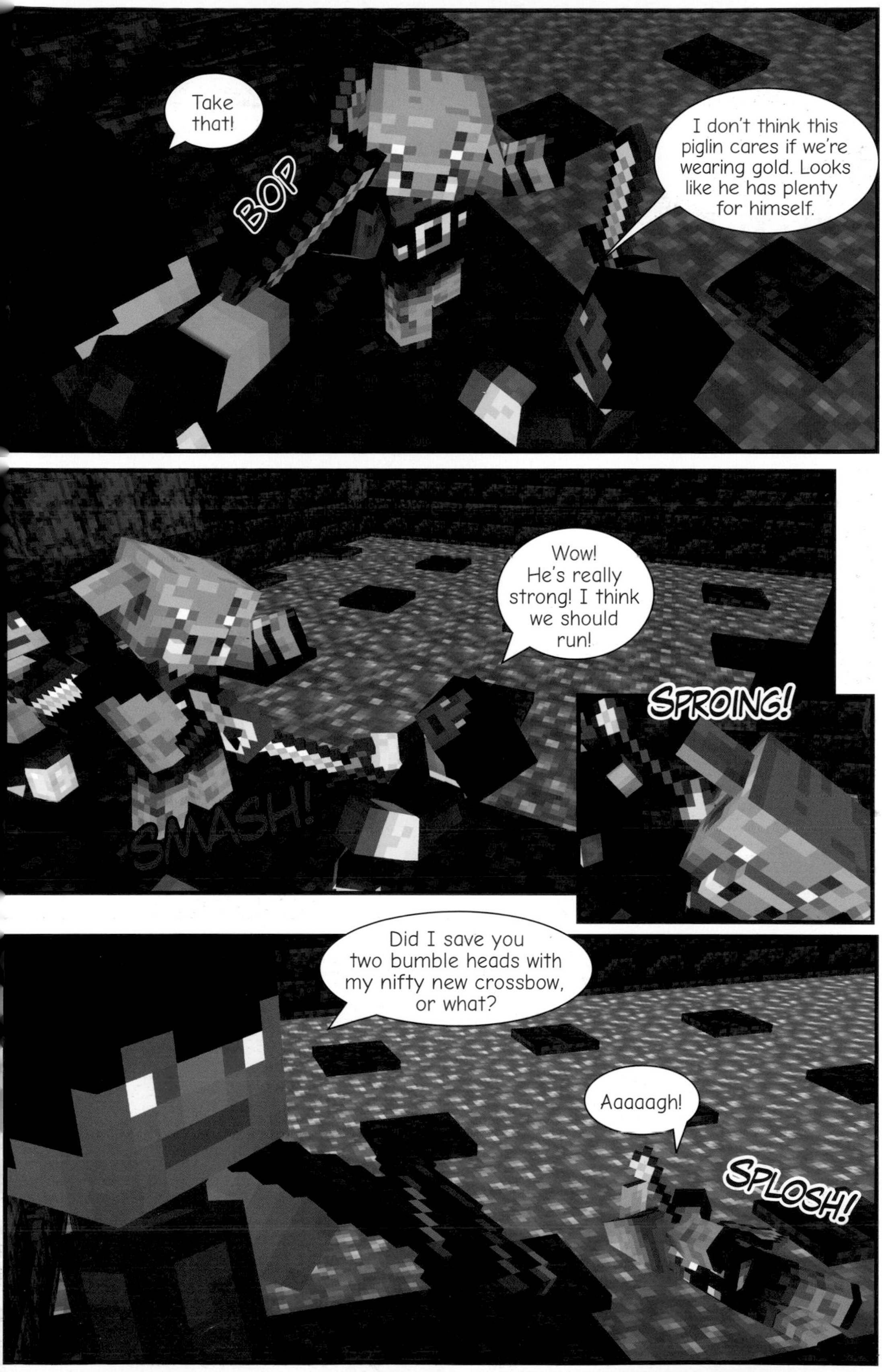
Take that!
BOP
I don't think this piglin cares if we're wearing gold. Looks like he has plenty for himself.
Wow! He's really strong! I think we should run!
SMASH!
SPROING!
Did I save you two bumble heads with my nifty new crossbow, or what?
Aaaaagh!
SPLOSH!

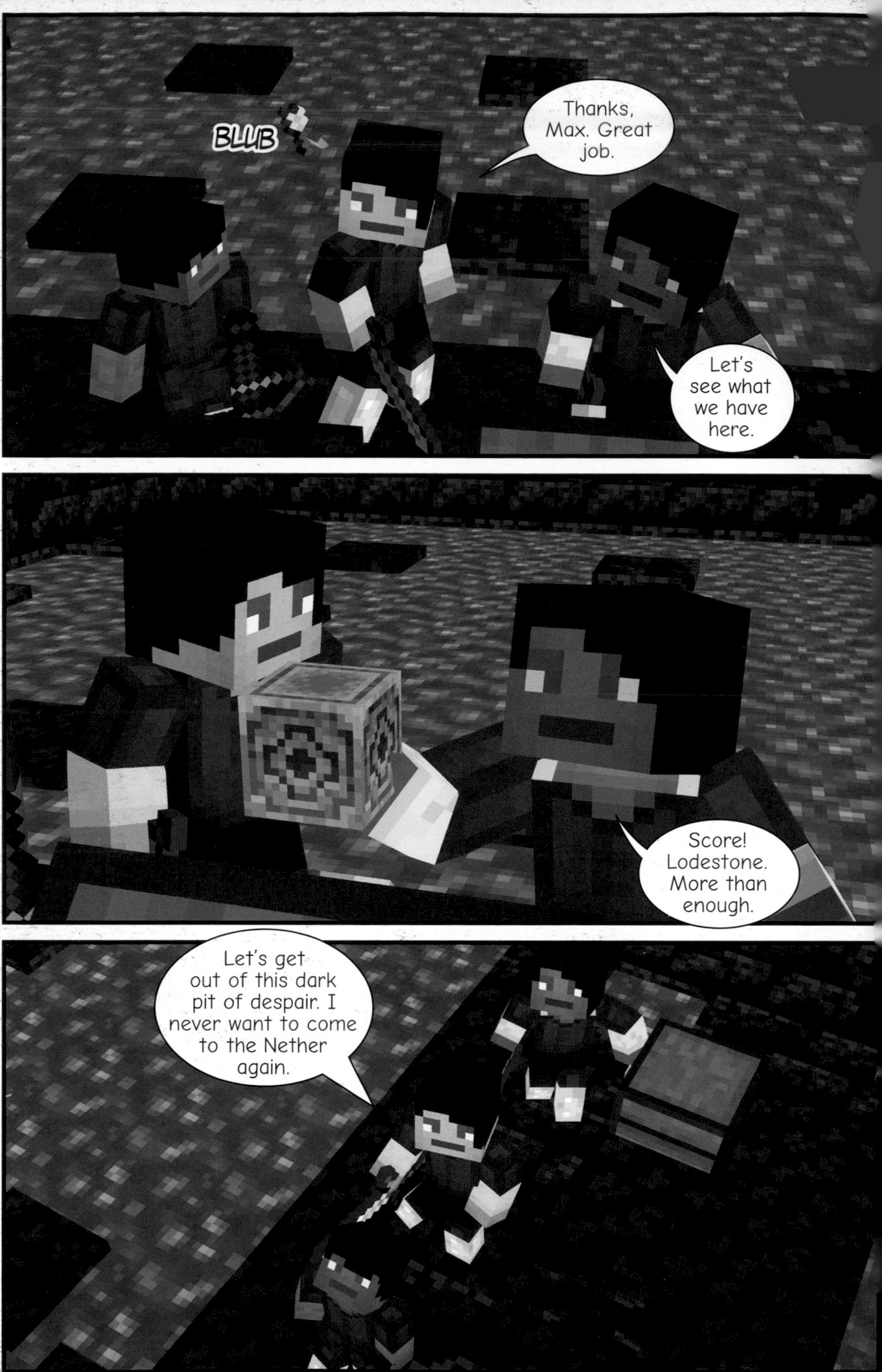
BLUB
Thanks, Max. Great job.
Let's see what we have here.
Score! Lodestone. More than enough.
Let's get out of this dark pit of despair. I never want to come to the Nether again.

Chapter 9
A Message
for Tara

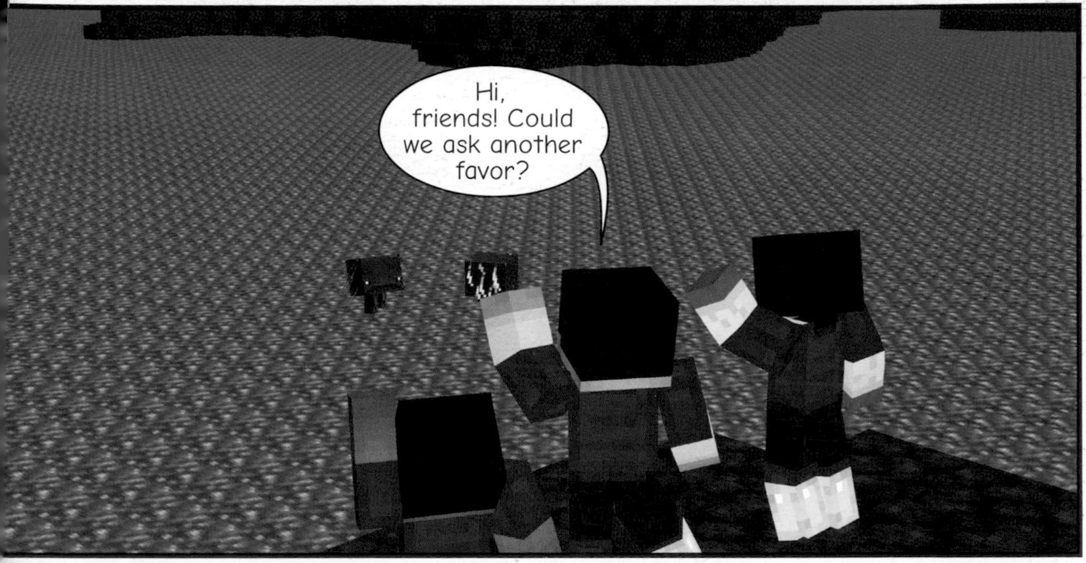
Hi, friends! Could we ask another favor?

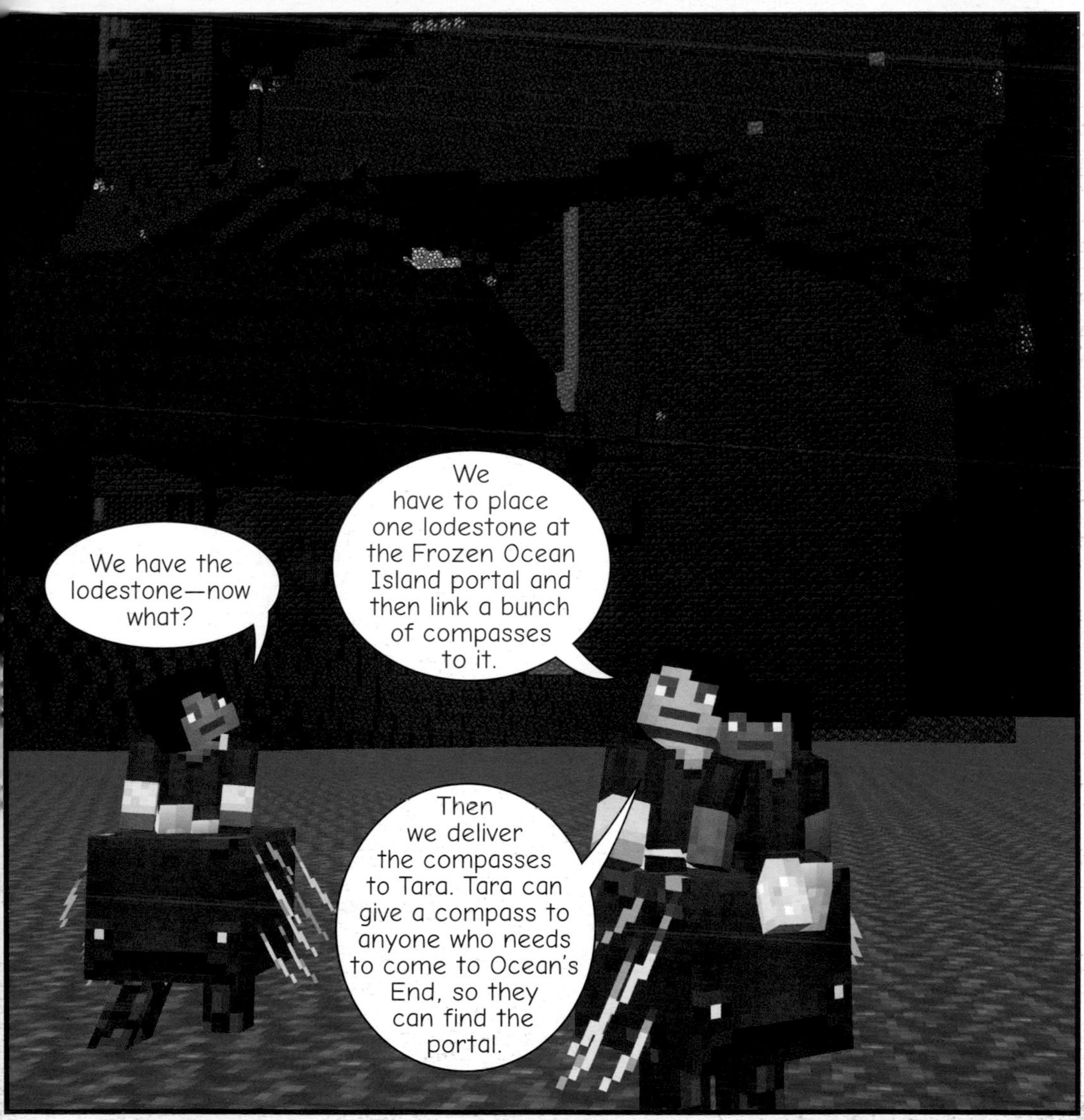
We have the lodestone—now what?
We have to place one lodestone at the Frozen Ocean Island portal and then link a bunch of compasses to it.
Then we deliver the compasses to Tara. Tara can give a compass to anyone who needs to come to Ocean's End, so they can find the portal.

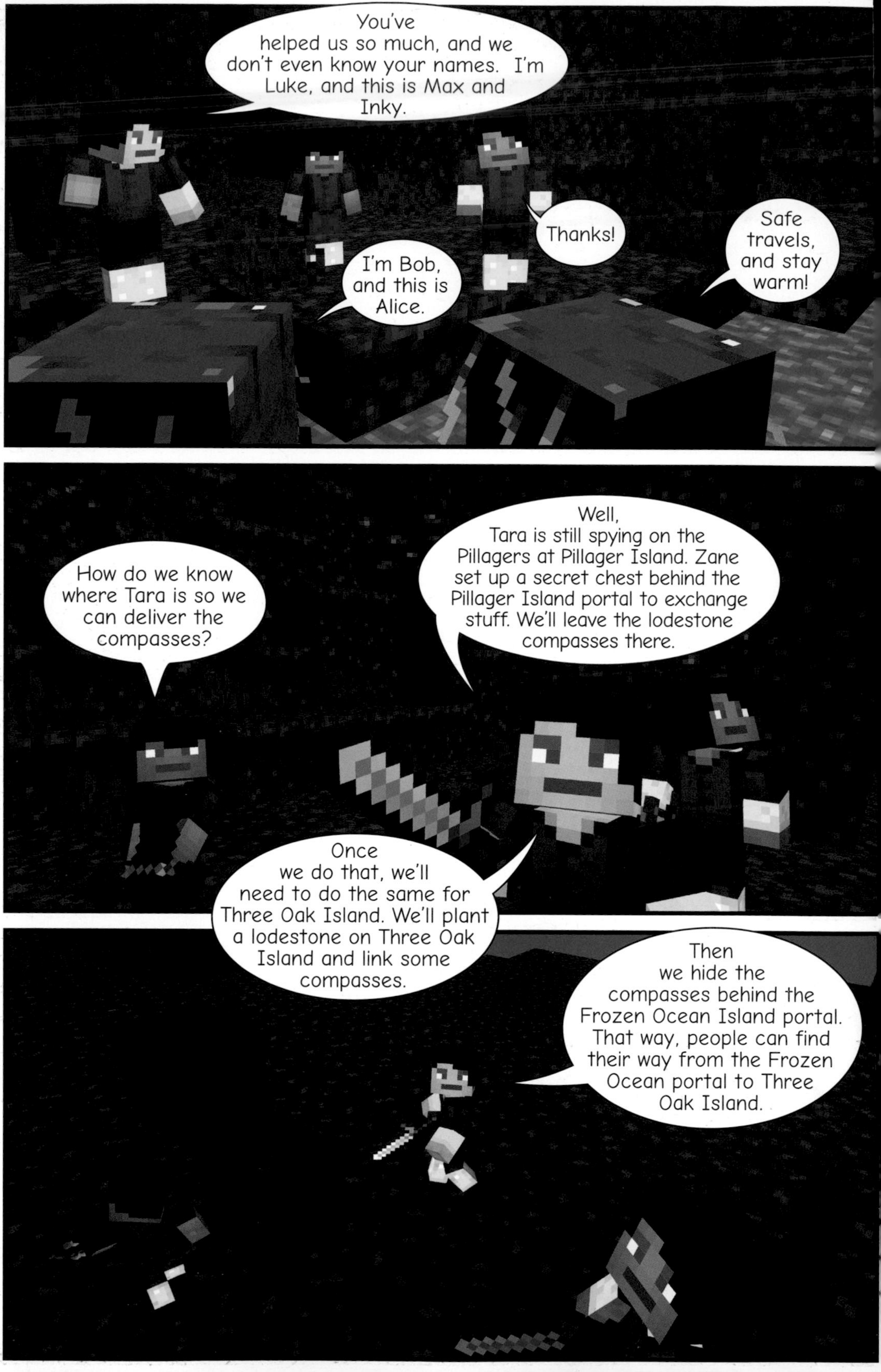
You've helped us so much, and we don't even know your names. I'm Luke, and this is Max and Inky.
I'm Bob, and this is Alice.
Thanks!
Safe travels, and stay warm!
How do we know where Tara is so we can deliver the compasses?
Well, Tara is still spying on the Pillagers at Pillager Island. Zane set up a secret chest behind the Pillager Island portal to exchange stuff. We'll leave the lodestone compasses there.
Once we do that, we'll need to do the same for Three Oak Island. We'll plant a lodestone on Three Oak Island and link some compasses.
Then we hide the compasses behind the Frozen Ocean Island portal. That way, people can find their way from the Frozen Ocean portal to Three Oak Island.

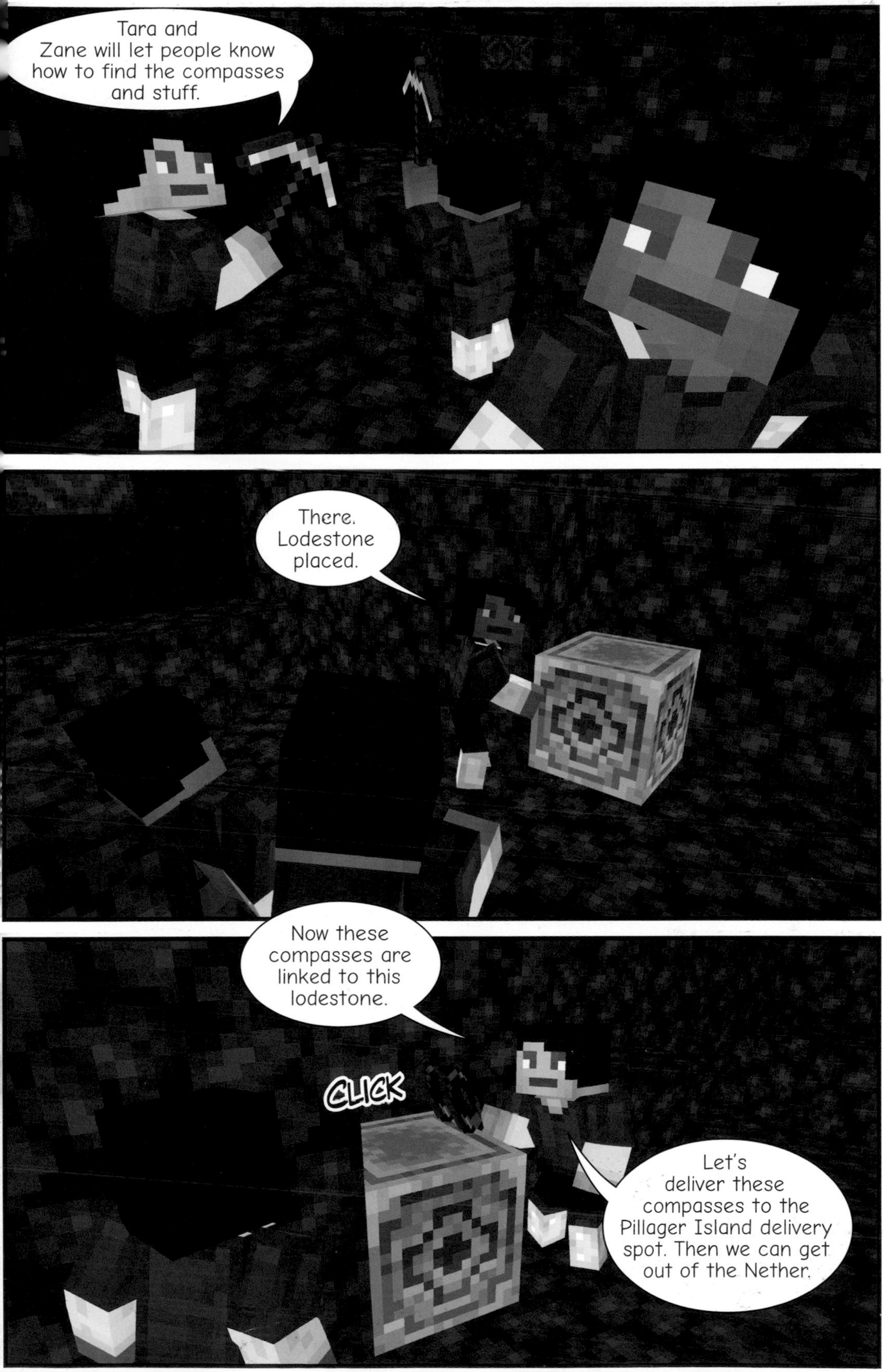
Tara and Zane will let people know how to find the compasses and stuff.
There. Lodestone placed.
Now these compasses are linked to this lodestone.
CLICK
Let's deliver these compasses to the Pillager Island delivery spot. Then we can get out of the Nether.

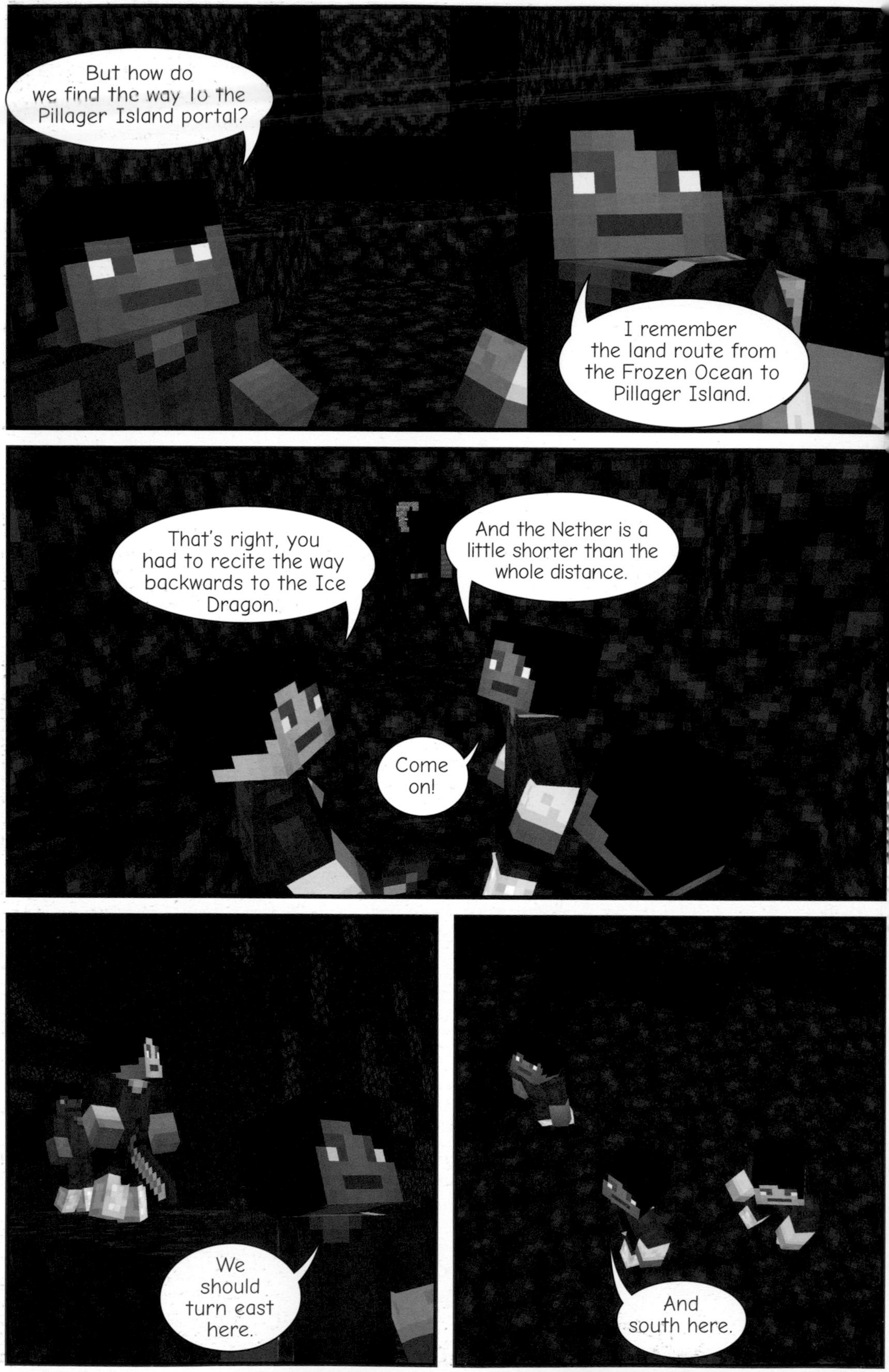
But how do we find the way to the Pillager Island portal?
I remember the land route from the Frozen Ocean to Pillager Island.
That's right, you had to recite the way backwards to the Ice Dragon.
And the Nether is a little shorter than the whole distance.
Come on!
We should turn east here.
And south here.

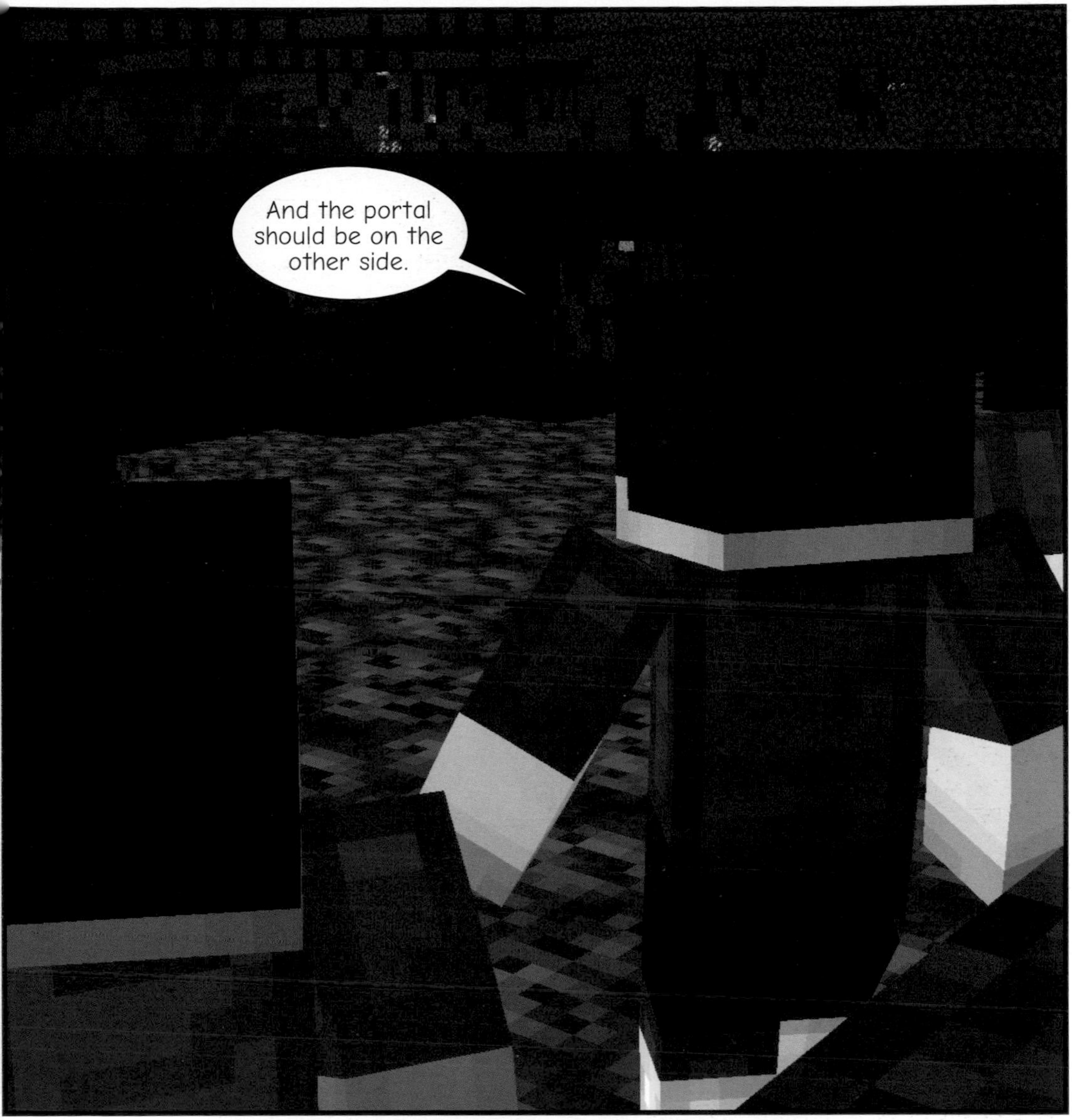
And the portal should be on the other side.

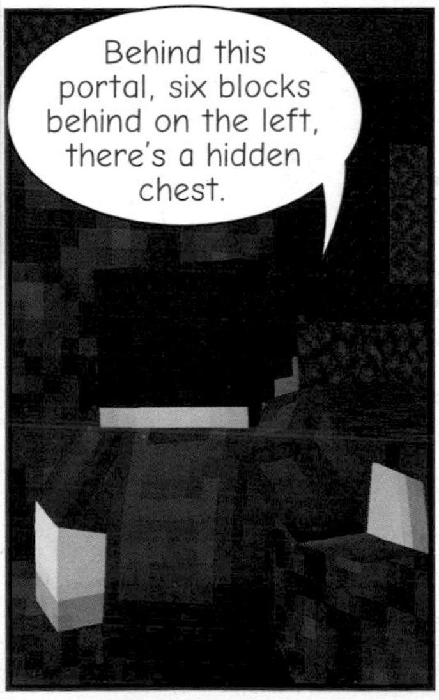
Behind this portal, six blocks behind on the left, there's a hidden chest.

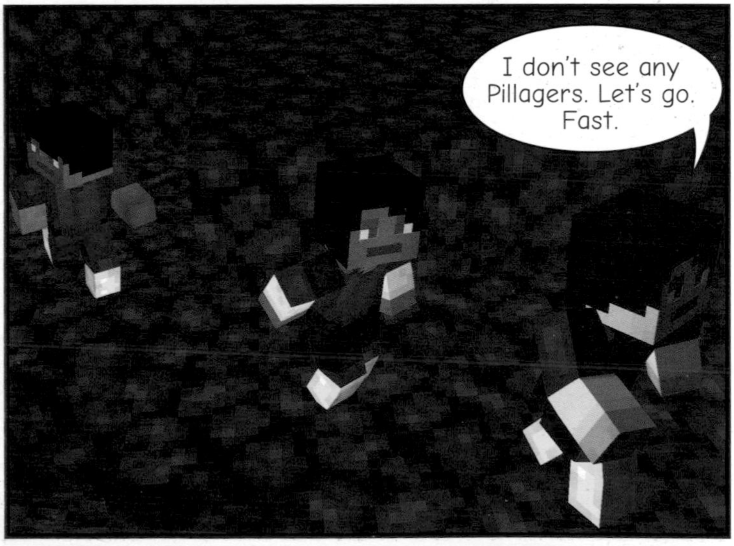
I don't see any Pillagers. Let's go. Fast.

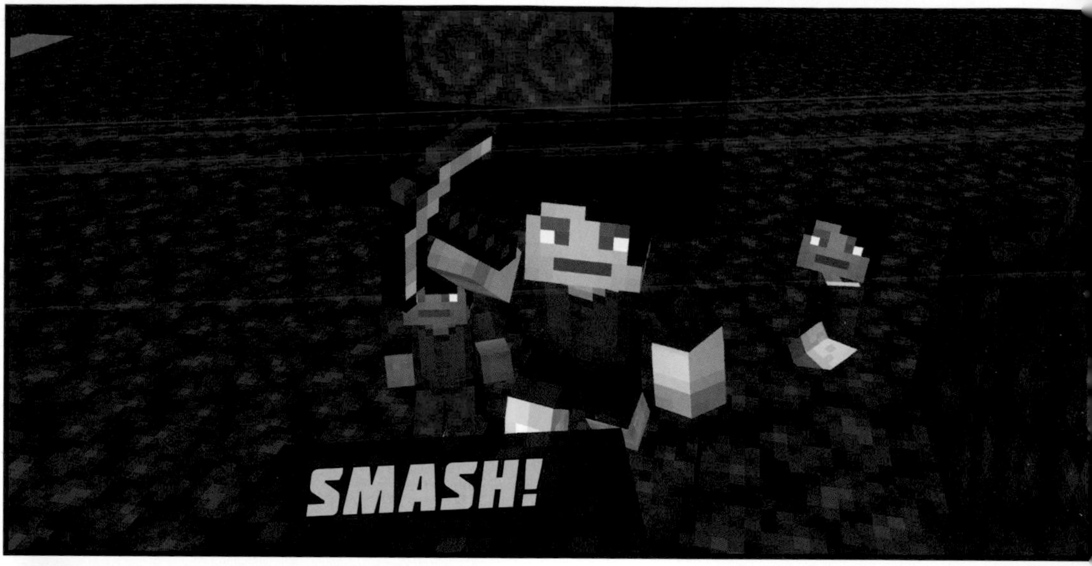
SMASH!

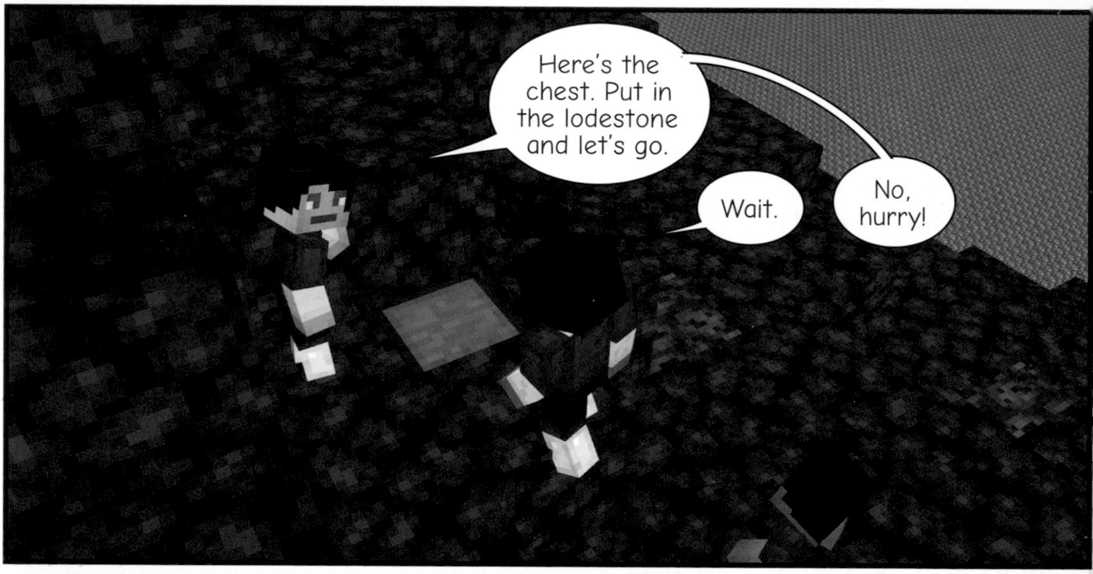
Here's the chest. Put in the lodestone and let's go.
Wait.
No, hurry!

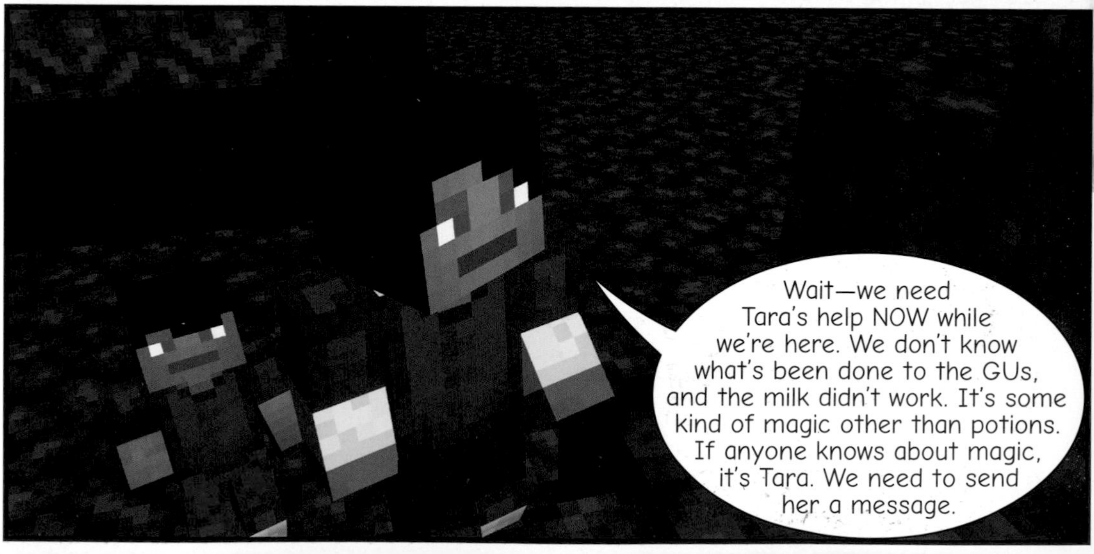
Wait—we need Tara's help NOW while we're here. We don't know what's been done to the GUs, and the milk didn't work. It's some kind of magic other than potions. If anyone knows about magic, it's Tara. We need to send her a message.

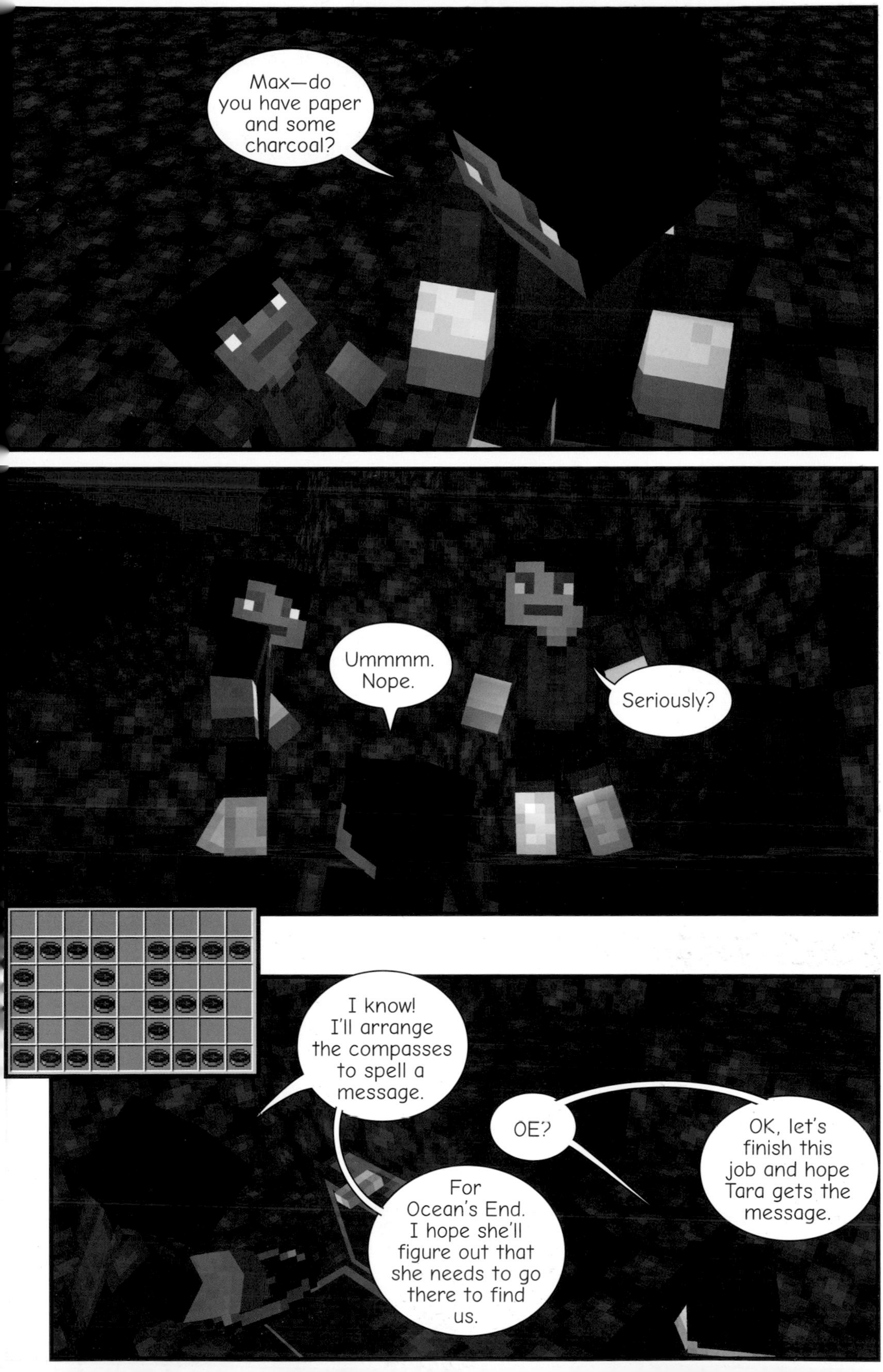

Max—do you have paper and some charcoal?
Ummmm. Nope.
Seriously?
I know! I'll arrange the compasses to spell a message.
OE?
For Ocean's End. I hope she'll figure out that she needs to go there to find us.
OK, let's finish this job and hope Tara gets the message.

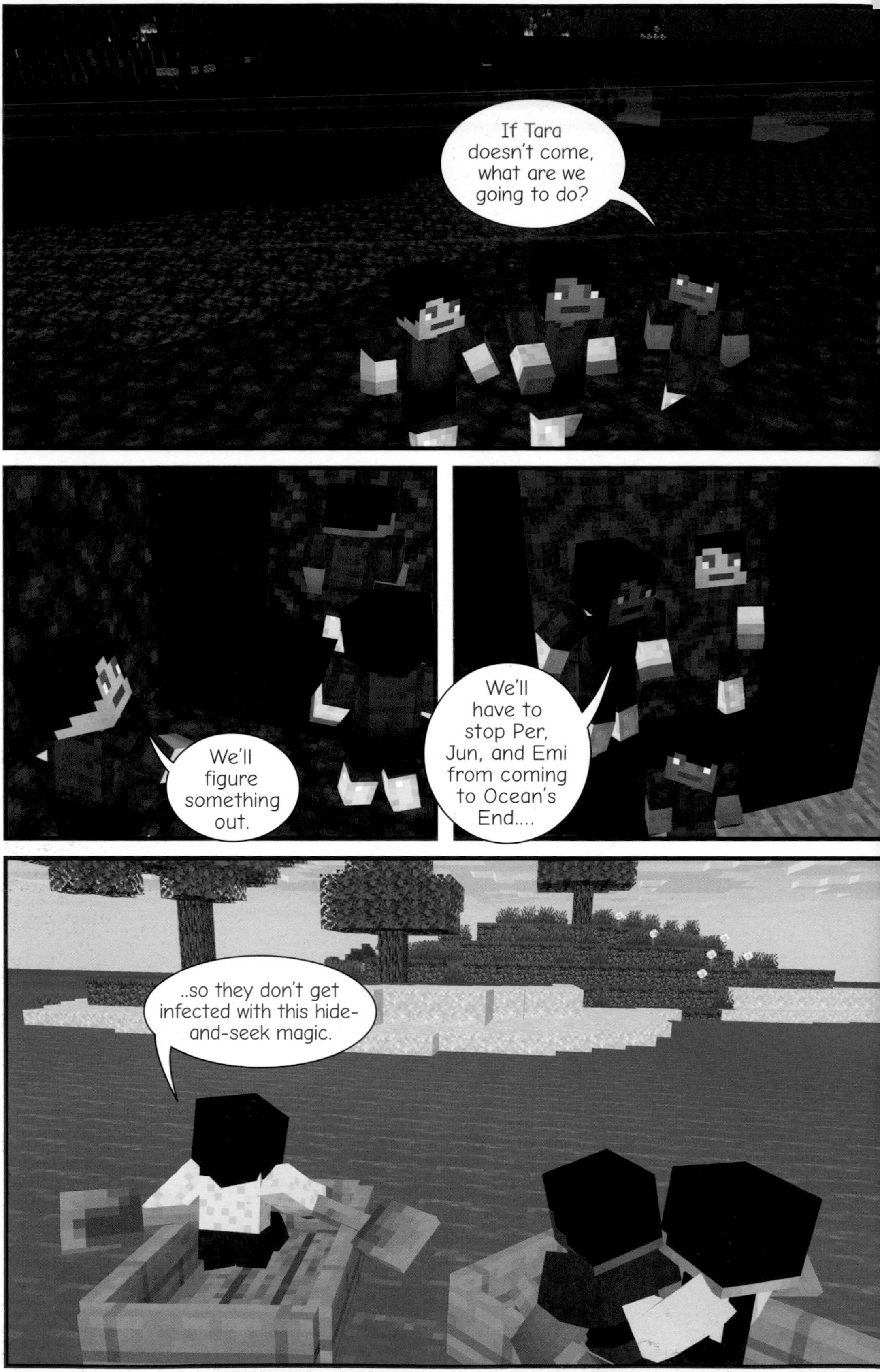
If Tara doesn't come, what are we going to do?
We'll figure something out.
We'll have to stop Per, Jun, and Emi from coming to Ocean's End....
..so they don't get infected with this hide-and-seek magic.

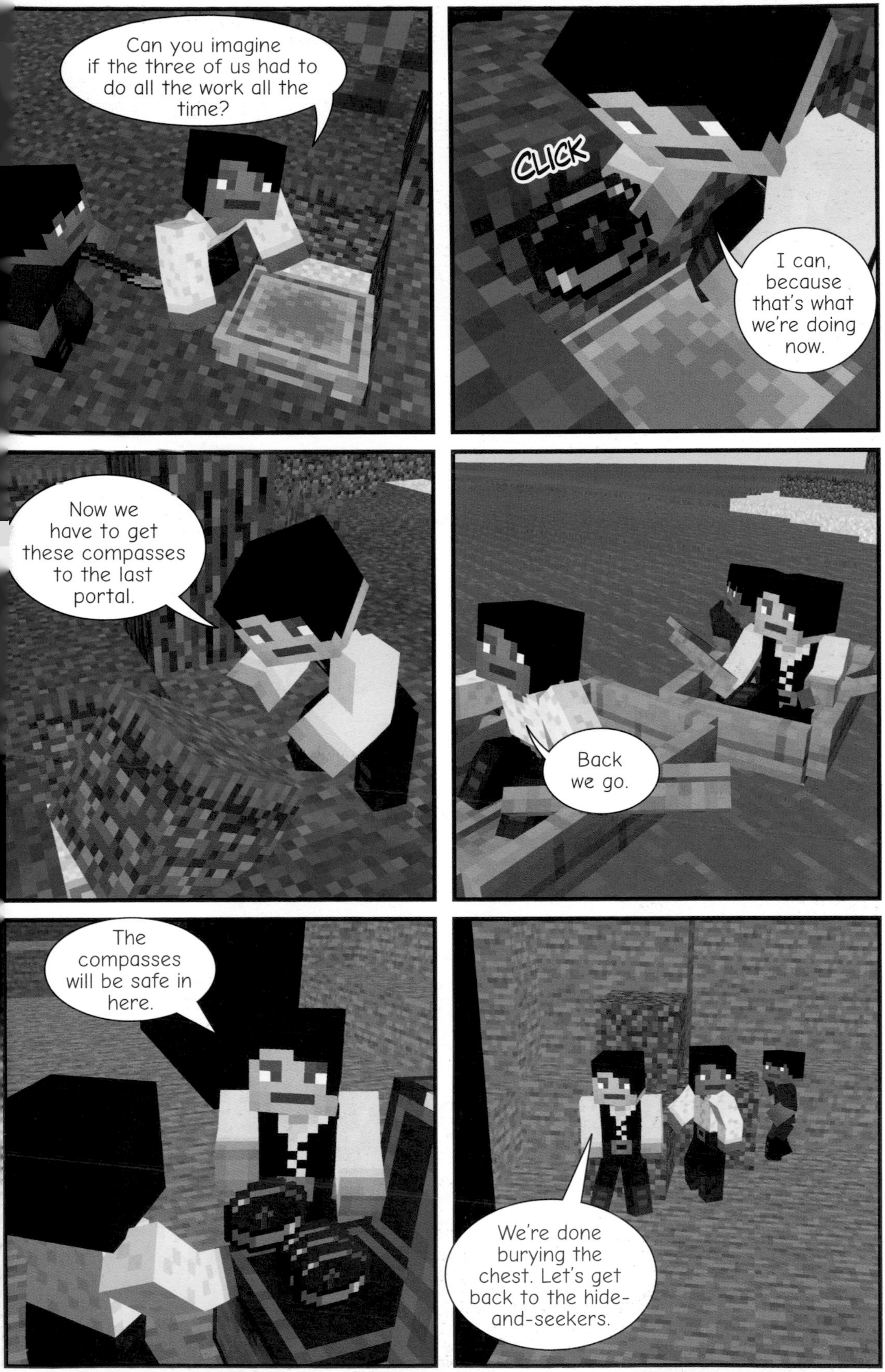

Can you imagine if the three of us had to do all the work all the time?
CLICK
I can, because that's what we're doing now.
Now we have to get these compasses to the last portal.
Back we go.
The compasses will be safe in here.
We're done burying the chest. Let's get back to the hide-and-seekers.

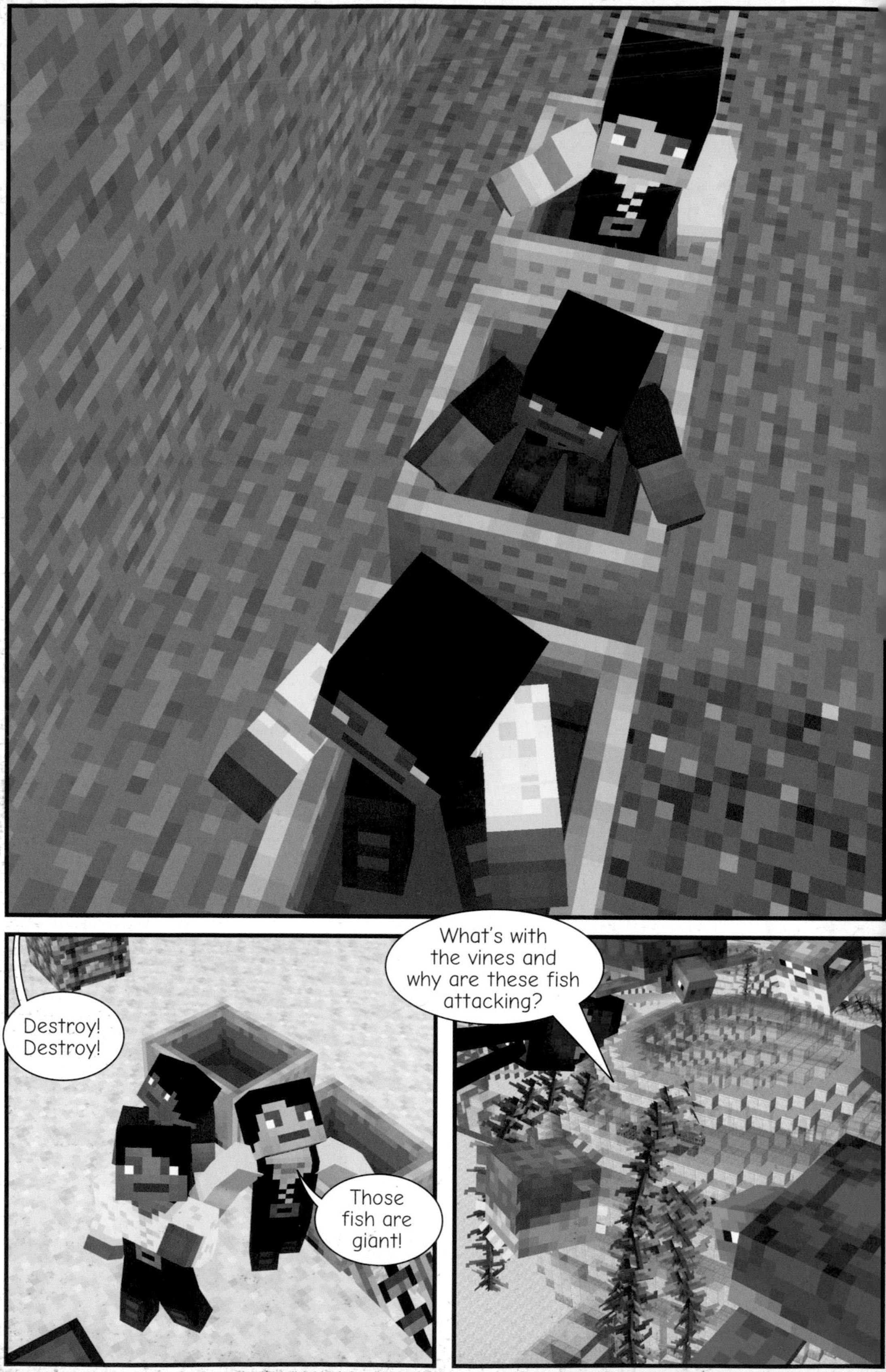
Destroy! Destroy!
Those fish are giant!
What's with the vines and why are these fish attacking?

Chapter 10
Return to Madness

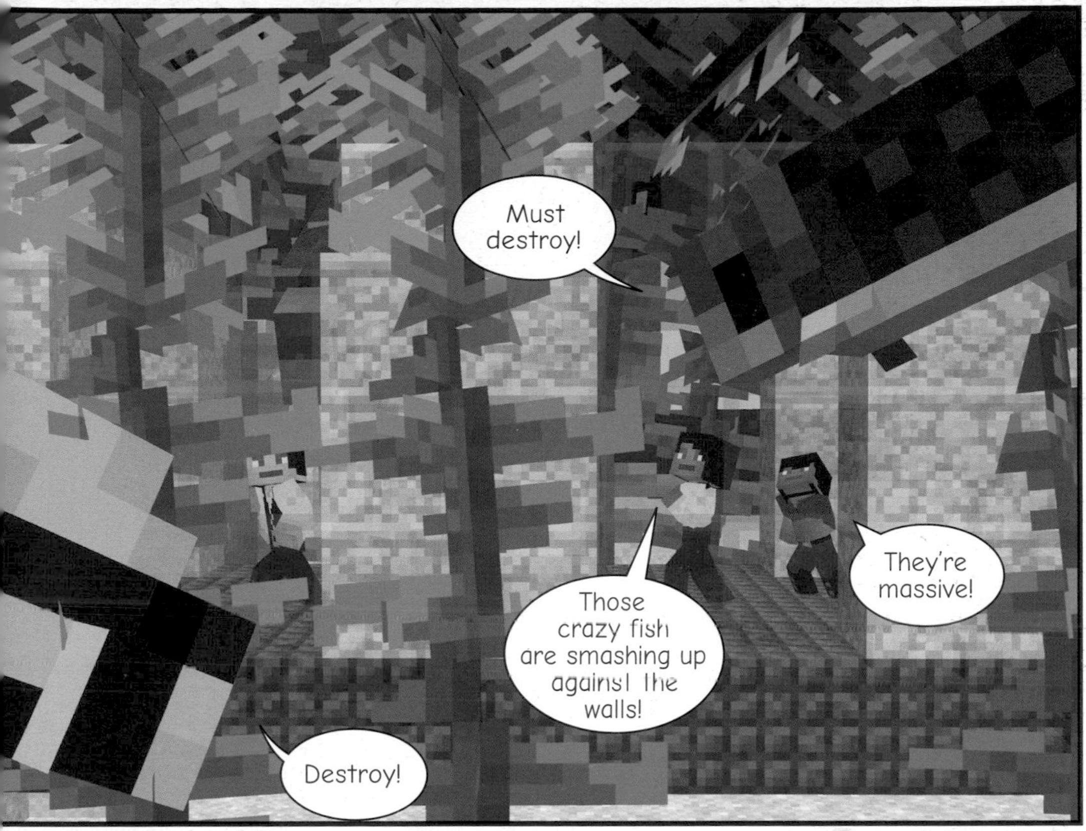
Must destroy!
They're massive!
Those crazy fish are smashing up against the walls!
Destroy!

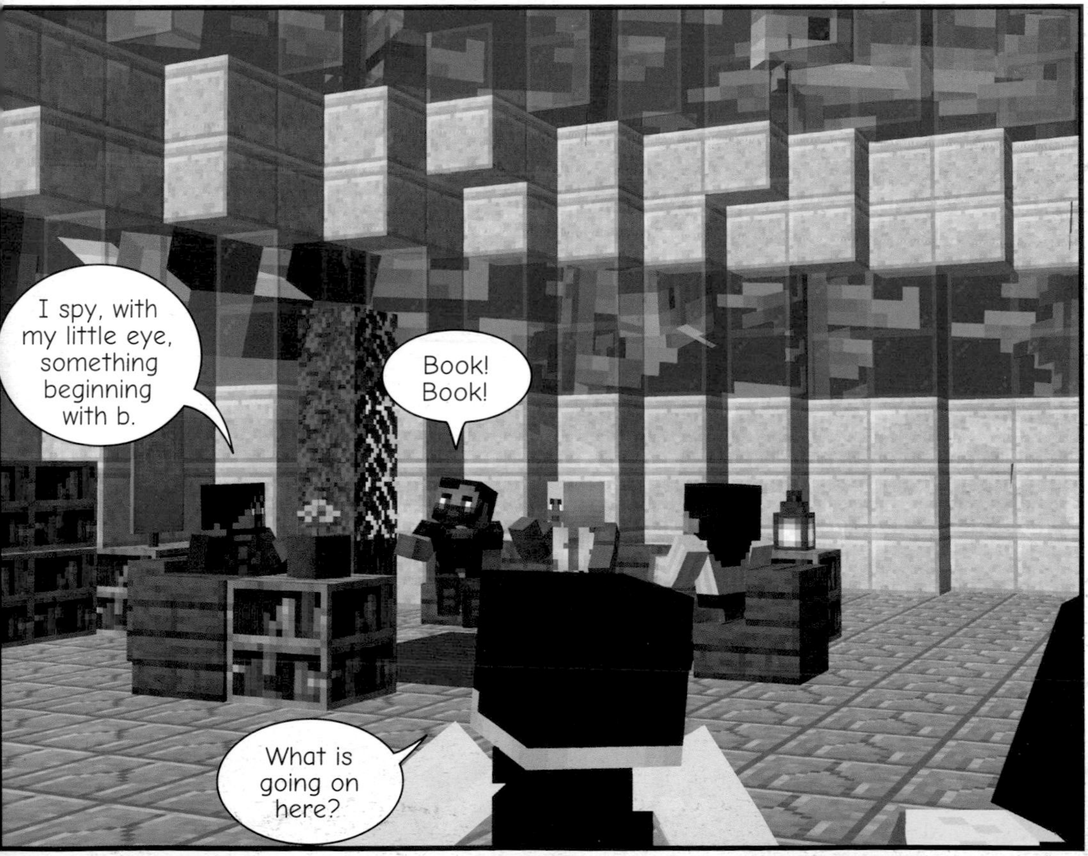
I spy, with my little eye, something beginning with b.
Book! Book!
What is going on here?

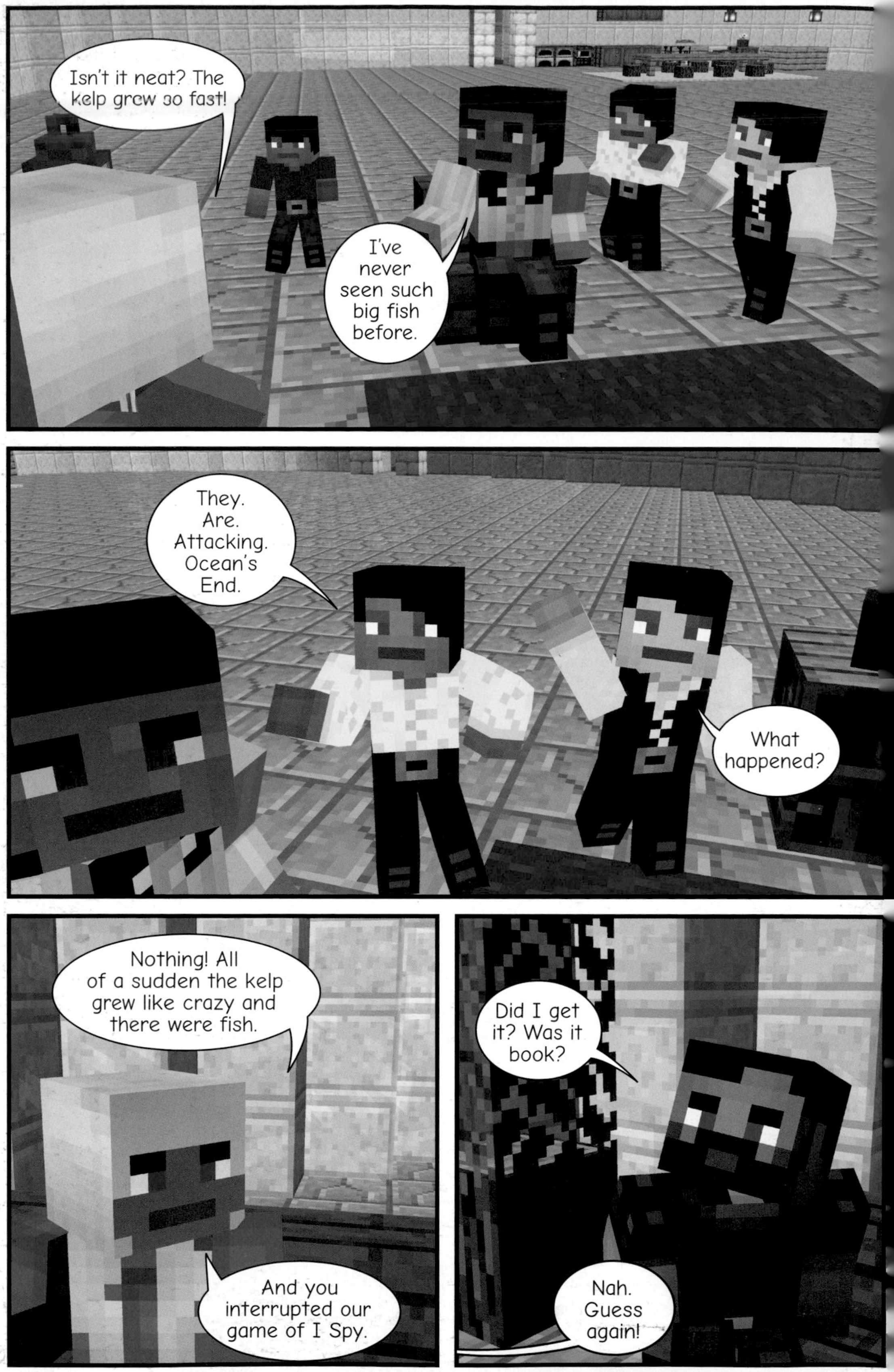
Isn't it neat? The kelp grew so fast!
I've never seen such big fish before.
They. Are. Attacking. Ocean's End.
What happened?
Nothing! All of a sudden the kelp grew like crazy and there were fish.
And you interrupted our game of I Spy.
Did I get it? Was it book?
Nah. Guess again!

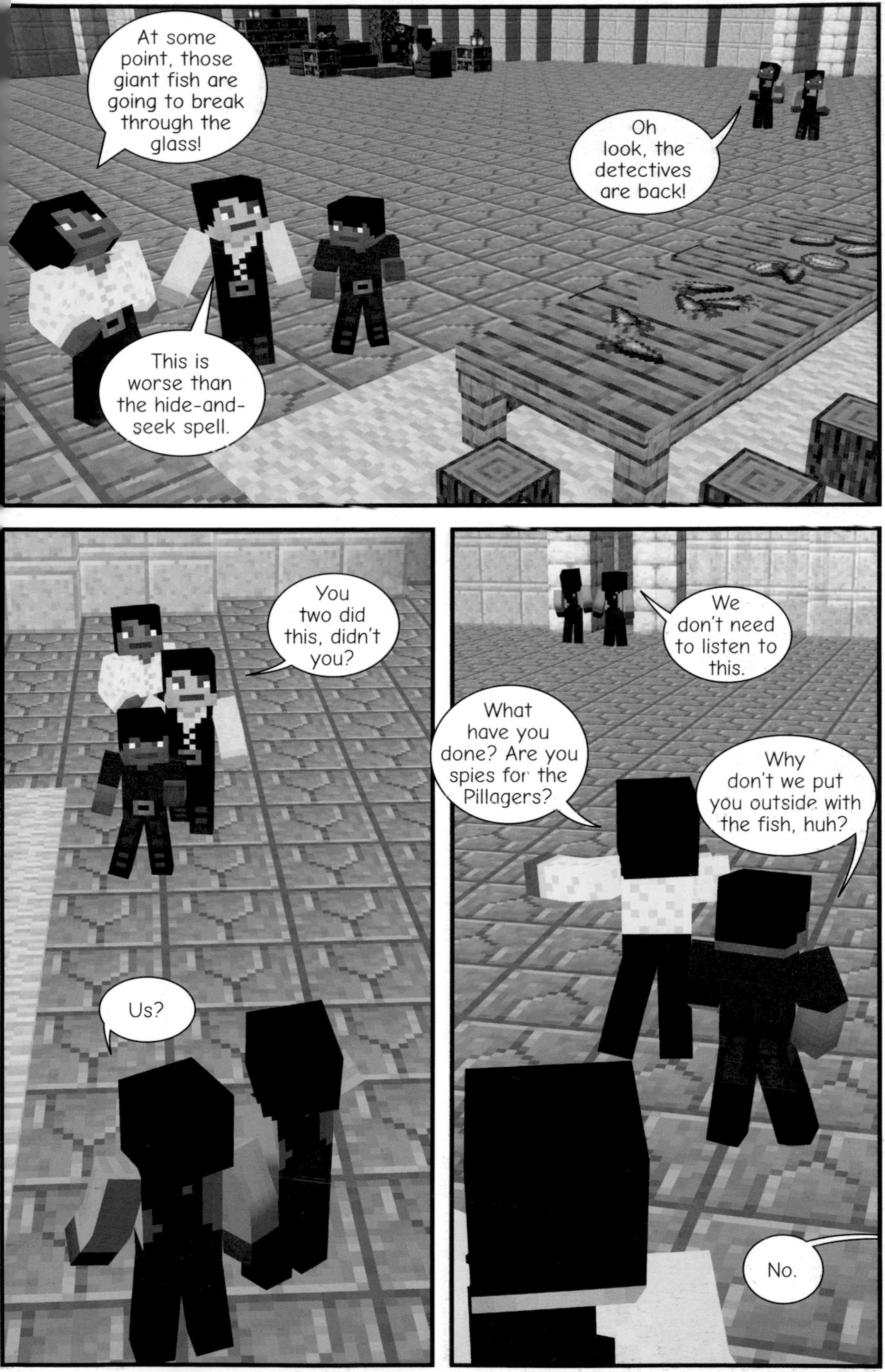

At some point, those giant fish are going to break through the glass!
Oh look, the detectives are back!
This is worse than the hide-and-seek spell.
You two did this, didn't you?
Us?
We don't need to listen to this.
What have you done? Are you spies for the Pillagers?
Why don't we put you outside with the fish, huh?
No.

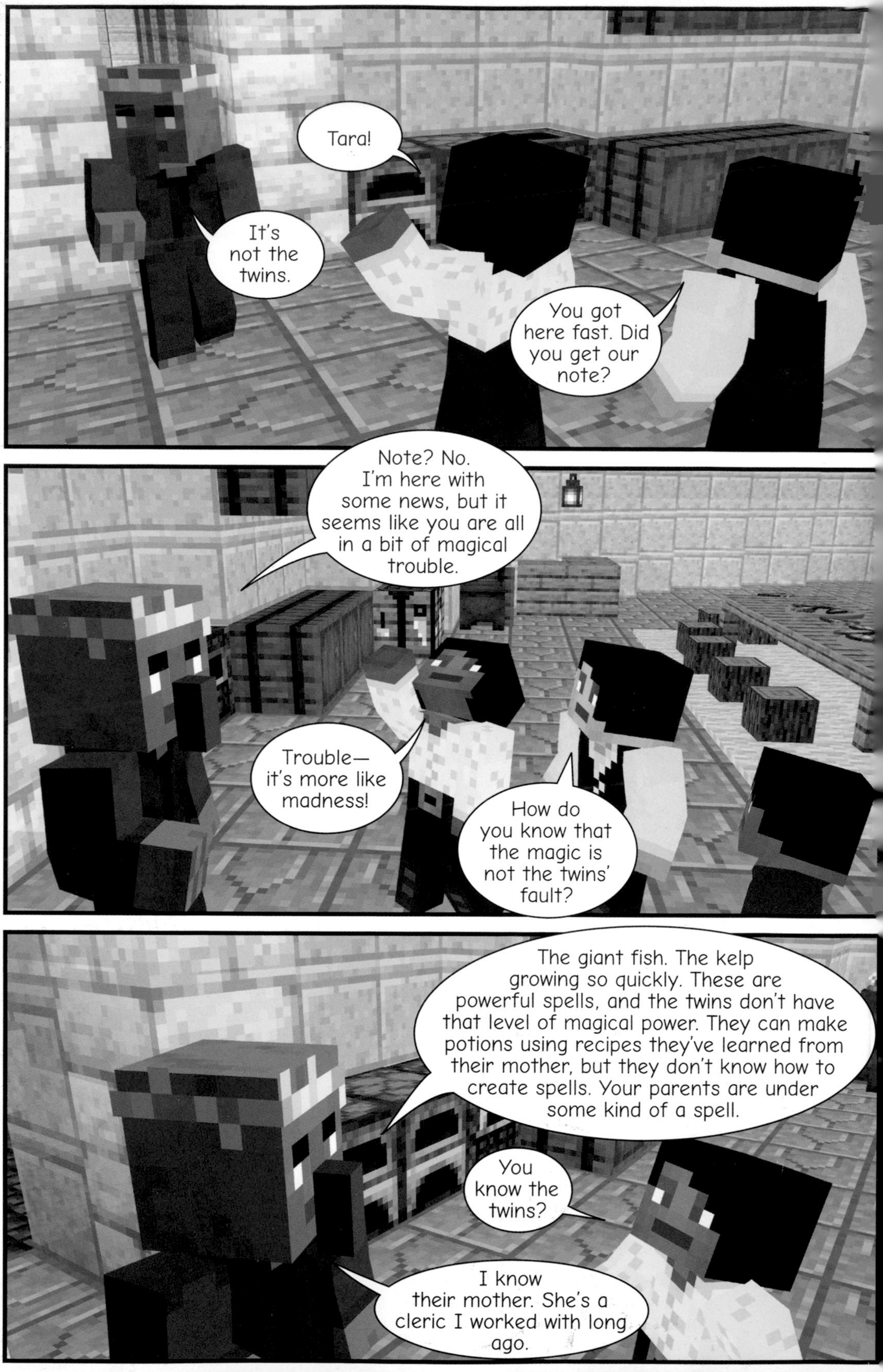
Tara!
It's not the twins.
You got here fast. Did you get our note?
Note? No. I'm here with some news, but it seems like you are all in a bit of magical trouble.
Trouble— it's more like madness!
How do you know that the magic is not the twins' fault?
The giant fish. The kelp growing so quickly. These are powerful spells, and the twins don't have that level of magical power. They can make potions using recipes they've learned from their mother, but they don't know how to create spells. Your parents are under some kind of a spell.
You know the twins?
I know their mother. She's a cleric I worked with long ago.

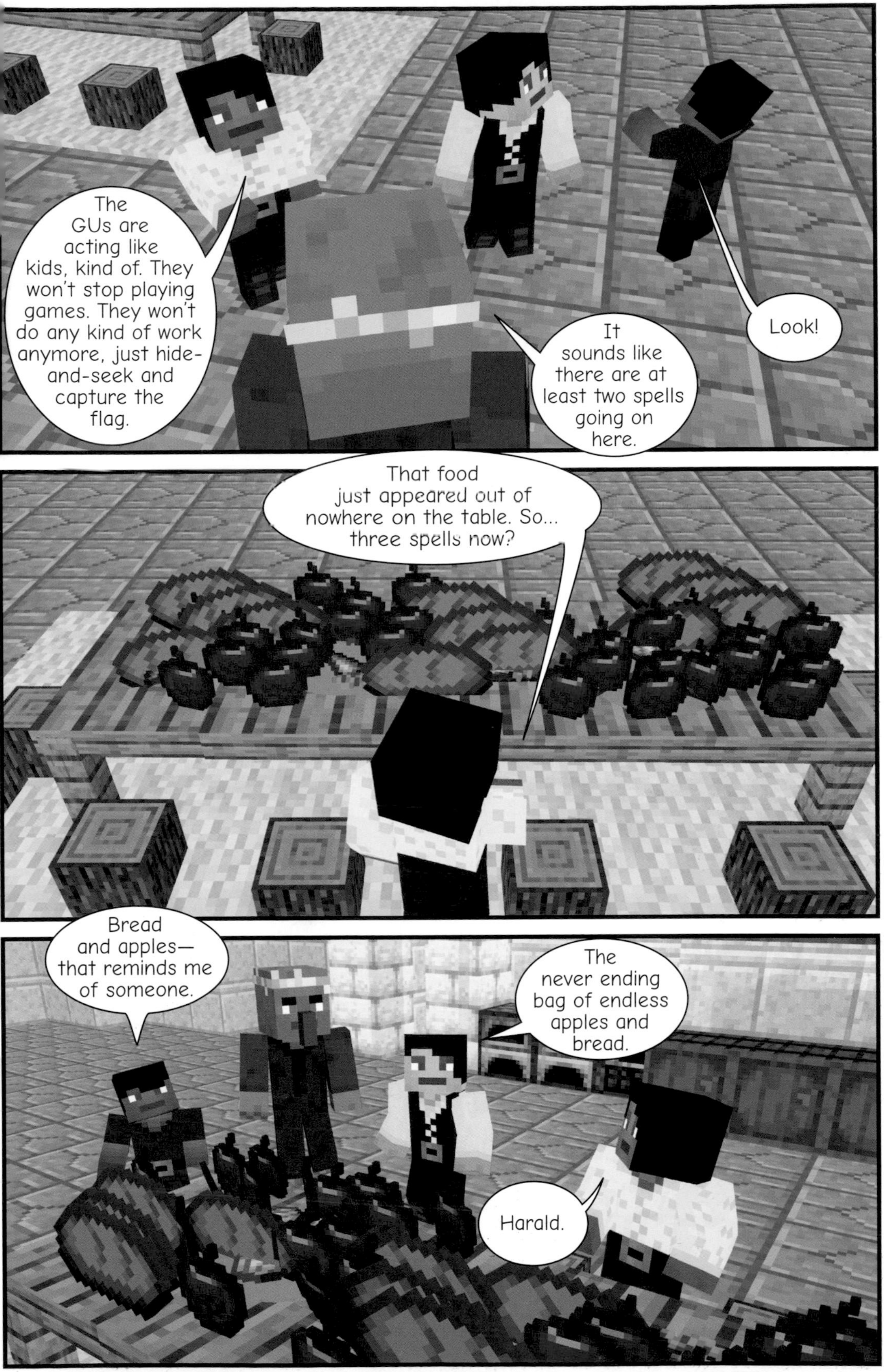
The GUs are acting like kids, kind of. They won't stop playing games. They won't do any kind of work anymore, just hide-and-seek and capture the flag.
It sounds like there are at least two spells going on here.
Look!
That food just appeared out of nowhere on the table. So... three spells now?
Bread and apples—that reminds me of someone.
The never ending bag of endless apples and bread.
Harald.

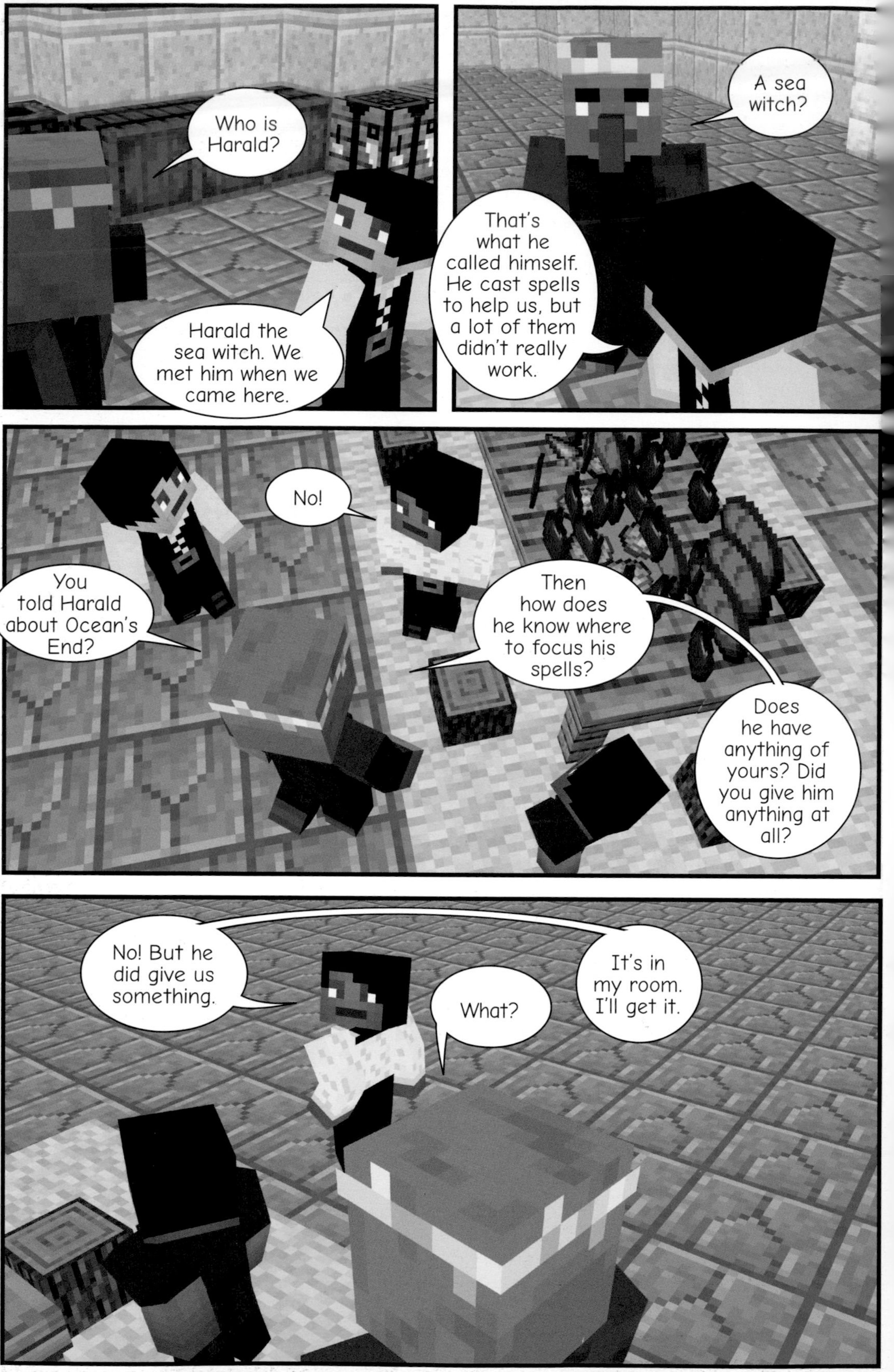
Who is Harald?
Harald the sea witch. We met him when we came here.
A sea witch?
That's what he called himself. He cast spells to help us, but a lot of them didn't really work.
No!
You told Harald about Ocean's End?
Then how does he know where to focus his spells?
Does he have anything of yours? Did you give him anything at all?
No! But he did give us something.
What?
It's in my room. I'll get it.

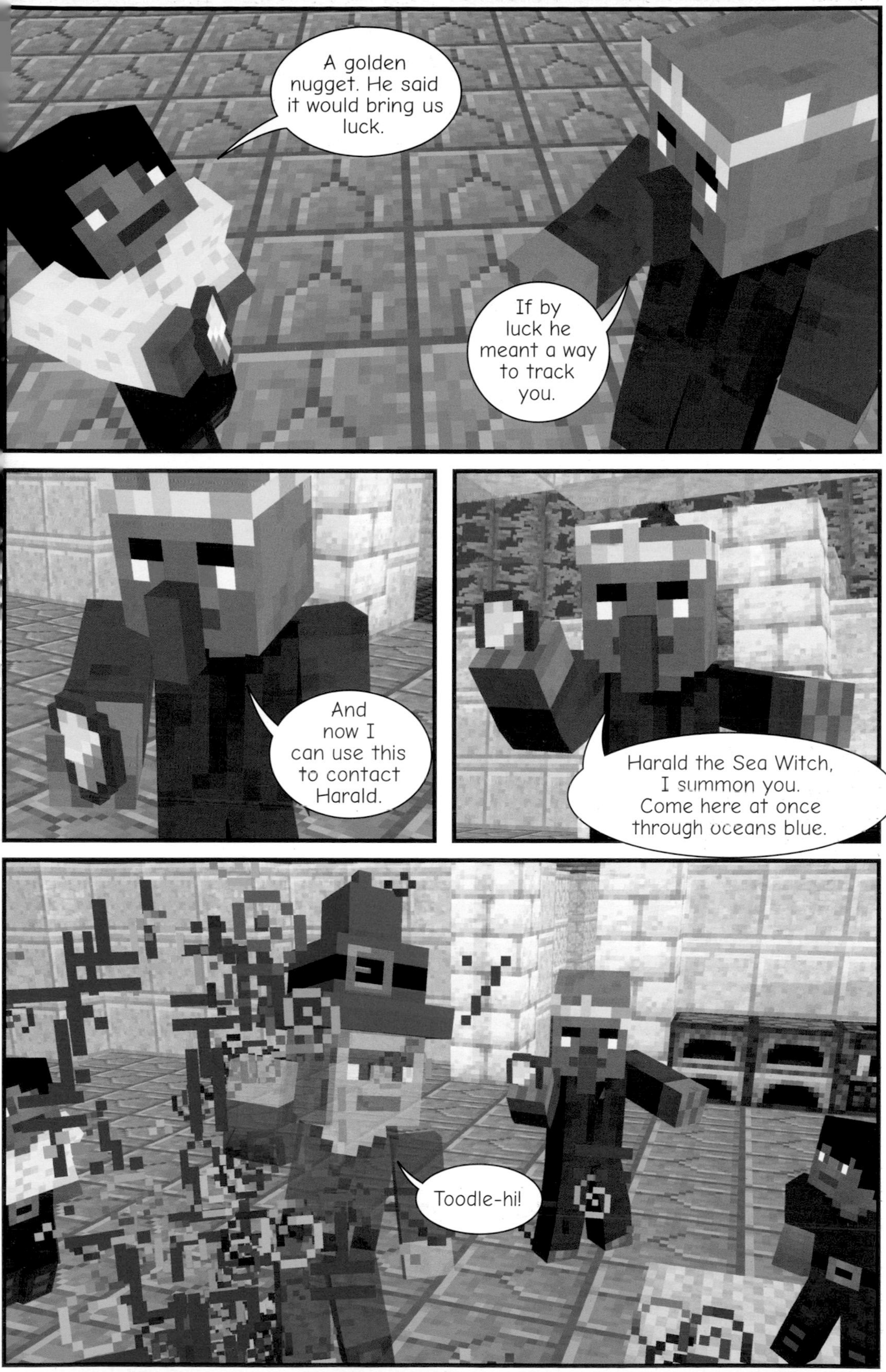
A golden nugget. He said it would bring us luck.
If by luck he meant a way to track you.
And now I can use this to contact Harald.
Harald the Sea Witch, I summon you. Come here at once through oceans blue.
Toodle-hi!

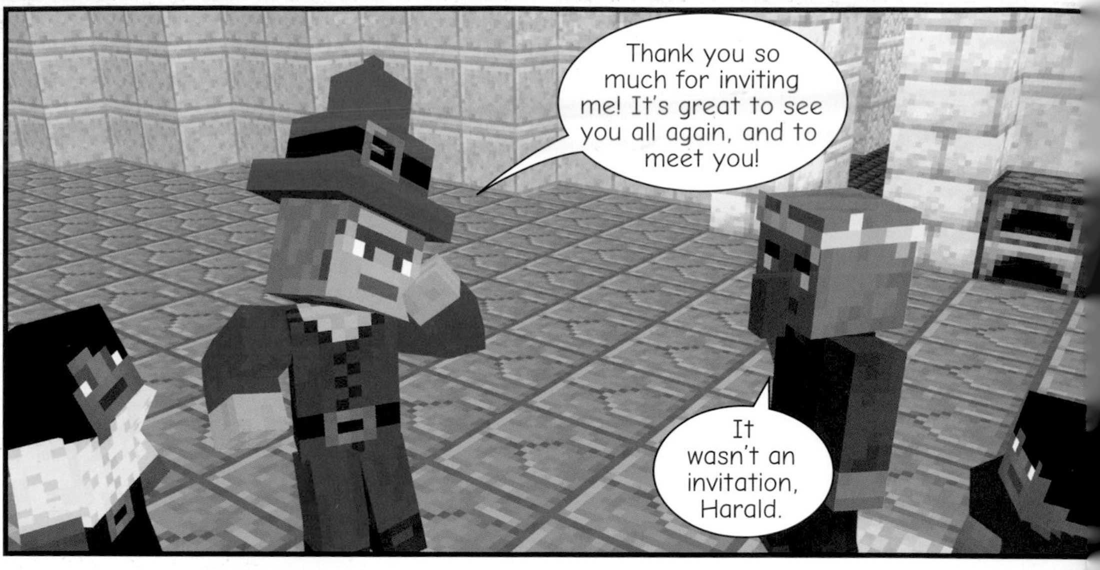
Thank you so much for inviting me! It's great to see you all again, and to meet you!
It wasn't an invitation, Harald.

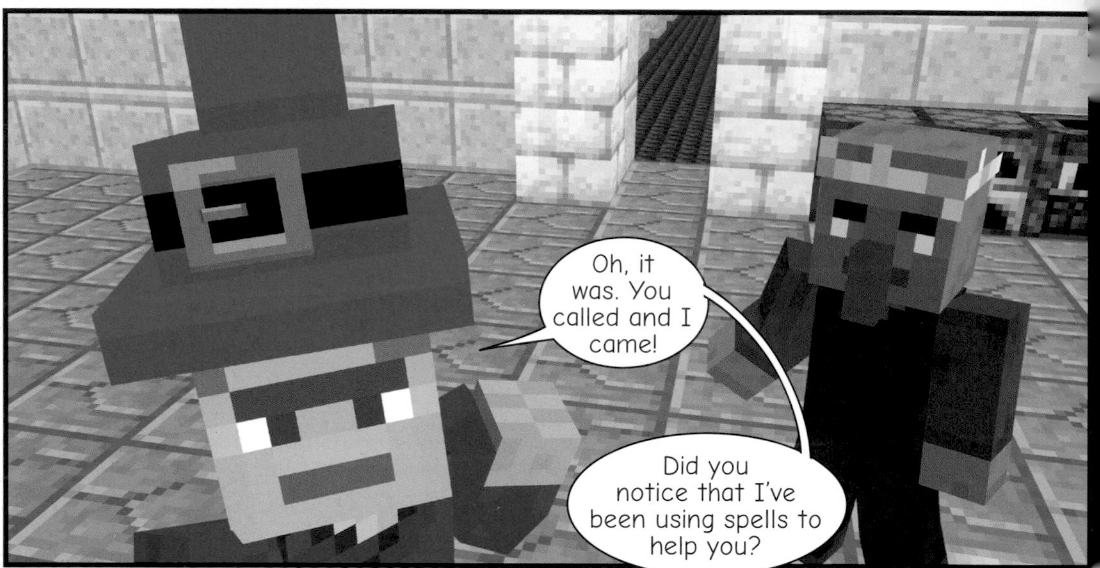
Oh, it was. You called and I came!
Did you notice that I've been using spells to help you?

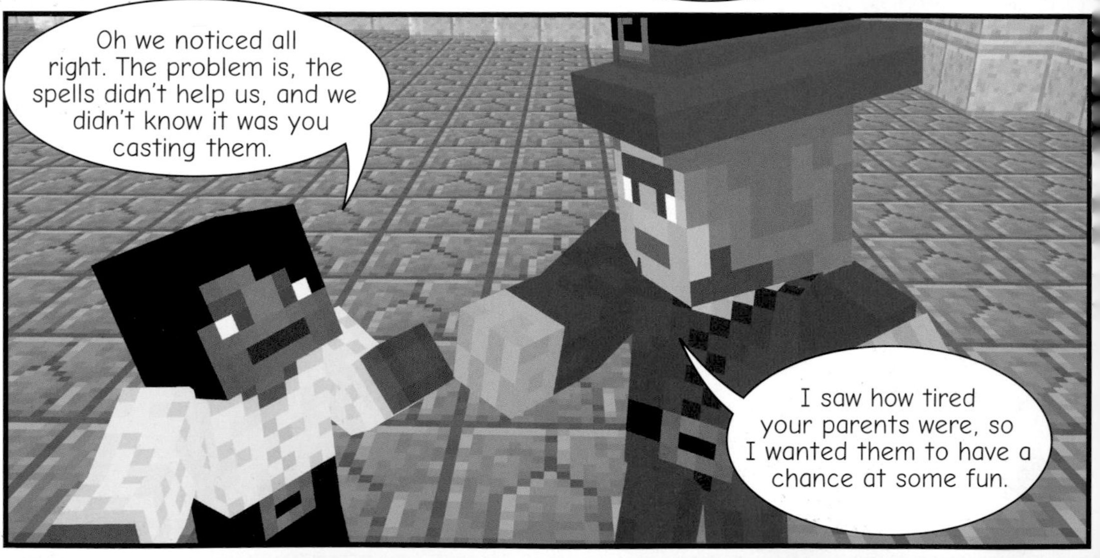
Oh we noticed all right. The problem is, the spells didn't help us, and we didn't know it was you casting them.
I saw how tired your parents were, so I wanted them to have a chance at some fun.

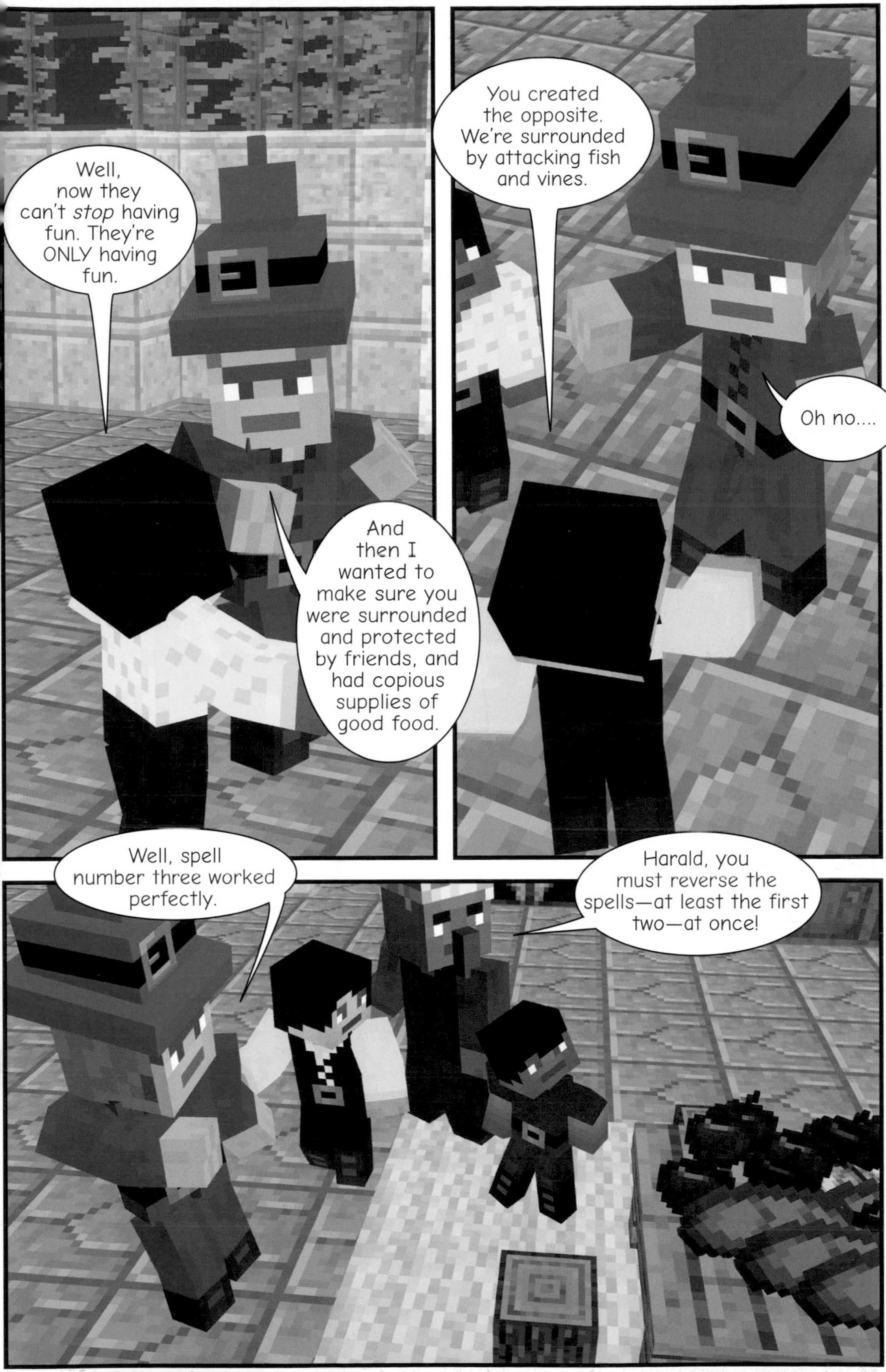
Well, now they can't *stop* having fun. They're ONLY having fun.
And then I wanted to make sure you were surrounded and protected by friends, and had copious supplies of good food.
You created the opposite. We're surrounded by attacking fish and vines.
Oh no....
Well, spell number three worked perfectly.
Harald, you must reverse the spells—at least the first two—at once!

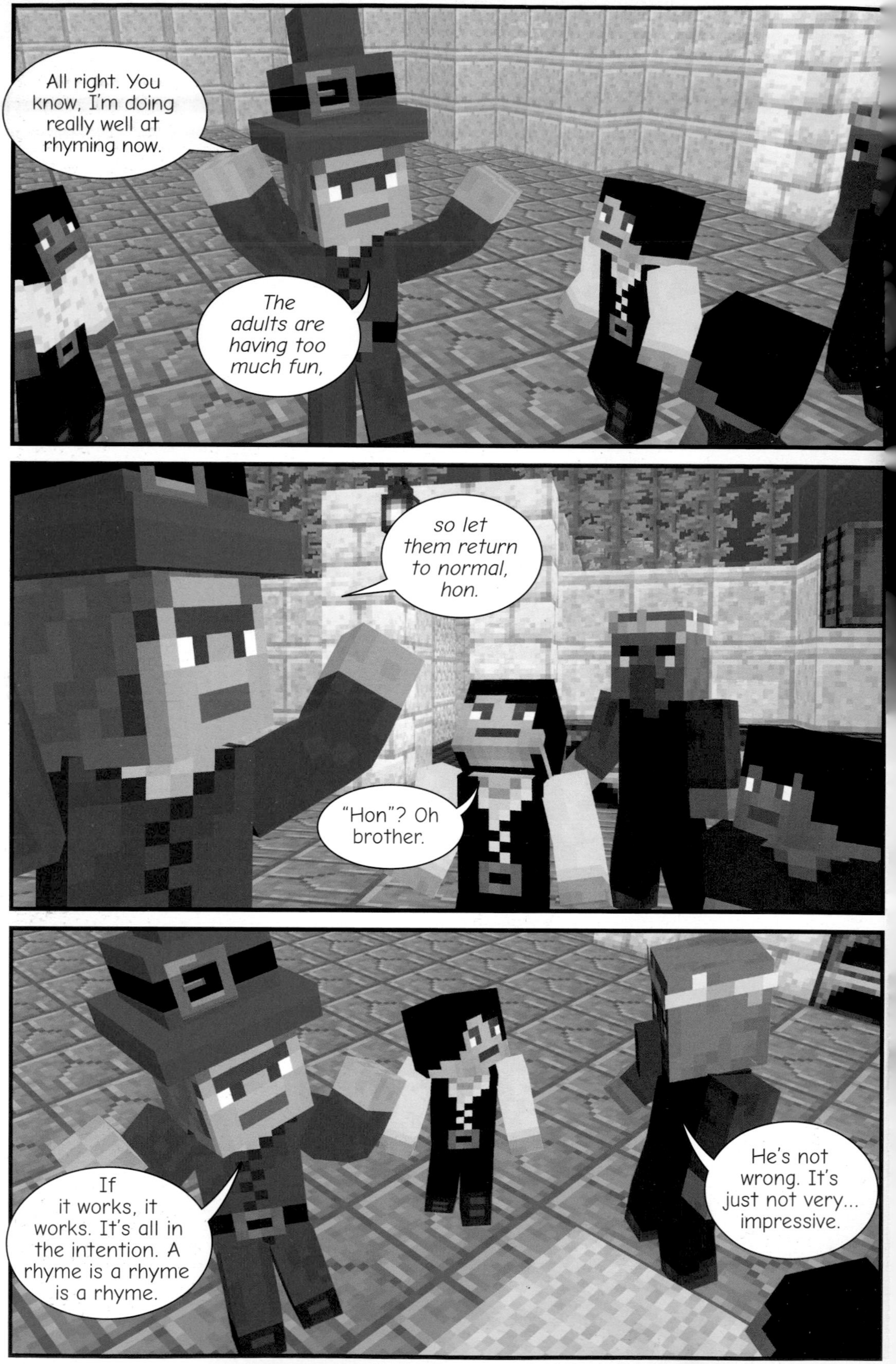
All right. You know, I'm doing really well at rhyming now.
The adults are having too much fun,
so let them return to normal, hon.
"Hon"? Oh brother.
If it works, it works. It's all in the intention. A rhyme is a rhyme is a rhyme.
He's not wrong. It's just not very... impressive.

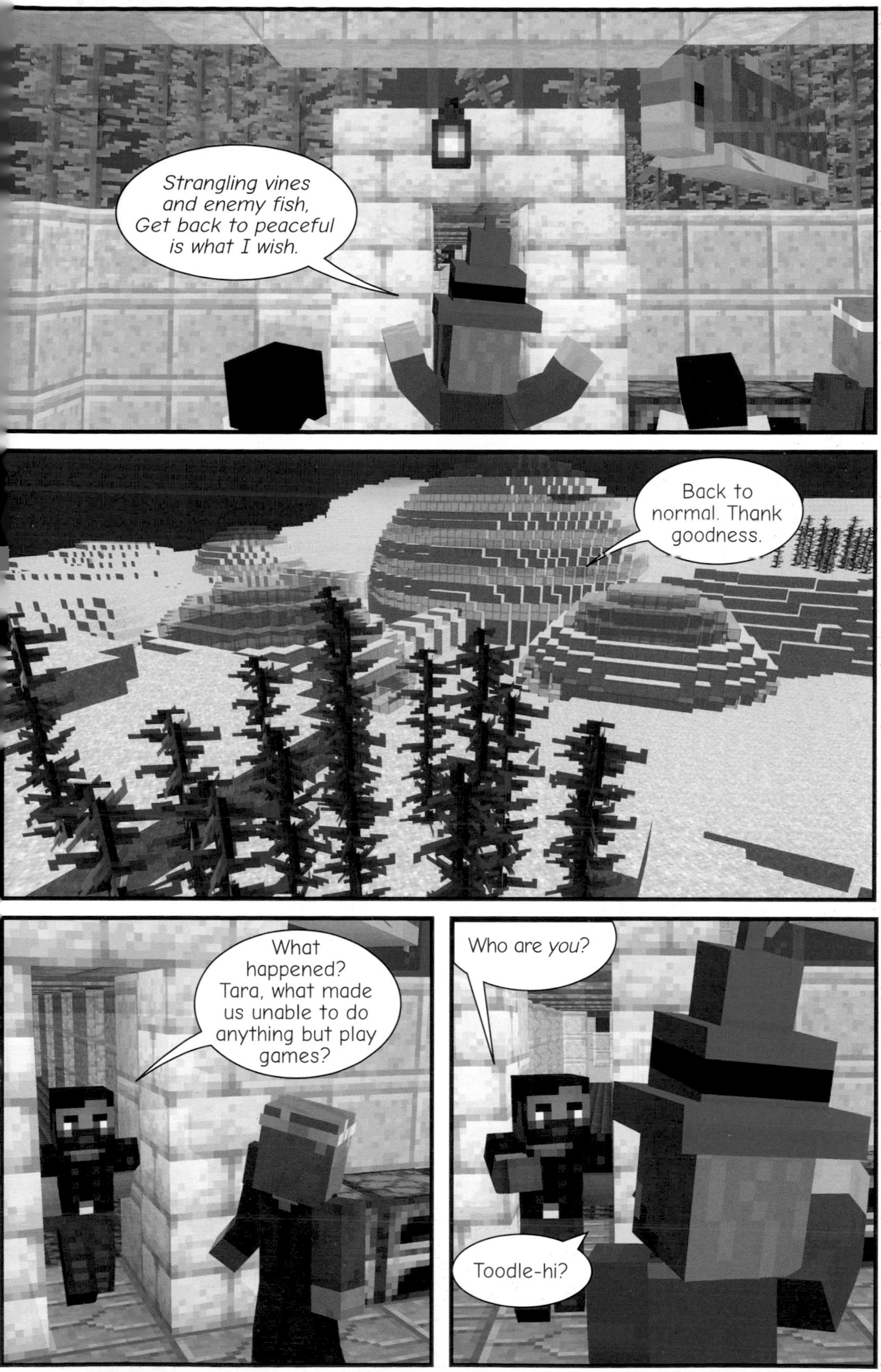
Strangling vines and enemy fish, Get back to peaceful is what I wish.
Back to normal. Thank goodness.
What happened? Tara, what made us unable to do anything but play games?
Who are *you*?
Toodle-hi?

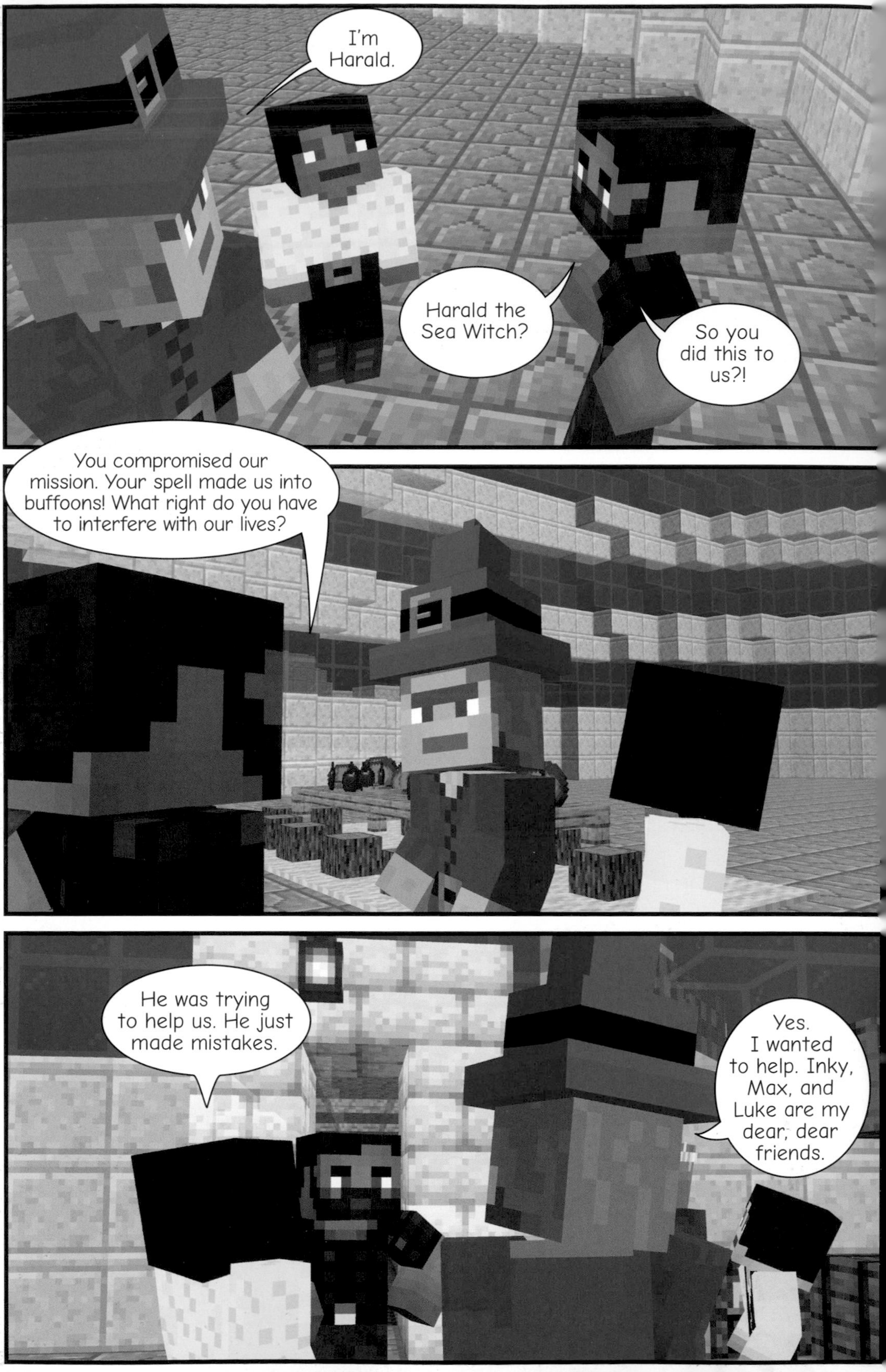
I'm Harald.
Harald the Sea Witch?
So you did this to us?!
You compromised our mission. Your spell made us into buffoons! What right do you have to interfere with our lives?
He was trying to help us. He just made mistakes.
Yes. I wanted to help. Inky, Max, and Luke are my dear, dear friends.

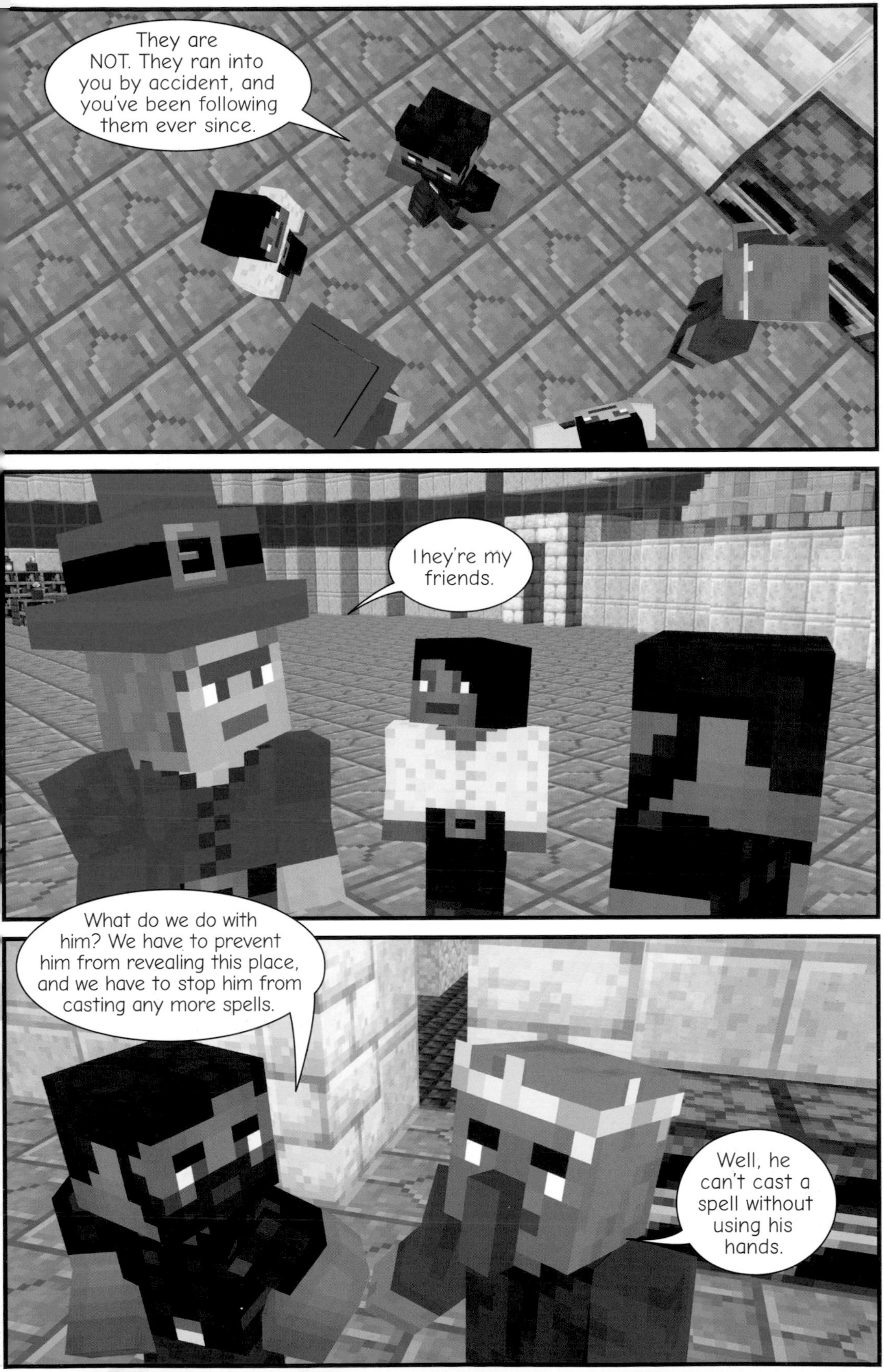
They are NOT. They ran into you by accident, and you've been following them ever since.
They're my friends.
What do we do with him? We have to prevent him from revealing this place, and we have to stop him from casting any more spells.
Well, he can't cast a spell without using his hands.

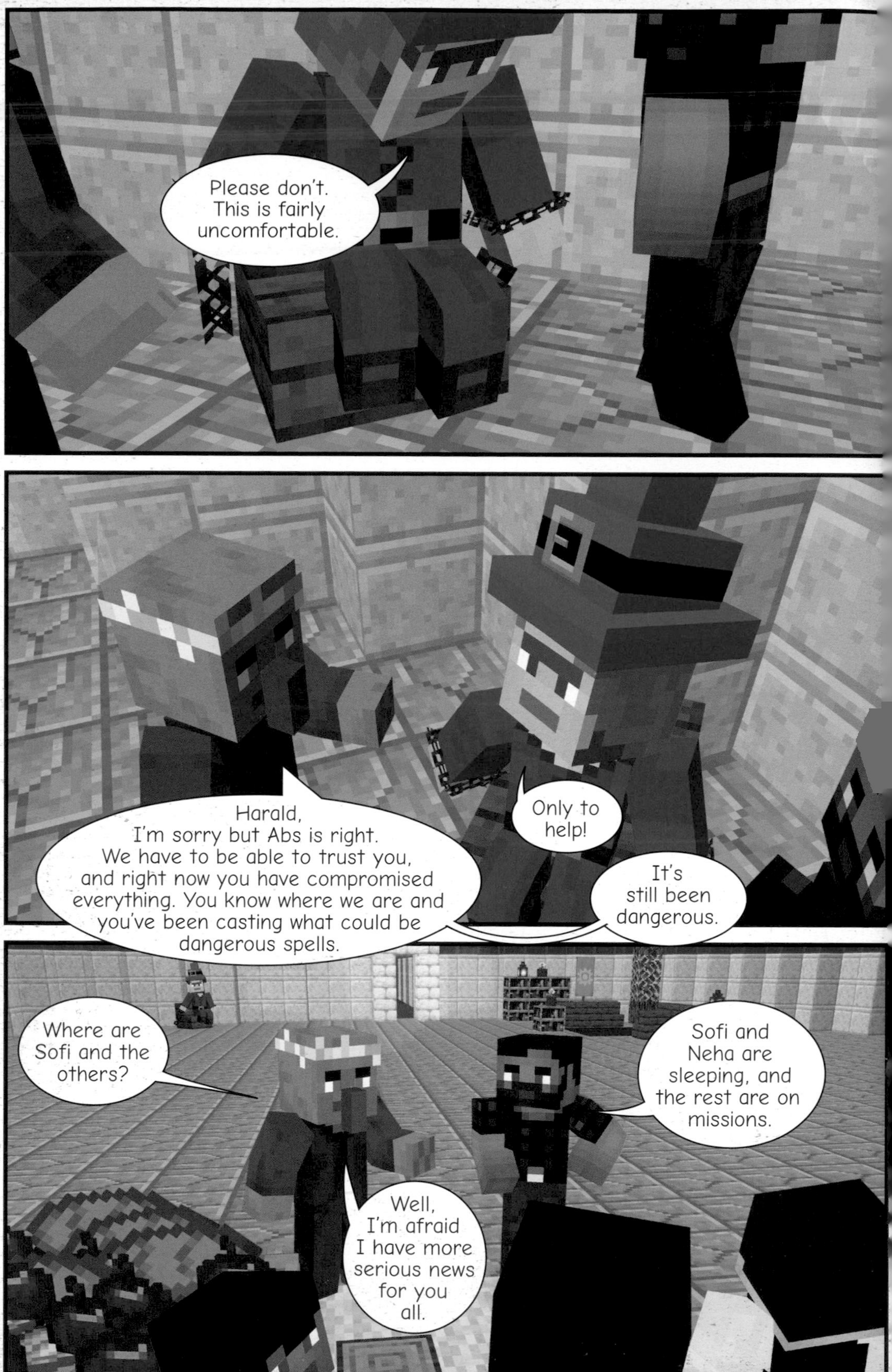
Please don't. This is fairly uncomfortable.
Harald, I'm sorry but Abs is right. We have to be able to trust you, and right now you have compromised everything. You know where we are and you've been casting what could be dangerous spells.
Only to help!
It's still been dangerous.
Where are Sofi and the others?
Sofi and Neha are sleeping, and the rest are on missions.
Well, I'm afraid I have more serious news for you all.

Chapter 11
Enemy Arrival

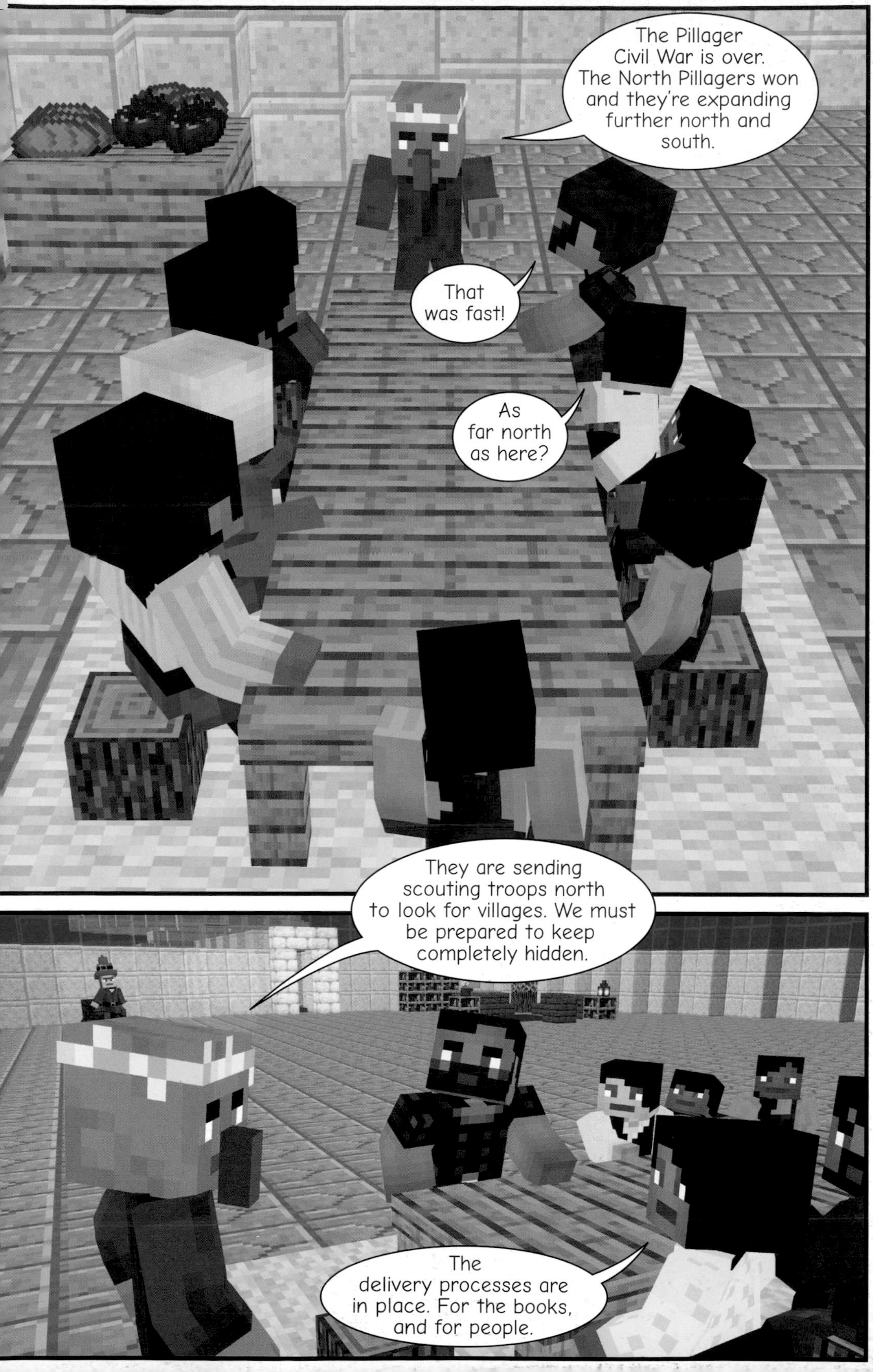
The Pillager Civil War is over. The North Pillagers won and they're expanding further north and south.
That was fast!
As far north as here?
They are sending scouting troops north to look for villages. We must be prepared to keep completely hidden.
The delivery processes are in place. For the books, and for people.

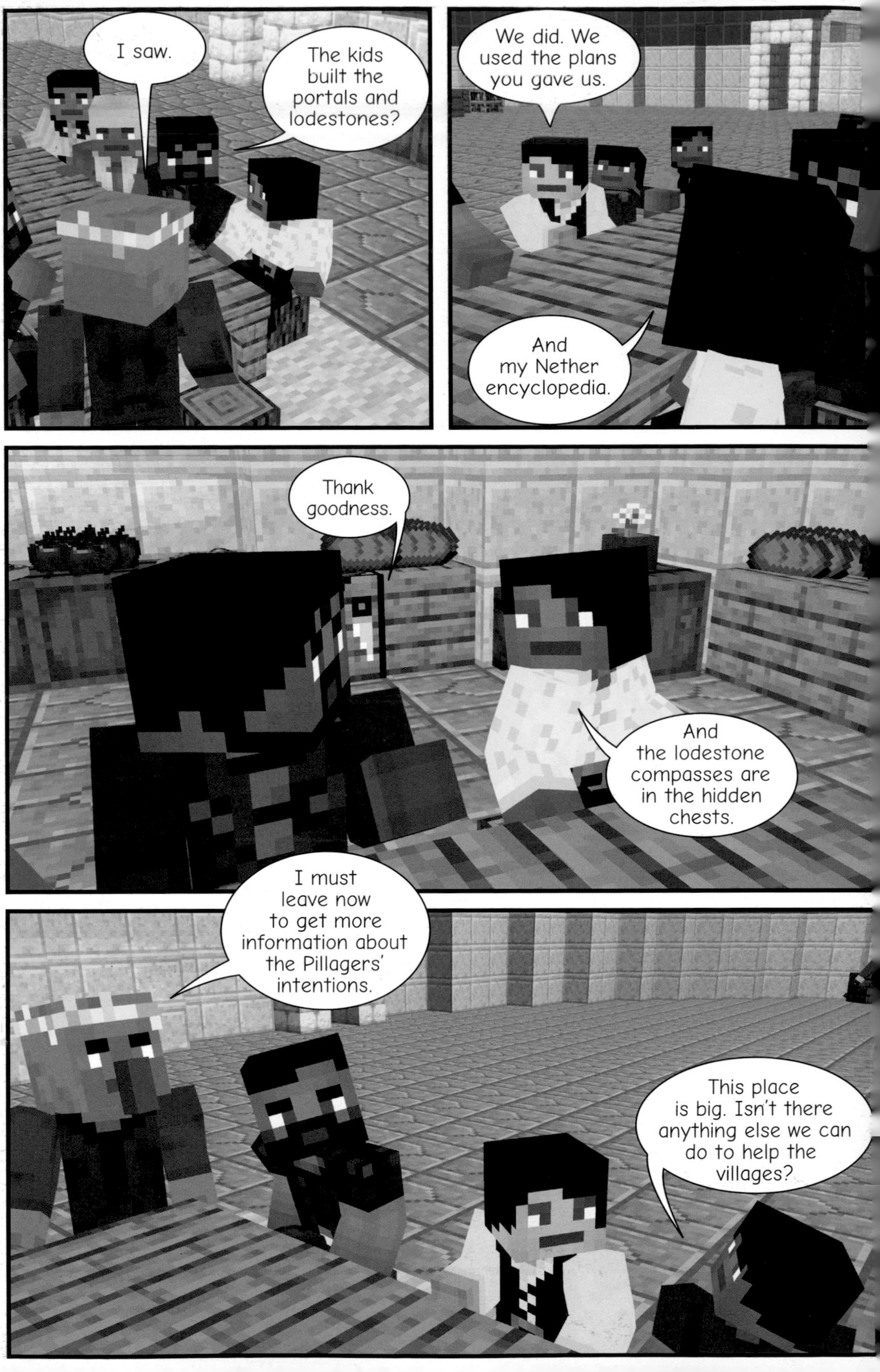
I saw.
The kids built the portals and lodestones?
We did. We used the plans you gave us.
And my Nether encyclopedia.
Thank goodness.
And the lodestone compasses are in the hidden chests.
I must leave now to get more information about the Pillagers' intentions.
This place is big. Isn't there anything else we can do to help the villages?

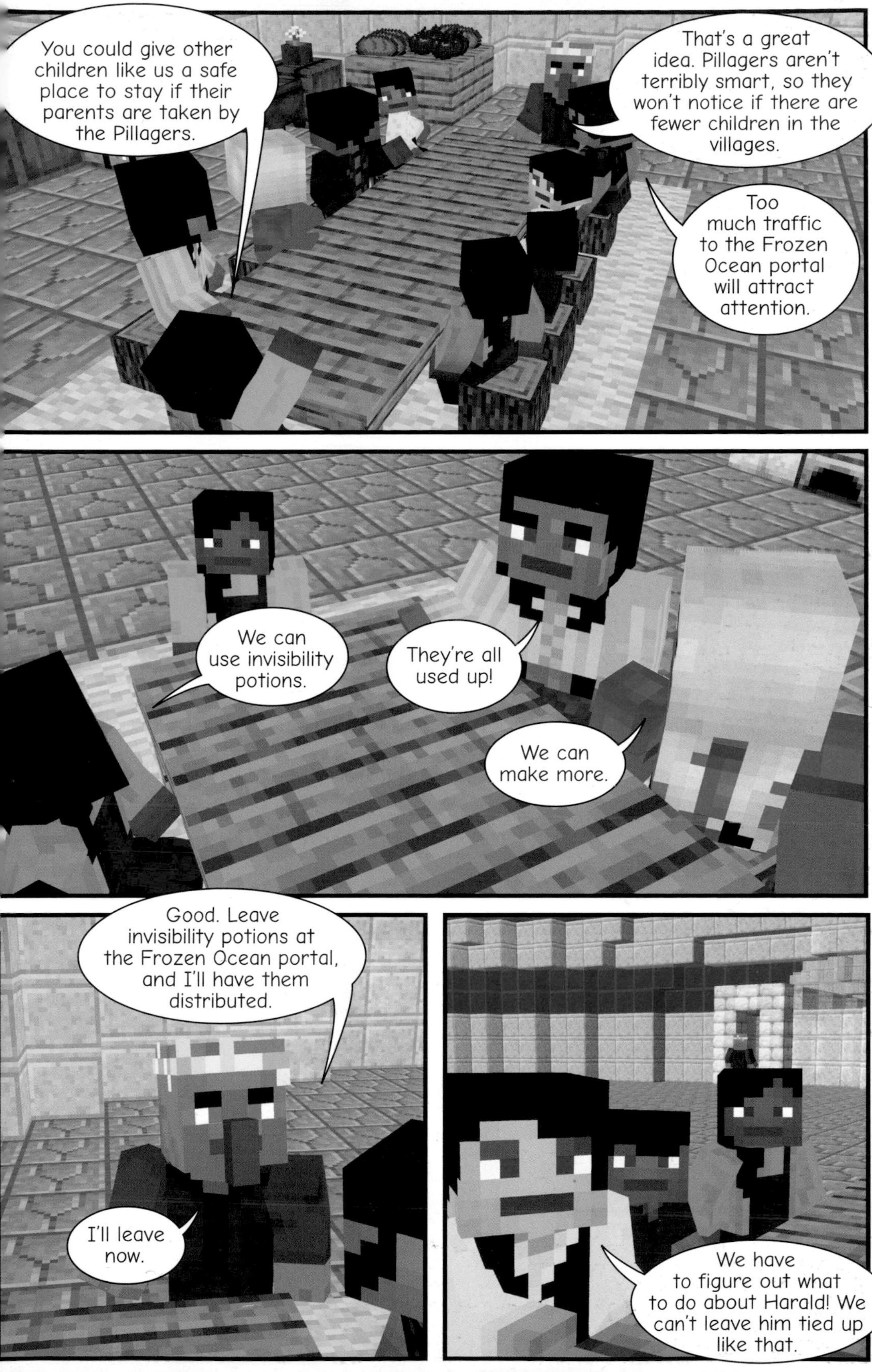

You could give other children like us a safe place to stay if their parents are taken by the Pillagers.
That's a great idea. Pillagers aren't terribly smart, so they won't notice if there are fewer children in the villages.
Too much traffic to the Frozen Ocean portal will attract attention.
We can use invisibility potions.
They're all used up!
We can make more.
Good. Leave invisibility potions at the Frozen Ocean portal, and I'll have them distributed.
I'll leave now.
We have to figure out what to do about Harald! We can't leave him tied up like that.

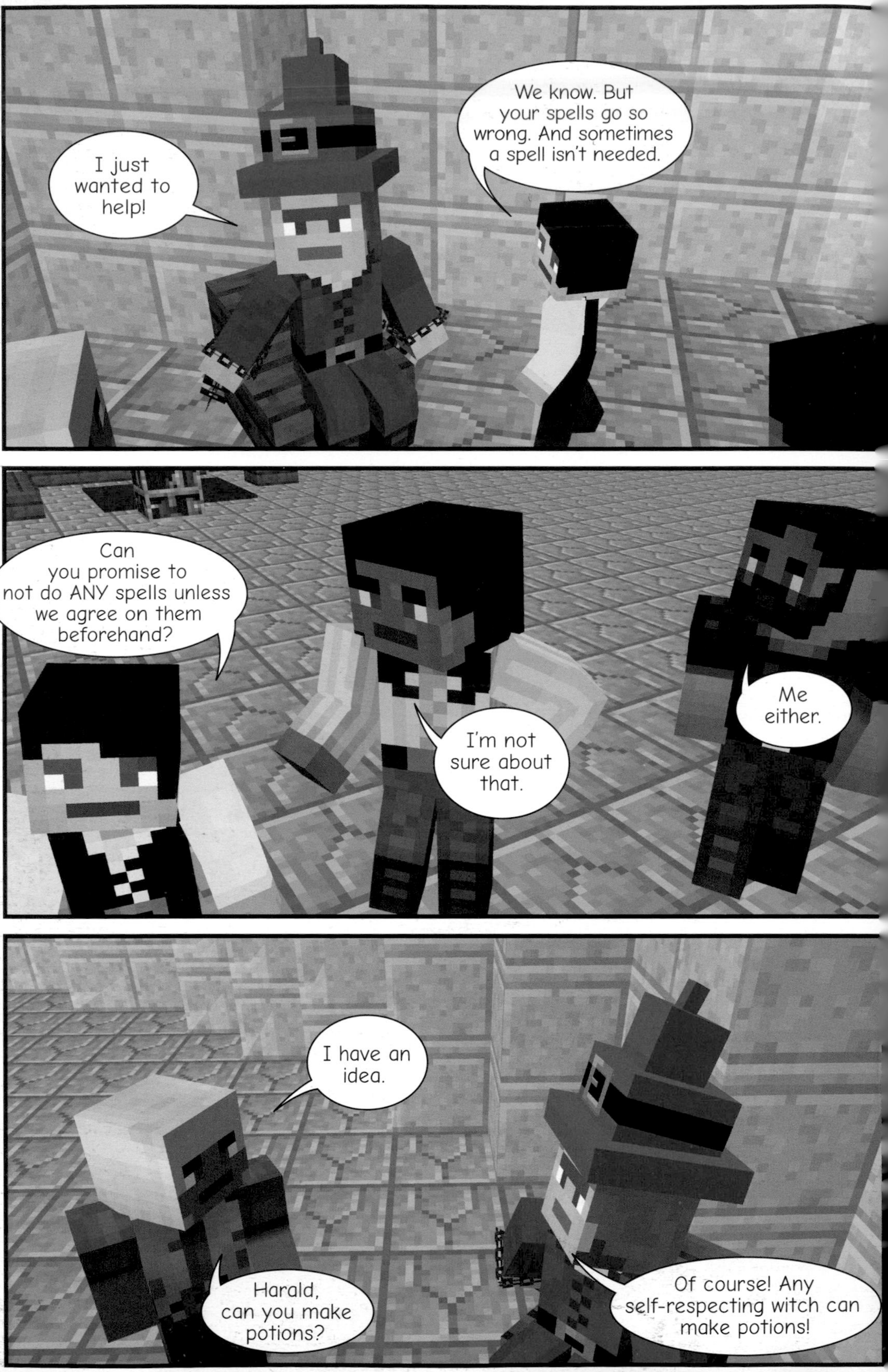
I just wanted to help!
We know. But your spells go so wrong. And sometimes a spell isn't needed.
Can you promise to not do ANY spells unless we agree on them beforehand?
I'm not sure about that.
Me either.
I have an idea.
Harald, can you make potions?
Of course! Any self-respecting witch can make potions!

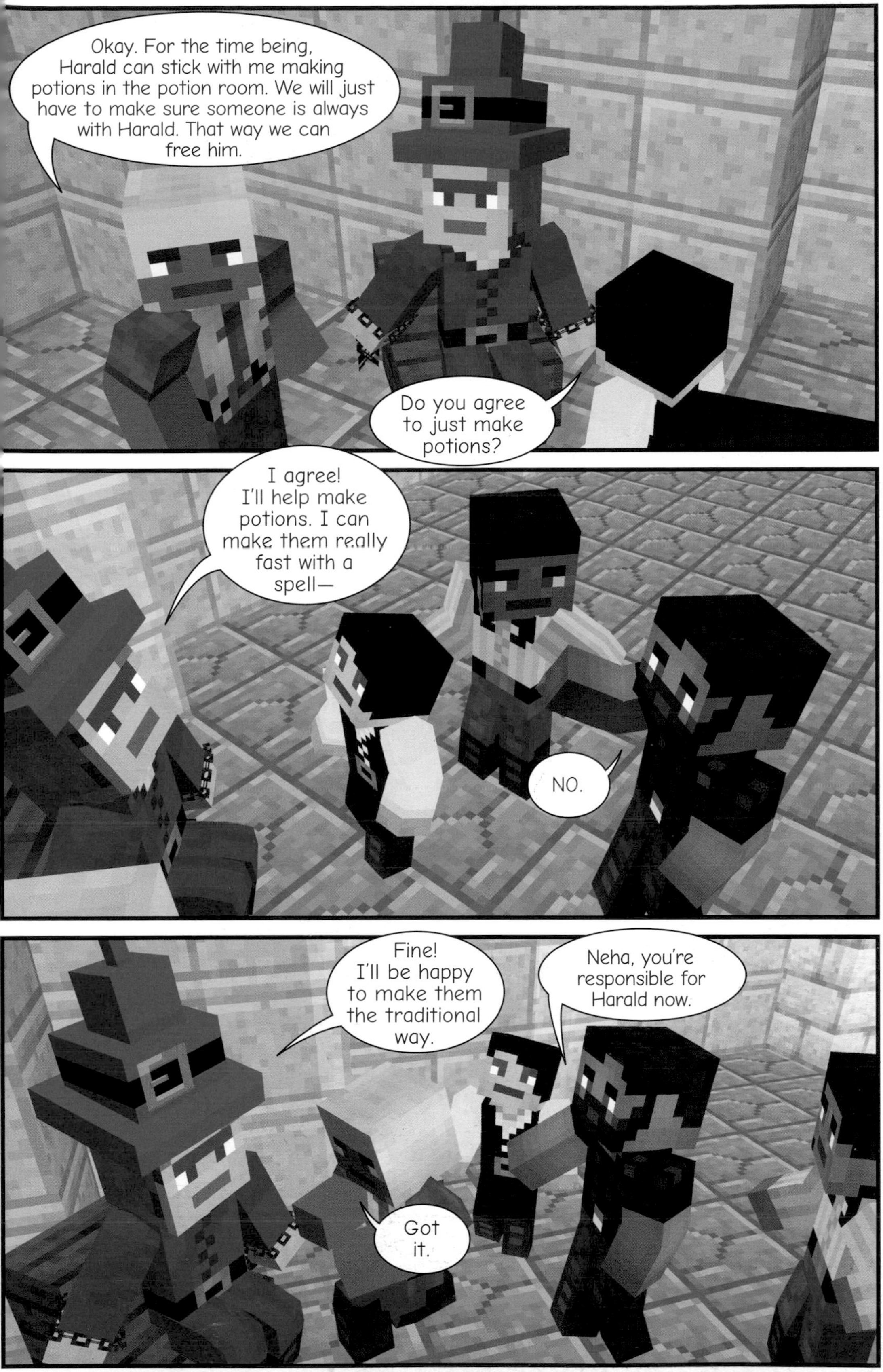
Okay. For the time being, Harald can stick with me making potions in the potion room. We will just have to make sure someone is always with Harald. That way we can free him.
Do you agree to just make potions?
I agree! I'll help make potions. I can make them really fast with a spell—
NO.
Fine! I'll be happy to make them the traditional way.
Neha, you're responsible for Harald now.
Got it.

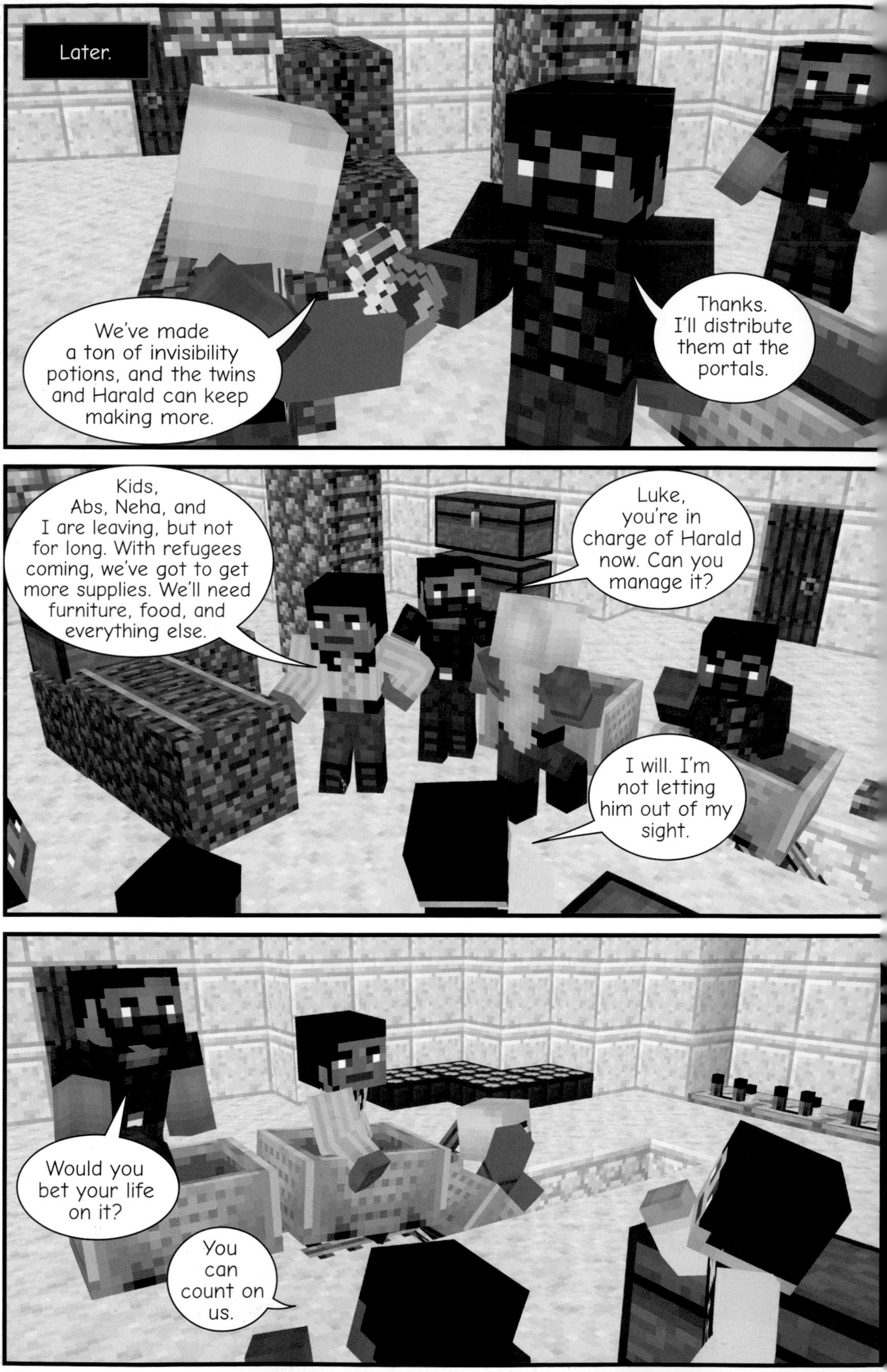

Later.
We've made a ton of invisibility potions, and the twins and Harald can keep making more.
Thanks. I'll distribute them at the portals.
Kids, Abs, Neha, and I are leaving, but not for long. With refugees coming, we've got to get more supplies. We'll need furniture, food, and everything else.
Luke, you're in charge of Harald now. Can you manage it?
I will. I'm not letting him out of my sight.
Would you bet your life on it?
You can count on us.

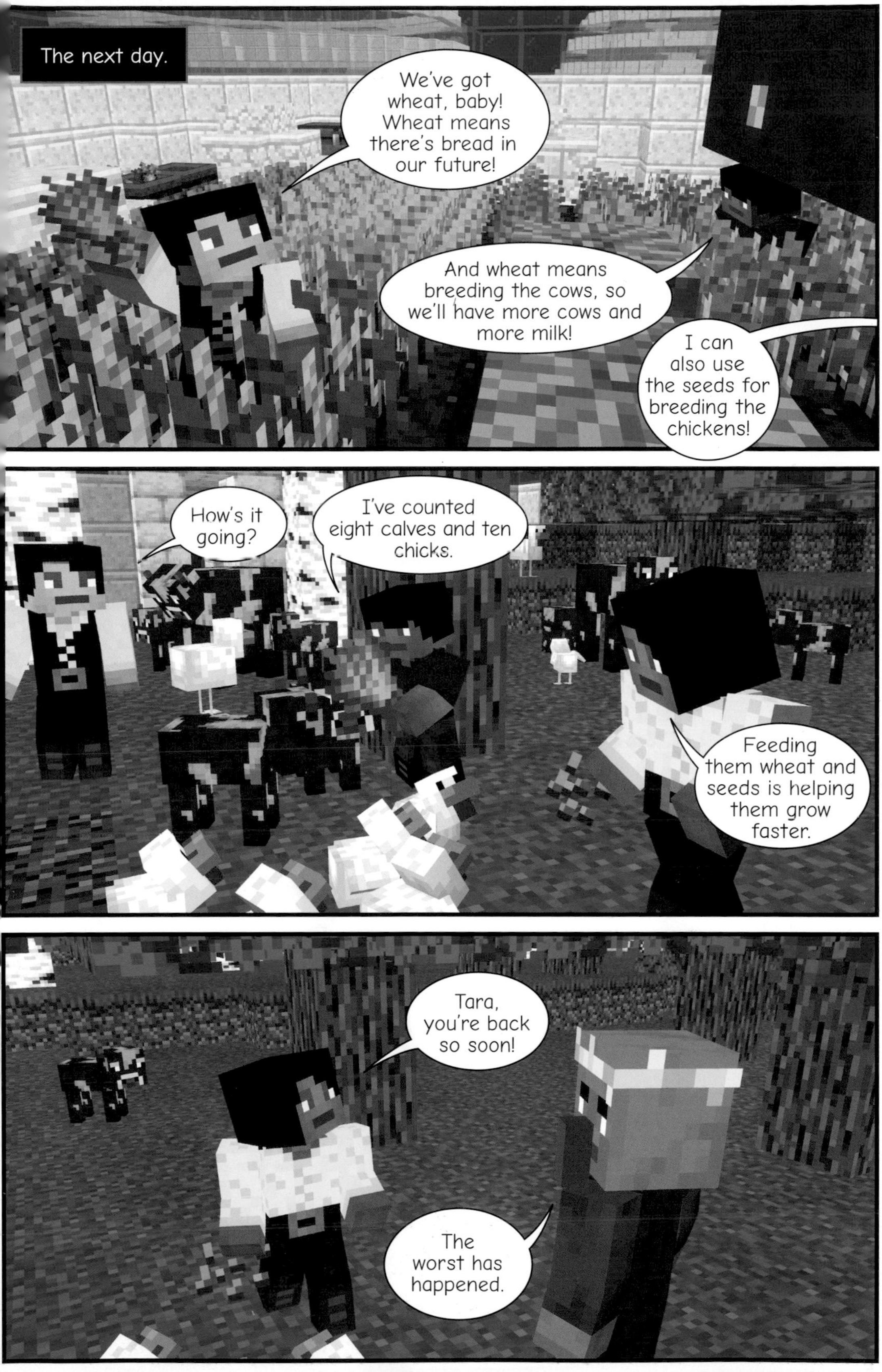
The next day.
We've got wheat, baby! Wheat means there's bread in our future!
And wheat means breeding the cows, so we'll have more cows and more milk!
I can also use the seeds for breeding the chickens!
How's it going?
I've counted eight calves and ten chicks.
Feeding them wheat and seeds is helping them grow faster.
Tara, you're back so soon!
The worst has happened.

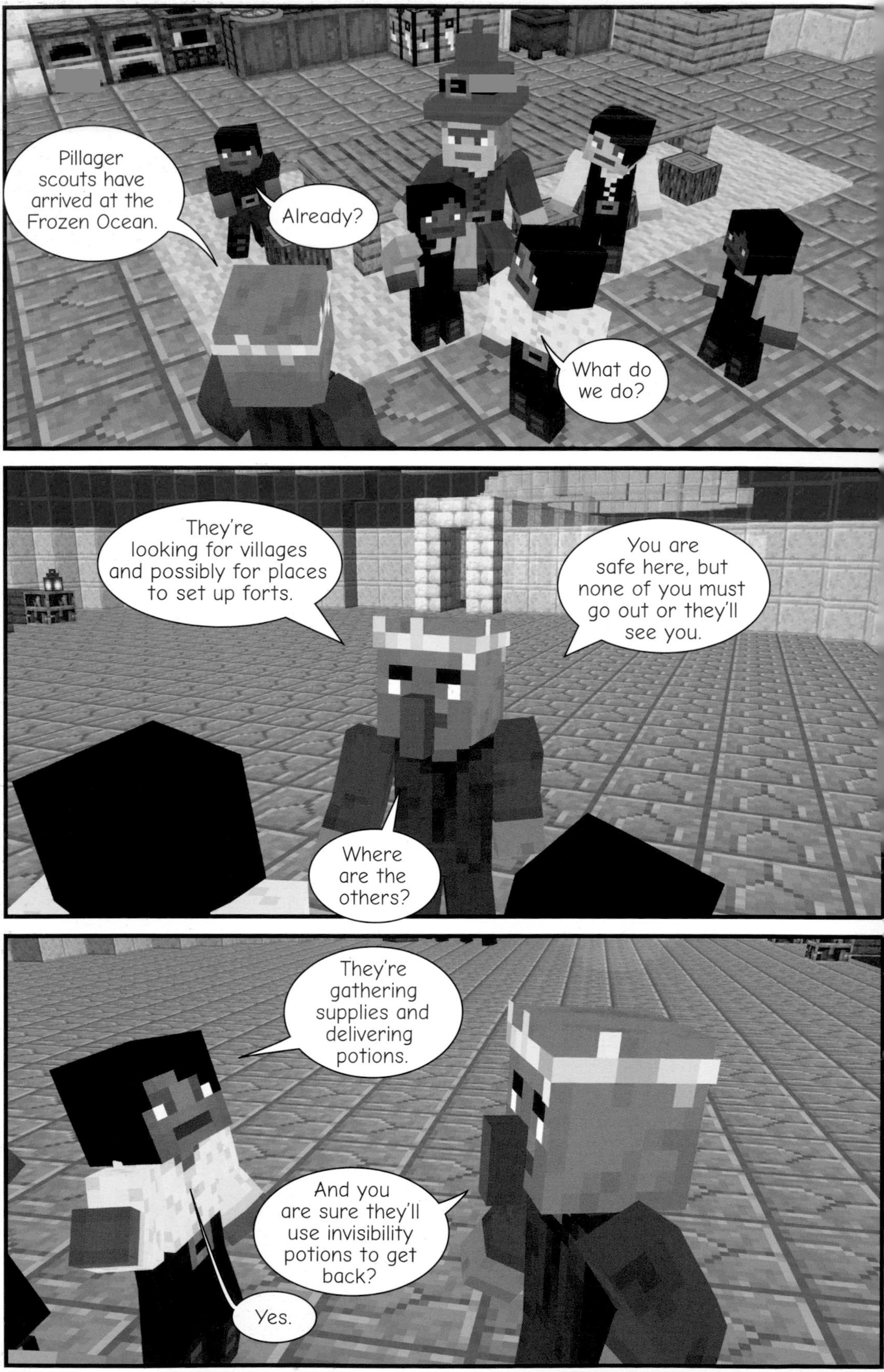
Pillager scouts have arrived at the Frozen Ocean.
Already?
What do we do?
They're looking for villages and possibly for places to set up forts.
You are safe here, but none of you must go out or they'll see you.
Where are the others?
They're gathering supplies and delivering potions.
And you are sure they'll use invisibility potions to get back?
Yes.

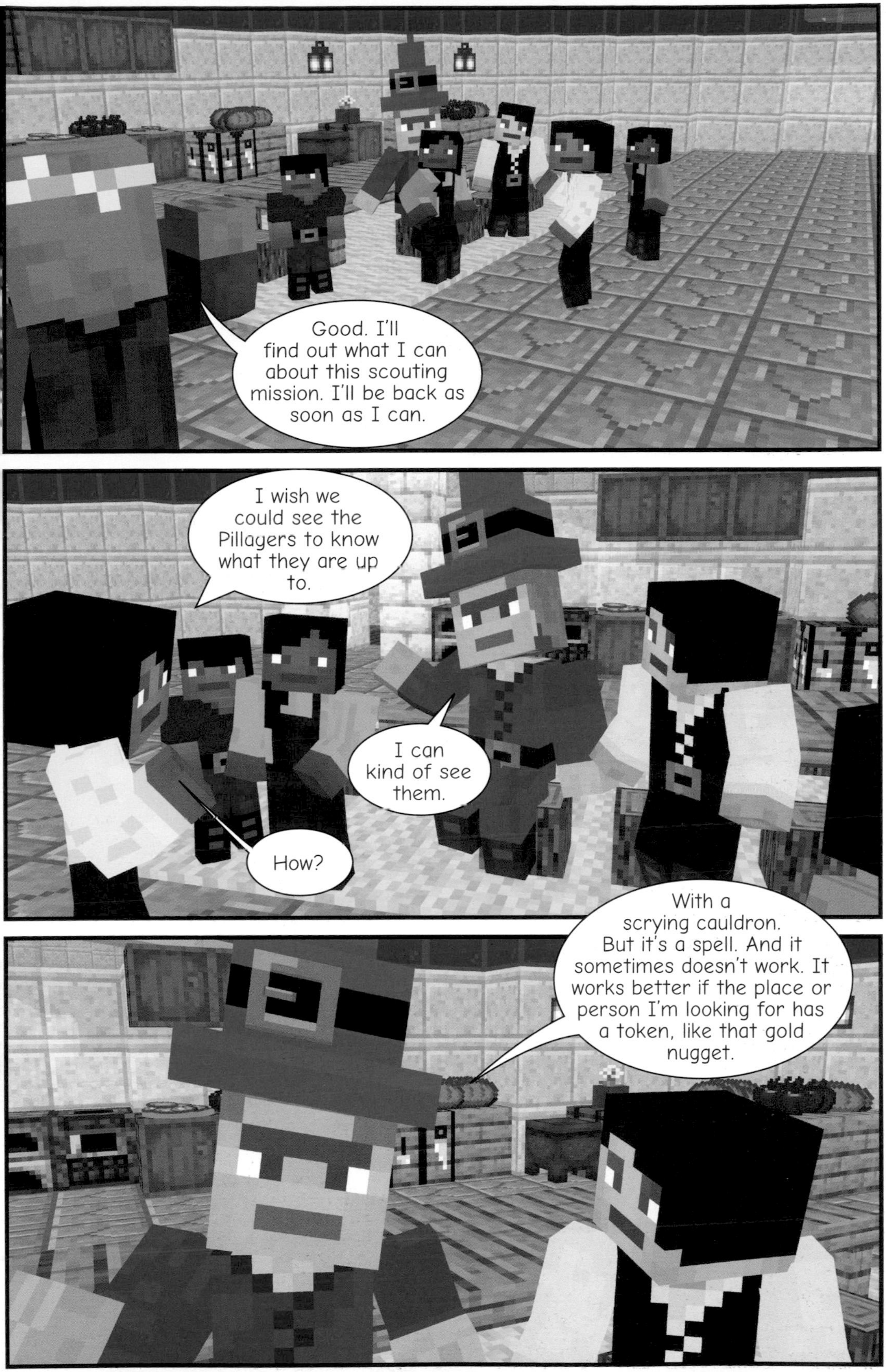
Good. I'll find out what I can about this scouting mission. I'll be back as soon as I can.
I wish we could see the Pillagers to know what they are up to.
I can kind of see them.
How?
With a scrying cauldron. But it's a spell. And it sometimes doesn't work. It works better if the place or person I'm looking for has a token, like that gold nugget.

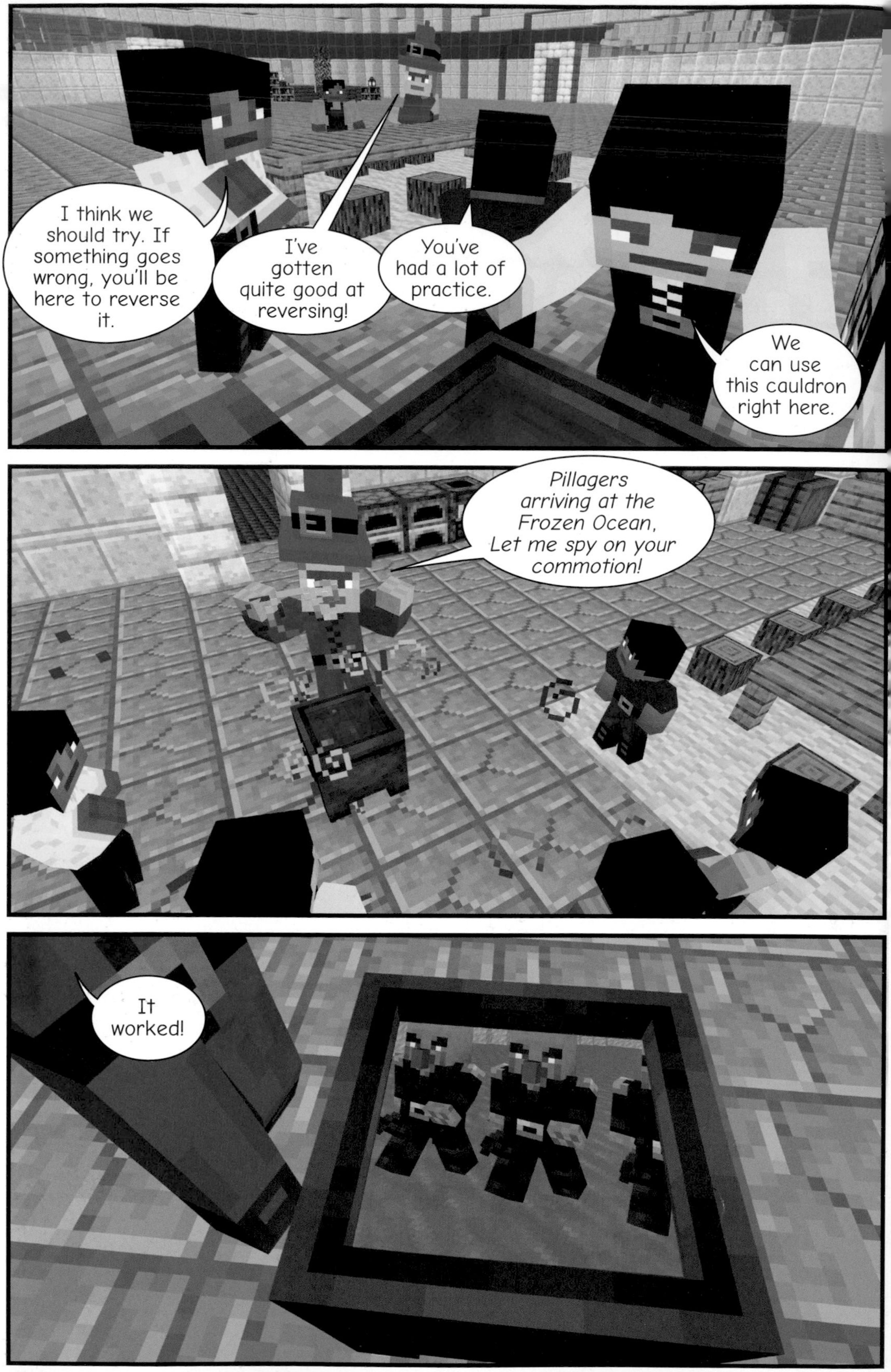
I think we should try. If something goes wrong, you'll be here to reverse it.
I've gotten quite good at reversing!
You've had a lot of practice.
We can use this cauldron right here.
Pillagers arriving at the Frozen Ocean, Let me spy on your commotion!
It worked!

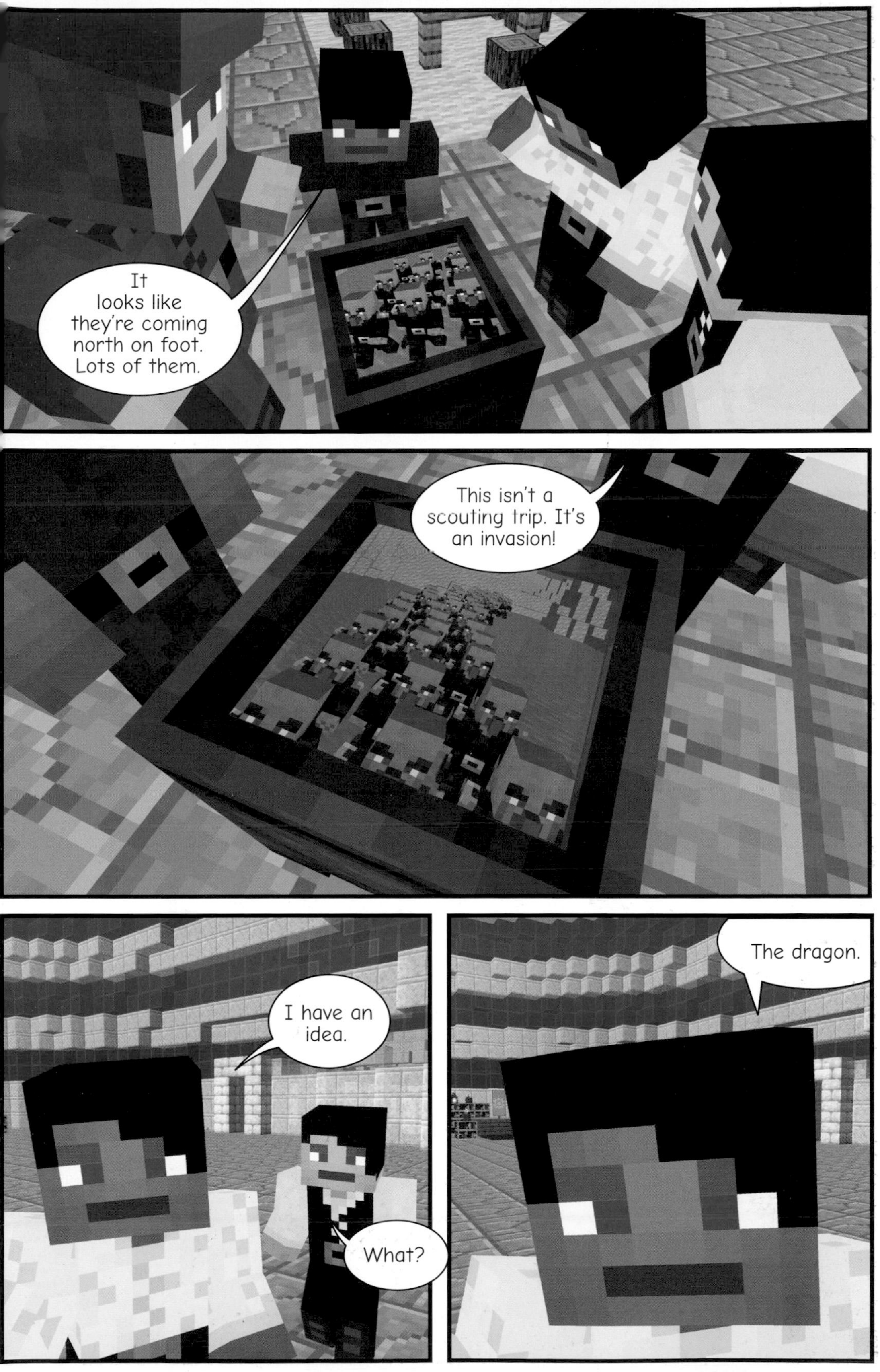
It looks like they're coming north on foot. Lots of them.
This isn't a scouting trip. It's an invasion!
I have an idea.
What?
The dragon.

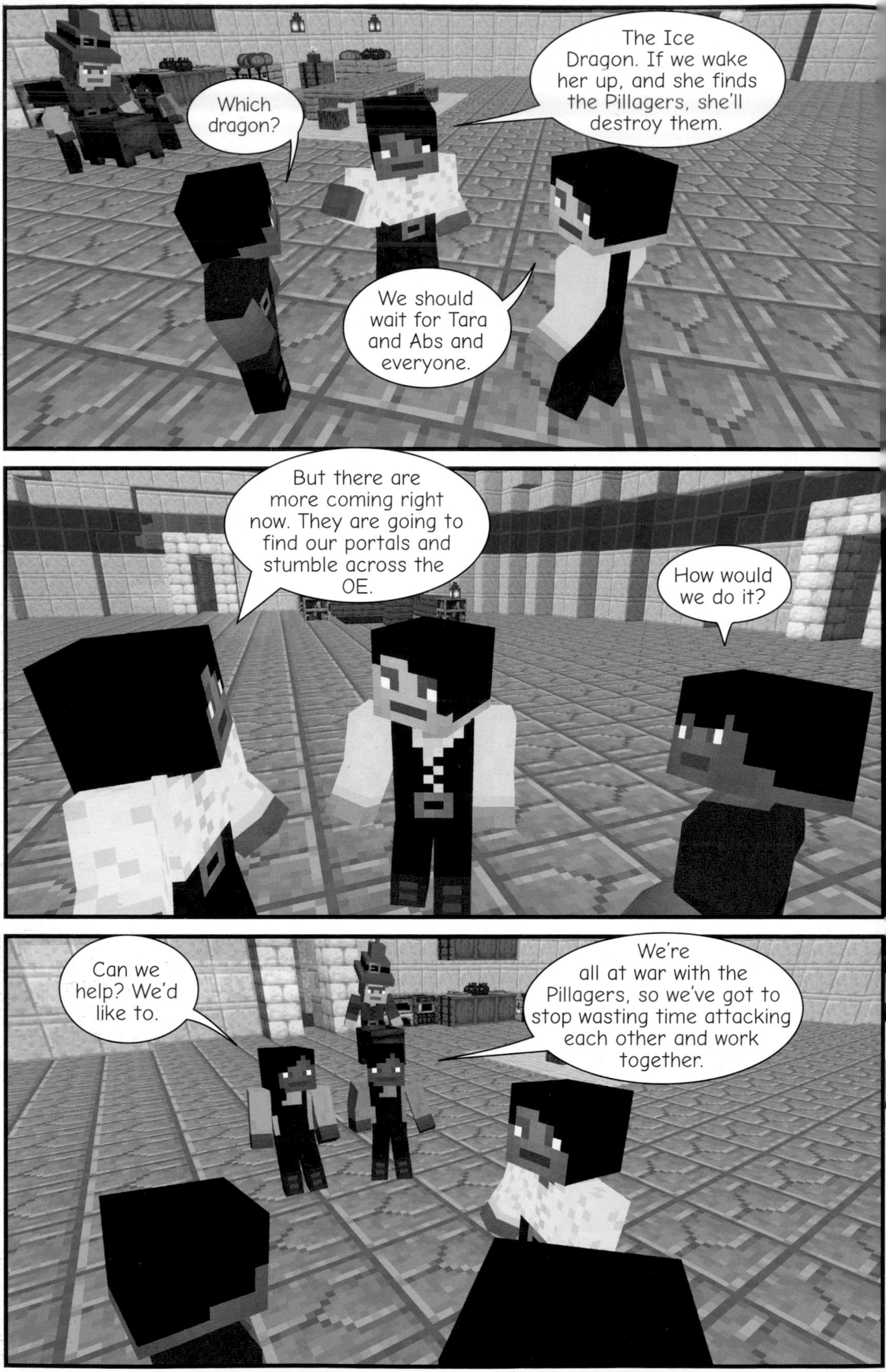
Which dragon?
The Ice Dragon. If we wake her up, and she finds the Pillagers, she'll destroy them.
We should wait for Tara and Abs and everyone.
But there are more coming right now. They are going to find our portals and stumble across the OE.
How would we do it?
Can we help? We'd like to.
We're all at war with the Pillagers, so we've got to stop wasting time attacking each other and work together.

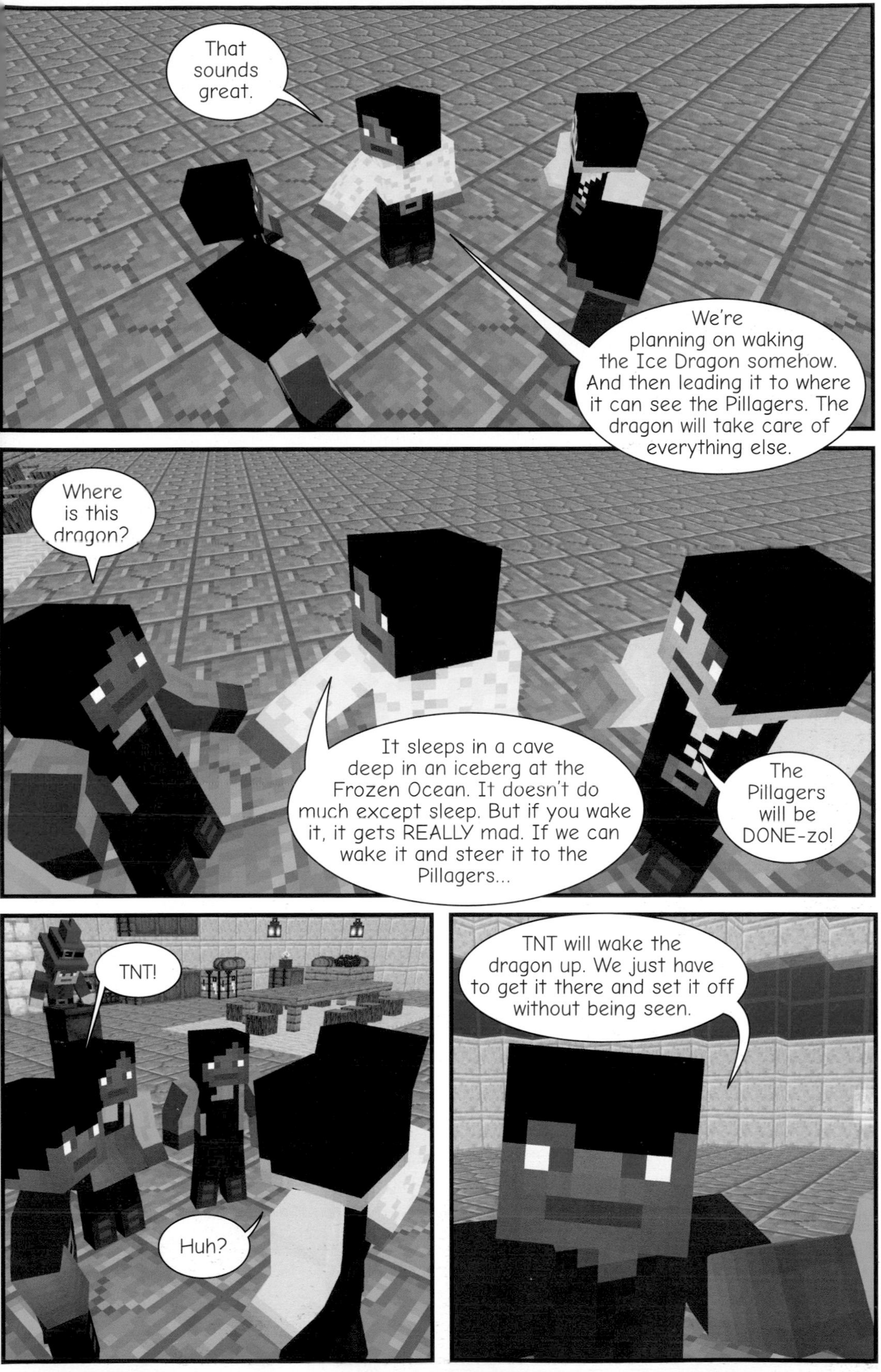
That sounds great.
We're planning on waking the Ice Dragon somehow. And then leading it to where it can see the Pillagers. The dragon will take care of everything else.
Where is this dragon?
It sleeps in a cave deep in an iceberg at the Frozen Ocean. It doesn't do much except sleep. But if you wake it, it gets REALLY mad. If we can wake it and steer it to the Pillagers...
The Pillagers will be DONE-zo!
TNT!
Huh?
TNT will wake the dragon up. We just have to get it there and set it off without being seen.

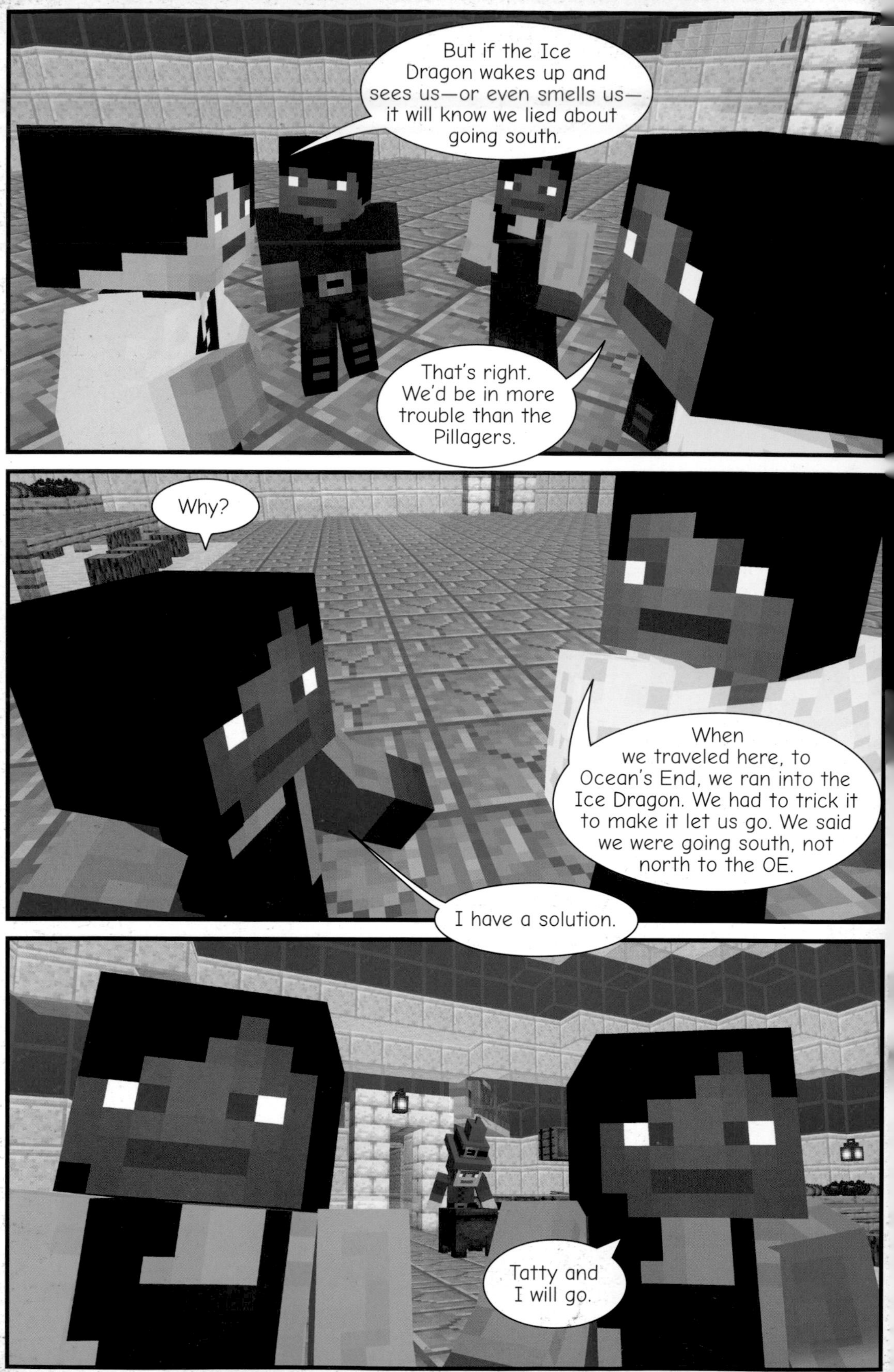
But if the Ice Dragon wakes up and sees us—or even smells us—it will know we lied about going south.
That's right. We'd be in more trouble than the Pillagers.
Why?
When we traveled here, to Ocean's End, we ran into the Ice Dragon. We had to trick it to make it let us go. We said we were going south, not north to the OE.
I have a solution.
Tatty and I will go.

Chapter 12
The Ice Dragon
Cometh

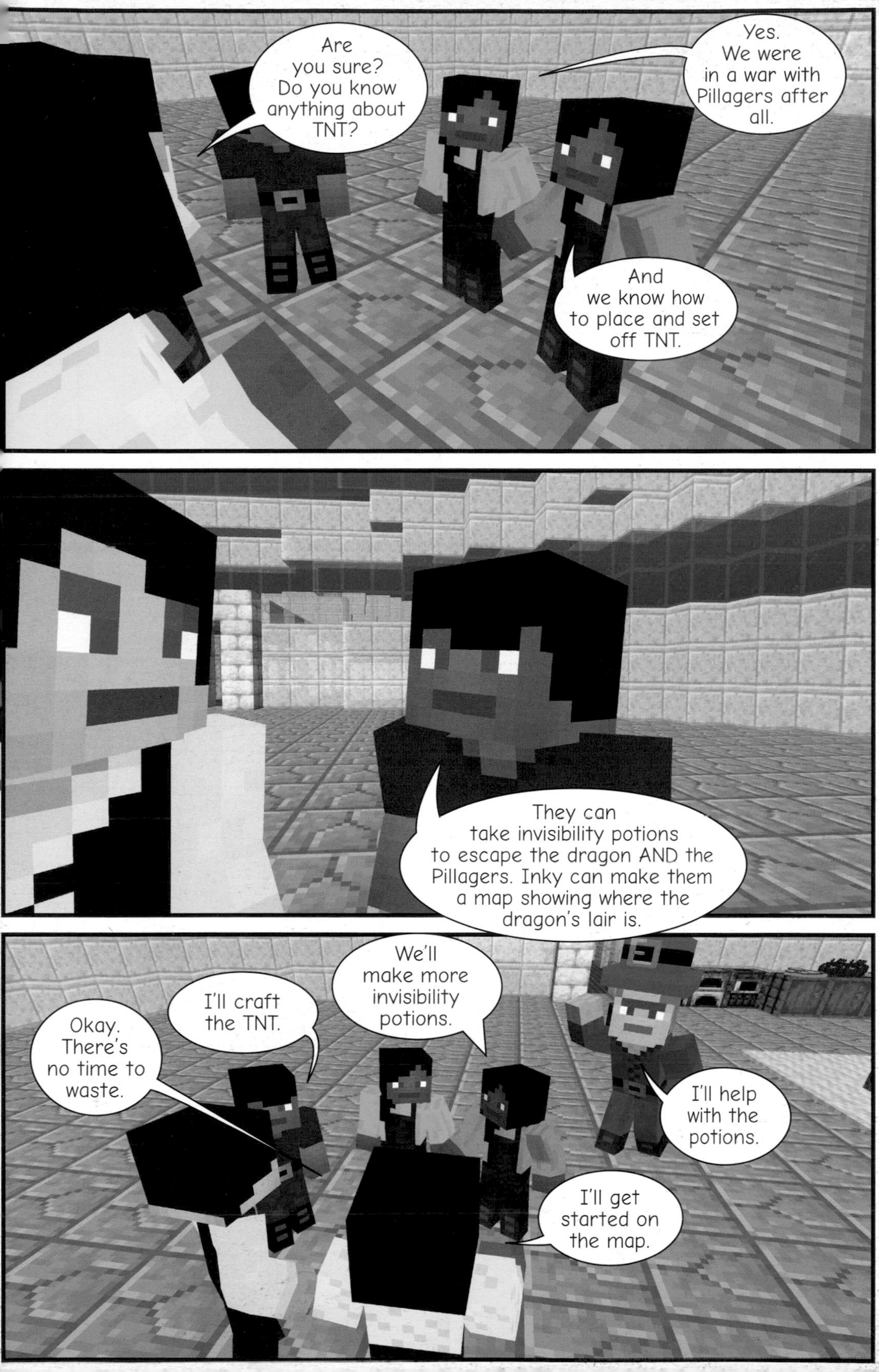
Are you sure? Do you know anything about TNT?
Yes. We were in a war with Pillagers after all.
And we know how to place and set off TNT.
They can take invisibility potions to escape the dragon AND the Pillagers. Inky can make them a map showing where the dragon's lair is.
Okay. There's no time to waste.
I'll craft the TNT.
We'll make more invisibility potions.
I'll help with the potions.
I'll get started on the map.

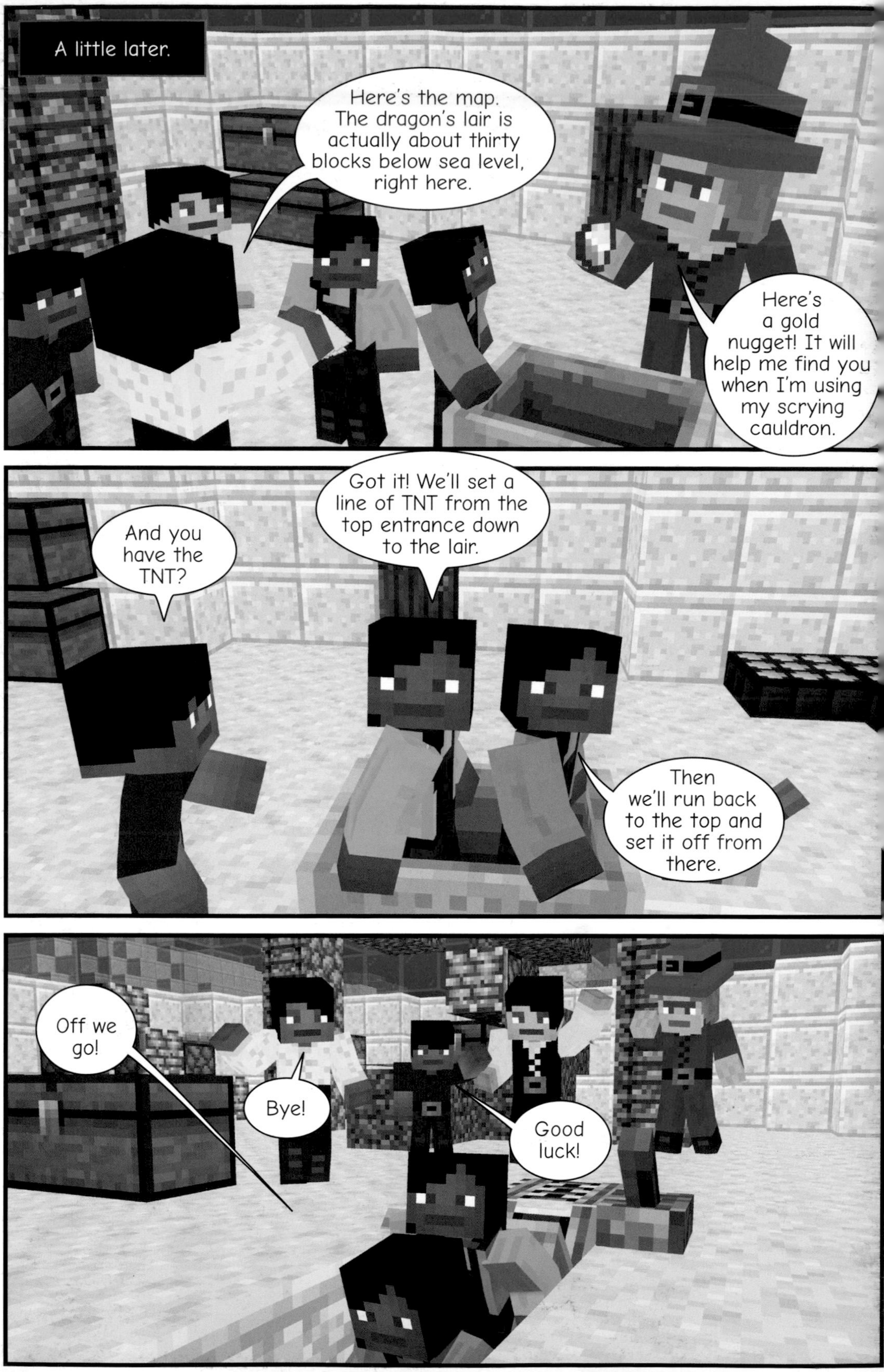
A little later.
Here's the map. The dragon's lair is actually about thirty blocks below sea level, right here.
Here's a gold nugget! It will help me find you when I'm using my scrying cauldron.
And you have the TNT?
Got it! We'll set a line of TNT from the top entrance down to the lair.
Then we'll run back to the top and set it off from there.
Off we go!
Bye!
Good luck!

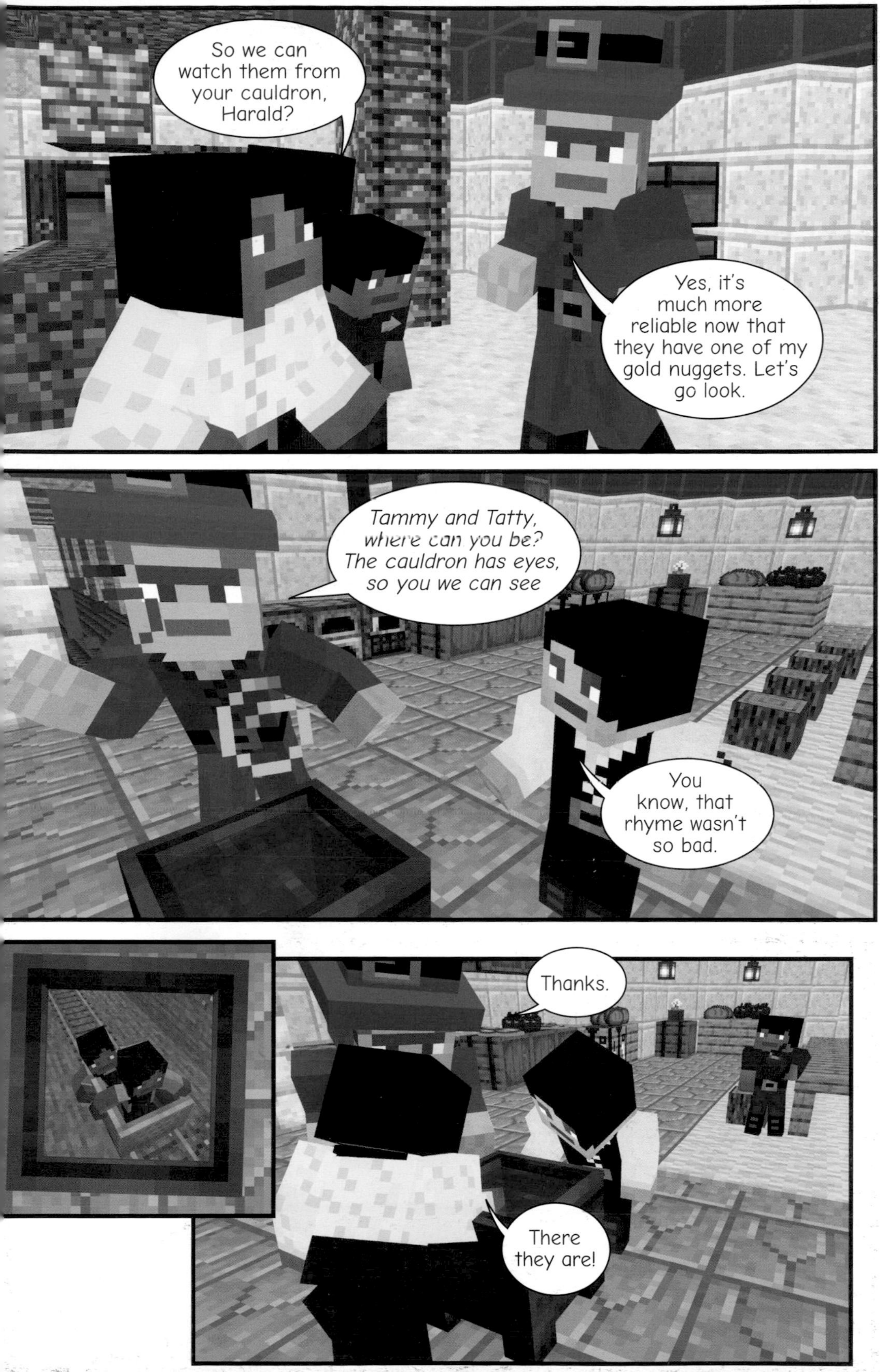
So we can watch them from your cauldron, Harald?
Yes, it's much more reliable now that they have one of my gold nuggets. Let's go look.
Tammy and Tatty, where can you be? The cauldron has eyes, so you we can see
You know, that rhyme wasn't so bad.
Thanks.
There they are!

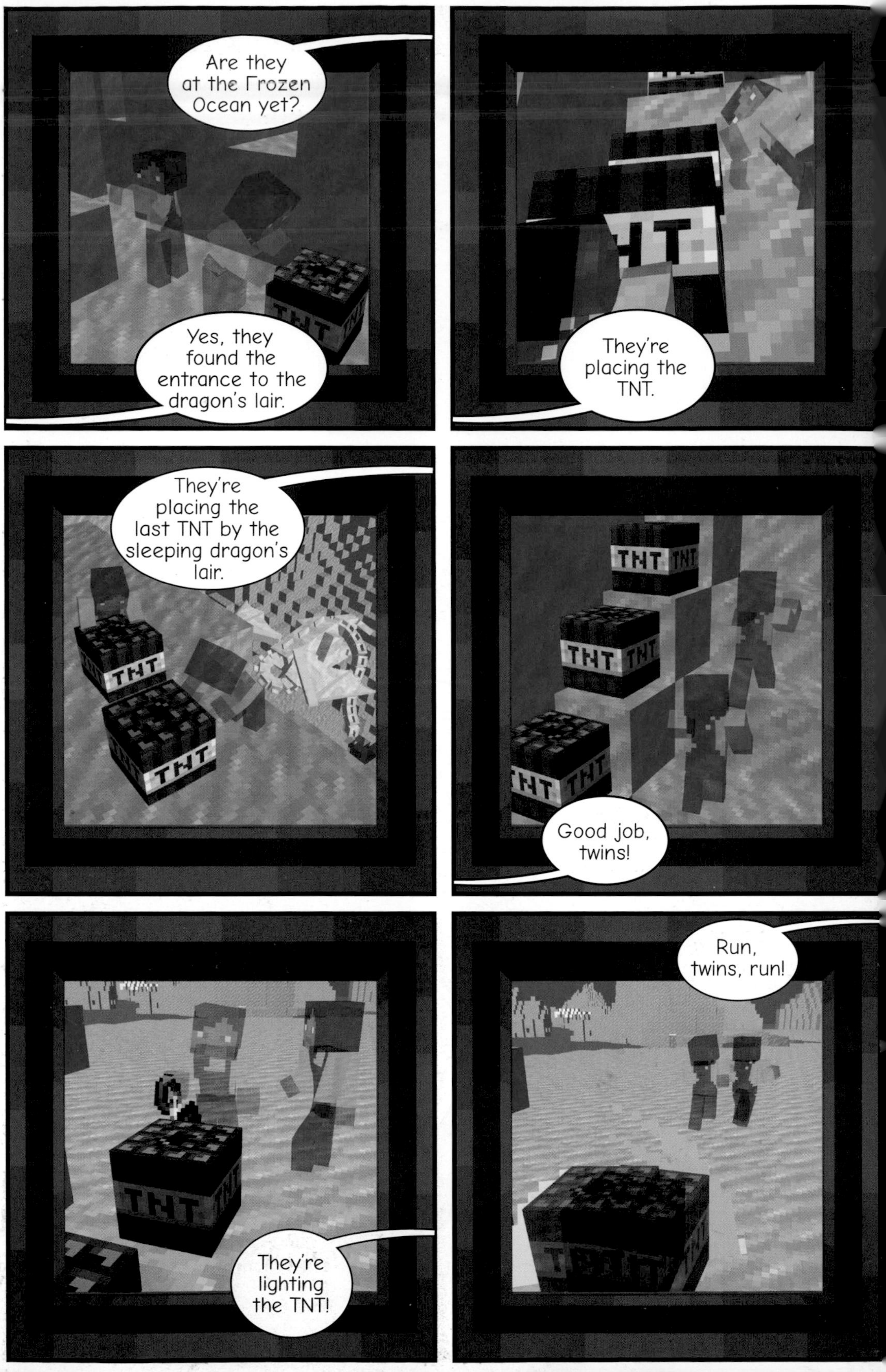
Are they at the Frozen Ocean yet?
Yes, they found the entrance to the dragon's lair.
They're placing the TNT.
They're placing the last TNT by the sleeping dragon's lair.
TNT
TNT
TNT
TNT
TNT
Good job, twins!
TNT
They're lighting the TNT!
Run, twins, run!

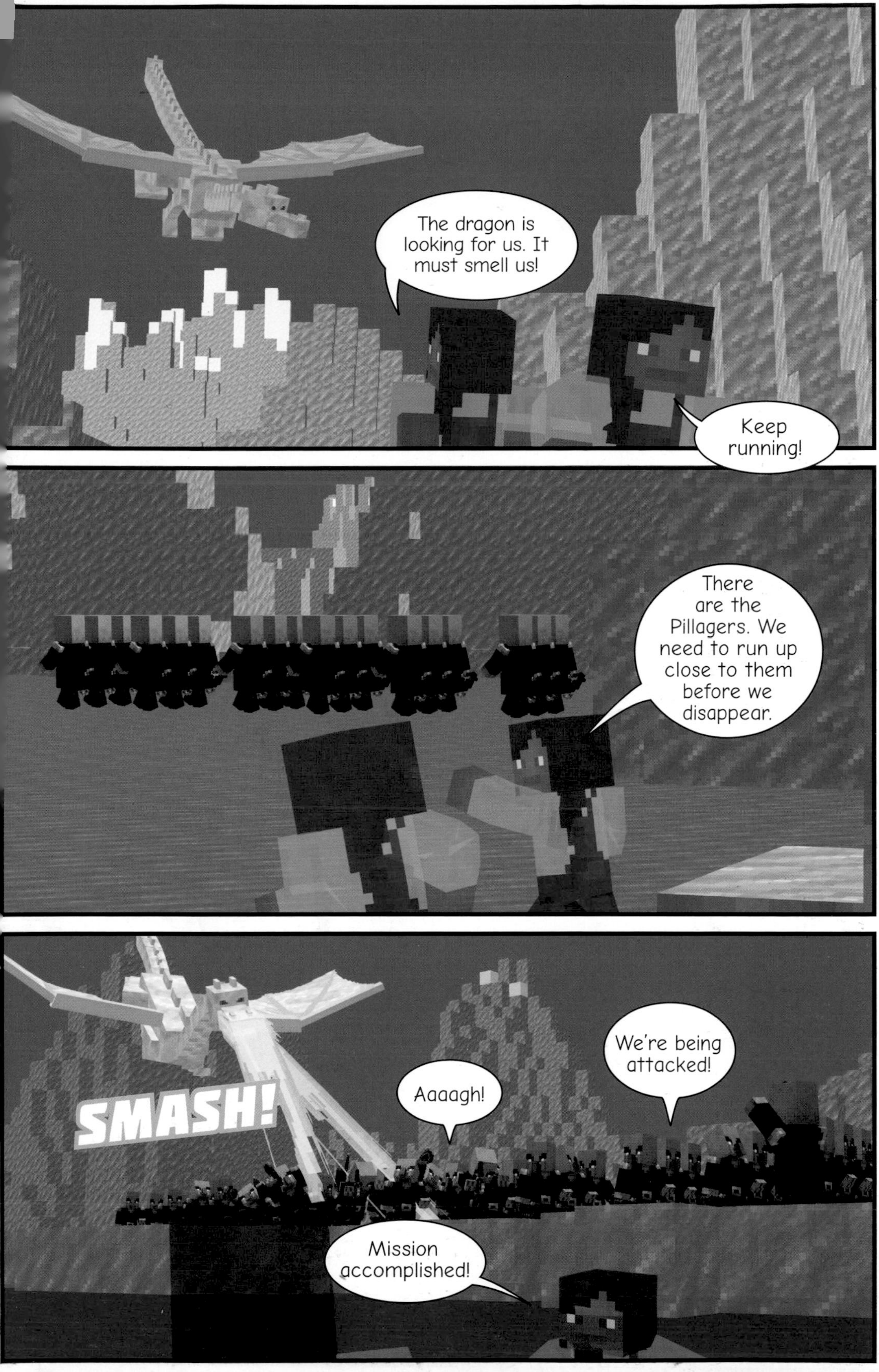

The dragon is looking for us. It must smell us!
Keep running!
There are the Pillagers. We need to run up close to them before we disappear.
SMASH!
Aaaagh!
We're being attacked!
Mission accomplished!

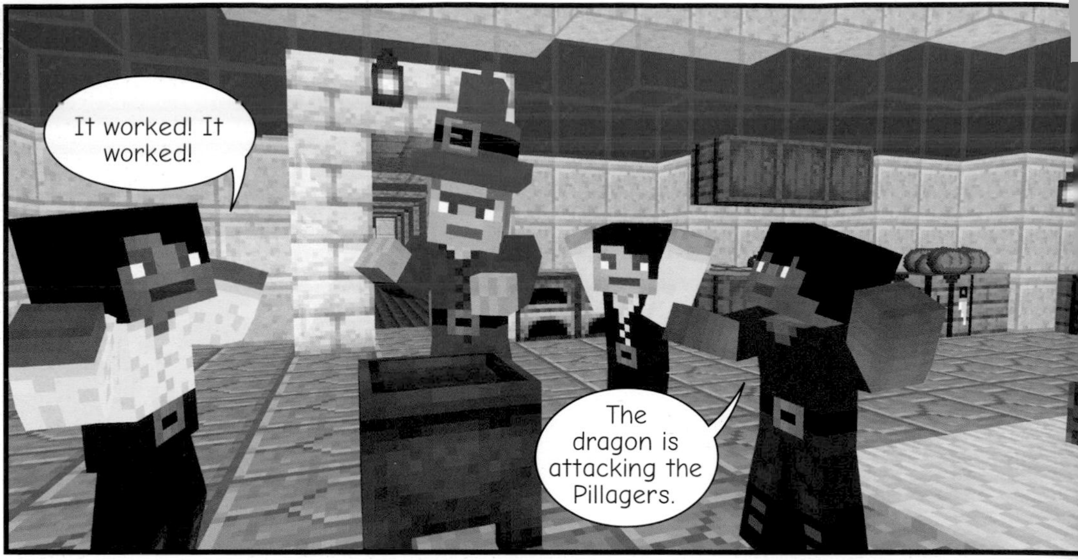
It worked! It worked!
The dragon is attacking the Pillagers.

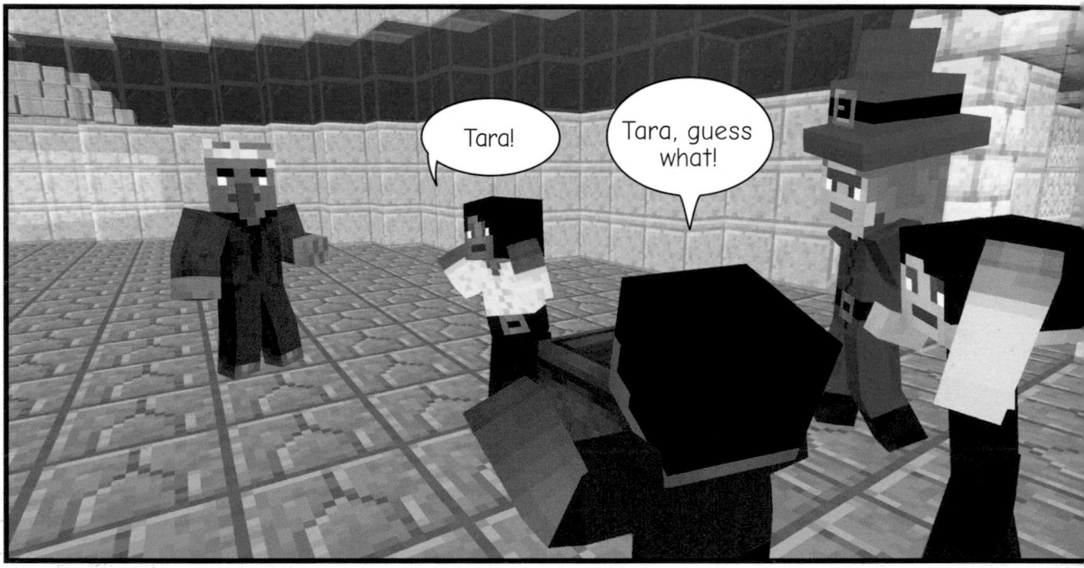
Tara!
Tara, guess what!

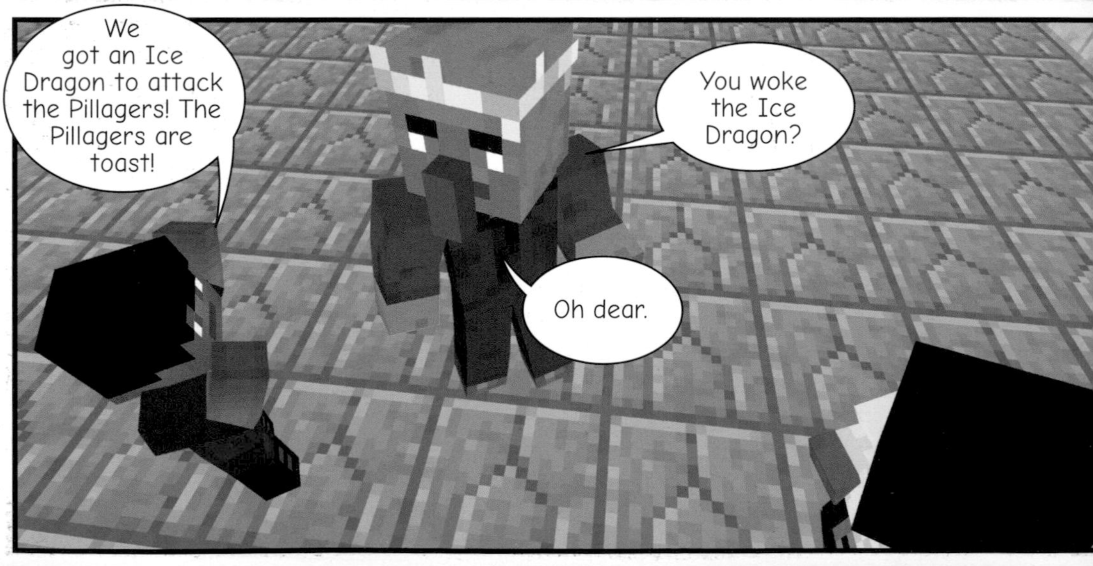
We got an Ice Dragon to attack the Pillagers! The Pillagers are toast!
You woke the Ice Dragon?
Oh dear.

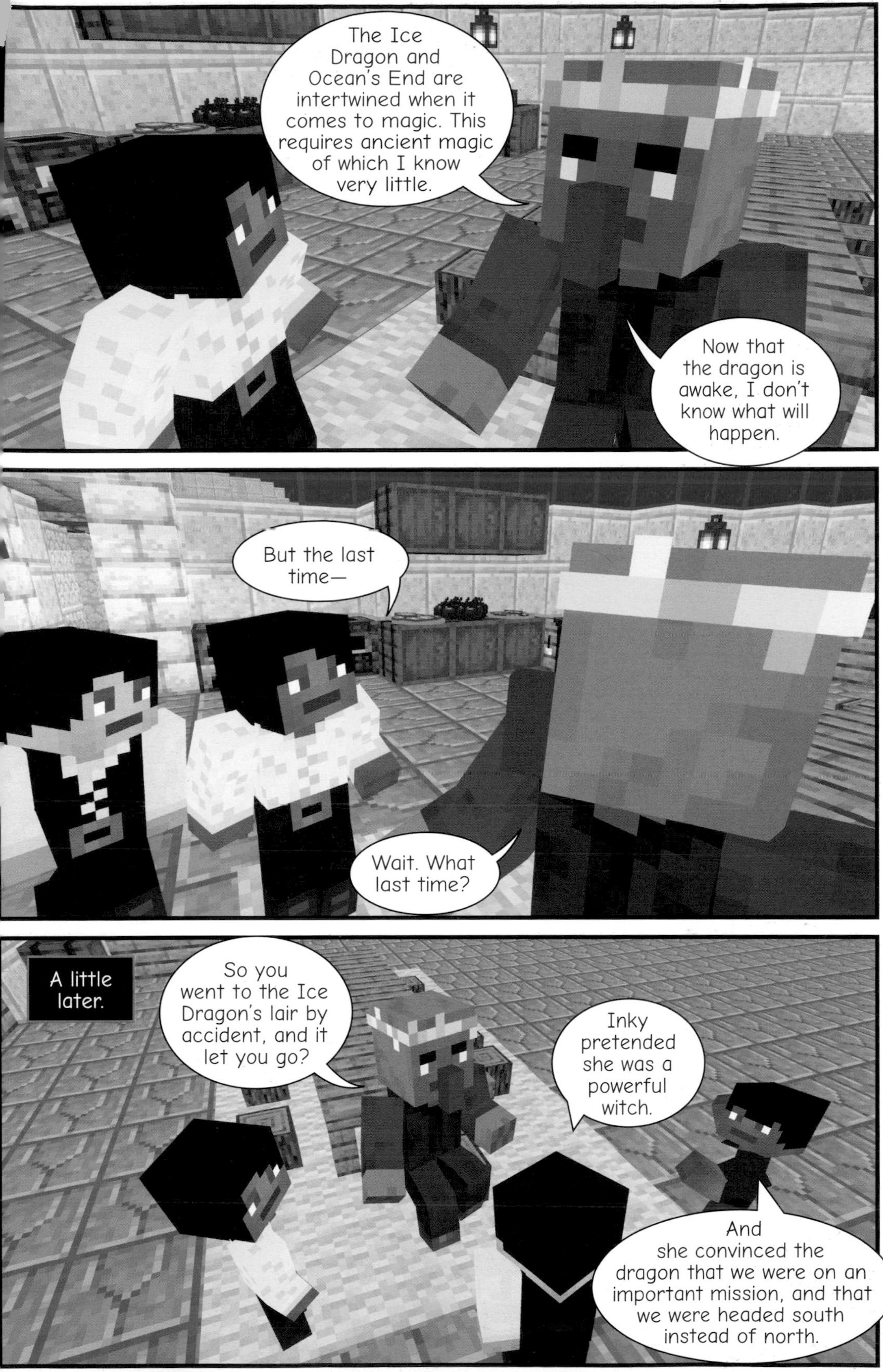

The Ice Dragon and Ocean's End are intertwined when it comes to magic. This requires ancient magic of which I know very little.
Now that the dragon is awake, I don't know what will happen.
But the last time—
Wait. What last time?
A little later.
So you went to the Ice Dragon's lair by accident, and it let you go?
Inky pretended she was a powerful witch.
And she convinced the dragon that we were on an important mission, and that we were headed south instead of north.

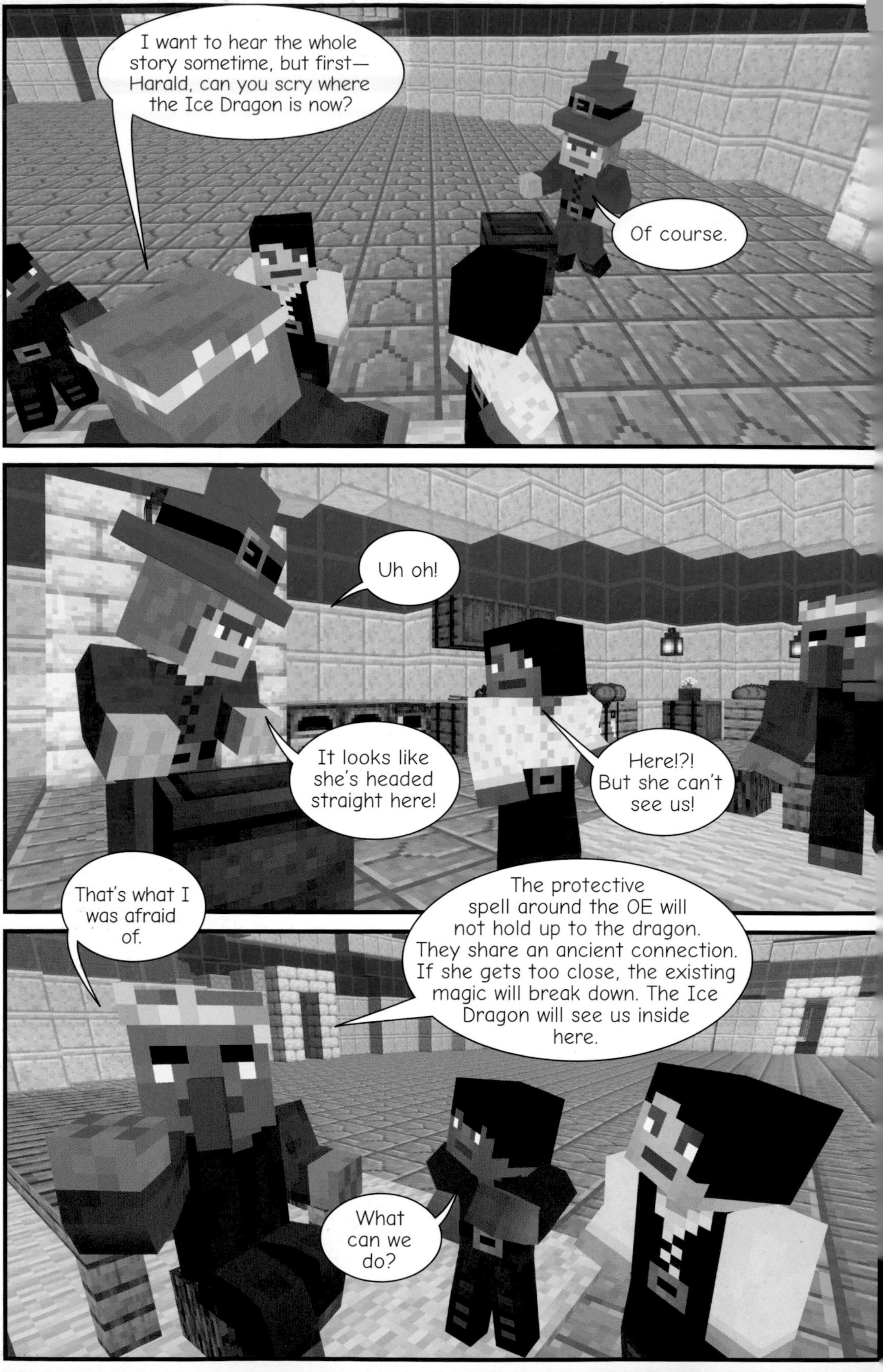
I want to hear the whole story sometime, but first—Harald, can you scry where the Ice Dragon is now?
Of course.
Uh oh!
It looks like she's headed straight here!
Here!?! But she can't see us!
That's what I was afraid of.
The protective spell around the OE will not hold up to the dragon. They share an ancient connection. If she gets too close, the existing magic will break down. The Ice Dragon will see us inside here.
What can we do?

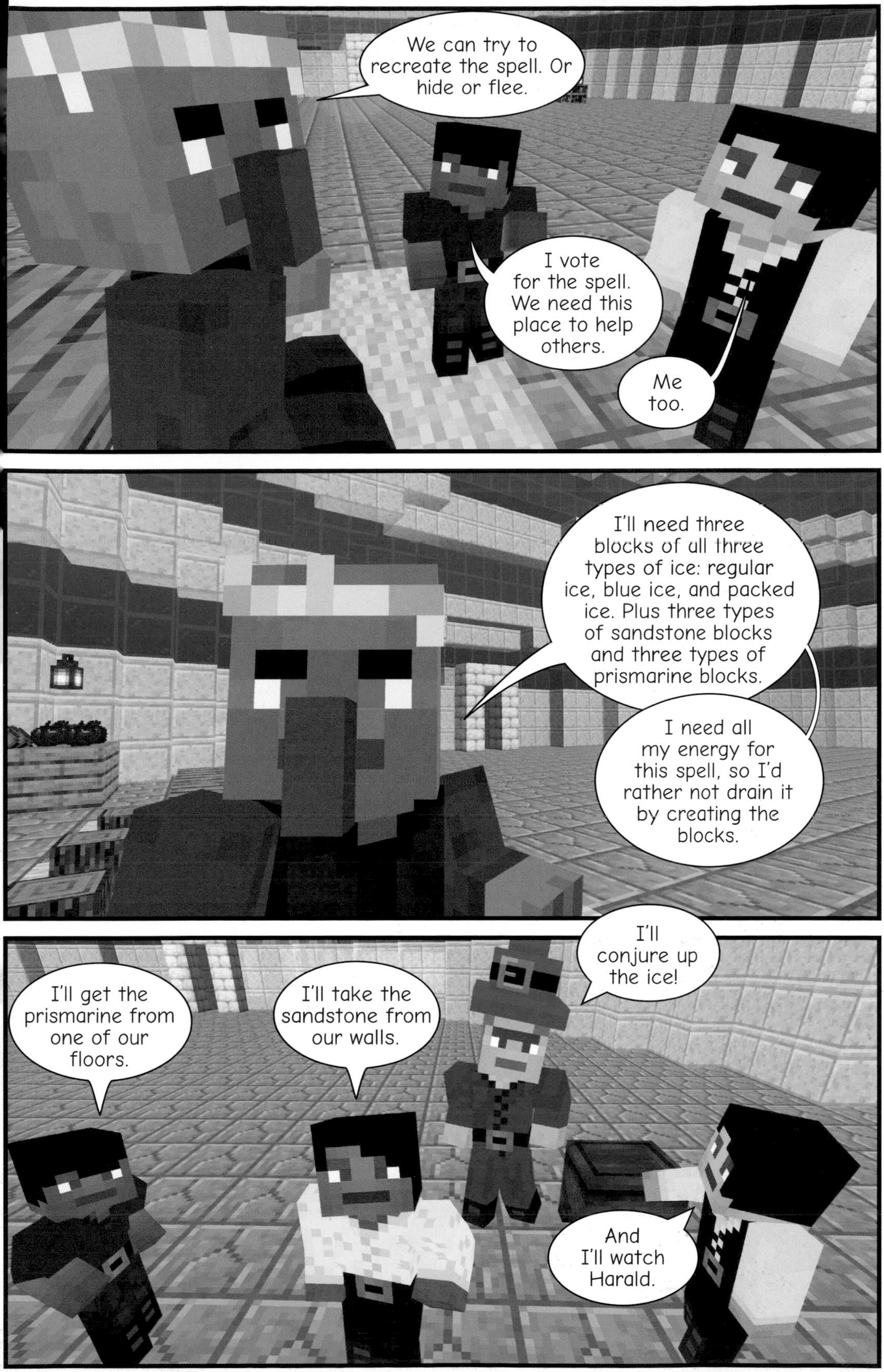
We can try to recreate the spell. Or hide or flee.
I vote for the spell. We need this place to help others.
Me too.
I'll need three blocks of all three types of ice: regular ice, blue ice, and packed ice. Plus three types of sandstone blocks and three types of prismarine blocks.
I need all my energy for this spell, so I'd rather not drain it by creating the blocks.
I'll get the prismarine from one of our floors.
I'll take the sandstone from our walls.
I'll conjure up the ice!
And I'll watch Harald.

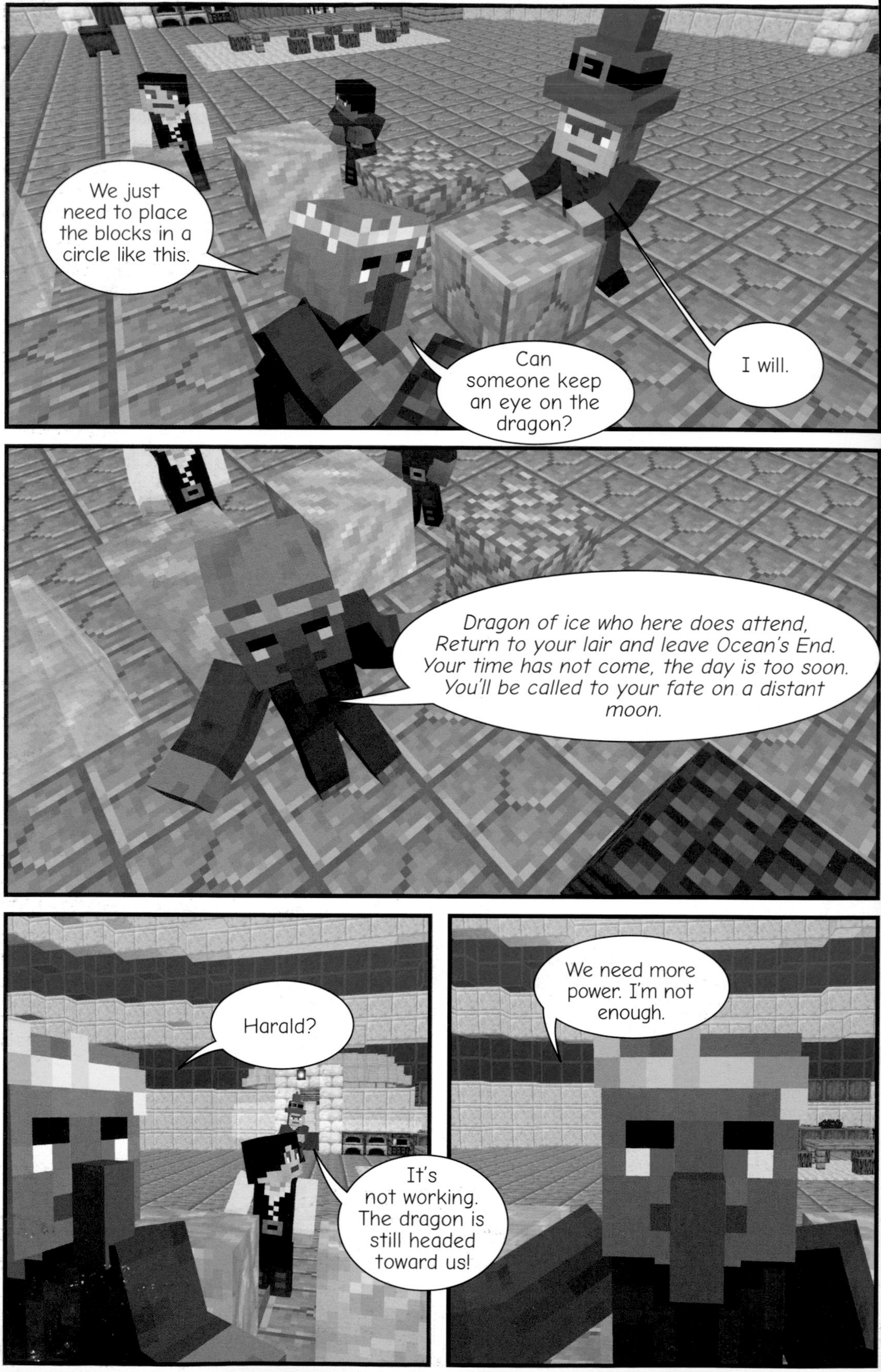
We just need to place the blocks in a circle like this.
Can someone keep an eye on the dragon?
I will.
Dragon of ice who here does attend,
Return to your lair and leave Ocean's End.
Your time has not come, the day is too soon.
You'll be called to your fate on a distant moon.
Harald?
It's not working. The dragon is still headed toward us!
We need more power. I'm not enough.

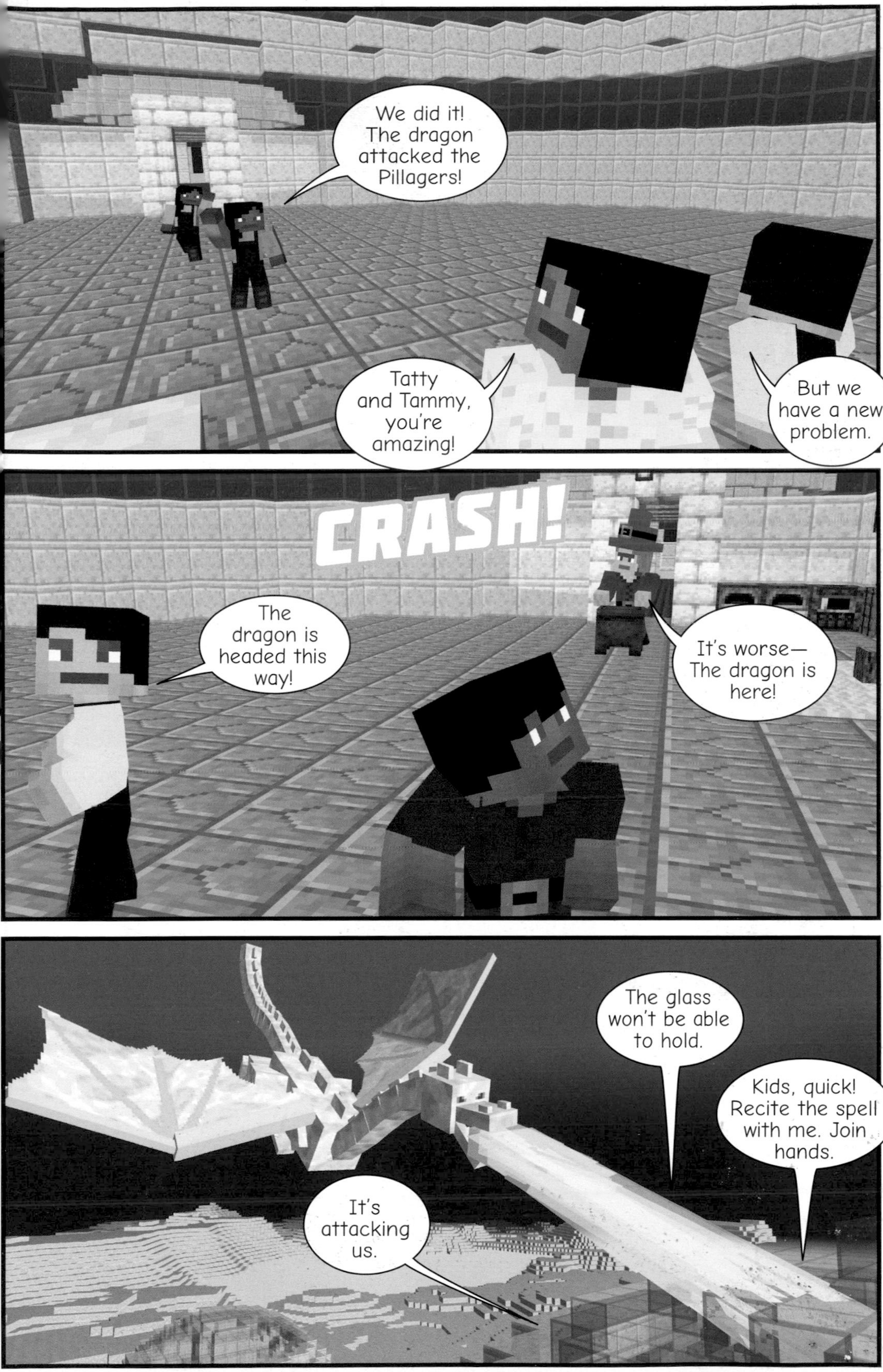
We did it! The dragon attacked the Pillagers!
Tatty and Tammy, you're amazing!
But we have a new problem.
CRASH!
The dragon is headed this way!
It's worse— The dragon is here!
The glass won't be able to hold.
Kids, quick! Recite the spell with me. Join hands.
It's attacking us.

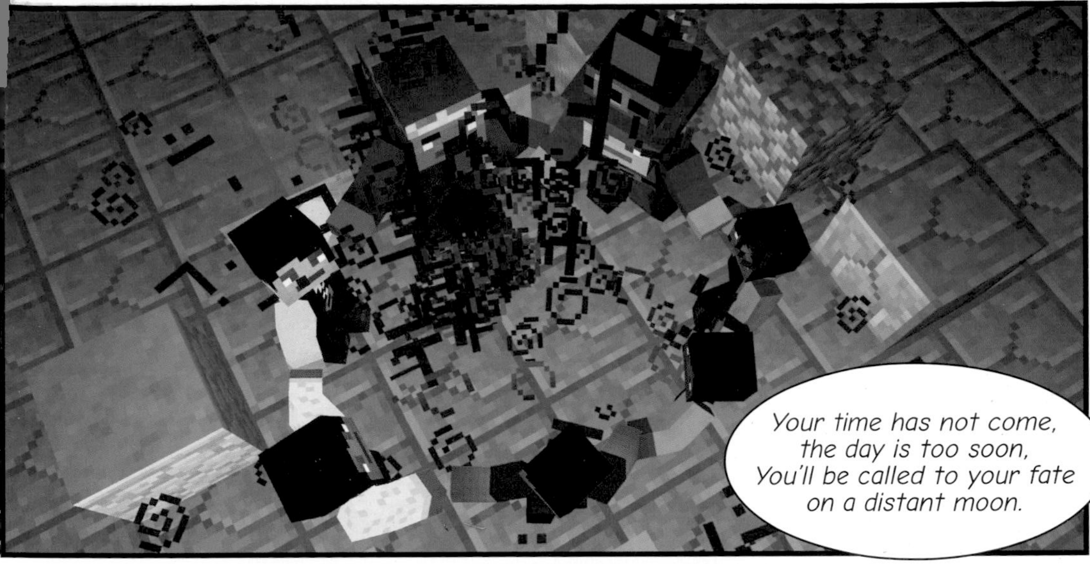
Your time has not come, the day is too soon, You'll be called to your fate on a distant moon.

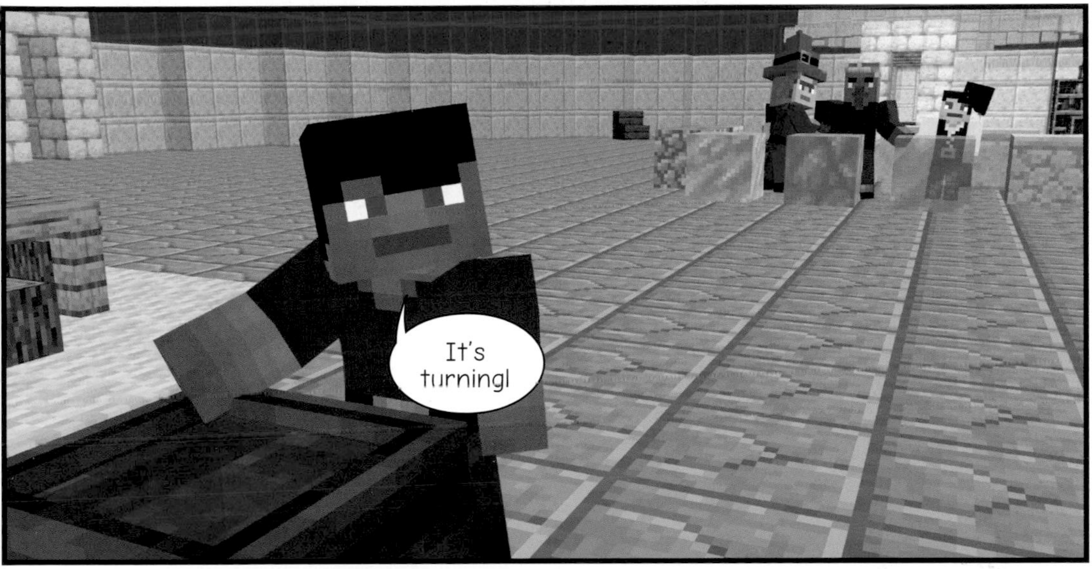
It's turning!

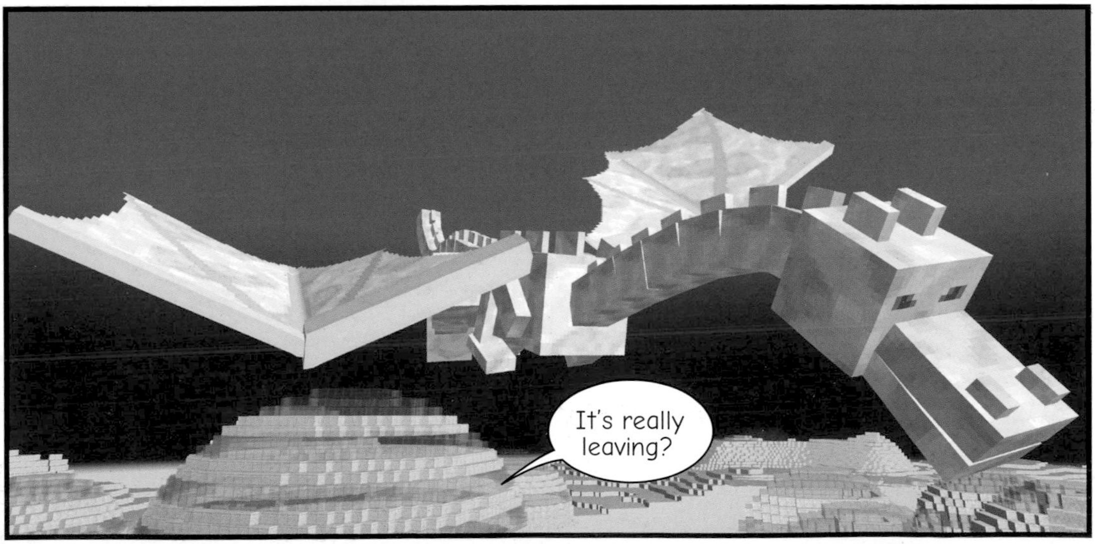
It's really leaving?

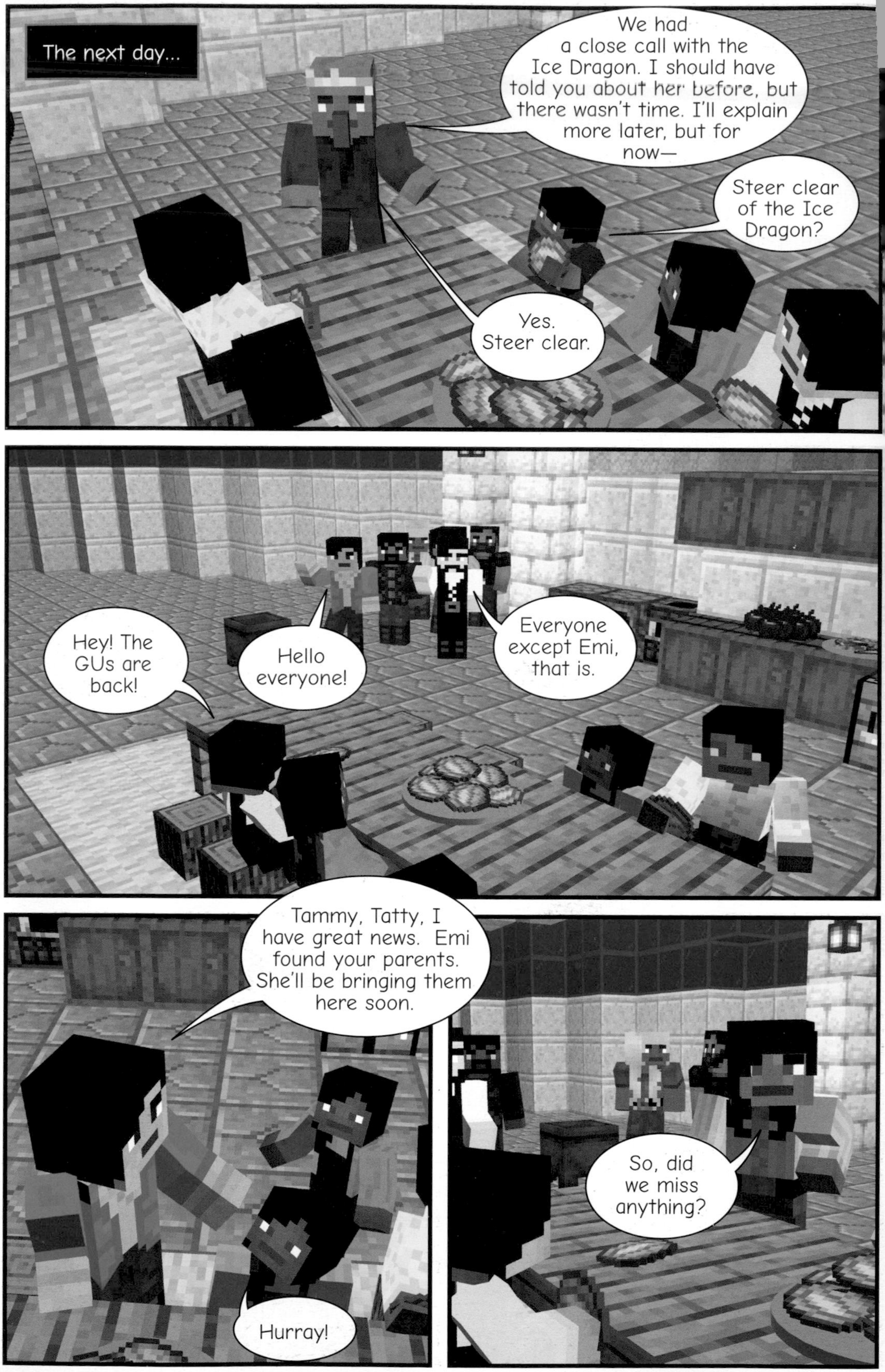
The next day...
We had a close call with the Ice Dragon. I should have told you about her before, but there wasn't time. I'll explain more later, but for now—
Steer clear of the Ice Dragon?
Yes. Steer clear.
Hey! The GUs are back!
Hello everyone!
Everyone except Emi, that is.
Tammy, Tatty, I have great news. Emi found your parents. She'll be bringing them here soon.
Hurray!
So, did we miss anything?

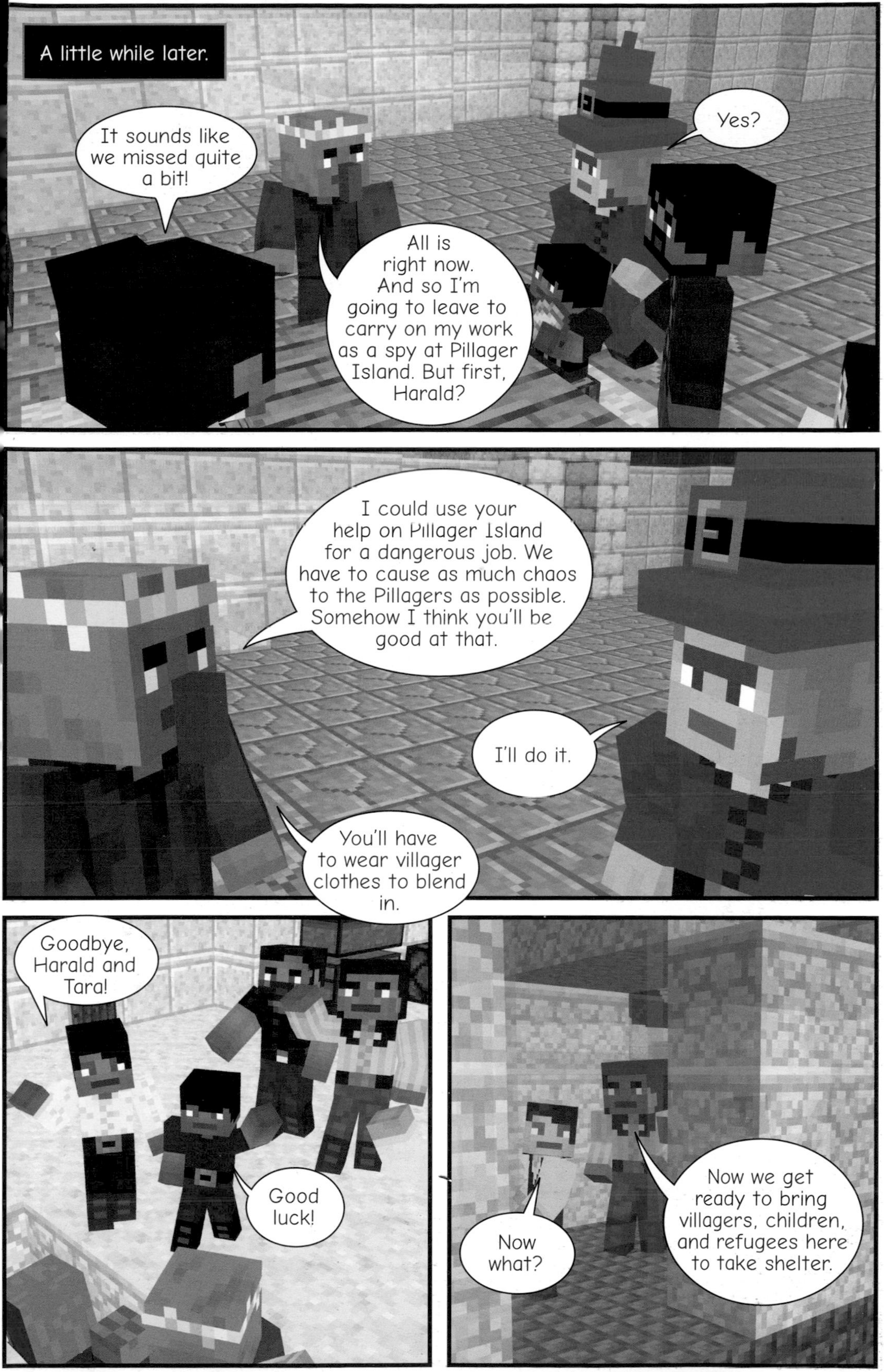
A little while later.
It sounds like we missed quite a bit!
Yes?
All is right now. And so I'm going to leave to carry on my work as a spy at Pillager Island. But first, Harald?
I could use your help on Pillager Island for a dangerous job. We have to cause as much chaos to the Pillagers as possible. Somehow I think you'll be good at that.
I'll do it.
You'll have to wear villager clothes to blend in.
Goodbye, Harald and Tara!
Good luck!
Now what?
Now we get ready to bring villagers, children, and refugees here to take shelter.

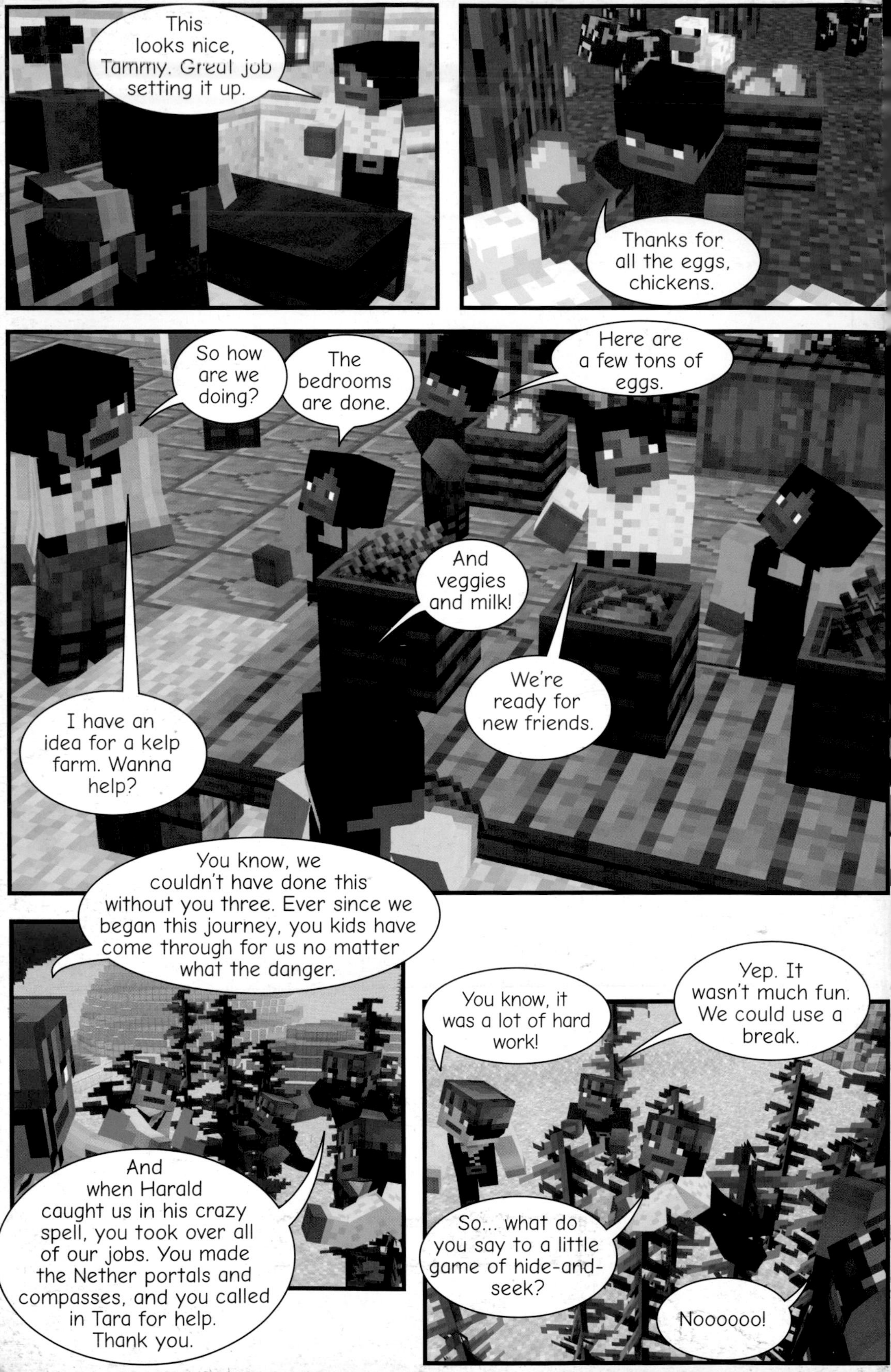

This looks nice, Tammy. Great job setting it up.
Thanks for all the eggs, chickens.
So how are we doing?
The bedrooms are done.
Here are a few tons of eggs.
And veggies and milk!
We're ready for new friends.
I have an idea for a kelp farm. Wanna help?
You know, we couldn't have done this without you three. Ever since we began this journey, you kids have come through for us no matter what the danger.
And when Harald caught us in his crazy spell, you took over all of our jobs. You made the Nether portals and compasses, and you called in Tara for help. Thank you.
You know, it was a lot of hard work!
Yep. It wasn't much fun. We could use a break.
So... what do you say to a little game of hide-and-seek?
Noooooo!